Mission Command

The Phoenix Rising Infinitology

Angela Timms

DEDICATION

For my parents who believed in me and the friends who have stood by me.

www.edendream.co.uk

ACKNOWLEDGMENTS

With thanks to Patricia Bertrand for editing this novel and also for her friendship.

1

Kel hesitated outside the door and took a deep, dry and slightly dusty breath. He held it for a moment to calm his nerves and then breathed out. Anticipation and doubts ran through his mind in a spiralling twist of excitement and fear.

He looked over his shoulder for a moment as his body tensed. The young man involuntarily brushed the bulge of the Kerillian Blaster that hung underneath his coat. He found it reassuring. He was alone on the dusty windswept veranda that circled the building. Kel could see both ways clearly as light flooded from the windows. This light illuminated a patch of boardwalk as if a spotlight highlighted something of value nearby. The only other illumination on the street came from the houses between the shops, the whorehouse down the road and the livery stable. The doors of the stable were open. Inside, the lanterns were lit and the owner was busily bedding down the horses as the last of them came in for the night, their riders trail worn and dusty.

Kel turned to focus on the weather beaten bare wood door in front of him. He was a tall man, broad shouldered and muscular. His black curls tumbled down his back over his black leather duster coat. As he paused at the door, the crow feathers woven into his hair moved about by the gusting wind.

The scent of old wood, stale alcohol and smoke filled his senses mixed with a vague aroma of sweet grass. He hesitated for a moment, his eyes flashing from left to right, trying to penetrate the darkness that hung between every building. Something in a latent memory was troubling him but nothing he could grasp, so he translated it as a feeling that someone was watching him. Deep down he knew it was just the unusual feeling of being outside after so many months on star bases. He mentally brushed it aside as irrelevant, though it lingered disturbingly on the edge of his consciousness.

His six foot six frame almost brushed the top of the doorway. When he opened the door, his muscular shoulders blocked the light from flooding out. He took a deep breath and strode inside. He scoured the room with his gaze, assessing the threat level before he turned slightly and closed the door behind him. With no hesitation, once inside, he took a step. His heavy metal shod boots were noiseless over the hum of conversation. He looked around the bar. The man's dark eyes did a visual sweep of the area. Determination accentuated his brow and thick set, handsome, slightly primitive features. Those who noticed him fell silent and looked away, trying not to get noticed. Others continued their conversation oblivious to the imposing, menacing stranger. He strode toward the bar, his coat sweeping just above the dusty sawdust strewn floor. As he walked it swung away to reveal his blasters which looked to anyone who was paying attention like a pair of Colt Peacemakers, one on each side. The belt of daggers across his chest glinted in what little light there was. Some saw the guns, some the daggers. Those who noticed either instinctively fingered weaponry to experience the reassurance of its proximity.

The candlelight cast an eerie glow over the faces of those who sought solace and entertainment at the Black Lamb Tavern. The wind outside howled around the buildings making the tavern sign swing. There was little left of the painting of a black lamb, it was blasted by the weather and bullet holes. The gusts of wind blew rubbish and vegetation down the street and around the small tavern in the outback town known as Whitewater on the planet of Kulak. It was a tiny planet almost lost in its solar system. It was an insignificant green and blue ball that nestled precariously between two far larger planets as the three jauntily orbited their shared sun.

On this tiny planet, the mining town buildings were generally built of wood as they clung tenaciously to the wide main street. Some had obviously been constructed in a hurry a long time ago and the planks of wood that had been nailed together, to make repairs, gave the buildings a patchwork appearance. Paint appeared to be as rare as gold, since those planks were as weather beaten as the others. The only paint that was visible was on the shop fronts where their owners had made a real effort. These were freshly done and a stark contrast to the shabby thrown together appearance of the rest of the town.

Across the road from the Black Lamb and on almost every corner there was a shop eager to supply those who travelled many miles for their specialist stock. The hand painted signs announced exotic bottled white water or other strange white water concoctions.

Inside the tavern Kel was looking around the room again and taking in faces. That made the inhabitants nervous and many tensed their hands involuntarily or voluntarily moved to where concealed or not so concealed weaponry was stored. Conscious that he was alone in a bar full of strangers who were probably all armed, he cautiously eyed his probable antagonists. His body tensed, expecting trouble at any moment. Then, as moments passed, Kel re-evaluated and then adjusted his impressions of this back water place. To even the casual observer it was obvious that what was considered a low level of technology by many, was actually quite the opposite. Although not overtly obvious, as Kel took in the scene, it didn't take him long to spot the technology. He noticed a watch here, a terminal there, a keypad in an open bag. He noticed one or two eyes that were too bright in the darkness, hands moving small black boxes around on the wooden table tops or wearing black gloves, their owners staring into space with an intent expression as their fingers moved almost imperceptibly. There was enough for him to realize that what seemed primitive concealed an underlying level of development he had not been expecting. He raised an eyebrow when it occurred to him that he was being scanned and targeted by many weapons that were carefully concealed.

Each table was lit by a candle dug into a mound of wax from previous candles and rows of candles hung from the ceiling at strategic points around the room. The tables were old, their wood worn by countless customers over the years and obviously mended many times. The tavern itself was rustic, the windows dusty and the floorboards coated with a dusting of dirty wood shavings meant to soak up the blood of hapless drunken warriors.

The bar stretched across the far wall of the room. Behind it the barman had been busying himself with washing glasses. Kel watched him as he broke off from his task to serve a couple of customers with a shot of whisky and a glass of a blue local drink before sitting down to chat with the lone customer seated at the bar. He had obviously noticed Kel but he was either being subtle or overtly ignoring him. As Kel got to the bar the barman hesitated, came over and put his hands on the bar, cloth in hand to meet Kel's glower.

The barman was a tall thin man in his mid-thirties. His face was clean shaven other than a neatly trimmed moustache and his short, neatly combed hair Although he seemed to be trying to master a friendly expression, all that came through was a weasel-like countenance and a nervous demeanor. A box of broken glasses behind the bar wasn't lost on Kel. Several lacerations on the barman's face and hands had all been noted. Kel suspected that more than a bit of dried blood on the floor belonged to the barman.

The bar was crowded. Every table was full or nearly full and the hum of conversation filled the air. Most of the customers were smartly dressed. The men favored black suits, waistcoats and thin ties fastened around mandarin collars. The women elegantly fluttered about in wide hemmed and frilled long dresses which were held out by hoops. The women's hair was generally dressed in curls which fell neatly to their shoulders.

In the corner a piano player was hammering out a tune and customers around the room involuntarily tapped out the rhythm with their fingers. It was only when the pianist reached for his drink and the piano carried on playing, the keys depressing by themselves that Kel realized he wasn't playing at all. To the right a poker game was in full flow. Some customers were playing, some watched and the chips were piling up in the middle of the table. To the left was a roulette table, the wheel spinning, the resident's financial fate hanging in the balance.

The barman took a deep breath and spoke in a broad accent. "And what can I get you sir?"

Kel looked about him, taking in the nervous expressions of those who were watching him, either overtly or covertly. "I'm looking for the Eridian Mercenary, Erasmus Deck. We received your narrowcast earlier today. I'm here to help."

The barman looked relieved. "Thank the gods that someone was paying attention. He is upstairs, room seven. He has my barmaid with him. Please be careful, she's a good girl. He arrived earlier today, demanded food and busted up a couple of my customers."

Kel nodded once and the customers in the bar who had overheard what he had said now visibly relaxed and went back to their drinks. He could almost hear those safety catches clicking back on the many guns in the room.

Kel took the stairs two at a time, pulling his blasters from their holsters and kicking the door in as he sprang cat-like into the room. He fired two shots before Erasmus knew he was there. The red beams cut through the darkness and ripped into the semi naked man who fell back onto the bed. The barmaid screamed and rolled away from the now dead corpse, grabbing what was left of her torn clothing. She covered herself and ran for the door, past Kel and down the corridor.

Kel crossed the room and rolled the man over immediately taking in that everything about this man was expensive. He went through the pockets of the man's clothes that were strewn around the room, pulling out ID cards and other items which he swiftly pocketed. Then he caught sight of a case in the corner. It was open and the contents lay on the table beside it. A radio transmitter and a small black box, a small book and what looked like a pen. Kel slipped these into his deep pockets, turned on his heels and left the room. He strode down the stairs and threw a glance at the bar which was now silent. All eyes were on him.

The barman looked up and opened his mouth as if he was going to say something, hesitated then spoke in a broken voice. "Thanks."

Kel strode on out of the bar, leaving a stunned silence as the door swung closed behind him.

The street outside was almost empty. Pockets of people stood around shop doorways and a couple of speeders which looked like carts without horses hovered along the dusty road. Kel stepped around the corner of the building as a Planet Hopper de-cloaked and the rear access ramp lowered. Its cylindrical chrome exoskeleton was starkly modern in contrast with the weather beaten wood of the buildings around it. A cat that had been stealthily stalking a mouse gave a loud meow and leapt to safety up a wooden wall and disappeared into the gloom.

Kel ran up the ramp as it closed behind him and the engines jumped into life. As he took his seat it glided effortlessly away with an almost silent swishing sound. Kel clipped on his seatbelt as the Hopper climbed sharply up out of the atmosphere, leaving the planet a blue and green ball ever decreasing in size.

The slight orange glow as they exited the planet's atmosphere played on Kel's face and illuminated the passenger hold. Everything was chrome and black, immaculately clean and efficiently stowed with the panels labelled to show what they contained.

The ship levelled out, inertial dampeners compensating for the acceleration of speed as it sped away from Kulak on the edge of the Nimbus Galaxy.

Kel smiled to himself as the intercom sprang into life and a silvery female voice spoke. "Welcome home Kel. I trust everything went smoothly?" "Indeed, without a hitch. Style and grace Shantara style and grace."

"No loose ends? Did you get what you were looking for?"

"He won't be carrying any more messages and I did, thank you. I trust the wait wasn't too tiresome." He smiled to himself. His sullen features brightened as he raised an eyebrow and waited for her to answer.

"Not at all, always a pleasure. After all I had Rowland for company." Unseen, Shantara scowled and contemplated the switches and buttons on the control panel.

A thicker male voice chipped in. "Thank you, very kind of you to say so." Kel nearly choked and stifled his laughter. He knew that even Shantara with all her meditation and training sometimes had difficulty around Rowland and his constant irrelevant chatter. "Our informant was right. He did have the communication devices. Now it's up to the tekkies to see what they can get out of them. What's on the screen Shantara, it's just figures to me. Anything I should worry about? The figures are red and they are counting up."

The intercom crackled slightly. Rowland's voice chipped in. "Nothing to worry about, I left it working on a power reading and forgot to switch back, it will just keep on ticking up until the numbers go green. That's the battery recharging its particles as we gather them on leaving the atmosphere and entering the inter-dimensional space."

Kel stared into space blankly but didn't answer. The intercom crackled and Rowland's voice came over it again, this time broken up. "It's showing the recharge rate of the Eion Drive. I really must fix that intercom. Hold on a second." It crackled and fell silent.

Kel cursed under his breath and shouted at the now dead intercom.

"Rowland just leave things alone. Great, now the intercom is broken and you are going to spend the next few hours trying to fix it. So what do I do now?" Then he realized he was actually talking to the dead intercom and shut up.

Shantara piped up. "Use the secondary intercom which only links to my headset. Its Rowland's one that is broken. He is not getting his hands on mine. So, what do we do now to pass the time until we get back?"

Kel smiled. "No idea. I prefer the Hoppers where there's a connection between the passenger hold and the crew cabin. Why didn't we take one of those?"

Shantara took a while to answer. "Sorry, just removing some wires from over my control switches. Thank you Rowland, leave that alone or I swear I will shoot you. Right, that was in case we had trouble. The shielding between the crew cabin and passenger hold on the other Hoppers isn't very strong, if you came in hot we could have been caught in the crossfire."

Kel shrugged. "Can't see why, they never worried on other missions. So, how long until we get back then?"

Rowland was mumbling something as Shantara clicked her intercom to speak. "Not long. So what are your plans for this evening?" Then she coughed nervously.

Kel looked down at the blaster in his hand and slipped it back into its holster and took the other one out. "I've booked the meditation room for a bit of unbridled sentimentality. It has been two years since the Followers raided my village. I thought I'd mark the anniversary. But I'm guessing you remembered that." Kel paused in contemplation, staring at the window. There was a lost look in his eyes. "Well, its time I did the Ceremony of Remembrance. Yes I am fine and no I don't need any company."

Shantara's voice was gentle, soft. "You want to talk about it? You've never said much about it."

Kel looked down the sight of his gun. "I don't talk about it but that doesn't stop me thinking about it, but that is my business. It's not something I'm going to forget in a hurry is it? Me and the rest of Mission Command I would guess. There isn't one person there who hasn't lost someone. You included."

Shantara clicked the intercom. "I doubt I'm the last of my species, someone had to survive. We were spread through many planets, as were your people. Don't think you are the only one and you know you aren't alone. I know it's hard to accept but there has to be more of us out there. The Followers take prisoners and they take slaves as often as they convert. Who knows the information in that box might give us a lead on where some of these people are."

Kel took a deep breath. "Your sentimentality is quite charming but I'm afraid your words are lost on me. It just might. Even if it doesn't it will give us the opportunity to even the score a little and perhaps get some people out before the Followers get to them."

In the cockpit Shantara was pouting and Rowland looked up momentarily then thought better of speaking. He went back to sorting out the bundle of wires on his lap.

The hours rolled by, broken up by the occasional crackle from the intercom as Rowland attempted to fix the problem. Kel passed the time by checking over his guns.

Shantara broke the silence. "What are you thinking?"

Kel looked annoyed. "I don't do much by way of that thinking lark. I leave that to you technological and sensitive types."

In the quiet solitude of the metal shell flying effortlessly through space Kel did think. In his mind he was back home where the camp fires burned brightly in the chilled evening air. The smell of cooking and the smoke from the wood fire, fur and leather mingled with the smell of animals and people to build such a strong memory that he could almost smell it now.

The ghosts of his life wandered again, laughing and living like he remembered them. But even in that moment of solace where he could imagine everything was alright, images came to remind him how far it was from reality. Unbidden came the images of its destruction, of his people dead. He was almost glad when Shantara's voice crackled across the intercom. "What was it like being a hunter in your tribe? Did you enjoy it?" There was a pause which hung in the silence as Kel scowled. "Look, what do you think? Life was simple back then. I liked my life. I didn't have people asking stupid questions. You've seen enough films where the hero loses his home and his family. Well, there you go. Yes I loved my life but it's gone. I'm not going into all that again, I've told you about it enough. You know very well that I liked the constant trips out to hunt Arlyx as that was the true test of a warrior. Life could have been a pleasure if that had been allowed to continue. So yes, I was happy back then, it was my life and I wish with every waking moment that it hadn't changed." His last words were almost growled.

Shantara was a slim woman who, if she had been human, would have been placed in her mid-thirties. Her hair and skin were a pale lilac, her eyes a vibrant purple. She smiled, her skin slightly flushed darker since Kel's last words. She was almost boyish in her looks which contrasted dramatically with her ample breasts. Her standard issue blue boiler suit clashed slightly with her skin and was unflattering. She looked at the tubby dishevelled individual who was still welding wires from the impossible tangle in front of him. He wasn't looking at her, he was trying to balance a manual on his knee and put out the small fire he had caused by igniting its pages with his soldering iron.

She looked away when the fire was out. "So what was your home world like? What was your village like? I saw it in a book I found in the library on base. Those pointed tents looked amazing with their poles ascending to the sky and the smell of the campfire and roasting meat must have been a regular thing. I went camping once on my world, just a night but I'll never forget that smell, the smoke, the fresh grass."

Kel scowled and clenched his fist. "All I remember now are those same tents burnt to the ground, my people lying dead and dying and me along with them. And yes I do wish I'd died there too and no I don't want to talk about it. They are all gone. My family, my wife and my two children, their bodies blackened and charred by the time I regained consciousness. I will never know what my unborn child would have looked like. I will never again feel Shakar's gentle touch and hear her mild wisdom both to me and to those who came to her for her words. Look these aren't memories I really want. I know you mean well but for now, can we just be silent." Kel's last sentence was more a command than a question. He thrust his other blaster back into its holster and watched the lights of the space between dimensions rushing past the window. He focused on his new home, Mission Command.

Within the hour the thrusters changed their vibration and the sparkles of the inter-dimensional space elongated as they re-entered normal space and he could see the starfish shaped base out of the window in the distance as they made their descent. Its silver tendrils spread over the moon's crust.

Shantara piped up. "I know you don't want to hear it, but you impress me. You never give up do you?" She took a breath as she considered her own situation, "Not much has changed really. I train people and then I see empty seats when their crews come back without them sometimes." Shantara spoke gently. "I don't know how you cope."

Kel laughed. "I bet you don't or you wouldn't keep asking and reminding me of everything. Nothing really makes me feel that much better but I have a need for revenge, it is my life. If that shocks you, stop asking."

Shantara's brow furrowed. "That kind of attitude can't be healthy. Haven't they sent you to the base psychologist?"

Kel bit his lip in frustration. "Shantara, not everyone needs to talk about things and not everyone sees it as a problem. Commander Zack no longer sees it as a problem. I've proven myself to be loyal and I am in control. They are as happy for me to kill Followers as I am. It makes me an effective killing machine, they appreciate it and they ask little more of me. I have a room, food and that is about the best I can ask for now. They don't have a problem with it, so why do you? You are going to have to stop trying to understand me. It is not the road to a deep and meaningful relationship. It was one night. You'll have to get over it."

She looked down at the controls as the ship brought them down to land. "Ok, I'll concentrate on landing, we'll speak later."

Rowland looked up. "Don't be silly. There's little to concentrate on as the computers handle all the minute calculations and adjustments. I can't see why you…" Her glare silenced him.

She was focusing on a terminal, her flawless skin furrowed by the scowl.

Her belt was pulled in to accentuate her slim waist.

Rowland was a middle aged balding man whose boiler suit mostly fitted him but the zip struggled slightly to keep his copious waistline in check. His thinning dark brown hair was unkempt as he constantly ran his fingers through it and his pudgy face was fixed in an almost constant smile. In front of him the communications array lay in pieces where he had taken it apart looking for the problem. Tools lay on the floor around him and wires pointed without purpose into the air.

Shantara cast a cautious sideways glance and almost sighed before she caught herself, focused forwards, relieved that she hadn't attracted his attention. Thinking that, at this point, silence was golden.

"Fixed it." Rowland's voice almost squeaked over the intercom which crackled into life.

Shantara's voice sounded strained. "We will be landing presently, better buckle up."

The Hopper lurched slightly as it negotiated the other traffic heading on and off base. Hoppers and other craft came and went. Transporters, supply ships and all manner of other civilian and military craft navigated their way around each other. They hovered slightly as Rowland keyed in the password and codes and then they waited, and waited. They were all waiting expectantly for that moment when the Controller gave them the go ahead to land.

When they got the landing code Shantara brought the Hopper effortlessly in on the outdoor landing pad. The clamps raised and the Hopper was securely grasped and moved forwards, sliding through the open doors of the hangar bay to be placed against the airlocks, one beside the cockpit the other covering the back bay door. There was a hiss as the pressures equalized and the back and side ramps descended to meet the immaculately clean white walkway of the Mission Command docking bay.

Kel sprang to his feet and strode out and down the corridor stopping in the glass booth at the end. Medical and other scanners sprang to life when they sensed movement. A red beam of light ran over the length of this body. He stood stock still as the intercom and recorded message sprang to life. "You are being scanned by the Inselink Medical Scanner, Reference Number SC2341566. Please stand completely still. This will not hurt. The procedure does not infringe your rights as an individual but it is an essential requirement for entering the base. Should you wish not to be scanned please return to your vessel and await further instructions. Thank you, you have been scanned and you are completely healthy. There is a slight strain to your right ankle and this has been logged on your medical record. Please attend a medical officer to have this attended to at your convenience. Welcome back to base KE237 Kel Elyn." The red light on the control panel switched to green and the door in front of him slid silently open.

He stepped out onto the polished blue floor on the other side of the compartment. His eyes ran along the photographs of planets. Although Kel had done this walk a hundred or so times, he always managed to notice something new. He breathed in deeply, the citrus smell of the floor polish filling his nostrils. The smell of home always conjured up many of the memories he had formed since he had been on the base. He took a moment to think about them, filed them in his mind and strolled off down the corridor. The glass door closed behind him. As he looked back the Hopper's ramps closed and large metal clamps reached down to encircle it before they took it off to maintenance.

At the second glass door which opened and closed in front of him he stepped out into the pristine white corridor which denoted he was in the main hub of the station. There were no photographs or pictures here, just white walls. He followed it as it turned the corner and rejoined Shantara and Rowland who had just come through the pilots' arrival lounge. Both wore military boiler suits with their rank and insignia of their planet of origin. Shantara wore the insignia of a pilot and combat medic, Rowland that of engineer. Rowland bore the insignia of Mission Command while that panel on Shantara's boiler suit was empty. Shantara smiled broadly at Kel and took a step closer while Rowland kept his distance and fell slightly behind, looking uncomfortable. He kept well behind as they strode off down the corridor. Shantara didn't notice, she was busy reaching into her pocket for a notebook. She fell in step beside Kel and they strode in silence down the corridor until they came to double doors on the right. Shantara tapped in her code with her elegantly painted fingernails, 4568, and the chrome doors swished effortlessly open.

The slightly damp air that met them carried the aroma of perfume and bath products. The room they entered was bustling with members of Mission Command. Rows of shiny black lockers lined the walls. Some open, most locked shut. There where twenty soldiers and civilians who were gearing up, dressing down or fetching things from their lockers. It was a communal room. Some individuals came and went from the showers, wrapped in towels or bath robes, retrieving clothes from their lockers before changing in the cubicles to the right of the room.

Kel went to his locker and ran his hand over the identification pad. The locker door swung open. Where other lockers were decorated inside with photographs and mementos of previous happy times Kel's was bare. He hesitated for a moment, turned and reached into his deep pockets and pulled out the items he had taken from the room on the mission. He looked at them for a moment and then handed them to Shantara. She took them from him, looking more at him than what she was doing, her other hand brushing his as she pretended to steady the pile of things he had placed on her hand.

Kel was oblivious to this, he took out his towel, buckskin tunic and leather trousers and disappeared through the door to the shower room.

Shantara and Rowland went to their lockers and took out their mission logs in silence. Rowland kept looking as if he was going to speak but as Shantara appeared busy and glared when he caught her eye he shut his mouth again. They left in silence and re-entered the corridor. A little further on they stopped outside a door to the right and again Shantara entered her code and the single door slid silently open.

The large room beyond was in two halves. The closest half was painted gunmetal grey. Pictures of different types of shuttles and ships hung on the wall. The light grey floor was a contrast to the white of the floor outside. Three long tables were set out parallel to each other and surrounded by chairs. A low wooden wall divided each table in half. The wooden dividers set at intervals provided private cubicles where terminals waited patiently for someone to use them. The screens displayed the standard Mission Command screensaver. Some were occupied, most were empty.

The far side half of the room had been partitioned off by a glass wall and a single glass door was shut. It was a smaller room and its main feature was a large black stone table with chairs around it which stood regally in the center. The room was currently empty and the table was set with notepads, bottles of water and glasses awaiting the next meeting.

They walked in silence to a pair of terminals next to each other, sat down and logged in their passwords. The logo disappeared and a screen appeared offering a list of choices. They both clicked on "Mission Report", the report template appeared, already filled in with the mission brief and as they began typing the boxes filled up and the auto correct kept their reports roughly readable. Shantara stopped typing and hesitated. "Why doesn't Kel have to file a report?"

Rowland smiled. "Kel can't read or write. The Commander got him a teacher but they gave up in the end. He'll do a verbal debrief later if there is anything worth reporting. He's not one for noticing detail anyway and his reports were very uninformative or so I am led to believe."

They sat in silence and typed, hit send and the job was done. They were about to log off when Shantara looked over at Rowland. "Isn't it about time that you told me a bit more about the Followers? Come on you are keen enough on your stories. We've got a little time while we wait for our next orders to come through."

Rowland looked a little stunned. "You know about the Followers. Come on, what is behind this? You mean you actually want me to tell you something? That makes a change. Well, ok then but I can't think that I know anything that you don't. I'll have to miss out specifics as you don't have full clearance yet. You will probably know as it is pretty much common knowledge that the Followers came to the Galaxies twenty five years ago. There was no record of them before then and most people welcomed them initially as a curiosity and then as a new and exciting ideal. They seemed to have good ethics which most people weren't that bothered about but they made people's lives better. People always like that and they tend to overlook a lot of they feel they are better off that way.

Looking back on it now they took what was seen as a healthy interest in the galaxies. Many of their people stood for positions in local government and eventually they got into positions which real influence on intergalactic affairs. Basically they worked their way into every level of government and their policy of having as many children as possible made sure that in a few generations they had control at all levels.

While they were the saviors of the galaxies that wasn't a problem but a few years ago things changed. Many people couldn't see it but those who did started to realize that perhaps these people were not the salvation they were made out to be. But of course by then it was too late. Mission Command was here for those who realized the problem. I think the rest is pretty much history.

Some planets had lived in peace for thousands of years without major technological advancement. They were progressing at their natural pace.

Suddenly they had technology thrust on them which in the most part wasn't a huge problem while everything was peaceful. But, when the Followers started having opposition they needed more resources and places to take them from where they wouldn't be noticed. They wanted to keep any conflict very quiet. This did not go well for the planets they harvested as they needed more materials and food to feed and provide for an ever growing population as well. They were left with an ecological wasteland as the planets were over farmed and didn't have the capability to replenish the soil. Many of them are dustbowls now, their inhabitants scratching a living where once they had rich pastures or they were wiped out to keep it quiet.

Wherever the Followers landed they "converted" new followers and those who would not convert were left as burnt corpses. Well that is what we know now. At the time it was all done very quietly. It was a join or die philosophy and often there wasn't anyone left to report what happened if you didn't convert. Of course once they had an uninhabited planet they moved their own followers there as new colonies. That much I think everyone knows now since there was a major broadcast by rebels a year or so back. Many planets rose up against this but most planets have just caved in and capitulated. The broadcast terrified the inhabitants of some planets into believing if they stood up to the Followers they would die. Which in effect means that the broadcast has backfired. Rather than weakening the Followers it strengthened their position and effectively neutralized the opposition.

In some places where the inhabitants joined them freely they are still heralded as the heroes who saved the worlds. Where they weren't so welcome they destroyed villages as a lesson to those who would stand against them and as their numbers grew and as they acquired better technology whole cities and even planets were wiped out. Their control of the media meant they were able to explain this away as a natural disaster or even as a good thing that was beneficial to the planet. That was the power of positive propaganda. Then they could impose their rules and regimes and as these came into play people lost their will to fight for free will as on the face of it they had great lives and everything they needed if they did what they were told.

The first thing they got rid of was the meeting places so that anyone who did have rebellious ideas couldn't spread them to others. Taverns on some worlds are banned. It is only on planets like Whitewater and the ones they haven't really worried about that you can still meet with other people. Where free spirits had met in pubs and taverns on the planets these became a thing of the past. The Followers banned alcohol where they could and their strict religious doctrine forbade their believers to touch it. From our point of view and with a bit of knowledge you can see why they did. There is something in alcohol which lessens the effect of their mind effecting drugs. We aren't sure yet how it works and it doesn't work forever but there is something there. The only places left to meet were the Follower Meeting Houses where obviously it was not possible to say a word out of turn. This in turn destroyed various small economies. Many businesses supplied the now non-existent meeting places. They went out of business overnight. In truth it drove drinking underground. People chose to drink in their own homes and this meant that they drank more and without social interaction there was a greater incidence of depression. This led people to reach for something in their lives and the Followers were more than happy to oblige. It was a win, win situation.

Where they encountered a non-technological planet they harvested it for its natural resources and left it a wasteland. Planets like Kel's ended up that way. As most of these were under-developed for a reason, be it harsh climate or their location they were unsuitable for colonization, harvested and abandoned.

Manipulating internal struggle for their own political advancement and using bureaucracy to slow everything down allowed them the opportunity to gain a foothold. Subterfuge and some incredibly ingenious minds allowed them to infiltrate all levels of government on those planets with a complex political structure and the resulting discussions they initiated meant that they could take over before there was a chance to rally ordinance and gather troops. In all it was a swift, well thought out and excellently executed take over that left governments in tatters and enough planets under their control after the initial invasion to quell any further organized resistance.

They also managed to manipulate other forms of technology which they managed to eliminate through the same use."

Shantara looked confused. "I think you'd better explain that last bit. You lost me there."

Rowland smiled. "Bad way of putting it. Basically we used to use teleport devices a lot. Matter was broken down to its basic particles, or strings, and then reformed at the new location. This was an ideal and very environmentally friendly way of travelling apart from the huge amount of energy required to break something down and reform it. Anyway, before we realized that they were tampering with it most of the major players were eliminated as they were scrambled when they reformed. That had a dual purpose. Firstly it eliminated people who were a threat without the followers getting the blame and secondly it meant that teleport transport was deemed too dangerous to use. That restricted people's movement and ability to get together. They already had every form of communication bugged and logged so it effectively gave them full access to any information that was typed or spoken. The technology was scrapped and those who made it were put out of work. It is safe to say that anyone who was in Research and Development disappeared shortly afterwards.

They have tried to cover their origins up but initially as you may have heard from Kel they were an environmentally friendly group. They brought about sweeping changes that were definitely for the better on some planets which were nearing extinction through overuse of their natural resources and pollution. They were known as "Fallow Earth" then. They took on the nickname "Fallowers" due to their preaching that it was better to leave planets and areas to recover, to be "Fallow" for a while and to let nature take over again and replenish its resources. I remember reading the writings of Erasmus Deck many years ago. He was an idealist and a visionary. He basically put into words what the rest of us were thinking. He was outspoken and many people believed he wouldn't last the year but he did. His writings about a Utopian Civilization where everyone could live in harmony with nature formed the basis of what is now the Followers' philosophy, albeit corrupted and implemented by force. I don't know what happened to him, he seemed to just disappear. No record of it anywhere. One day he was here, the next he vanished. If you want my opinion he is in a Follower research establishment somewhere.

Way back they started removing some cities that were decaying after relocating their inhabitants and planting whole areas with trees and reintroducing wildlife. That was also how they got into such positions of power. People liked it and even where they had to be voted in it was normally a landslide in their favour. Then it all changed.

They played on the mistrust that they could easily create. Followers look no different to anyone else and wear no insignia or use identifying equipment. Anyone could be a Follower and it was well known that they had "sleepers" everywhere who didn't even know they were Followers until they were activated. So, who could be trusted? It was mostly the conspiracy theorists that worried about this obviously. The general public was pretty oblivious or was pretending to be. They may have said they weren't worried about the

Followers being everywhere but in general I think that they were happy with their lives and didn't want to rock the boat. Not everyone wants to be an individual and their controlled lives were very comfortable. It was hard to question them as well. What could anyone really say? They gave everyone a better standard of living. No, I correct myself, they gave their chosen few a better life and those were generally those who were useful.

Only now that we think that they have progressed into genetic engineering do we have a distinct enemy and something that people find distasteful. Their bone soldiers are easy to recognize. Their exoskeleton makes them look like they are wearing a skeleton mask. Few have been caught and when they have their self-destruct ensured that there was little to analyse. As to what they look like under the mask, or if that was a mask and not a part of them, that is unknown. What is known is that their great strength and speed makes them a formidable enemy, totally loyal to the Followers and unstoppable other than destroying them when they were carrying out a command. We have lost a lot of good people to them.

Mission Command only survived because it was well hidden and the genius minds that had gathered here managed to keep it that way. It had been created for just such an occurrence, initiated by a lone scientist many hundreds of years ago. How he knew I cannot hazard to guess. He had been heralded as a nutcase by his peers but thankfully he had been a very rich nutcase with a very clear idea of what he wanted to create. He had set up "The Foundation" and they had then set up Command bases around the galaxies to protect against the event of an incursion such as that of the Followers. Each was a different design and hidden in a different way. There was no communication between them and each was unknown to the others until they were needed.

I remember it well and it had not been long ago that I and Lex, a Sharathian Warrior, you know the Lizard folk."

Shantara looked blankly at him.

Rowland smiled. "Oh well, never mind, they have green skin and slightly reptilian features. Anyway, we had been seated in the Debriefing Room for a meeting with Commander Zack. Just like any other day really. That was the day he had informed us that everything had changed. The Followers had demanded conversion and had spent time preaching their beliefs. From then on they had another way of spreading the word. They had created a drug and an implant that cut that process out and removed any free will in the matter. Those who were taken were removed to their research facilities and put in pods. The implant was injected and they spent time being indoctrinated with the Followers' belief system. That way they could guarantee loyal followers and they could also know if there was a spy in their ranks. The implant was not only detectable, it was coded to the person it had been implanted in. They could track any of their followers at any time. Well that is how I heard it back

15

then.

The implant was relatively small but the chemical that was also introduced has proven almost impossible to analyze as we have never managed to get hold of any in a large enough quantity to isolate its properties.

The only positive news that comes from this is that if we could develop the technology then we could possibly be able to detect who is a Follower. That doesn't apply to the "Originals", those who came to be Followers because they actually believed and those who had fully converted without the implant and the drug. It is hoped that on one of our missions we will find some intelligence that will give us a way to counteract the drug. Until today we had to work with what we had. That was why today's mission was so important. That mercenary was an undercover Follower. What he carried was a report but I don't know what was in it. So you'd better go and get that delivered to Commander Zack." He pointed to her orders flashing on the screen to report to Commander Zack.

Shantara looked down at the items that Kel had given her. "I suppose I'd better." She got up and left the room.

2

Commander Zack was in his office sitting at a desk piled high with files. He was almost hidden from view as he looked through a few of the papers contained in one of those files. The room was square, large and painted a pale military grey. The floor was covered with a practical black rubber material to ensure antislip and anti-electromagnet issues related to the planet's atmosphere. Behind his head there was a painting of a coniferous wooded valley with a Planet Hopper flying over it with a dramatic sunset highlighting its chrome metal hull with oranges and yellows.

To the right there was a long dresser filled with trophies and awards with the Commander's name on them. The wall above this was almost completely covered with certificates and framed awards for bravery and other military honours.

As Shantara knocked and entered he looked up and smiled kindly. She stepped forwards nervously across the expanse of floor, taking small calculated steps. Then, she stood to attention in front of his desk, holding out the items that Kel had given to her on top of her hands, palm upwards.

The Commander was in his early fifties. His uniform was immaculately pressed. His grey shirt crisp and recently laundered, his grey military issue trousers ironed with a razor sharp precision. His shoes shone and his insignia was immaculately polished. His balding head was slightly shining, reflecting the light above him and what was left of his receding hair was immaculately cut. His deep blue eyes were sharp and took everything in and his face though round was decidedly bird like.

He was slightly rotund in his smart uniform which was a stark contrast to the pictures of the lithe young man that adorned the wall but the warm smile was the same. Now as then his collar was neatly buttoned, his tie just so. His military honours were pinned to a black pad in the centre of a frame amongst the other awards on his shelf. He wore the basic uniform and rank insignia.

He was surrounded by papers, piles of files and maps and looked up with a pen in his hand. Shantara's file was open on the desk in front of him. She caught a glimpse of the rather strictly posed photograph of herself clipped to the top left hand corner and the printout of her skills that she had helped Elana, the Personnel Officer put together to fulfil the protocols.

Commander Zack cleared his throat. "Shantara, you have been with us for three months now and your contribution to the crews you have accompanied has been very much appreciated. I also appreciate your great skill in flying our Planet Hoppers and your contribution as a Combat Medic. In that respect it is felt by myself and Central Command that you should receive your full membership of this facility and that your probation period be considered over. So, it gives me great pleasure to be able to present you with your statutory insignia, making you a full time and permanent member of this crew.

I realise that your information has been necessarily limited over this time. Our survival as you know depends on secrecy for us and our operatives. Rest assured you will be fully briefed on issues you need to be aware of now.

I trust in your time here your fellow crewmembers have brought you up to speed on the basics. I am not underestimating the value of your previous knowledge either. Your reports were extremely informative and detailed. But, recently information has come to light and you will now be granted access to that information.

The Personnel Department will be speaking to you about allocation of a permanent room and you will receive full pay and pension rights as well as being able to access the amber restricted zones."

The smile on Shantara's face was like none that had been seen in many weeks. She stepped forward, held out her hand and took the offered pin and shook the Commander's offered hand. She immediately unclasped the pin and attached it onto her uniform.

Commander Zack nodded and smiled. "I understand you are flying evac missions this afternoon. I would like to wish you every success. Thank you, you may go."

She turned on her heels smartly and left the room, shut the door, leaned against it and took a deep breath. The smile was still all over her face as she walked away.

The corridors were crowded with crew members going about their business. A siren went off, its tone alerting certain members that they needed to get to the Hopper Bay and prepare for an emergency mission. Two middle aged men in boiler suits immediately turned and ran in the Bay's direction. Those in their path got out of the way, including Shantara.

She made her way along the maze of corridors until she came to a door marked "KR2316A CREW ROOM". With her hand on the door she hesitated a moment, took a deep breath, opened the door and stepped over the threshold.

Rennon, the Science and Research Officer, the fourth member of their team was smiling his usual warm and inviting, bright eyed smile. It flashed through her mind as she entered and saw him that he always seemed to be smiling unless there was a real crisis. He was a striking looking man. He looked small compared to Kel but he was at least six foot tall. His elfin pointed features and wildly unruly spiked hair made for a handsome slightly mischievous, roguish look that he was happy to maintain and live up to. His face lit up as she came in. He had a selection of equipment laid out around him and a laptop which was scrolling down what looked like an endless list of figures. He smiled broadly and spoke quickly in his broad Scottish accent. "Shantara, our wee lassie, I see you've got a new piece of jewellery on that suit of yours. Welcome to the Unit."

Kel was sitting by the window, his chair tipped back, his feet crossed on the table with a cup of steaming coffee in his hand. His blaster hung down by his side, his long coat was draped over the back of his chair and he looked relaxed as always in his native buckskins and leather trousers. He looked up, his deep brown eyes sincere as always.

Rowland the engineer was sitting on the other side of the table opposite Kel. He had been trying to fix a scanner and bits of it were set out on the table in front of him. His features were lost under an unkempt mop of dark brown hair, his beard was straggly and tatty. He looked up and grunted. "Well done."

Rennon bounced from his chair and went over to congratulate her.

Rowland grudgingly stepped up to congratulate her as well.

Kel put his cup down, looked up and rolled his legs around, stood up and went over to her slowly. She looked up at him expectantly staring far too intently into his deep brown eyes so he was forced to look away. He smiled and in his deep voice spoke slowly, "Well done." He pulled himself up to his full height as Shantara stepped far too close to him. "I am pleased for you."

She looked disappointed as she froze in the middle of reaching to hug him, "So formal from our native hunter?" She laughed nervously. "You won't be able to get rid of me now. I, like you have been accepted, we're both aliens who found a home here. As I told you, I want to be part of the team. You'll appreciate me one day, you know that. Perhaps we can all move forward now. I feel it, now that I'm no longer on probation, now that I'm one of the team. If it was that you feared I was going away?"

Kel scowled. "Do not spoil your special moment. I am pleased for you. You have a home here." He caught her hand and gently pushed it down to her side. "I do not wish to get rid of you."

Shantara looked hopeful while Rennon and Rowland gave each other nervous looks.

Kel looked from one to the other then back to Shantara. "You are a member of the team, a valued member. We are all pleased you are able to stay. I am sure Rennon here agrees with me too. After all he is in exactly the same position as we are."

Shantara pouted and Rennon looked relieved but the smile soon faded when Kel looked at him expectantly.

Rennon swallowed hard. "We've all lost people but there are people out there who need to be found. Ours and others. Kel is right, don't spoil your moment. Tonight when you get back we will celebrate properly, won't we Kel?"

Unseen by Shantara, Rennon gave Kel a knowing look. Kel looked awkward. "Indeed, we can do that."

Shantara looked a little deflated. "Thank you, I'd like that. I'm due in the Hopper Bay right now, though." She gave Kel a meaningful look which lingered far too long, turned and left.

The door closed and the three sat in silence for a long time. Rennon went back to his scanners and Rowland to his bits and pieces.

Later, Rennon looked up. "It is good news, she's a brilliant pilot and I can't fault her as a medic either, though we know who gets her fullest attention."

Kel flushed a little red as Rennon smiled broadly at him. "She will get over it."

Rennon frowned. "I'm not so sure. I looked up her race on the expanded Elofoalak database. They are long lived and form firm attachments, especially after your little union the other month. You really didn't help your arguments there did you?"

Kel growled. "Last thing I need to hear. Well she will have to un-form them. That was stupid, I accept that. I told her that. The more she annoys me the less likely I am to want her anyway. And no, no matter how much we celebrate I'm going to be a lot more careful about how much I drink and what I do this time. I thought she felt the same way. I thought it was just a bit of fun."

Rennon pressed a button and the screen changed. "Do you want me to talk to her again?"

Rowland looked up momentarily.

Kel took a mouthful of coffee and swallowed. "It didn't do much good last time. Why should it be any better now?"

Rowland looked up. "You could always date her and ditch her. Then she'd have to get over you. At the moment you are throwing excuses in her way. To a woman that is going to look like she's got a challenge to fix the broken man and be the one who saves you from your enforced bachelorhood."

Rennon glared. "If he dated her as well that would make it worse.

Akashonians mate for life. If he takes that place in her life he will never get her to take a step back."

Rowland shook his head and sighed. "Sounds a bit clingy to me. What was her psych evaluation like?"

Rennon looked shocked. "I haven't looked."

Rowland smiled. "Well perhaps you should. You could be playing with fire here. She's a woman after all. They are dangerous by nature."

Kel grunted. "Don't remind me. Actually that's not such a bad idea. Rennon, can you access her file?"

Rennon looked up for a moment. "Not officially but that has never stopped me before."

Kel looked from Rennon to Rowland. "It's in all of our interests to know if she is going to take this to another level and turn psycho on us."

Rennon was staring intently at his laptop. "On,"us"? That's an interesting way of putting it. Erm, perhaps not a bad idea considering what I've just read here. It says that despite a generally rational outlook it is necessary to keep a close eye on her in view of previous mental instability triggered by traumatic events in her life."

Rowland laughed. "Kel, you had better remember to lock your door at night."

Kel stared out of the window at the stars and blackness of space. "I don't want to hurt or upset her. I just don't want her in the way she wants me to. That night showed me that. Now I have to live with it."

Rennon shut his laptop. "Well we had better come up with a way to gently convince her that she doesn't stand a chance. If you are sure you don't want her."

Kel's glare silenced Rennon.

After about an hour Kel got up and went off to the gym to spar and train. Rennon returned to his laboratory and managed to put Rowland off, sending him to the hanger bay to check on a faulty Hopper.

Kel was the first to get a message, it came over his personal pager and he laid down his weapons and picked it up. "Report to the Commander". He bowed to his sparring partner, a tall, blonde haired man dressed in a regulation issue track suit, then, left for the showers.

Rennon got the message next. He was eagerly pouring over his computer screen analysing a list of data when his pager went off. He reached for it without looking down, clicked on the read button and raised it so he could see it on the screen then hit "save". He shut off the laptop before heading for the Commander's office.

Rowland was in the hanger bay reading a novel. The Hopper was in the bay in front of him, its components spread across the floor in untidy heaps. He heard the bleep of his pager and finished his chapter before lifting it from his pocket to read his message. Hastily he rammed the bits of the Hopper back into place and screwed the panel back. Finding a spare piece he unscrewed the panel again and reinstated the missing piece before screwing the panel back again. As he was hastily leaving he met a trainee engineer on the way in. "Hawkins, run a full diagnostic on Hopper seven, I think there's a problem in the basal wiring." Too right he thought as he strode off down the corridor, leaving Hawkins to redo his handiwork.

Rennon arrived at the Commander's room first. There was a young Marine on the door who knocked for him, opened the door and let him in. The Commander was standing looking at the painting behind his desk and turned to face him. "Ah Rennon, good, take a seat son."

There was a knock on the door and Kel came in. They then had to wait nearly a quarter of an hour for Rowland who stepped through the door, flustered and red faced.

The Commander cleared his throat and looked at them with concern. "Now this is not good news. Shantara's shuttle hasn't returned after the evac run. She's three hours overdue and I want to send a recon mission. As you are her usual crew I want you on this as soon as possible. I've allocated five Marines to go with you. There is a possibility that the planet was over-run. Our intel told us we had days before the Followers arrived, there's a possibility this information was flawed or it was a trap.

The last report we had was that they were approaching the planet and everything looked normal. They were on final descent and due to report in within the next hour. They missed that report and they are now three hours overdue. We have reason to believe that we may have been compromised. Intel has reached me today that we may have a spy on the base. As you know everyone here is screened before entering and you all have regular evaluations. We thought we were clean but apparently not.

The shuttle came down and its transponder is still beaming a signal but they are not responding to the radio. I'm afraid I could be sending you into a trap and I want you to be aware of that.

Kel, I'm making you senior officer on this one as it's more your expertise. Your tracking skills should be very handy.

When we scanned the planet about a month ago we didn't see anything other than the settlement we have been trading with. It is not impossible that there are people living in the mountains but the people of the village denied any other occupation and we questioned them fairly extensively. We've also lost contact with the village. They are a primitive people but they did keep a radio there for communicating with us. There is no signal from it now."

Rowland looked annoyed. "Don't we have a long range scanner? Surely that would be safer than committing more people."

Kel looked at him in horror. "What do you mean Rowland? Shantara is a team member."

Rowland looked up at him. Their difference in height was very noticeable.

"I meant that it was best to check if she is alive before we risk more resources. We don't know what is happening there."

Kel grunted. "No, that is why we need to find out. If you don't want to go I'm sure the Commander will find someone else."

Rowland smiled. "Well there is bound to be another engineer who will fill in. I'm not sure what use I'd be to you anyway."

Rennon piped up. "Rowland, you have to be kidding me. You are keen to be part of this team, now you want someone else to step in. Either you are with us or you are not."

Rowland didn't look too happy. "Don't be ridiculous, she wasn't on a mission with us when it happened. We're not joined at the hip. Well some of us aren't." He looked from Rennon to Kel. "I'll go, alright, you win."

Kel shook his head and cast a glance at Rennon. The Commander closed his file. "Gentlemen, you have a go. You have permission to go off base." He picked up a pen and noted Rowland's comments and attitude on his file.

Kel and Rennon were walking down a corridor. Rowland had gone another way to return to his room to sort something out first. Both had fixed expressions.

Kel turned to the right and Rennon followed close on his heels. "Rennon, what the hell is it with that guy? Either he's a member of this team or he's not."

Rennon shook his head. "When we were taking him on, before you joined I read his file. He's just like that, he's not a team player but his references were good and his qualifications astounding. Well according to his file anyway."

Kel grunted.

An hour later the Hopper hovered over the planet and the smoke from the wreckage of the shuttle rose in a plume into the air. Debris was spread over a clearing and from the air they could see bodies strewn amongst it. They used their scanners but they could find no life signs in the area. Rennon held his new scanner cautiously and pointed it toward the ground. He pressed the on button and the machine began to beep and bleep. The screen flickered into action and a map of the ground appeared on screen.

Rennon tapped it. "No biosigns, there's nobody alive down there and there's no sign of her subcutaneous implant. I've extended our scan to the village. No life signs there either. This is not looking good."

Kel took the Hopper down and gently landed it next to the damaged shuttle. He used the ship's scanner to scan from the ground but found nothing. The ramp slowly rolled down and the clear spring air filled the inside of the Hopper with a fresh clean aroma of the countryside. Birds were singing and everything seemed peaceful. It was the perfect country scene other than the downed shuttle and the dead crew. The smoke was being blown by the breeze away from them and there was only the feint aroma of the burning ship.

Cautiously Kel took the lead, followed by Rennon. Rowland hung back and waited for the other two to step outside. Weapons were at the ready, safety catches off. They scanned their surroundings over the barrels of their guns. Back to back they made their way forward while Rowland made his way backwards into the shuttle and checked the pre flight protocols. The Marines fanned out, covering the area and soon half were back in the Hopper wondering what to do next.

Rennon sent an encoded message back to Mission Command.

Kel was still outside searching around the debris with the Marines. Rowland was sitting in the passenger hold. None of them saw or heard the cloaked ship as it hovered above them and then glided to land over the ridge. The scanners were unable to detect it. The only clue was a feint movement in the trees.

Kel was looking at the ground so he missed it. He spotted some tracks and an indentation which had bothered him from the moment he saw it. He checked around the area and followed the tracks as they went to and from what he assumed was a shuttle or some sort of craft. He went over it and over it until he found the track he wanted. One set of returning boot marks was slightly heavier than the rest and he hadn't detected a heavier one going out.

Kel stood at the bottom of the ramp. "I've found some tracks on the east side of the wreck. It looks like a Hover Shuttle may have rested there and another group have been in the area. They have left very little trace. These guys are very good. We haven't been the first to this crash site. There are signs that one person may have been carrying something back.

There was a sound outside and Kel turned and saw three Followers in full Follower regalia. They were of a matching height, tall and thin. Their long black robes fluttered in the gentle breeze and only one wore the signature leather cape with high collar that had become so recognisable. All had their hoods up and the gauze that hid their faces gave them an eerie undead look. Kel was immediately hit by a stunner before he could react. He reeled but was hit by two more before he sank to the ground. The others were firing at the Hopper and blasts hit the inside, one very close to Rowland's head. Rowland did not hesitate, he jumped into the cockpit and hit the emergency button and the Hopper shut its doors. Rennon made a leap to catch Kel's unconscious body which slid over the edge of the closing ramp. The hopper took off leaving Kel at the feet of the Followers as they approached blasting at the retreating hopper.

Rennon leapt into the cockpit and tried to override the controls but it was too late. The system was automatic. Once the button was depressed the ship would only return to its hanger bay. Rennon screamed at Rowland who looked stunned at his response. He then punched him, knocking him back against the control panel before he slid unconscious to the floor. Rennon fumbled with the controls in a vain hope that he could override the auto-return. Then he fell back hopelessly into the pilot's chair and grabbed the radio.

Rennon's voice was broken. "Rennon, S4542, Recon Mission. Rowland aborted mission with auto return when Kel got stunned. Kel has been abandoned on the planet. Three Followers in attendance so immediate assistance is requested."

Kel woke up somewhere cold and dark. He tried to move. It felt like every part of him hurt. He was not restrained. He sat up and waited for his eyes to adjust to the dim light and took in the stale, damp and slightly metallic aroma in the air. As his eyes focused, the only illumination was coming from a small window located high up in a bare metal wall. It cast a bright square on the floor and gave off an eerie glow which illuminated just a small part of the room. Once he was accustomed to the dim light he could see that the room appeared to have solid metal walls on three sides although the back of the room was difficult to see. The fourth was constructed from sturdy bars behind which he could just make out a dark corridor and a blank wall beyond. There was an old light fitting high above him but the bulb was broken. He could see that there were items of furniture near the back wall and these cast dark shadows.

Immediately he sprang to his feet. Nothing seemed broken but he staggered a little. He ran to the bars and cautiously tested them to make sure there wasn't a current running through them. He then rattled them wildly with all his strength but they held firm. In desperation he threw himself at them but all he got was a badly bruised shoulder as the bars vibrated but held firm.

As he slid to the floor clutching his bruised shoulder he noticed something move in the shadows. It was only a slight flicker out of the corner of his eye. He moved across the floor with lightning speed and grasped into the darkness. His hands met warm soft skin. He grasped what turned out to be an arm and pulled a woman out from her hiding place behind a pallet bed.

She pulled away from him but relaxed as he pulled them both into the dim beam of light. Once in the dim light he tried to see what she looked like but it was almost impossible. He could see that she was dressed in a thin white dress which was covered in dirt and blood. She was trembling.

She looked fragile but he felt muscles like iron in that delicate arm. Her voice was silky and gentle. "Easy Tiger, I am a prisoner too, they brought you in yesterday morning unconscious. I am no threat to you. I have medical training and I've checked you over. You are in pretty good shape, they must have just stunned you and brought you here. You were lucky."

He released his grip and she relaxed. He offered her a hand, she took it and he helped her over to a bench. They both sat down. He spoke as gently as he could, seeing that she was still shaking. "Sorry. You spooked me. I'm not in the habit of grabbing women that way."

"I'm glad to hear it. You are forgiven. This is truly a spooky place though. I am Kyla Deralis of the Eltalashi. May I ask who you are?" Her voice was a little more assured now and she rubbed her arm where he had grabbed her.

"I am Kel Elyn of Eldoria." He bowed his head slightly and smiled at her.

"I have known quite a few of your race over the years, many have been good friends." Her voice was sincere and her expression gentle.

"So, what can you tell me about this place? How did you get here?"

"I don't know how long I've been here. I was stunned when I first came here so I don't know how long I spent unconscious. I was on a pilgrimage to Ha'Ka'Tash when the village I was staying in was attacked. I have taken a vow of non violence until I attain the final order of enlightenment as a healer. So I was taken without a fight. There were four of the villagers in here with me but one by one they have been taken away and they weren't brought back. They took them down the corridor dragged unconscious.

This cell is sound locked by what I can guess as I have tried various ways to call out or get someone's attention but I haven't managed it. There is no echo and as the place is silent, it seems that they do not want to hear us. I would assume there must be others but I can't tell how many. I have seen many carried past the bars by the soldiers though.

The guards are the Soltari Death Knights, the genetic creations of the Followers. You look puzzled. They are the same usual skeletal faced warriors but they have been mutated or manipulated in some way. They use them as guards and for basic tasks. They aren't particularly bright but they don't need to be. They fulfil a function and they can be very nasty." She involuntarily rubbed her shoulder and he could see the black bruise which covered much of her neck and chest.

"The walls are metal as you can see and they can run a charge through them so you were right to be cautious. It's a high voltage charge but obviously not lethal. It will give you a serious jolt and knock you out. I don't know how long I was out when I first tried it and got shocked unconscious.

They don't open the bars without stunning you first. There's no point hiding as the stunners have an area effect."

Kel was watching her intently. Her eyes were red from lack of sleep, her dark brown hair was matted with dirt and her face streaked with mud and dried blood. Despite the dirt she was still classically attractive. Her green eyes were intense but her whole aspect was that of one who was totally exhausted.

She looked directly at him, meeting his stare without fear. "I don't know what planet we are on or where we are. They speak a language I don't understand so I don't know what else I can tell you.

They haven't tried to convert me as far as I know but I've no idea if they used their drugs on me as I've been stunned often. I have to assume that they have as should you.

By what I've seen that skeleton like bony carapace is actually joined or fused to their face. I haven't been conscious when they have been too close but I'd hazard a guess. How about you?"

"I was on a mission to recover some of our people lost on an evac mission and got stunned when we were overrun."

"Welcome to wherever this is. I'm afraid I can't offer any hospitality. It's a bit cold, it gets worse at night."

"We won't be here long, my people will rescue us. Aren't you cold? That dress isn't exactly warm."

"That is the best news I've had. I have no intention of staying here any longer than I have to. Neither do I want to turn my back on two years of pilgrimage by being forced to fight them so I'm not much help. I have been colder than you can possibly imagine. You are right, this dress offers precious little protection from the chill in here." She gave him a tired smile.

"You won't need to fight when my people get here. We'll soon get you out of here to somewhere warm."

"They check on us about once a day, not at any regular time. They don't come in and if they do they stun first."

"They will get us out, don't worry." Without thinking he put an arm around her. She didn't flinch although he hesitated just before he made contact. She felt like ice. "We'll get out."

She looked up at him and smiled then rested her head against him. "I hope so, I really hope so."

The hours passed by and the light from the small window faded to dusk and then night. They spoke about many things, of Kel's home world, of Kyla's. They talked about happy memories, feasting, hunting and fishing. Kel kept his arm around her and tried to warm her up by rubbing her hands which were like ice. As the last light faded Kel turned to Kyla. "I think we ought to try to get some sleep. I will keep watch."

Kyla put a hand on his arm. "If they are coming for us they will stun us so there is nothing we can do about it. I've been too scared to sleep properly and it feels like I haven't slept for a lifetime."

Kel rolled onto a stone pallet and fell asleep. The sound of his snoring rumbled in the darkness and echoed off the walls.

Kyla smiled to herself, the snoring was somehow reassuring and for the first time in ages she drifted off to sleep despite the biting chill of the room.

Kyla woke up. The room was bright as day. The light had been fixed and was on and there was no sign of Kel. The room looked the same, only a little different. She couldn't place what was wrong with it.

There were skeleton warriors all around her. They stood in a circle. As they stepped forwards they raised bony hands and removed their skeleton masks. The face beneath was blackness, the only feature she could see was an open mouth filled with long pointed fangs.

As they bore down on her they ripped the flesh from her bones while she watched, unable to move. She tried to scream, she couldn't as she was paralysed with fear. She focused, gathered her inner calm and called on her training.

The scream she let out was blood curdling. Kel fell off his pallet bed in his haste to get up. He leapt to Kyla's side as she screamed in her sleep. He lifted her from the bed and shook her awake.

In her dream Kyla had been eaten to the bone before a robed figure stepped through the parting sea of skeleton warriors. He carried robes and a mask. The mask was outstretched in his hand and he reached towards her. It went dark as the mask covered her face despite her desperate struggling.

The mask fell off as the skeletons shook her then she realised they were gone. It was all gone. There was only Kel there.

Tears rolled down her face. He wiped them away with his thumbs while cradling her head with his hands.

Kel smiled at her as her eyes glistened with tears. "You are awake now. It was only a nightmare, only a dream." She looked up at him and he pulled her head to his chest and wrapped his arms around her. "You are not alone. Come on, lay down, you will be fine. Come on, rest now. You need the sleep. Do you want me to stay with you?"

She rested her head on his chest, the tears running down her face and she was still shaking. "Yes."

They lay down together and she finally drifted off to sleep again. All night he held her, both waking occasionally, jolted into wakefulness before drifting off to sleep again.

They woke when the light flooded through the tiny window. Kel woke first but stayed where he was as Kyla was still asleep. He lay there watching her sleeping. She awoke with a start, looked up at him and smiled.

The guards came and went, once a day, every day for nearly two weeks. In that time Kel and Kyla had plenty of time to talk and to share experiences from the past. They laughed, they cried and they started to become friends. Every night he held her in her sleep and tried to keep her warm despite the cold. He found comfort like he never had before just having her there beside him. Her straightforward conversation with no demands on him or agenda in what she was saying was welcome and despite his surroundings he actually began to enjoy having her there. She for her part enjoyed his company and having someone she could talk to. She liked the straightforward way he saw the world and that he didn't expect anything from her other than her company.

Then one afternoon down the hallway a metal door swung open, grating on the uneven floor. Marching feet stamped towards them and five Follower Warriors stood in the darkness. Their bone faces glowing white in the dim light. They did look like they were wearing masks as the bone carapace seemed to stand away from what looked like a face underneath. Their black shiny metal insect like armour reflected what little light there was. They raised their stunners, fired and both Kel and Kyla fell unconscious.

Kel awoke on a table in a brightly lit white tiled room. He tried to move but he was restrained with metal bands across his wrists which held him down to a metal table. He wildly tried his strength against them, growling at his captor as the skin on his wrists broke with the ferocity of his attempt to escape. He looked around the room wildly in a panic, looking for Kyla. She wasn't there. There was blood on the floor, he saw that and fought ever harder driven on by his anger.

A small man with a bald head and very bird like features walked cautiously across the room. "I wouldn't struggle, those bands will hold you. You might as well relax and accept this. Do you know what this is? No of course you don't." He giggled. "It's something new and you are going to be the first person to try it. This is a drug I have perfected. It will suit you perfectly. One dose of this and you will attack anyone. What do you think of that?"

"I think if you take these bands off I'll happily attack you drug or no drug." Kel growled at the man.

"No, I'm afraid that I'm not the subject. There's no point me trying this out with someone you might want to attack. I thought it would be much more appropriate if you attacked someone you might not be so keen to take your anger out on. Like your cell mate. She is a much more suitable opponent for you. I heard your conversation, of course your cell was being observed. You are a man of honour from a planet well known for its vicious fighters. She is a healer and defenceless. It couldn't be more perfect. This will be fun to watch. You won't have any control over yourself but she won't know that. Just to make it even more upsetting for you we are going to chain her to the floor as well. Then we're going to put you back in with her and you can watch her suffer with the injuries you have given her and the only medical assistance she will have will come from you. You are more than likely going to have to watch her die. What do you think about that?"

"Bastard." Kel fought the bands like he'd never struggled before, willing them to break.

"I thought as much. Well, here we go. No point in struggling. He picked up a stunner and fired. Kel fell back unconscious.

Kyla had come around in a concrete room. She immediately tried to stand up and found her ankle was chained to the floor. She tried to get free of it but the chains were too thick. She could vaguely see that there were people above her behind glass panels. "Let me go, what do you want me for?" She shouted as loudly as she could but nobody answered. She stood there for

29

what seemed like hours when in fact it was barely half an hour. She sat down again and tried to keep herself calm.

Kel woke up in a circular room with no windows and no apparent door. The walls were white painted concrete, blood stained in places. There was no visible door or escape route. Above him, around the walls, well out of reach, there were faces pressed to the glass watching him. Uncontrollable anger arose in him and he wanted to kill them. A wild feral feeling took him over and the need to inflict pain on anyone in his path ran through him. He reached for his blaster. It was gone. On the floor in front of him there was a baton, about a meter long and studded with nails. He grabbed it and tried to jump to break the glass. The onlookers stood up and cheered. He could hear them clapping and commenting to each other in anticipation. They were all now on their feet trying to get the best view they could. Kel growled and howled but there was nothing he could do. He ran at the wall and tried to climb but his hands could find no purchase on the smooth stone. He tried again and again but that just made him more and more angry.

Kyla tried to reach him but he was on the other side of the room. She knew that something was wrong. He looked wild. His eyes were staring and his veins were standing out on his face. He started howling at the people behind the glass. Then she got to her feet. He had not yet noticed her. She had a few feet of movement but no further. She moved towards Kel. Reaching out, she put a hand on his arm when he got close enough. He was looking towards the windows and ranting at the onlookers after trying to climb the walls so he hadn't seen her.

He felt the warmth of her hand on his arm. His feelings were confused. Then a red mist seemed to come down over everything and all he could think of was that she was his enemy. She was dangerous and he had to kill her. He growled at her, then balanced himself and pulled his arm back to take a swing.

Kyla looked at him in horror. "Kel, you know me. I'm no threat to you." In a rush of movement that seemed to happen in slow motion she looked into his wild eyes, his pupils were still dilated and his veins stood out with the strain of extra blood pumped around his system by the drug. Something was wrong with him, she was sure now. Her body tensed immediately. Thoughts rushed through her head. She tried to make sense of what was happening. She made every effort to control herself so she didn't look like she was going to attack in any way, calling on all of her discipline as she took a defensive stance. All she could think about was what she would lose if she failed this great test of her own resolve. She must not fight back.

He took a swing at her, well aimed and if she had not moved with seemingly unnatural speed he would have taken her head off. She screamed at him to stop. He ignored her and hit her full force on the shoulder. The baton knocked her to the ground, her blood spilling in an ark around her. Then he leapt on her, punching wildly, before standing up and kicking her.

She lay still, feeling the pain from each blow. She feigned unconsciousness, using all her calm and skill to try not to react to the pain from the blows until he stopped. He lifted her now limp body over his head until the chain that bound her pulled her down. He reached down, pulled with all his strength and broke the chain before swinging her around and throwing her to the edge of the room. She hit the wall with a sickening crunching sound and could feel her bones breaking. She wanted to cry out but she bit her tongue rather than do that, knowing that if he thought she was still alive the punishment would continue.

Above the crowd went mad. They were standing and applauding as white gas filled the room and Kel and Kyla lapsed into unconsciousness. Kyla's last thoughts were of the healing she pulled into herself in the hope of staying alive as she felt the life slipping away from her.

Kyla woke back in the cell. She opened her eyes and her head felt like it was going to split in two. The pain she felt was unbearable and she was about to move when she caught sight of Kel sitting on a bench on the other side of the room. His head was in his hands and his hair fallen down over his face. His crow feathers lay in a broken pile on the floor in front of him and he stared down at them. Seeing that he wasn't looking, she tried to move, but the pain was so great it made her cry out. That got Kel's attention and he looked up at her. She froze, terrified that he was going to attack her again. He didn't, he got up and rushed across the room to her. She tried to get away but that just caused more pain. Flashes of light nearly blinded her and she could feel that her legs were broken. She tried to move her arms but they were broken too. The pain in her back was sharp and she felt cold, everything from the neck down hurt but somehow that was reassuring. All that she could hear ringing in her ears was that horrible crunching sound as she had hit the wall. Kel crouched over her as she lay on the pallet. She tried to open her mouth but she could feel that her jaw was broken, as well. The sight of him took the words away and the pain was unbearable.

There were tears in the big man's eyes. "I didn't mean to. It wasn't me in there, it was the drug. They drugged me, they made me hurt you." He put a hand on her arm and the pain was terrible.

She took a deep breath and summoned all of her strength. She was about to speak but the pain silenced her. She opened her mouth but at that point everything went black.

The evening passed into night. Kel wanted to hold her, to keep her warm but he knew that every touch was agony for her. He sat on the pallet with her and watched her as she slept. Occasionally she would wake, wide eyed and in pain. He gently stroked her forehead and reassured her.

The days passed by and he did what he could for her. He had no medical supplies but he fed her as gently as he could around her broken jaw and gave her water when she needed it.

Kel heard a sound and looked up. He felt an excitement of hope which became intense when he saw Rennon and four Marines, armed to the teeth and just about to blast the lock off the cell bars. "Boy am I glad to see you guys."

Rennon smiled. "I thought you might be. We had to get you home in time for Rowland's Courts Martial. I thought you might like to give evidence about how he left you for dead on this planet."

"He what? That snivelling little weasel. I hope they throw the book at him."

Rennon stepped into the room. "Don't worry, they will. Commander Zack will see to that. Now, let's get you out of here and this wee lassie too. It looks like they did a real number on her. All the other cells in this block seem to be empty." Rennon had rushed over to Kyla and was gently checking her over.

Kel looked at his feet. "Be careful with her, she's had a rough time. It was me, I did that to her. They drugged me Rennon, I had no control at all over what I was doing."

Rennon looked up, his brow furrowed. "Look my friend you aren't going to like this but I'm going to have to cuff you. We have no way of knowing if you've been brainwashed and there is a command word to set you off. That drug is probably still in your system. When we are back to the base I'll get a diagnostic run on you and find out. If it is then we'll get it out of you. For now, I'd rather get us out safely than you start turning on us."

Kel held his hands out. "I'll come quietly but can I carry her? You haven't got a gurney and I'd like to. I can't harm you if I'm carrying her. It will leave one of the marines free to fight."

Rennon slapped two sets of hand restraints onto him and joined them together to give him more flexibility so that he could carry Kyla. Rennon bent over her and took out a knock out shot from his belt. He broke the cap off of the needle and inserted it into her arm as she looked up at him pleadingly. He squeezed the rubber ball which contained the fluid and watched as she drifted back into a painless sleep. "That should make it easier on her if it gets a bit rough on the way back." He then lifted her gently into Kel's arms. Kel looked down at her blood stained dress, her pale face streaked with the blood from the many deep cuts he had inflicted on her. He took a deep breath and followed the others.

They were met by five skeleton faced armoured warriors coming down the corridor. The marines fired and before the assailants could get a shot off they were on the floor. They were slow and no match for Rennon and the marines. The crew stepped over them and continued down the corridor to the now open door. Outside they encountered another twenty warriors who died in the same way. They were passing a door and Kel caught a glimpse through the glass window. "Rennon, stop a minute. This is the lab, this is where he's making the drug."

Rennon reached into his bag and put a hand on Kel's arm as he heard sirens going off around the base. "Stay back. No time to deal with it any other way. The research guys are going to kill me but…" The Marines formed up around him as he opened the door, his body to the side so that all anyone firing randomly through the door would hit was the back wall. The scientist looked up from his table where he had been grinning insanely as he mixed two vials together. The resulting green liquid foamed slightly. He was about to drink it as a small round metal object rolled across the floor. He looked at it. Sudden recognition crossed his face as he realized that the object was a grenade. Rennon called to the others "Fire in the Hold". Rennon shut the door and as it went off the scientist, the room, his experiments, notes and chemicals were blown to pieces. The blast blew the doors open and burning debris flew out into the hallway and fell ineffectually onto the stone floor. Inside the lab everything was burning.

Rennon waved them on. The crew ran around a corner where they came to an open window. Rennon turned to Kel, "Now this is where we came in. The Hopper is outside and it will uncloak when they see us. I'm going to take her from you. You climb out and I'll pass her out to you. When you have her run and don't stop. Get in, buckle her up and yourself. We'll all get out if we do this as smoothly as possible. Now go."

3

Dr Samson looked at the readings on the screen and shook his head. His sandy short cropped hair was neatly combed. He had gentle "boy next door" with a touch of the rogue features. His face was set in concentration. He ran his fingers through his hair, messing it up before pressing a button and calling up more readings. He was in his early forties, his white coat immaculately clean, his retro stethoscope hung decoratively around his neck.

In the isolation room Kel was screaming at the walls and trying to break his restraints. He bellowed and screamed and fought with a ferocity that caused his bed to bounce around. Red bands were appearing on his wrists and ankles despite the amount of padding and bandages that were there to protect him. His eyes were wild, the veins standing up in his neck and face.

Commander Zack strode up to the exhausted doctor and looked over his shoulder. "So, what is the diagnosis Samson? Can you isolate the drug?"

Dr Samson looked up, his features worn with care and too many hours looking at the screen. "The drug is definitely ravaging his system but that is pretty obvious to everyone. The strange thing is that this time there is no device. It seems to have a part of it that has reacted with the part of the brain that produces adrenaline, the basic fright or flight part of the brain triggering an almost constant need to go into a form of kill frenzy which we can't bring him out of. Isolating the drug has become a problem as it seems to involve a protein which has bonded with his genetic structure. The laboratory it came from has been destroyed so getting any more is unlikely. I ran a full scan and I have the technical readout for the drug, it seems to be multiplying in his system. If I can't check its multiplication he is going to be locked in a constant rage and the corresponding wear and tear on his organs will lead to shut down. In short, it's going to kill him if I can't come up with something fast."

The Commander looked at the nearby computer screen with the technical readouts displayed. "Is he lucid at all?"

Dr Samson turned around. "He knows that there are people there but as to whether he knows who they are or not, I don't know. Everyone seems to be the object of his hatred, fear and need to attack. I think there was more going on there than we originally thought. I think we were either expected to rescue him or he was going to be turned loose at this point, probably at some location where we would be sure to pick him up and bring him back here. That drug makes him a bomb waiting to go off. He was lucid for nearly a day and then he just flipped into what you see now. It is also possible they were using some form of neural inhibitor to keep him manageable. The effect of that has now worn off. For now all I can do is try to administer a similar neural inhibitor and buy ourselves more time. That is him with the inhibitor, that's the best I can do. It does at least make him lucid on occasion. Whether that is going to be any better for him emotionally I don't know. He's pretty cut up over what he did to that other prisoner."

The Commander put his hand on the table and turned around. "I know you are doing all you can. You can only do your best. If you need any resources or equipment just let me know. What about the woman. How is she?"

"Unfortunately Kel is a very efficient killing machine and I have no idea how she has survived her injuries. She has her arms and legs broken, most of her ribs, two lumbar vertebrae and her lower jaw has had to be wired. Her fingers were broken and she has a shattered pelvis. Most of her internal organs have sustained severe damage. But she's still with us and strangely enough her vital signs are strong. I put her in a chemical coma to give her body a chance to heal. With that amount of injury the pain was just unbearable and any painkillers I was able to give her were just not enough. She's resting now so her body can do its work. I've set the bones, pinned and wired what needed to be pinned and wired and we will have to see how she comes on. I got a chance to talk with her before I put her under and despite the pain she was very logical about it all. Her main concern was to let Kel know that she knows it's not his fault and she doesn't blame him. She made me make a recording just in case she doesn't make it through. I found it quite remarkable that her only thoughts were so practical considering the pain she was in."

"Did you find out anything about her?" The Commander looked concerned.

"Very little, the pain was so great that I kept her sedated most of the time." Samson looked worried.

"Do we know where she came from?"

"Yes, I've written it in my notes. It could be worth making contact with her people and letting them know she is alive. She said she didn't know how long she'd been in there but I've tracked it back by knowing when she was captured, she'd been there a little over six months." He picked up his notes and looked at them. "Not a lot else to say really but we have her home world so that is a start."

The Commander left the room and sent a communiqué to Kyla's home world. It was answered and three hours later Rennon was dispatched in a Planet Hopper with a couple of Marines.

The Hopper flew over the lush woodland and rolling plains until it settled in a clearing next to a village made up of mud huts. They did the post flight checks and the ramp lowered. As they were stepping outside they noticed a party of people advancing towards them. They were walking slowly and deliberately. It took a while but eventually the party got to them. It consisted of an elderly woman who appeared to be the village elder by her clothing. Her feathers hanging from long white plaits, animal skins and trinkets hanging from her woven brightly coloured loose fitting clothing which swayed as she walked with the aid of a stick. She was being supported by two muscular young warriors armed with spears and blasters. Two middle aged men walked behind. They moved to stand on either side of the elderly woman when she got close enough to the Hopper to speak to them.

"Welcome to our village. I am Maran, Onoshari of the tribe. This is Erlis and Ren, she indicated the middle aged men and these are my helpers Sher and Irol. I have been expecting you and if you would join us we would like to invite you to enjoy our hospitality."

Rennon stepped forward. "I am Rennon. I believe we spoke over the radio. Thank you for your hospitality. We would be delighted."

He fell in behind the welcoming party, the Marines fell in behind him and they walked to the village.

The village mostly consisted of dome topped mud huts constructed in various shapes with added wood and materials. Each was elaborately decorated with feathers, painted wood and carved bone which hung like mobiles moving in the wind. The wood that supported them had been intricately carved where they could see it through open doorways. In the centre of the village there was what looked like the main meeting building, another dome. It was colossal and towered over them as they approached. As they stepped inside, the huge vaulted ceiling took Rennon's breath away. It was completely painted in rich colours. The light which filtered through canvas panels created an atmosphere inside that was distinctly magical. In the middle of the room there was a raised platform on which there was a large fire burning in an ornate metal fire pit. Behind this there was a large throne. Benches and tree trunks were set out around the walls and the central area in a circle around the outside of the room. A table had been set up beside the fire and drinks were brought on a wooden tray for them. Maran seated herself at the head of the table and they were brought food which looked like a cake made of meat and vegetables.

Rennon bowed his head slightly as a good sized portion was put in front of him and a drink placed to the side of it. "I thank you for your hospitality."

Maran smiled. "Eat, drink, young one. It has taken courage to come here."

When they had eaten their fill and were relaxing with a warm drink Maran waved the rest of her people away. Rennon did similarly with the Marines, leaving the two of them in the silence broken only by the crackling of the fire.

"I thank you for taking care of Kyla, she is like a daughter to me. You have done much for her but I'm going to have to ask you to do more. I have a problem here now and the safety of the tribe is in jeopardy. Without your intervention the problem would not have arisen so I am asking you to help me to sort it out.

You may or may not know that Kyla has for many years been our leader. She has ruled by right of birth and has done well. I am very proud of her as she could not have done any better had she been a true born daughter of this tribe. That is the problem. Since she has been away the tribe has been well cared for by Andalon, son of Alathon. He took over her rule temporarily by right of birth. He would have been leader had it not been for Kyla and her prior claim. He has faced a minor challenge from Desash who also feels he should command the throne and what little resistance there has been has been quickly quelled as he fears Kyla's return. It will not be so once the truth comes out that she will be unable to retake her throne. I'm telling you this in confidence as there is nobody else I can see who can help with this situation. Either way I will have to tell the tribe now that she will not be returning before the moon is at its full tomorrow night. That is when she must reaffirm her right as ruler or it will pass to open battle.

This could not have happened at a worse time. She has been away on her pilgrimage which was supposed to finish with her return for the full moon. The White Lady would then have granted her full mastery of the last order and all would have been well. That mastery is greater than even I, in all my years, have been able to attain. Nobody would have dared to have challenged her as that would have given her unquestionable rule for the rest of her life rather than the annual renewal she has to perform currently.

Kyla cannot be here for the reaffirmation so her rule is at an end one way or the other. There is nothing we can do about that. Nobody can take that promise for her. I cannot speak with her so I am going to have to be strong in my faith that I know her well enough to know what she would do. This is also an opportunity to put right a wrong that I did many years ago. It is an added complication but it could be the solution as well. Despite her belief that she is, Kyla is not of this tribe. The elders know of this but it is unknown to the rest of the tribe. It was decided many moons ago to leave the situation as it was when she proved to be such an effective leader. Her mother died giving birth to her but she was a visitor here. I took her under my protection when she arrived in a damaged shuttle and she had been healing with me when the birth started. I did all I could to save her, much as I did for Tyrannon's baby who also died that same day. It seemed such a harmless thing to do, I took the baby without a mother and gave her to the mother who had lost her baby, she never knew.

But, all actions have repercussions. At that time the Followers were unknown to us and her position in the family was so insignificant it was deemed as a mercy to allow the childless mother to have the baby. But by the time Kyla came of age all her adopted family were dead and that left her next in line for the tribe leadership. She sat on the throne by assumed right of birth when in truth she does not carry the bloodline. Her bloodline must be noble though or she would not be able to use the Stone of the Seer. That was my saving grace as there was nothing to betray what I had done. But, this might actually help us strangely enough. If she is not entitled to the throne then it would fall to the one next in line. That will bring peace.

Andalon must assume leadership of this tribe at the full moon tomorrow night. I believed that if I took Kyla through the right of the healer she would have a purpose if the truth ever came out. If it did she would in any case have to leave the tribe or accept Andalon as a mate. As she is not of the tribe it is not possible for him to claim her. That is a great sadness as they would have made a wonderful couple as they do have an affection for each other and would have had many strong children.

If Andalon claims the throne now it will be challenged. Then the title would most likely pass by rite of combat. They should fight it out but that is not that coward's way and he fears Andalon who is a fierce warrior. He will prefer to take the way of gaining people behind him and then take the tribe that way. It will divide us all and create a bloody battle for the throne as others will die on his behalf.

I honestly had planned to reveal the truth to her on her return after she had completed the rite of the healer and been given her sword and right to fight back. As High Priestess of the White Lady she would have taken her place within the Higher Order and been accepted into the Chapter House.

It was a sad truth that once the truth was discovered she would have had no option but to stand down at the affirmation if she would keep peace in this tribe. But by her rights of status her word would have been law. As I've already said this would permit her to declare Andalon as the new leader and if he is challenged to accept that challenge for him. Andalon must not ascend the throne with blood on his hands or an ancient prophecy will be fulfilled and whether it is true or not there will be dissention within the tribe. Once he is safely on the throne, reinforced by right of birth, then I could have revealed the full truth. Once he has taken the oath at the appointed hour nothing can be done to change that and my deception may well in time have been forgiven.

What I need you to do is to find someone who will fight for her. I intend to ensure that this is the only way that the throne can be taken. This is not to be undertaken lightly as the battle will be bloody and to the death. It is undertaken in the mountains in a cave which provides a natural amphitheatre and there will be no quarter given. The challenger is an accomplished warrior and will fight very dirty as this is everything he has ever wanted. I need you to find me someone who will be able to fight him with no mercy, he must die. Can you do that? You explained to me the situation and how she came to be harmed. Will her attacker take on the fight that she now cannot?"

Rennon looked thoughtful. "I'm going to have to return home before I can make any decision as it is not my choice to make. We cannot speak with Kyla, her injuries are too severe. We have put her in a chemically induced coma and it is not known whether she will survive. If she does we are unsure what sort of a life she will have left."

Maran's eyes filled with tears. "If she had not been on her quest the result would have been very different. She is a fine warrior. She has truly proven herself worthy of mastery and I would ask you to take her sword back with you, whether she lives or dies. She must die a warrior. But for now the one who harmed her must take her place for that fight. I can only ask you but considering the situation I would be very disappointed if you refused."

Rennon looked down at his hands. "He has taken the drug and the effects of it could kill him. Its effect on his system is taxing and he cannot take much more."

Maran smiled. "Bring him here and I will heal him if I am able. We will work on bringing him back to his old self once the safety of the tribe is assured." The smile fell from her face. "Return to your people and make the arrangements and make your decision. I will be waiting for you." She got up and left. Rennon followed her and found his men outside the door.

In the Hopper on the journey home Rennon piloted the craft solo so that the Marines could take part in a game of Battlestones in the back. The Hopper glided effortlessly into the docking bay and the passengers disembarked.

Rennon went to the mission briefing room. There empty chairs were not lost on him. It was merely days since they had been filled. Now there was just him, Dr Samson and the Commander sitting there discussing what was to be done.

The Commander took a drink of his coffee and put the mug carefully down. "What they are asking is for me to put Kel's life on the line. What is your medical opinion on this Dr Samson?"

Dr Samson looked down at his notes. "In my opinion Kel is under more strain because he isn't fighting. It is in the drug's nature to make him want to fight and holding him back is putting strain on his body. If we can restrain him and take him there then he could well do what they want but it is exposing him to the possibility of being killed. It is also putting him in a position where he can in some way make amends for the damage he has already done, albeit not his fault. It will give him a better chance of healing himself mentally and forgiving himself."

The Commander looked up, surprised. "Well, under those circumstances you have a go. Arrange containment for him, fetch his weapons and return to the planet. I want you to go with him Dr Samson and at the first sign of trouble sedate him and get him out of there."

Dr Samson closed his file. "I will get him contained and moved this afternoon, by what you say there is little time to lose. I am assuming here that Maran is going to do all the talking."

Rennon smiled. "Maran sounds like she might be able to do the talking for all of us."

The Hopper touched down gently on the planet and a tracked vehicle rolled down the ramp, carrying the containment unit with Kel inside. His weapons were strapped in a box to the side of the unit and Rennon and Dr Samson walked beside the vehicle, checking on the readouts and making sure that everything was working.

Maran came out to meet them, accompanied by her two helpers. "I am glad that you have come. I have been using the Orb this afternoon and I have discovered much. The signs are good. This was all meant to be. It will work out for the best, I am sure of it. Bring him, the gathering is about to commence. I will do all the talking. All you need to do is to let him out of the box at the correct time and all will be well."

She led them around the outskirts of the village and up into the mountains. They followed a narrow track which was just about wide enough for the vehicle to cautiously make its way along. Below them they could see the vast coniferous forest that surrounded the village stretching out into the distance and the mountains on the other side of the valley rising to their snow capped tips. The air was fresh, it was slightly chilly and the wispy clouds scooted across the turquoise sky. Up and up they went following a well worn track. Occasionally there was a flat stone, placed against the wall and carved with a symbol.

Finally Maran stopped in front of a cave opening and led the way inside. They followed with the vehicle and Rennon stopped in his tracks as the cavern opened up. It was vast. In the middle there was an arena circled by a fence and then seats which rose like an amphitheatre to the back wall.

The cavern was full of hundreds of people waiting expectantly as they rolled the vehicle inside. The elders of the tribe stood facing them. The two contestants stood facing each other in the centre of the arena.

Maran walked into the centre of the arena and raised her walking stick. "People, I have much to say and I will say it if it is the will of the elders." She looked at the line of dignitaries, dressed in fine embroidered silk robes. One by one they raised their ornamental stick and said "Aye" in agreement.

"That is good." Maran walked up the steps and took her place on a stone balcony beside the elders. "Now, we shall begin. As you know as oracle for this village I have the right to speak at these gatherings." The candlelight was flickering and it cast shadows on her face making her look even older. "As you know the Chieftain cannot be here tonight to oversee the handover of her rule. As is our law she may appoint a champion to fight and a voice to speak for her. By right of position I have taken on the right of speech. By virtue of my age I have waived my right to fight for her. If fighting is necessary it shall be done by the creature who took her strength, who violated her and who put her in a state of near death."

Rennon had made his way to the seat that had been set aside for him. He went to stand up when he heard her words and he felt a sharp blade against his spine. Maran's bodyguard leant forward and whispered in his ear. "Move and you are a dead man."

The room was in uproar. Warriors hurled loose masonry at the box, most hit, making it rock precariously. Maran raised her hand and silenced them. "Be still, we will see how tonight unfolds and we must adhere to Kyla's wishes spoken through me. Step forward Andalon, come and take your rightful place on the throne."

Andalon stepped up to the throne and stood in front of it. He was a tall and well built man, about six foot two and muscular. His dark features were somewhat similar to Kel's heavy brow but he had a lighter bone structure. Immediately he was challenged, a sword was thrown to the ground, its tip dug deep into the impacted soil. "I challenge!" The challenger was a smaller man, his frame lighter and he had long light brown hair which was braided with feathers and animal skulls.

Maran raised her stick and all fell silent. "The Challenge has been issued. You will fight the beast for the right to take the throne."

"I challenged Andalon."

"Your challenge to Andalon has been accepted by Kyla, the one who harmed her must fight in her place as punishment for his crimes. That is the law. Are you standing against me?"

"No Maran, I would not do that."

"Good, then you will fight the beast. What honour would you have left if you refused to fight the one who violated your leader?"

Rennon relaxed. The bodyguard leaned forwards. "I trust you can see why she worded things as she did."

All but the challenger left the pit and the gates were closed so the Challenger and Kel were fenced in. Rennon pressed the button that worked the remote door opening device and the door swung open.

Kel came out of that box like a wild thing and his weapons were released onto the floor. The Challenger was hit full force and flew backwards against the pit wall twenty feet away. Before he could get to his feet Kel was upon him, unleashing the frustration of over a day of being tied up with all the pent up aggression running through his veins. The Challenger literally did not know what hit him, again and again. He was thrown about, punched, kicked and thrown off balance. Then he found his footing and the fight was much more evenly balanced. The fight went on. Kel regained his weapons and from punching the injuries escalated as they both used their swords and daggers to good effect. An hour passed, and another, and another. Both men were tiring but none stepped in to stop the fight. It was a fight to the death and that was how it had to be.

Kel scored blow after blow on his opponent. The other fought with a ferocity that matched his. They were evenly matched. Blow after blow was dealt, blood was spilt and the sand ran red with it. Neither would stop and there was no chance of surrender or mercy.

Finally the Challenger made a mistake. He sidestepped into a punch and then slipped on the ever growing pools of blood on the floor. Kel saw his opportunity, caught the opponent's head and neatly snapped his neck. He roared and dragged the corpse until it fell lifelessly to the floor. Rennon had his stunner ready and as Maran stood up and nodded to him he blasted Kel a few times. Kel fell to his knees, fell forwards and was still.

Maran raised her stick. "Now I proclaim Andalon leader of this tribe. Does anyone else challenge?"

There was silence.

"Good, well I would ask the Elders, is Andelon leader of this tribe?"

One by one they stood up and shouted "Aye".

"So for the second and final time I proclaim Andalon to be leader of this tribe."

Andalon took his place on the throne and Maran placed a circlet on his head. He then stood up and everyone cheered. He raised his hand and the room fell silent. "People, I will do everything in my power to be a good leader to you as Kyla and others have been in the past. As my first act I would call for Kyla's attacker to be brought to justice. This uncontrollable beast should pay for what he has done to one of our people by the Rite of Ast. I also call for the Aionarie. I would claim Kyla as my mate by ancient law and by all that I hold true."

Maran looked stunned. It took her a moment to gather her thoughts before standing and raising her stick to silence the raised voices of the assembled host. Maran's assistant leant forwards and spoke into Rennon's ear. "Aionarie hasn't been declared in centuries. It is an oath bond which states that the woman is being asked for as an equal. That would have made Kyla co-leader of the tribe." Rennon was reaching for his blaster and his Marines were doing the same. "People, much as I would have dearly loved to have seen Kyla with such a worthy mate it cannot be. For the sake of the tribe a great secret was kept from you for many years but it must be revealed now. Is it the will of the Elders?"

Again they stood up in order and shouted "Aye".

"Then I will speak my truth. It was before Kyla was born that her mother came to this planet by shuttle. It crash landed here as it had been badly damaged by the Antastari when she had left her home world. Kyla's father was killed before they left Eldorian."

Rennon gasped and looked at Dr Samson who raised an eyebrow.

Maran carried on. "He was part of the security force trying to keep the Followers from overrunning the planet. They were one of the last shuttles off of the planet. Her mother arrived here injured and despite my best efforts the injuries were too great, she died in childbirth. Kyla's given mother had just lost her baby that same day and it was agreed that she should be given the baby. She never knew that Kyla was not her natural child so she spoke her truth all the days of her life. May she rest in peace with the spirits.

By our law that means that Andalon may not claim her as his mate as it is forbidden for a Chieftain to claim any mate who is not of the tribe. He also may not claim the blood of her attacker as she is not of our blood. It is known to me that her attacker was under the influence of the Followers when he exacted such damage on her and violated her body by breaking her limbs. I would also ask of those who brought him here, where is he from?"

Rennon had not seen this coming. He was stunned when all eyes were upon him. He stood up and cleared his throat. "He who you see before you is not usually the ravening beast you saw tonight. He is a loyal and honourable friend who would sooner kill himself than harm an unarmed woman who was bound before him. But, this is the result of an experiment carried out by the Followers. They have given him a drug which is binding with his own body to make him the beast you see before you. Despite our best efforts we have no way of unbinding this drug which is multiplying in his system. He will die if we cannot do anything about it but rather than him die in vain we brought him here so that what may be his last breaths may be used to defend the woman he would never have wished to harm. Not least because she is of his people, one of the few left. He too is of Eldorian."

The cavern had fallen silent. Then two of the guards unlocked the pit gate and entered. They carried Kel out and Rennon followed. Maran followed on behind and Andalon was left to speak with is people.

They carried Kel higher into the hills and as it got steeper the path got narrower until it was merely a goat track. Still they ascended until they came to a cave. The mouth was covered by thick animal skins and as they stepped into the darkness inside Maran hastened to light candles.

"Here, lay him here. I will see what my medicine can do. Now tell me, what did you find out about this drug?" She brought over stuffed animal skins and fleeces to make Kel as comfortable as his unconscious body could be.

Dr Samson who had kept silent until this point stepped forwards. "It is chemical based and is multiplying in his system, growing and linking with his organs and glands to produce adrenaline."

Maran furrowed her brow and reached for a leather bag. Dr Samson was about to stop her but he hesitated when she pulled out a bioscanner and ran it over him. She looked up at him and smiled. "What you thought I was going to pull out a magic stick and make it all better?" She ran the scanner over him and waited for the results. "Alstoic, they've used Alstoic, how cunning. I've never seen it used in this way. Its from the Alstoic Bug which has a sting which makes the victim angry, afraid and more likely to leave the insect alone and go off and attack something far larger. It's a cunning little bug too, hates sunlight and tends to move into other animals' dens. Of course if it's challenged it simply bites them. It is unlikely in their rage that they will see a small bug and they go and attack someone or something else. That then gives the bug something to feed upon. Very cunning. Now, what to do with it? You are going to need an antidote. I actually wish Kyla was here as she's really good at this sort of thing.

The bug's eggs are carried in the sting venom. The venom also has a component which is a parasitic algae which forms the bond between the venom and the body. We need to break that bond. Very well, so now we've got to find an antidote to egg cells floating around a system, latching on to anything that creates adrenaline. Ah, I've got it, a bit of healing could go a long way here. If you would be so kind as to lay him on his back I'll use healing energy to bring his adrenaline levels down. Once they fall below a certain level the eggs will not be able to feed on the adrenaline so they will start to deteriorate and will certainly stop multiplying. I would make yourself comfortable, it's going to be a long night."

They all sat down and Maran arranged herself in a position where she was propped up and could keep her hands over Kel without having to strain muscles over the many hours she had to sit there pumping her healing energy into him and keeping him calm. From time to time Dr Samson administered sedatives and combining the two by dawn Kel's heart and breathing rate were far lower and he was beginning to lose the tight veins that had been showing all over his body.

Dr Samson picked up the scanner and ran it over Kel's prone body. All sign of the eggs had gone, his system was clean. They had broken down in the night and been flushed by the blood stream and into the kidneys. So, gradually he reduced the sedation so that Kel could have a chance to come around.

Kel opened his eyes and looked around blinking. "What hit me, I feel like I've been run over by a shuttle."

Maran put a reassuring hand on his shoulder. "Don't you worry, you've had a rough old time of it over the past few days but hopefully the worst is over now. You are going to be weak for a while. You may want some help to get back down the mountain but in a day or so you should be fine. I'm sure that Dr Samson here will take good care of you. Now, if you don't mind I'd better be getting back to see what is going on in the village. We will go down the mountain together but I suggest you leave this place and do not return until you have Kyla with you. The people of this village may have believed what I said but they have a strange sense of justice sometimes and may see you as their enemy until she personally puts them right. I will try to contact a friend of hers who will be able to help. He may well visit you."

Kel grunted. "Thank you for what you did though." He looked up at her, his expression peaceful.

Maran smiled. "You are welcome. You still have the hardest task ahead of you." She put a hand on his shoulder.

Kel looked confused. "What's that?"

Maran gave a really enigmatic smile. "Telling Kyla."

Kel swallowed hard. "I guess so. Do you think she will ever forgive me?"

Maran looked at each of them. "Kyla will forgive you, it is in her nature. But will you forgive yourself? Now it is time for you to leave if you wish to get back to your craft before the hunters start out for the day."

They followed Maran down the mountainside in silence at her slow pace. They parted with Maran at the village and went back to their Hopper and glided away into the infinite depths of space.

4

Kel and Rennon sat in the crew room and the door opened. Dr Samson stepped inside.

The Doctor poured himself a cup of coffee from the urn and sat down. "I've just come back from a meeting with the Commander. It would appear that I'm on your team now."

Rennon took a sip of his own hot coffee. "Welcome, it will be good to have you along with us doc. But, how do you feel about it?"

Samson took a mouthful of his coffee and pulled a bit of a face. "Nothing like the coffee back home is it? Me, well I feel that I would be better placed in the Infirmary doing the job I was trained for. I'm no combat medic. My aim is lousy and I am definitely not the outdoors type."

Kel barely raised a smile. "You'll do fine. How is Kyla? Fix her and you can go back to the Infirmary, I've heard she's a medic."

Samson looked down into his coffee. "I heard and I'm counting on it. Although I don't know if she would choose to stay after what happened. We'll have to see." Rennon glared at him as Kel's face dropped. Samson smiled nervously. "Physically she is healing far faster than I would have expected and I'm really pleased with her progress. I adjusted my program when I found she was one of your race. It worked out, she responded far better. I did a test by the way, matching your DNA, she is definitely of the same race as your good self. After treating your injuries for so long I know what you can take, she's not doing too badly either, I'm impressed. She is strong willed and her body is strong but I am worried about her. He body took a heck of a lot of punishment sustained over a long time. She has also suffered from the cold. I've skin grafted where I can so there shouldn't be any scars if she does survive or perhaps a little minor scarring but nowhere that would generally show. It's her emotional health I'm worried about. Even if she does survive there is no way of knowing what that sort of stress will do to her mental state. We do not know what she was like before the injuries so it will be difficult to judge her emotional state when she is finally reawakened but I can guess how you'd react.

It has been nearly a month now. Her limbs are on auto movers to stop atropine in the muscles and electrical pulses are maintaining her physically so there is little to worry about there. What does worry me is that her neural activity is unnaturally high for someone in a coma, in fact for someone who is not. There is a lot going on in there and I've no way of knowing what that is."

Kel's cleared his throat. "When are you going to wake her up?"

Jack faced him. "It is likely that I'm going to bring her round in the next week or so. She will still be in extreme pain but that is better than risking long term emotional problems. I'm glad that you are sitting with her Kel, I have no way of knowing how much she can hear. As I've already said, her brain activity is far higher than it should be, there's a lot going on there despite the coma. She may well be able to hear every word you say."

Kel looked horrified. "So she may be unable to move yet able to think. That would drive me nuts."

Jack nodded. "That is why I can't keep her in a coma until she is fully healed. I'm worried what that lack of movement is doing to her."

Kel looked thoughtful. "Maran may know something we can do. Shantara told me something about meditation and that sort of thing. I wasn't really listening. Kyla is a Master. She may well be in some sort of meditative state or wandering off somewhere spiritually."

Rennon put his coffee cup down. "I still can't believe we couldn't find Shantara."

Kel looked up from contemplating his coffee cup. "It was like finding a needle in a haystack with nothing to go on. We did our best and we will find her, someone somewhere is going to know where she is and when we find out, we will go and get her. Whoever took her is really going to pay. If they had taken her with a good intent she would have been in touch by now. You know our best people are on the case when we can't be. She could be anywhere on any planet. If only we'd had the time to search that planet properly before we had to evacuate."

Samson took a deep breath. "That planet was overrun pretty soon after you took off. I can only hope we will get her back. But, hoping isn't enough is it, we need some leads. Look, I don't mean to put the idea down but I'm a medical man, I've no way of knowing and until proven I can't accept the spiritual theory, but I'm prepared to do a few tests just to find out. What I will say is that her vital signs do react to you being in the room and talking to her so she does know you are there."

Rennon looked surprised. "Kel, so that is where you have been."

Kel turned to him. "I needed to be there. I feel good talking to her and it helps to explain things to her. She is one of my own after all and I did put her there. Look we're due out on a recon this afternoon why don't you come with us doc to get a feel for it all?"

Samson choked over his coffee. "Like I've got a choice."

In the infirmary Kyla's body lay motionless on the bed. Machines monitored her vital signs and unnoticed her neural activity accelerated dramatically.

Out in space a ship approached Mission Command. It was glisteningly smooth, an almost liquid silver outer hull reflecting the starlight as it silently glided through space. Its nose cone was pointed and it tapered at its tail, like a diving water bird and just as elegant. It moved effortlessly and with purpose, heading directly towards the base.

The ship had made no effort to evade being noticed. It was flying directly towards the base and slowed to hover almost motionless above the central hub of Mission Command. Once there it presented an open channel and began hailing. It was only when it arrived that those watching realised that it was twice the size of their space station. Its huge bulk blocked out the stars. It just hung there in the air, silent and intimidating. The control room was already by then in a state of high alert and the Commander had been called. He sat on his chair and stared intently at the screen, watching the craft as it hovered above them.

Dreafas, a middle aged man with a mop of curly black hair, who was doing his shift on the comms piped up. "We are being hailed." He flipped switches and turned dials.

The Commander nodded. "Patch our visitors up on screen."

A man appeared on the screen. He was elegant, slim faced with well defined high cheekbones. His features were fine, his skin immaculate and pearl white. His bright steely blue eyes darted about taking everything in, his shoulder length blonde hair was waved slightly and swayed with his movement as he spoke. "I am Lord Joniel, Commander of the Elthsantia and Master of the Order of Brax. I come in peace under Section 457 of the Intergalactic Treaty to talk about trade and to visit a friend who is injured and is recovering within your facility. I request permission to come aboard."

The Commander hesitated momentarily as he keyed the name into the central computer and awaited a response. It came back with a Code Purple which meant highly dangerous and extremely influential but all information Clearance Gold which was above Commander Zack's extremely high clearance. Commander Zack attempted to hide his surprise but the visitor smiled slightly. "I am Commander Zack, Commander of this base and it is an unexpected pleasure to speak with you Lord Joniel. I am assuming that you speak of our guest, of Kyla? Permission is granted and you may come aboard. Will you be requiring a docking port?" Before he could take a breath at the end of his sentence Joniel stood in front of the Commander who jumped slightly. "I had assumed that you would land by ship and I could have met you at the airlock."

Joniel smiled. "I am sure it would have been with every courtesy and full protocol and I thank you. I must apologise if this way of transport is not your way, I forget sometimes. I find this a more elegant way to travel. Now, if I may visit my friend I would be very grateful and it will give you time to assemble your negotiators so that we may speak about trade treaties and how we may help each other. These are difficult times, I hope that any previous enmities and distrust can be laid aside."

He stood a few inches taller than the Commander. His long black cloak hung from his broad shoulders, the leather body armour beneath was skilfully crafted with swirls and points. The Commander looked up at him, pulling himself up to his full height. "I will arrange for an escort to take you to the Infirmary. May I ask why you would visit?"

"I would visit Kyla of the Order of the White Light." He turned on his heels as the Commander called for his guard. "She is beloved of Maran and I owe both of them a life debt."

The door to the Command Centre opened and Kel with three Marines stepped inside. Kel stopped in his tracks when he saw the visiting stranger who looked at him making him physically shudder. Those eyes were piercing and seemed to cut into his very soul. Kel could see a hatred for him and it gave him a chill that ran down his spine.

Joniel spoke slowly and deliberately. "I understand you were the one who inflicted these injuries on her?"

Kel strode over to face Joniel. "I was. I trust that Maran has given you all the facts."

Joniel put a hand on Kel's arm which made him reach for his weapon. "She has. There is no need for that. Put your weapon away. We both know what a real war is like as we are fighting men. No need to show your prowess now, we have nothing to prove to each other. I trust my reputation precedes me, if I wanted you dead you would be now, I could easily have administered poison by this touch." He smiled wryly. "There are necessary casualties and there are those that we have to kill. Rest easy, I know of your reputation and the truth. The only wisdom I can speak for you today is this. Look to yourself and your obvious skill, you could easily have killed her which was their intent. You did not, even though you were drugged. To have even that level of control while under the influence of that type of chemically induced passion says a lot about your strength of will. You have nothing to fear from me on this day though one day we may spar for the sheer enjoyment of it. My time is limited here, take me to her."

Kel smiled. "You do have a point. In the situation I could so easily have killed her. Something must have stopped me." He felt strangely comforted by the intimidating stranger.

Joniel nodded knowingly and waved away the comment with a velvet gloved hand. "I have no doubt."

They walked to the Infirmary and the way had been cleared. The corridors were empty so they were able to talk on the way.

Kel walked beside Joniel. He kept taking sideways glances, sizing him up. Joniel strode along the corridor. He made no sound, his boots silent, his cloak billowing out behind him. Kel took a breath. "You have known her for a long time? How come you have a life debt to them?"

Joniel smiled. "I have known her for many years. We met when she saved my life on the twin moons of Keldar. I have known Maran some four hundred years. Kyla is of the White Light, as such she would normally have been unlikely to help my kind. Her compassion for another in need set her above many of her order in my eyes. I am of the Eanesti, my race kill without remorse, we have destroyed whole civilisations over the years and we are not known for our compassion. I am asked to be here by Maran, I will do her bidding, this once. Kyra called me also, she has the powers of the White Order now and she was able to contact me during one of my meditations. I am sure that she will be a great asset to all of you if you choose to allow her to stay and if she chooses to stay. If that is not your intention then she will always have a place on my ship. For now part of a debt will be paid. It is sensible that our people co-operate as we now have a formidable enemy so it is not purely on this matter that I have chosen to visit you. So, I will speak later with those of you who arrange such things. Although it is not normally my way I am being open and honest with you in all of this. You need information and I would not wish you to spend valuable time looking for these answers out of mere curiosity."

They turned a corner and were at the Infirmary. Dr Samson was waiting by the door and they stepped inside.

Joniel stepped towards the prone woman. "Leave us." His voice was commanding although it waivered slightly as he put a hand gently on her shoulder.

Dr Samson took a deep breath. "She is my patient, I will certainly not leave her with you, a complete stranger."

Joniel smiled. "Your courage is commendable. That is brave talk as I can feel your fear. You have nothing to fear from me at this time. I will allow you alone to stay Dr Samson until I have completed all that I must physically do and that which medically she needs. After that I ask for time alone so that I may speak with her. You may keep the monitor on but without sound. You will see things that will not be to your liking and know this, if you try to interfere I will kill you and anyone else who may enter the room. I do not usually explain myself but it is important that you know the use of this vial I am going to leave with you." He passed a small glass vial to the doctor. "You must use this wisely, use too much and she will instantly die. Our race uses this toxin to paralyse or it can kill but used properly it will numb her pain and allow her to heal much faster. She is a healer, let her heal. One ml once a day at precisely the same time, not a minute sooner or you will overdose her, later and the effects will wear off and she will be in exquisite pain that no pain killer will sate if you get it wrong, so don't. Now, I would suggest that you leave the room and Dr Samson that you ready yourself for what you are about to see."

He waited while the others left the room and Dr Samson took up his position where he could clearly see what was going on. Joniel looked down at the prone woman, his sharp eyes softening slightly. "I must feed on her to be able to introduce the venom into her system. You may find this unnerving. Do not move as disturbing my concentration could be lethal for her. I will have to curb my natural instinct to kill and control the dose I am giving her. This initial dose cannot be given through a syringe and I must also exact my payment. It is what was promised."

He bent down over the prone woman and gently put his hand on her chin, tipping her face sideways. He ran his fingers over her cheek, gently stroking it and lifted her. He sat on the table where she had been laying, cradled her in his arms gently, then he bent down and bit into her neck. His teeth met slight resistance as he broke through the skin and sank his now extended fangs down into the vein in her neck. He shuddered slightly as the warm blood flowed into his mouth and he felt the warmth of her body close to him.

Dr Samson checked himself as he almost stepped forwards. Joniel didn't see him as he was bent over her.

Joniel remained almost motionless for what seemed like an age. Then he laid her down and stepped back, gasping for breath, wiping his mouth with a silk piece of material he pulled from his pouch. He steadied himself with a hand on the examination table. "I have taken very little. You may bring her around any time that you wish now. I will leave that to you. I would appreciate if you did so now, as I would speak with her and my time here is limited."

Dr Samson stepped forwards and busied himself taking her pulse and checking the monitors, his hands shaking slightly.

Joniel watched him with some amusement. "The blood will be made up swiftly so she will not feel its loss. If you are ready, bring her back to consciousness."

Dr Samson went to a cabinet on the wall and lifted out a small glass bottle, taking a syringe he drew off some of the clear liquid and injected it into the liquid feeding into her arm. "She will wake shortly."

Kyra opened her eyes and looked up at the two of them standing over her. She smiled and the pain seemed to have gone from her face. Her face was still swollen and black from the bruising as was her neck and any part of her skin that was visible. The wires around her jaw caged her mouth. She looked exhausted and there were dark circles under her eyes.

Joniel bent down. "Kyla, do you know me?"

Her voice was weak. "Yes." Her eyes seemed brighter and she looked at him longingly.

Joniel spoke to her in almost a whisper. "I heard your call and I came in answer. Can we consider our life debt played out now?"

Her voice was broken and she winced in pain. "Yes. Can you get me back to the Affirmation before the full moon?"

"No, that time has long passed. Our ability to manipulate time was lost in a battle with the Followers, the ship was destroyed. It is good that the debt is settled." He sat up and spoke slightly louder. "Dr Samson, I would have time alone now. I trust you have completed your preliminary tests?"

Dr Samson bowed slightly and backed out of the room, switching the sound off on the monitor before leaving. He was ashen white and still shaking slightly.

Joniel sat on the bed beside Kyla and took her bruised hand in his. "Now we will be bound as equals again, not as one with a debt to pay to the other. You would be welcome on my ship and I would have you come with me. End this eternal torment I beg you. But it is your choice. If you do not find a home here, come to me whenever and however. You would find a good life with me."

Kyla looked up at him. "I would dearly love to, now as always, but the bonds that tie us are still the same. I have my duty, you have yours."

Joniel looked away, carefully making sure his lips couldn't be seen by any monitor. "I know that one day it will be different." He bent down and kissed her on her forehead.

He looked up and motioned for the others to return. Kel and Dr Samson came in immediately. Joniel smiled at Kyla then looked up at the pair of them. "Take care of her. Now I will return to your Commander and we will talk about trade agreements. Dr Samson, I believe Kel would like time alone with her. They have much to discuss. Remember that you must administer the dose every 24 hours to the minute until the vial is empty. Farewell." With that he touched the pad on his wrist and vanished into thin air.

Dr Samson rushed forward and began to do more checks on his equipment and took readings. "I cannot find anything that he has done other than to administer the venom and drain a few pints of her blood. I've checked the chemical formula and it is what he said, feeding venom. It will keep her in a state of euphoria, she will feel no pain but she will be able to communicate and be conscious while still healing. How do you feel?"

Kyla smiled slightly. "Better, I feel numb. And she is still here. Talk to me not about me."

Dr Samson picked up his clipboard and turned to go. "Sorry about that.

52

You are still tired, take some time to talk to Kel and then I want you to rest. I will come back later and make sure that you are comfortable and I'll bring you something to entertain you as well."

"Thank you." Kyla turned her eyes to face Kel. "It is time we talked."

Dr Samson left the room and the doors swished closed.

Kel shifted his feet.

Kyla spoke, her voice quiet and she spoke carefully so that she didn't have to move her jaw too much. "You have said all you needed to say while I was unconscious. I heard every word and I have my answers and you may have your forgiveness. Now forgive yourself so we can get on with being friends."

Kel looked uncomfortable. "You heard everything?"

Kyla was quiet for a moment, trying not to smile. "I heard every word. Andralon will be a good leader. So, what are our people like?"

Kel stepped closer. "I will tell you later and I'll bring you photographs of the planet you would have called home. One day we might even go there. I'm sure you will be welcome here if you choose to stay. You should rest now. I'll come back and see you later if you would like me to."

Kyla looked up at him. "I would like that."

Kel put his hand on her shoulder gently and looked down at her for a moment before he turned to walk away. "I'll be back later. Try to get some rest."

Kel left the Infirmary and went to Rennon's lab. Rennon was at a terminal scrolling through information. He ran his hands through his hair making it stand up and be even more spiky and unruly. "I'm just looking up something. I'm working on trying to get a way of detecting Followers. What I need is a comparison so we need to catch one of them so that we can find the differences. Are you up for a Follower hunt?"

Kel smiled. "Now you are talking."

Rennon picked up his bag. "Good job I've already got the go ahead to go off base and for the mission. Dr Samson can't go with us as he's tied up in this meeting with Joniel as they seem to have medical supplies that we could do with. Come on, let us go and pick out a Follower for ourselves. I would suggest that we go to a non technological planet and grab one from there."

Wordlessly they went to the crew room, kitted up and when the go ahead for the Hopper came up on the screen they made their way on board and slipped off into space.

Nearly an hour later the silent cloaked Hopper glided across the night time skyline of Elanos, a small planet within the cluster known as Eukatius Minor. Below them the wide tracts of forest spread in the darkness, broken by the mountains and the many villages and settlements that clung to the valley sides and nestled in clearings. The village they were looking for was one of the larger ones, set on the east side of the planet.

Rennon checked his screen again. It had been reported that there had been Followers sighted there though not in full force as yet. As they circled the village everything seemed quiet and nobody was about. The sun had set many hours ago and other than the meeting hall there was little movement although candles burnt in every window.

Kel looked up. He had been thoughtful for the whole journey and they had hardly spoken. "So why did you choose Elanos?"

Rennon was reaching for his scanner. "It has been occupied for almost five years though not with a full force. It had been a mid level technology planet that had been welcoming advancements, now it seems to have slipped back to low technology. The Followers have made few if no developments. They have just removed the technology that was already here. Do you see, the communications array still hasn't been repaired, can you see it there blackened and twisted. That burnt out warehouse housed the village's heating and power supply as you can see is beginning to be grown over. I can't believe how little they actually do for the people they take over. The people on this planet nearly froze to death last winter as they had no heating. Similarly with other planets, the Followers have allowed them to slip back technologically.

I'm just going to check if they have any scanners working. Our scanners will pick up the distinctive signature of their bio scanners and protective shields. That is a bonus, there is nothing showing on screen. You see those watch towers, they are registering as empty. Everyone seems to be in the big meeting room, elsewhere there seems to be nobody about."

Rennon looked up from his hand held scanner. "Everyone seems to be in there, there seems to be a meeting going on. It will give us a chance to get into the village fairly easily. No, hold on, not so easily. There are heat signatures in the woods around the village and I have no way of knowing who or what they are."

Kel was pressing buttons and preparing the Hopper to land. "There's one way to find out. Might as well take this down and go in and have a look around."

They glided the Hopper silently over the ridge line and brought it down in a clearing not far from the village. The trees were tall evergreens with very little ground cover growing under the towering canopy. The distinct smell of the pine forest filled their lungs with clear air and the damp aroma of the rotting needles and other vegetation as the rear ramp of the hopper descended.

They cloaked the hopper so that it remained invisible and moved swiftly as there was no real cover other than the trunks and soon enough they were making their way over the ridge and into the inhabited forest close to the village. The trees were deciduous there and there was much more ground cover. They moved as a pair, silently and swiftly, alert and ready for anything that might jump out at them that they had not noticed.

Kel caught Rennon's arm and they dropped to the ground. Kel scuttled off sideways and rolled into the undergrowth. The next thing that Rennon knew was when he heard a loud thump to his right as a body hit the ground and rolled beside him.

The body was bulky, about six feet tall and dressed in a carapace of armour. Seeing it close up he could see that what had looked like solid metal when he'd seen these creatures before was actually a type of fibreglass that would not stop a bullet. The unconscious body was one of the Followers' skeleton faced soldiers. Rennon was just reaching out to touch when Kel leapt on the body and with a great deal of force managed to cut the creature's throat. He then ran a scanner over it. "I can't find a transmitter but I know there is one. Don't look at me like that there's no way we could take one of these things back to the base. I'm sure there's a transmitter on it but I just can't find it. They have an internal self destruct. Take him home and he'd blow a hole in the place." He held out a hand held scanner which was showing a reading in red letters and numbers.

Rennon pulled out his biodetector and ran that over the body. "That's because whatever they use is not metal, it is some sort of grown organism. I'd reprogrammed this scanner to look for this sort of thing. Don't ask me when, I can't remember but I've seen something like it before. Wait a moment."

He pulled out a small roll up kit and unrolled it, taking out a scalpel and tweezers. He cut the tendons that held the exoskeleton onto the skin and lifted up the plate and then cut down into the white dessicated flesh below. After digging around under the near featureless face for a while he held something up to the torch light. "Et voila! There it is, a small transmitter. I've just had a thought, if this sends back life signs they are going to know we're…"

His timing was perfect. He almost finished his statement as they heard noises in the woods all around them. They were surrounded by more of the soldiers. It was impossible to see how many in the darkness, but more than five. They started blasting into the darkness at any movement they saw. Then they came under fire from the woods as laser blaster beams flashed a deadly green through the darkness of the night. The first bit deep into Rennon's arm, the second into Kel's leg. Rennon let out a howl of pain, Kel bit his lip slightly but they both kept firing. They were firing blind into the woods with little hope of hitting anyone except by a lucky shot.

They rolled to a position between two tree trunks and kept firing at the soldiers they could see. The shooters in the woods still hadn't revealed themselves but the occasional blaster beam reminded them that they were still out there. Another soldier fell but moments after Kel took a blast in the shoulder from one of them and there were others coming out of the wood now to join them. They were trapped.

Rennon swallowed hard. "So, what do we do now?"

Kell replied, his voice monotone. "We keep firing. They are getting ready to rush us. Just keep firing."

Rennon smiled. "Fair enough." He kept firing alright and hit a soldier clean in the chest. It fell and was replaced by one coming up behind.

Kel roared as he took another blast in the shoulder. He leapt out of the overestimated safety of the fallen trees and charged the woods. The firing stopped.

Rennon had also stopped firing as he tried to evaluate the situation and to work out where Kel was so he didn't shoot him. He was still peering into the darkness when Kel landed beside him having leapt over the fallen tree. "Did you miss me? Thankfully they did. Come on, they won't be confused for long."

He grabbed Rennon and they rolled out from under the trees. They then ran. Zig zagging through the trees they made it to the Hopper. They found it by running into it, felt their way around and the door opened, they jumped inside and Rennon leapt into the pilot's chair. "Straight home?"

Kel landed beside him. "Straight home."

Rennon hit the auto-return as Kel reached for the medical box.

Kel bandaged Rennon's arm. "How does it feel?"

Rennon winced with pain. "It feels like I've been shot. If you are really lucky the doc will put you in a room with Kyla."

Kel looked at him. "What do you mean by that?"

Rennon's smile faded. "You have to be kidding me. She's one of your people and when those bruises fade I wouldn't mind putting money on it that she's going to be worth a look. You've been saying right from the start that you would not consider any other woman than one from your home planet. Ah, I get it now. That was your get out of jail free card when they got too close wasn't it?"

Kel pulled Rennon's bandage comfortably tight and taped it so it didn't unravel. "This isn't the time to consider things like that. I want her on our team, anything else would complicate matters. What should happen, will happen. For now she must recover and if we don't get up to a full crew soon we'll end up being divided between other units. We're three, we need to be four, even five to get our own missions. This one today would have been better with a full crew. Neither of us are human in the way the base considers human and the Commander will probably want to assign us a new leader. Better that Kyla joins us before we are assigned someone else."

Rennon had just finished bandaging Kel's leg where he couldn't reach it. "I can see your point. She's not human either though. Well at least Dr Samson is going to be happy, I guess his trip out is cancelled now."

The Hopper flew in autopilot and landed effortlessly on the landing pad.

A medical team was there to meet them and they were taken to the Infirmary.

5

Rennon looked up from his notepad where he had been doodling a design for an auxiliary power unit for his hand held modulator. They were in a meeting in the briefing room and up until that point it had been the same old round of protocol and administration. Now he'd heard something that had really made him sit up and listen. "Could you repeat that please sir?" He almost made himself jump as he said it.

The Commander cleared his throat and turned to Rennon. "Certainly, we have been informed that Shantara may well be on the Planet of Alexandrinos. We have been working with Kyla and she has managed to activate an ancient piece of technology which has boosted our scanners enough to pick up Shantara's implant."

Rennon raised an eyebrow. "Kyla?"

The Commander smiled. "Yes, we had been aware for some time that a mystic can activate various pieces of technology. We are fortunate enough that she appears to be particularly talented in this field. On a scientific level as you may know that is basically what her training was all about, attuning the mind's vibrations to access the technology. Her DNA is quite remarkable and allows her to be able to access artefacts that others have had no luck with. If you remember the transcript of the day she came here, Maran clearly stated that she could access the Orb on that planet. That means she has what they call the "Noble DNA". While she has been recovering we have been working with some of the pieces we have been unable to activate until now. It seems our new guest is proving very useful."

Kel grunted. "How did you know you wouldn't kill her? She is still very weak."

The Commander turned to face him. "She is willing to help and understands the risks involved. We need this technology and she is happy to do anything in her power to help us. It will come as no surprise to you all that I have extended an invitation to her to join us here. I am waiting on her reply.

I am putting together a team to investigate the planet and to try to locate Shantara. This will have to be a more diplomatic mission than the ones you are used to. This is not an occupied planet. It is a highly developed civilisation with a very well established political and governing system. They have managed to fight the Followers off. That in itself makes them interesting to us. We have tried to open diplomatic channels but we have received no reply as yet.

I have spoken with High Command and they have suggested that we send a small reconnaissance party to go and take a look around under the guise of traders. They have also informed me that there has been a lot of activity in that quadrant of late. They would like to find out more about what is going on there.

I'm taking it as read that Rennon and Kel will be willing to be part of this expedition. Dr Samson I would like you to go too. This is a peaceful planet so you'll need to tread carefully."

Kel laughed.

Commander Zack put his papers down. "So your usual style of interrogation will have to be toned down, won't it Kel?"

Kel swallowed. "Yes Sir."

Commander Zack picked the papers up again. "As I have already said, Alexandrinos is a highly developed technological planet and a highly developed civilisation. It is well known that they have been gathering some of the brightest minds from all over and taking them there. I have no intelligence as to whether this is willingly or unwillingly but it is known that slavery is legal on Alexandrinos. You may find this distasteful but you must under no circumstances try to interfere. If Shantara is being held as a slave then your orders are to secure a price and buy her back. It is possible that Shantara was taken there as she is able to read many languages. Far more than anyone I have ever met. That would immediately appeal to them. Until we know the situation your directive is to investigate and report back."

Rennon was taking notes. "So, you think they took her to translate and to work on languages. Surely they would let us speak with her."

Zack turned to face him. "Not if she is a slave who has been taken against her will. They are yet to answer any of our hails and diplomatic overtures. They are also a closed world. Little is known about them so you would be going in blind and reporting back is not going to be easy. But, Rennon, I am sure you can find a way."

Kel had been folding a piece of paper, he stopped. "So how are we going to get in there?" He looked concerned.

Zack looked serious. "They may not accept outsiders going in there without a good reason. It is known that we are against slavery so it is not possible for you to use this as a form of subterfuge. Our only alternative that I can see is for you to take Kyla with you. Her ability to activate the artefacts would make her a valuable commodity. I don't have to tell you that you would have to protect her while she is there but she is willing to go. I have spoken with her former home planet and they already had trading relations. The emissaries from the planet have dealt with her before so no doubt will be more than willing to deal with her again which gives us an "in". She has never been to the planet despite countless invitations from them. Their eagerness to get her to the planet is something of concern in itself. That is where we're going to have to be exceptionally careful as no doubt she is a prize they would like to keep. I don't think any of us would like that to happen. In order to give you all a reason to be there I have arranged identities for you. You Doctor will be travelling as Kyla's personal physician. She is still recovering and I want you there in case anything does go wrong. Rennon as her brother and business partner it would be acceptable for you to accompany her and with Kel as her husband we can ensure that you have access to any quarters they may allocate to you so that she is protected at all times. It also assures her marital status. It is part of their law that a woman can be claimed if she is single. As her planet is part of the Ert'la'Karis Consortium this would leave her vulnerable to falling foul of this law."**

Kel threw the paper aside. "You would put her in that sort of a danger to get Shantara back?"

Zack put his knuckles on the table and stood up. "That is not the situation. I have discussed this with Kyla and she is prepared to go with you. She appreciates that we want to get Shantara back and is happy to help us retrieve our team member."

Kel stood up to face him. "So you'd send one of my people who is still recovering from her injuries into danger? We can find another way. Surely she doesn't need to go?" His hand was hanging over his blaster and his face had flushed slightly red.

Commander Zack was beginning to flush a little red in the face himself. "Now I think you need to calm down son and look at this logically. Kyra is due to be signed out of the Infirmary any day now and I have already spoken to Dr Samson about her medical fitness. I think you will confirm what I am saying Dr Samson?"

Dr Samson nodded as Kel glared at him.

The Commander shuffled his papers about the table. "He has given her the go ahead to leave the Infirmary and to take on missions. I am counting on you to help her and to look after her. This is not negotiable, we need Shantara back. Her knowledge of this base puts every man, woman and child here in danger. You have twenty four hours to prepare. Dr Samson you will return to the Infirmary to get Kyla on her feet and ready for the go. Rennon I have information set up for you that will help you to know your way around.

Our information is limited. If there are no more questions you have your orders."

He slipped his papers into the folder and ignored Kel's stony stare. He got up and walked calmly out of the briefing room, leaving Kel, Rennon and Dr Samson to talk.

Kel turned to Dr Samson. "Surely she's not…"

Dr Samson cut him off. "Kel, you can't keep her safe in the Infirmary forever. I know you have been there every step of the way and your daily help with her has been invaluable. I have appreciated it and you have given her a lot of strength. But, you know she's walking now, she's involved in research and artefact investigation and she was instrumental in finding the location. You have to let go and let her get on with her job here. In my medical opinion she is well enough to undertake the mission."

Kel stood up.

Rennon grabbed his arm and got glared at. "Where are you going?"

Kel pulled his arm free. "I'm going to speak with Kyla and to try to talk her out of this."

He strode out and his fixed stare reflected that his mind was racing as he strode down the corridors. People got out of his way without being asked, the dark menacing look on his face was enough. He reached the Infirmary and the doors just about managed to swish open as he strode through, down the ward and to the private room at the end which Kyla now pretty much called home.

Kyla was sitting on the bed watching something on the screen. She looked up when he came in and smiled. "Kel, good to see you. I thought you were in the meeting?"

"Kyla, you can't come with us." He sat down on the bed beside her and took her hand. "You have to see reason, you aren't well enough yet. Who knows what we will meet on that planet."

Her voice was calm, gentle and hardly more than a whisper. "Shantara was and is a member of your crew. You have always said that you cannot leave anyone behind. Also, I have heard that she trusts and cares for you. That makes it all the more important to find her and bring her back."

Kel turned his stony glare on her. "I never said I wanted to leave her behind. We are going. What I said was that you aren't coming with me. I mean us."

Kyla stood up and faced him. Her hazel eyes flashed bright green. "Who are you to stop me? You may have helped me but you do not own me." She pulled her hand out of his but he reached and caught it back, pulling her down to sit on the bed. "Is this what you are really like? Am I truly seeing the real Kel now rather than the kind soul who has helped me all these months? I don't think so."

Kel let her hand fall to the bed and looked down at the floor. "No."

Kyla took a deep breath. "I am glad that you are worried about me but I have seen pictures of that planet. It is highly civilised and its people are devoted to knowledge, art and wisdom. It is not a war zone. On the practical side I may stand a better chance of getting in there than any of you because I can operate the artefacts. I also have experience dealing with people and negotiating trade agreements. By what I've heard that may just be the way to get her back. If she is a slave she is a commodity and commodities can be dealt in. This may be the only chance that Shantara has. It has been more than three months now. I have traded with these people before many years ago and others who have traded with them recently have said that they are hospitable and more than friendly. I'm worried enough about this as the subterfuge that is necessary may well be our undoing. Kel, please don't make it any worse.

I had a long talk with the Commander today and he has asked me to stay. When we get back I'll make my decision. He has also given me the opportunity to use your library and to work with various artefacts. If I stay I'd be working mostly in the laboratory with Rennon." She stood up and took a step away and almost lost her balance. "Is that quiet enough for you?"

Kel stepped in and caught her, lifted her effortlessly back onto the bed. "This is exactly what I mean. You are not ready."

Kyla smiled. "I lost my balance." Her voice was firm and commanding.

Kel turned to go. "If you won't listen to me there is no point in me staying here is there. I'll see you at the mission briefing tomorrow. Have a good night."

Kyla reached out and caught his arm as he was almost out of reach. "Don't go, not like this."

Kel turned back like a rag doll and sat on the bed with her. They sat in silence, the film on the television screen playing to itself as they both looked at the screen but neither saw it. After about half an hour Kel turned and put his arms around her. "I'm sorry, I was just worried. When you have so little left, what there is becomes so much more important."

Kyla brushed a stray hair away from his face as he sat back. "And if you worry too much about something you make the very thing you are afraid of happen. I know you will be there to look after me and I'm not planning on doing anything too stupid. It's a recon mission and if we are lucky a trading mission where we'll come back with her."

After he left the Infirmary Kel went to the gymnasium and knocked the hell out of a punch bag. He then felt a lot better, showered, returned to his room and rolled onto his bed.

Rennon had spent most of the evening in his laboratory with the information he had been given. At around midnight he closed down the laptop and headed to the Infirmary with a small wooden box that had sat on the table in front of him all afternoon.

Kyla was still awake, watching something on the television and trying to make sense of it. "Rennon, good to see you. What do you have there?"

Rennon sat on the chair beside her. "Sorry to disturb you but I wondered if you knew what this is? I can't see any notes on it." He opened the box and Kyla took a look at the block inside. "I think it is a puzzle box. We couldn't get it open earlier but it buzzes when I touch it. Why?" Rennon took the block out and handed it to her. "It comes from the planet we're going to and I wondered what it was."

Kyla turned it over. "Where did you get it?"

Rennon thought a while. "I'm not totally sure and the notes with it are very sketchy. Someone wasn't doing their paperwork properly. We're assuming that it is from there as those markings are typical of the scholar's writing from scrolls we have from the place."

Kyla turned it over in her hand. "I wonder." She held it in her hand and concentrated and the box began to hum.

Rennon looked surprised. "Now that's new." It vibrated and opened up, leaves of it unfolding like an onion skin. "Wow". "Now what do you do?" It vibrated and almost jumped in her hand. Where before it had looked like a large dice now it was opened other bits opened out until it laid out flat. There were markings on it and as Kyla turned it over it became obvious, it was a map.

Kyla turned it over and over in her hands. "Well, that makes it a bit clearer. A map of what is what we should be asking?" As she asked a hologram appeared above the map and technical data began falling as if running down a screen.

Rennon grabbed a camera from his pocket and began to film the screen. "Wow, this is going to be interesting. So much for sleeping tonight, this may well be important."

Kyla tried to keep her hand as still as possible. "I guess so."

The text fell for nearly an hour until it started to repeat. When Rennon had a full copy they took the camera and they walked to Rennon's laboratory where he plugged in the camera and the symbols turned up on the screen. He looked at Kyla. "So, how is your Alexandrosian?"

Kyla smiled. "Lousy. You haven't had a chance to read the reports of the artefacts we looked at this afternoon have you?"

Rennon was watching the images on the screen. "No, I haven't had a chance yet."

Kyla took a seat as her leg collapsed but Rennon wasn't looking so he didn't see. "We found a translation device which has been docked into that laptop over there. It's a stand alone terminal so if you put a copy of that program into there you might be able to read it. Look, I've got an idea. Hopefully that is some serious information we may be able to trade or use."

Rennon downloaded the information onto a disc and carried it to the other laptop and plugged it in. Immediately the symbols turned into words they could understand. Rennon ran through the text. "Wow, you are right, this seems to be some sort of ancient poem, just the sort of thing that may be currency to get us in there. Did Kel speak to you?"

Kyra sighed. "Yes, he seems very concerned. I'm still going with you tomorrow though."

Rennon pressed a button and made copies of the poem. "He sees things very black and white sometimes. I would not let that worry you. He'll get over it and once you are doing regular missions you'll prove to him that you are ok. If you are. How are you feeling? Be honest."

Kyla smiled. "In truth a little shaky, a little apprehensive and a little worried about all this. When I was in the Infirmary that was one thing, now everything is real."

Rennon put his arm around her. "Don't worry, you'll settle in."

Kyla looked up into his gentle grey eyes. "I think so. Let us get this first one out of the way and we will then see how things go. What needs to be done here?"

Rennon looked down at the keyboard. He was typing furiously. "Not much more. I've done a report, filed copies and sent a copy of my report to the Commander." He smiled and hit send and the information flashed as message sent. "Now I'm going to hit my bed and get some sleep before tomorrow. I would suggest that you do the same."

Kyla headed for the door. "You are right, see you tomorrow."

The morning dawned like any other in space. With no weather and no sun to rise or fall everyone filed about according to MC Time. One by one they filtered out to breakfast until the four of them were sitting by the window, the vastness of space their backdrop occasionally disturbed by a passing shuttle or transporter.

Kel sat directly next to the window, deep in thought so that a piece of toast suspended between his fingers was already going cold and the butter solidifying. Rennon dug into his breakfast with his usual gusto and Samson was reading some notes while thoughtfully munching on a piece of bacon. Kyla sat there watching them. She opened her mouth to speak and then closed it again.

Rennon looked up for a moment. "Look I know it's a different team but nothing has changed really. We're going off base to achieve a goal. This one might not involve getting ourselves shot and knocked about though."

Kel smiled and took a bite from his toast. "Sure, just another mission." He gave Kyla a meaningful glance and smiled at her.

Rennon pulled a small notebook out of his pocket. "They are basically a peaceful race until they need to fight. Their advancement in science and technology is quite spectacular and their army organised and disciplined.

Although they are technologically advanced they have chosen to live a life that is gentle to the planet. They use candlelight at night of choice though they do have the option of other light sources and heat their houses with vast under floor heating systems powered by sustainable fuel. Of course all this is maintained by their vast number of slaves. I wouldn't worry too much about the slaves. They are given comfortable board and lodgings and by all accounts they are looked after far better than most of the poor on other planets. They are bought and sold but within their structure, the slaves that is, not their masters, they gain status by what they have raised in the open market and what they are worth.

In general their architecture is magnificent and their statues and art unrivalled in any galaxy. These are scholars and teachers with a standing army of thousands of well skilled fighting men. We could learn a lot from them."

Kyla looked up. "Indeed, in my experience they are very polite, very civilised and have not allowed their advancement to spoil them. They delight in luxury and hospitality and their alcoholic beverages are also unrivalled."

Kel spoke with his mouth full, his words muffled. "I don't care, we get her, we get out, end of story."

Their breakfast done they put the trays on the trolley and went to the crew room to get ready for the mission. There were rails there and on those rails the costumes that would help them to fit in with the locals.

Kyla lifted her dress on its hanger. "Where did they get this from? Its beautiful." The dress was loose fitting, tied in under the bust with a gold thread to form a high waist and a loose skirt. The material was floating and colourful, a vibrant gold.

Kel smiled. "There is a department on base here that makes whatever is needed from information they have on a database." His outfit was more martial. His waist length breastplate of shining metal armour had been emblazoned with a rearing goat. The leather panelled skirt that protected his lower regions was metal shod and almost met his long metal faced boots. To finish that outfit off he had what looked like a complete wolf pelt to throw around his shoulders. "Lord's Robes" it said on the label.

Rennon's outfit said "Merchant" and consisted of long purple robes with a cloak suspended over one shoulder. As a physician Dr Samson was presented with long blue robes with a belt of pouches which buckled around it. Kyla smiled and disappeared into the changing room.

The men changed in the communal room, throwing the robes on and flouncing about in front of the mirror. The jokes done they settled down to concealing an appropriate amount of weapons and getting themselves mentally ready.

Kyla stepped out of the changing room and all three of them stopped in their tracks, Kel's mouth fell open and none of them could take their eyes off of her. She seemed to glide into the room, her slim waist, ample figure and muscular shoulders were complemented beautifully by the elegance of the dress. It was such a contrast to the plain blue boiler suit she had been issued with that they couldn't help but stand and stare. The dress was draped over one shoulder only, leaving most of her neck and one arm bare. There were no sign of the black welts now and her skin was pale white. Her dark brown wavy hair was now tamed and held back from her face with a circlet of braid. She grabbed the shawl that was still hanging on the rail and hung it around her shoulders. "Well, will I do?"

Kel opened and closed his mouth but no words came out. Rennon stepped forwards put a hand on her arm and faced her. "My dear you look delightful. You will charm them I am sure."

She stood back and looked at them. "Wow, what a difference! We will all do very nicely. Come on before I change my mind. Let's see what sort of a ship they have found for us."

They walked side by side down the corridor to the Hopper Bay. Beyond its doors there was a slightly shabby trading vessel. It resembled a sea going ship with a prow and bow and huge flying fish like fins which were folded to its side. It was slightly tatty and had seen better days but as Rennon gave it the once over he smiled and patted it on the side. "She may look tatty but there's life in the old dog yet."

Rennon took the pilot's seat, Dr Samson the co-pilot's, leaving Kel and Kyla in the passenger seats behind. They didn't waste any time, they blasted off immediately they had the go ahead.

After a three hour journey they neared the planet and began hailing. It was a predominantly grey and blue planet hanging between a moon and a sun. Another twelve planets were in orbit around the sun. As they watched many shuttles and spacecraft were coming and going. They followed a path which filed them neatly in and neatly out. Rennon transmitted the code he had been given and they waited. There had been no reply for nearly half an hour. They were about to try again when they received landing codes and directions to switch their ship to automatic and to allow the planet's pilot to bring them down onto the planet. Rennon hesitated then switched to automatic. Checking all communication was shut down he looked around the others. "We have no alternative, to hesitate or to try to keep control would alert them that we are suspicious and that something may be up."

The ship glided through the atmosphere and the planet's shields and came in to land on an obvious landing pad on the edge of a great city. It was a vast great expanse of stone built on platforms of stone. It connected to the roof of one of the many ornate buildings. Other buildings had turrets and many porticos and minarets in contrast to the landing pad which was flat and functional. As they alighted from their craft the floor below it opened and it disappeared from sight, the doors closing over it.

Kel stepped to Kyla's side and took her arm to support her as she swayed slightly as she stepped out of the ship. She felt slightly feint and was glad of his arm for support. She could feel he was tense. Rennon fell in behind her while Samson stepped up to her other side and looked slightly concerned. They were all very vigilant as they crossed the landing pad to a large grey veined marble flight of stairs which ascended from the landing pad to a huge rectangular balcony on the front of an ornately carved top three storeys of a colossal building. The part of the building they could see consisted firstly of a flat plain balcony. A second balcony with a huge fountain on it could be accessed from the back of the first and at the back of that there was access up more stairs to the top a balcony which had a roof supported by sturdy marble pillars. On top of the roof were three pyramids. It stretched a good two hundred feet across the end of the landing pad and towered into the sky above as well as down many more levels to the planet's surface below. They could see that it stretched into the distance as well. The balconies were just the front of it.

As they reached the top of the first flight of stairs they were able to see a large bronze statue of a noble warrior dressed in a similar fashion to Kel's costume. It stood on a plinth at the back of the balcony, raised up out of a fountain fed by four sea creatures. There were two wide marble stairways which ascended to the next level on either side of it. They crossed the first balcony and ascended to the next where they were met by soldiers wearing heavy duty battle armour. On this balcony there was another fountain carved to represent a huge statue of a man with a serpentine tail. He was twisted around a huge sea creature which fed the fountain from its mouth. Each balcony was edged with pillars with a stone rail on top.

They crossed the balcony to meet with the soldiers who stood in front of a columned entrance to the building. At the back of the balcony to their left and right were ornate and extremely ostentatious marble rooms fronted by more columns which supported a pointed roof.

The soldiers stepped aside to allow a dignitary dressed in ornately embroidered robes depicting the sun and moon to step forwards. He looked slightly nervous and looked them over cautiously. "Welcome to our fair city. I hope that you enjoy your stay with us. If you adhere to our laws and rules while you are here then I am sure that you will find this a profitable and rewarding visit. I must excuse myself for the scanning I am about to do. These are as you know difficult times. I assume I have your permission?" He raised his hand, there was a metal spider like piece of equipment that was wound around his right palm and it glowed red as he moved it over Kyla. He took a step back. "My lady, we are honoured that you would grace us with your presence. May I offer you our hospitality and we would of course be delighted if you would stay with us in our palace during your stay on our fair planet."

Kyla looked nervously at Kel who was watching the dignitary's every move. She turned her attention back to the City Official. "I thank you for your hospitality and extending me such a warm welcome. I had sought to visit this place in a way to be able to enjoy all that your City has to offer."

The official coughed slightly. "My lady, I am afraid that would be totally impossible. Now that the galaxies are changing we have had to do much to protect ourselves from would be infiltration from the Followers and their allies the Yxathon. There are scanners and detectors everywhere and almost every household and business has their own. Your royal blood would be detected as soon as you step outside the palace. You would be much safer staying with us, there is much dissent on the streets and we would not wish a diplomatic incident."

Kyla bit her lip and smiled. "I thank you then for your hospitality and we would be delighted to accept."

The Official rose to his feet and bowed. "If you would follow me I will take you to the baths so that you may take your ease."

They followed him in silence and the guards fell in behind them. They were led across the vast marble hall with its huge vaulted ceiling and they could not help but look up. The ceiling was completely covered in paintings of the gods ascending and offering solace down to man. The artwork was truly magnificent. The deep rich oils of the paintings seemed to come alive as they watched. It looked like it may well be truly someone's life work.

The huge ornate metal shod doors on the far side of the room opened smoothly as they approached and beyond the galleried corridor was carved from marble. Statues adorned the base of every pillar of the gallery.

Kel looked up. "The perfect kill zone."

Kyla glared at him and then smiled when she noticed the Official watching her. "My husband is constantly worried for my safety. I could not ask for a more devoted mate."

The Official smiled, his smile was genuinely warm. "You are both truly blessed. Male and female bathing is separate. Female bathing is to your right, male bathing to your left. If you would leave your clothes in the antechamber they will be returned to you when you leave. We have provided attire which I hope you will find quite appropriate."

They looked at each other nervously and Kel was left standing watching Kyla go through the ornate gold door. He then turned and followed Rennon and Samson through the other door. The men were bathed and massaged by beautiful women who left them to relax in the warm mineral bath area once their task was done. Rennon and Samson were enjoying themselves and relaxing in the soft water. Kel looked on edge.

Rennon splashed over to him. "What's the matter with you?"

Kel looked over, his black curls soaked, his muscular chest glisteningly wet. "What do you think is the matter with me? The first thing we do when we get here is allow her to go off by herself and let them take all our concealed weaponry."

Rennon smiled reassuringly. "We are here on a recon mission, this is not a war zone. We had to give a little here. That scanner would have revealed whatever we had hidden. We were lucky he neither commented nor reacted to it."

Kel climbed out of the bath and a leggy blonde stepped from the walkway behind to wrap him in a soft warm towel. He grasped it and headed for the steam room, the only way out of the baths. The others grudgingly followed him.

Kyla emerged to join them smiling and looking relaxed. She was dressed in a figure hugging floating red gown of a similar style to the gold one she had left behind. A handsome youth followed her and wrapped a deep red silk cloak around her shoulders. He lingered far too long as he fastened it about her neck, his fingers brushing her porcelain skin. Kel growled under his breath and Rennon laughed. Kel elbowed him in the stomach so he had to struggle to regain his breath.

Kel held out his hand. "My dear, I am glad you enjoyed your experience in the baths." He turned to the youth. "I thank you for taking care of my wife." He emphasised the last word.

The young boy bowed. "It was indeed my pleasure." He turned to go with an impish look on his face.

Kyla caught Kel as he stepped forwards to follow the youth. "Leave it, I have been safe and well looked after. I have an audience with the General. He has been informed that I carry the Noble DNA and that I was once Chieftain and he has requested a meeting. He wants to introduce me to someone. As my husband you would be expected to accompany me but I can't get Rennon or Samson in with us."

Samson emerged from the baths just as the Official emerged from a corridor. "If you would like to follow me I will take you to your rooms so that you may rest and I will then return later to take you both to see the General. I have arranged that you can visit the Gladiatorial Stadium this evening. I trust you will find it entertaining and you will of course be the General's guests of honour."

They followed the Official down the corridors. The rich purple deep pile of the carpet was so soft under the soft shoes they had been given to wear. Purple drapes hung on the walls and the plinths that lined the corridors were adorned with busts of regal looking men. The Official began explaining who they were in great detail with excruciatingly long anecdotal dialogue and although Kyla attempted to look interested, Kel had long since lost interest and was lost in his own thoughts. Rennon was fascinated and Samson couldn't help focusing on the well armed guards following them down the corridor.

When Kyla and Kel were on their own in their room Kel walked over to the bed. He turned around and fell backwards onto it and sank into the deep well filled mattress. "Now you are talking, this is comfortable. I could enjoy this."

Kyla had gone to the window and was looking down. "There are so many people here. Look down there, the street is teeming with them. How will we ever…" She hesitated and turned to Kel. He glared and shook his head and she immediately went back to looking out of the window.

Kel looked over to where she stood, silhouetted by the golden light of the fading sun. "Don't worry, I am sure that the negotiations will go well. We are after all prepared to be fair and would hope that our hosts would be also."

Kyla tensed up. "Look, look, down there, something is going on. Oh by the stars look at that, Followers, there in the street."

Kel leapt to the window and looked down. His arm snaked around Kyla and he pushed her back behind him. "Get back." Down in the street there was a group of black robed figures striding down the street blasting anyone in their path and in windows. Bodies fell like rain. In the corridor outside there was a scream. Kel ran to the door, opened it carefully and nearly came face to face with a black robed figure just about to come in. Kel reached for his blaster, it wasn't there, he'd had to leave it behind. He did have a sword he had been given so he drew it. The blade glistening in the evening light from the window as it smoothly exited the scabbard. Kel took a step back and swung his sword and the head fell from the black robed Follower. He nimbly dodged the blade of a second who stepped in as the first fell. His blow hit flesh, severing the arm that had been left exposed before smoothly turning the sword in an arc to slice the torso with an upper cut. That one too fell and Kel found himself facing the City Guard. They nodded to each other politely. Kyla ran to the window and looked down.

In the street below everything seemed quiet. The bodies of the Followers were being loaded onto a wagon and as she watched the blood was scrubbed from the ground until there was no sign that anything had happened.

Moments later the Official was at their door. "I am so glad that you were not harmed. You may see the General now. He has asked that your two companions also accompany you. In light of the incursion you may feel more comfortable remaining together." He stood and waited for them to follow him. He stopped again at Rennon's room and Samson's then led the way through a maze of corridors.

The General's room was adorned with gold and red drapes. He was seated behind a huge gold carved desk and large gold statues stood guard around him. As they came in he looked up and they were offered chairs facing his desk.

"Please sit." The General's voice was grave and deep. He waited for the Official to leave then turned to face them. "I am sorry that you had to see that. You may not know that we have had trouble from the Followers for a few years now. As have you I do believe. Nowhere seems safe these days. But as you have seen we are dealing with the problem when it arises. I do believe you came to discuss trade. We are always keen to make new trading partners. May I ask the nature of your interests?"

Rennon sat up straight in his chair and looked to Kyla. "May I speak for us my lady?"

Kyla smiled. "You may. I give you the authority."

Rennon clasped his hands together. "We are looking for a translator who can decode some ancient texts that we have found. Do you have such a person among your slaves?"

The General appeared relaxed. "Such a person would be a great asset and would command a high price. We have such people but we are unlikely to be able to spare any. We may however be able to arrange a trade in that you could bring what you need translated here."

Rennon looked at the General without blinking. "We need someone who can translate Ancient Akapraxian."

The General coughed. "That however is a little more difficult. I will have to consult with my Slave Master and the records. I would assume you have something valuable to offer in trade should we have such a rare commodity?"

Rennon smiled. "Indeed we do. We have an original copy of the Codex Ker Alapatha. I believe that would be a more than adequate trade for such a person."

The General looked slightly stunned momentarily but he regained his composure. "I will think on this."

There was a knock at the door. The Official came in, his face ashen white. He stepped forwards and waited.

The General turned to him. "You may speak."

The Official was out of breath so his words were slightly muffled. "The Followers have landed in force. That was just an advance guard."

The General stood up and strapped on his sword which was leaning on a stand beside the desk. "Muster the Legions and sound the City Alarm. I have little time. I brought you to speak with me as I had hoped that you can operate the ancient artefacts Kyla. It seems that any possibility of negotiation and trade is a little irrelevant now but you can still help. There are artefacts we have that could help us in the battle that is just about to start, one in particular. Would you join us or shall I order one of my guards to escort you to your ship?"

Kel stood up and looked at the others. "Well, shall we help?"

Kyla looked up. "I would help."

Rennon nodded.

Samson jumped up. "If I can help in the hospital I would be glad to."

The General stepped back. "Good, I will arrange for you to be taken to the field hospital that will be set up. I will give you rank and right. Follow me."

He strode out of the room and down the corridor to a room where others were strapping on armour. They followed suit, Kyla reached for a woman's breastplate and Kel put a hand on her arm. "No Kyla, please no." There was something in his eyes that stopped her in her tracks. She felt a shudder run down her spine and inexplicably she did what he wanted and stepped away from it.

The General took the armour from the stand and handed it to her. "She would be safer. If she is to die, let her die with honour and join us in the Elyseum Fields."

Kel was about to object but he saw the intense look on the General's face. He looked away and went to put his own armour on.

They joined the lines of troops marching swiftly down the corridors. Lines of chariots waited outside the palace and they jumped on board the one behind the General's. The charioteer cracked the reins on the paired horses' backs. They reared slightly and leapt forwards. He took the strain and held them under control as they joined the other chariots heading for the battlefield. They held onto the sides of the chariot tightly as they sped through the streets. Dust billowed up and got in their eyes and mouths. They were racing down the main thoroughfare. The huge white marble buildings rose impossibly high on either side, the statues on their roofs silhouetted in the last of the rays of the setting sun.

They raced through the elegantly practical marble City Gates whose doors were open wide. They raced across the open plain outside. In the distance they could see fires, explosions and blaster beams going off at nearly regular intervals. Lines of men and women formed up and as they got closer they could smell the cordite, leather, blood and animals. Banners fluttered in the air and fell as flaming balls filled the air, breaking the battle lines, leaving huge gaping holes which others stepped in to fill. Somewhere in the air a craft screamed down out of orbit and blue laser bolts rained down on the General's troops.

The General's chariot was beside theirs and other chariots raced alongside as he shouted orders and commanded his forces into position. Men and women jumped to his every command. He ordered them left, right and to circle. With well practiced ease his voice boomed out and their movements anticipated the Followers actions, holding them back as soldiers fell on either side. He rode into the thick of the battle, his sword slashing from left to right. The chariot horse rose up on its hind legs, its metal cased and sharpened hooves cutting into those in front of him. He bit and reared with the ferocity of a lion, his serpentine tail swishing from left to right. The horses fought as a line, the chariots moving between their own men who fell in beside them. The force of their charge knocked the front line of the enemy force over and decimated it, allowing the General's troops to push through.

Using weight of numbers they crushed the second rank of fighters back tightly against the ranks behind so they were unable to fight. The charioteers and second rank of the General's army fought over the top of their horses, using the chariots as a platform.

From where they were they couldn't see the enemy now, all they could see were the backs of the troops as they stood in the shield wall and the bolts flew from behind them towards the enemy and towards them from the ranks of archers within the enemy lines. Some fell but they were replaced by others who stepped in and they started advancing. The rhythm of their marching and the clatter as they hammered their swords onto the back of their shields became deafening. They were ready for the hand to hand battle that they were moving towards. They came up behind the chariots ready to step into any spaces left by those who fell.

A hovering platform sped towards the front line and the General leapt up onto it, his chariot continuing on with the fight, his charioteer ably taking the reins. The General took the controls of the platform and hovered over their chariot. "Kyla, if you would join me I would be delighted to have your assistance."

Kel screamed. "No." But his voice was lost in the cries and explosions that went off all around them.

Kyla took the General's hand and stepped up onto the platform. The platform sped off towards the front line.

Kel watched it go, hanging onto the side of the chariot as it rattled its way towards the front line. Rennon was beside him and they looked at each other in horror. They reached the front line and Kel leapt from the Chariot and joined the troops fighting on the ground, the shield wall broken now, they were hand to hand with the enemy. Smoke billowed everywhere, choking them. It got in their eyes and made it hard to see. They were looking for colours. The black of the Followers made them stand out from the scarlet of the General's men. Eventually they were slashing at anything black as they were pressed together and pushed forwards. It took every bit of strength to stay on their feet. No skill was required. Luck and taking any available opportunity was the only option. Bodies pressed around them and everyone was having the same problem. There was no chance for finesse, no chance for fighting. All that they could do was try to slash and hack whatever they could and just hope they didn't hurt someone on their own side.

Kyla held onto the ornate supports on the platform. They rose up like giant plants, the leaves forming the protective wall around the edge. The General handed her a flat box. He was screaming orders and moving troops about. The platform lurched at his touch, moving to dodge blaster bolts. The bolts were cutting into the bottom of the platform and it rocked slightly when a fiery ball exploded at its edge, showering them with sparks. The General stopped shouting and turned to Kyla. "Use it, open it. We need it."

Kyla put her hand on the box and opened the lid. Inside was a keyboard and she turned the terminal on. A blue light flashed momentarily, covering the battlefield and scanning everyone and everything.

The General looked down momentarily. "Very good, now let me look." He looked over her shoulder. He reached down and began to type. "I need you to press that button there and when you've done it, throw the box over the side of the platform. Do not hesitate or we will die."

The General pressed more buttons and then went back to flying the platform. "Press it."

Kyla pressed the button and threw the box. It was hit by a blast and bounced back onto the platform. Without thinking she kicked it over the side but in so doing, her other leg gave out under her and she slipped over the edge of the platform. She missed the safety rail and found herself falling through the air down onto the battle below. The General saw her fall and cried out in shock before manoeuvring the platform underneath her to catch her again. She landed on the platform with a loud crunching thud and lay there, unconscious. The General swore and pulled the platform up, struggling against the steering bar with all his strength to get it up away from the Followers who were now hanging onto the side of it.

The box flew through the air, the blue beam intensifying, scanning and locking onto the biosignatures it had been commanded to find. Beams flashed from it and those it touched clutched their chests and fell to the ground, lifeless. Only some were unaffected but the attacking troops had lost nearly three quarters of their number and those who were left were stunned and demoralised.

The Followers clinging to the platform as it rose in the air were hit by the beam. All but one fell to the ground dead. The one who clung on looked in disbelief as the General kicked his hands off of the safety rail. He fell backwards, his mouth open to let out a final scream before he hit the ground.

The local warriors fought with a passion. They were organised and methodical in their actions and slowly but surely moved across the battlefield until all the attackers were dead or unconscious.

The General brought his platform down to land and Kel and Rennon jumped onto it while the General leapt onto a passing chariot. The platform sped off. Kyla was coming around and she tried to stand up. Kel stopped her but she pushed him away. "I'm fine, I just slipped that's all." She staggered but with Kel's help and holding onto the rail she managed to stand.

In the skies above the stars went out as a huge vessel bore down towards them. It was hit by beams from space. Gaping holes appeared, revealing several floors and levels in its infrastructure. Sparking led to fires, which led to explosions until the whole ship erupted in a ball of fire. Debris rained down on everyone below, huge chunks of it crushing those it fell on. Before their eyes many thousand died where they stood, unable to get away. The ship was falling like a stone towards the planet. Then it stopped, caught in space in a giant tractor beam which radiated around it and carried it away from the planet and cast it into space. It exploded harmlessly causing a dramatic light show of sparks and burning debris.

Renon grabbed the platform controls and flew them out of the immediate battle area. Kyla was trying to hold on but her arms lacked the strength and she skidded across the platform. Kel caught her around the waist, laid her down and lay across her, holding her onto the platform as the inertia almost slipped them both off. He grabbed part of the control panel and his great strength stopped them sliding. Rennon was concentrating on navigating them past the falling debris of the ship. At one point he almost flipped the platform over when he had to make a really tight turn to avoid a falling fireball. His knuckles were white as he gripped the controls tightly. The fireball hit the top of the platform as it was tipped up. The liquid from it ran down the flat surface spreading its sticky burning liquid. Rennon jumped out of the way up onto the command box as it flowed into the control area. Kel had to roll Kyla out of the way as the liquid flowed over where they had been. Rennon flipped the platform the other way. The liquid began to flow away from them just as he flipped the platform to avoid another fireball. Kel and Kyla skidded across the platform and almost went over the side as there was nothing to hold onto. Another turn and they slipped over the edge. Kel caught the edge of the platform as they went over, his other hand slipped around Kyla's waist as she began to fall. He caught hold of the straps of her armour and held on tight.

Rennon saw what had happened and gently lowered the platform until they were on solid ground. They leapt back onto the platform and he took off again and sped off towards the City. "We've done all we can, lets get out of here." His voice was slightly high pitched, his face strained, his hair blown back from his face by the wind that rushed past him.

6

The City was peaceful again. Darkness had fallen. Everywhere lights twinkled, illuminating statues and giving the city a mystic air. The moon was obscured by cloud cover. It began to rain. The water cascaded in a torrent and splashed on the balcony outside Kyla and Kel's room. Kyla reached out to close the window, feeling the chill of the wind which blew in through the billowing curtains. As she turned Kel caught her arm. His grip was firm, his eyes pleading, questioning, he looked worried.

Kyla was the first to speak. "So much for a peaceful mission," she said, a slight smirk on her face. She looked into his eyes, reaching for something, trying to convey a lightness that she knew the minute she looked at him was hopeless.

Kel answered her, stony faced but his eyes said otherwise. "You could have been killed."

Kyla half smiled but let the smile fade when she saw the seriousness of his expression. A dark cloud seemed to hang over him. "Anyone out there could have been. That is what war is like. You know that." She tried to take her armour off but she couldn't reach the straps. Pain she had ignored until now bit into her ribs and she gasped slightly.

Kel took a step forwards. "Let me help you. That is all I'm trying to do. You have to see it from my point of view. Let me help you get that armour off and we can talk." There was a great sadness in his eyes.

She let him help her. Strap by strap he undid the armour, letting the pieces fall onto the thick carpet. Finally he lifted the breastplate over her head, catching her hair on one of the buckles.

Someone had laid out a dress on the bed. It was a delicate blue, plain with a high waist and tied with another braid, used as a belt. She walked over to the bed. "You could turn around."

He did but the mirror behind him was not lost on him and he couldn't resist looking as she pulled the rough gambeson and padding off and let her hair fall down her bare back before lifting the dress and slipping it on, letting it fall into place before tying it to define her waist. She pulled her hair out from down the back of her dress and picked up a second braid which she used to tame her wild curls. She looked around for the mirror and Kel froze, like an animal caught in a bright light he knew he had been caught out.

She smiled at his discomfort and he stepped aside so that she could pick up the hairbrush on the dresser and began to brush her hair. She looked at him and handed him the brush. He took it and gently brushed her hair, pulling the wild curls into some sort of order. Kyla sat on a stool and relaxed, enjoying having her hair brushed. When she was happy with the hair she took the brush from him and laid it on the dresser.

Kel untied the wolf pelt. It was coated in dried blood, the once soft fur now stiff and hard. He unbuckled his armour with practiced skill and let it fall into the pile in the middle of the room. Kyla stood up. "Let me." She unbuckled the rest of his armour and moved the pile to beside the door. A silken robe had been laid on the bed for him. He grabbed it and stepped to the bowl of water waiting on the wash stand and began to wash the blood off. "You have to understand the way I see it."

Kyla sat back down, she turned around on the stool and watched him as he ran the cloth over his muscular chest and neck, washing the blood from his torso. "Explain to me then so that I do understand."

Kel hesitated then washed out the cloth. "Two years ago my life was very different. There were nearly thirty thousand people on my planet. Our planet. We fought the Followers and would not surrender and those souls died. We nearly all died and for a year I had begun to believe I was the last of us. There are others, I know that now but very few. How can I explain how I felt when I found out about you? It can't mean so much to you, you never knew your people did you? They are gone now, in their thousands. How can I put it into words?"

Kyla stood up and crossed the room silently and took the cloth off of him, washed it out and began to help him wash the blood from his back. She ran the soft cloth over his shoulder blades and felt the taunt muscles underneath and ran the cloth down his spine. He visibly shuddered and his muscles tensed up. She spread the cloth and wiped around his side. He reached and caught her wrist with his hand. "You don't need to. I understand now. You have to understand my thinking too. If we fall to the Followers then all is lost and we'll die anyway. I'd rather die fighting. But I'd rather not die at all."

Kel turned slowly to face her and slipped his arm around her waist. "Thank you." He swept a stray curl from her face with the other hand and rested his palm on her cheek, curling his fingers around her head. She looked into his eyes and he looked down at her and bent down towards her.

She was already pulling away from him when there was a knock at the door and they jumped apart. Kel went to the door, sword involuntarily in hand he opened the door and the Official stepped in. "I trust that everything is to your liking. The gladiatorial games have been cancelled. It was felt that a celebration banquet would be more appropriate. You would be very welcome to attend. I am also to tell you that you have been summoned to an audience with His High Excellency in the morning." He smiled, turned on his heels and left.

Kel grabbed a towel and began rubbing himself dry. This done he slipped the robe on and turned to Kyla who was using the powders left on the dressing table for her. She stood up and he took her hand, they went to the door, opened it and followed others to the Banqueting Hall where they met Rennon and Dr Samson.

They recognised the General, he was sitting on a long table which stretched across the far end of the room. He was deep in conversation a dark haired elegantly dressed noble looking man who was rubbing his chin thoughtfully with one hand. He looked very dignified, his mere manner was that of a ruler. His neatly trimmed black beard and hair were cut differently to the others in the room. His robes too were of a different style. His well cut jacket was gold brocade, he had an elegant gold cravat fastened with a diamond pin. Occasionally the dark haired man took a glance around the room, taking it all in.

The seat of honour was a large red velvet padded gold edged throne. It dwarfed the heavily robed man who sat there. He barely filled half the seat and was clearly propped up on a large red velvet cushion. He was painfully thin, his features pointed and his blonde hair long and thin. He waved his hands about constantly giving orders to serving staff and summoning guests who came to stand before him. He would speak, they would laugh or nod their heads vigorously and he would send them away. The dark haired guest was looking around the room smiling enigmatically.

There were many round tables set about the room, leaving a wide open space in the middle where entertainers and dancers were performing acts of great skill. As they walked past a fire eater blasted a gout of flame in front of Kel. Kyla only just managed to catch his arm as he turned, he continued walking, staring at the man who was looking very worried until Kel sat down in his seat.

The hall was immense and every seat at every table was full. There were many hundreds of people there and the hum of conversation almost drowned out the subtle music that was being played by a band of musicians in a gallery to the left of the head table.

The hall was vaulted and the ceiling intricately painted with rich oil paint. Gods were celebrating and the edge of each of the panels was painted as a grape vine. The central painting was a well built and well fed almost naked man pointing to a small stone which was painted to be glowing at his touch. Around his head there were many hundreds of flying doves. The ground at his feet was strewn with flowers. In his right hand he held a sword which was painted to be on fire. Behind him stood a beautiful, elegant, slim woman who had a hand on his shoulder. Her hair was ornately trimmed, rolled to curls and then hung down in a curl over her shoulder. Her dress was of a similar style to the women in the room. With a high waist and full skirt, although the material was so soft that if fell smoothly over her body, as the dresses did on the women in the room. The painting was a centre piece, other paintings spiralled away from it in triangles, some one way, some the other to fit inside the huge domed and vaulted ceiling.

Other than the entertainment area the rest of the room was covered in a dark red deep pile carpet. The tables and chairs dug down into it and they could feel it underneath their boots. The walls were painted gold with panels of other oil paintings depicting men and women undertaking various official tasks.

Kyla was mesmerised, she couldn't help looking around with her mouth open. Kel seemed totally unbothered. Rennon kept looking things up in a little book that he was constantly thumbing through and Samson couldn't help eyeing up the ladies.

They were being led to their table by a young woman who wore a similar dress to the rest but like the serving women she had a short skirt, her legs bare to the small gold sandals on her feet. She showed them to a table and they sat down.

Immediately bottles of rich ruby wine were opened and set in front of them. Cut glass goblets were set in front of them and Kyla gave Kel a worried look. He smiled. "Don't worry, I have been to dinner before, I've learnt a lot while at Mission Command."

Kyla laughed. "I didn't say anything."

Rennon shut his book and put it back in his pocket. "You didn't have to, we were all thinking it."

Kel looked offended. "This really is not my thing."

Rennon laughed. "What drinking too much and watching scantily clad dancing girls?"

Kel looked interested. "What really?"

Rennon pulled his book out again. "Well according to this, these banquets are renowned through the galaxy as being something to experience. The man on the throne there is the High Emperor Maxillius VIII, Supreme Ruler of this planet. Those at the table will be the dignitaries and honoured guests, mostly here for diplomatic reasons. This Hall is the "Hall of the Gods" and was built by his great, great grandfather as a place for celebration. Maxillius however has taken that celebration to a whole new level, you can expect a severe amount of drinking tonight.

Kyla was looking around the faces in the crowd, most of whom were now looking to the Emperor who had stood up. There was silence.

The High Emperor spoke. His voice was high pitched but very loud. "I would like to welcome you one and all. Please, take your rest, take your ease and take your fill. I am delighted that you were able to join me on such an occasion, please, let me not keep you from what you really want to hear. Let the banquet commence."

Serving girls scurried about carrying plates of food to different tables and the bubble of conversation had resumed.

Kyla was still looking around the room. Rennon caught her arm. "What is the matter, you look nervous?"

Kyla looked down at the plate that had been put in front of her. It was steaming and the meat and potatoes, vegetables and rich red sauce looked very tantalising. "Something isn't quite right, it is just a feeling but I can feel something."

Rennon looked down at his plate and thanked the serving girl. "It could be that you aren't used to being around this amount of people."

Kyla shook her head slowly. "I don't know, perhaps."

Their conversation was much curtailed as course after course of fine food arrived accompanied by fine wines, brandies and other local delicacies. Kyla was just about to dip her spoon into a chocolate mousse like ornate pudding that looked like a work of art when she caught something out of the corner of her eye, a face she recognised.

Joniel was sitting about four tables down from them with a group of men in black robes. He too wore heavy black velvet robes, his face almost covered. She had only caught a glimpse for a moment but he had noticed her and turned to face her. He smiled and leant forwards said something, put his spoon down and got up.

Kyla put her spoon down. "If you would excuse me for a moment I must do something."

She got up and walked out. There were many other guests wandering about as well as serving girls. A troop of swirling dancing girls had just launched themselves into the room and Kyla found it really easy to slip out without being noticed too much. She walked slowly down the corridor outside, not really sure why or what she was doing.

Joniel passed her going in the opposite direction, back to the Hall. He stopped for a moment and bowed. "My Lady." He made a grand gesture. "May I say that you look delightful tonight, more lovely than a summer flower." He bowed close to her, kissing her on the cheek as he whispered in her ear. "I wanted to speak to you. There is something going on here. Do you know who the guest of honour is?"

Kyla looked into his sincere eyes. "No." She whispered then spoke a little louder. "My Lord, it has been some years since we have met, please, walk with me a while, you may escort me."

Joniel bowed deeply and took her arm. He looked down at her, smiled slightly and raised an eyebrow once they were alone in a corridor. "You really should look into some research before you come walking into politically explosive situations. Do you have any idea what is going on here? I am guessing that you don't. It is dangerous Kyla, it could get you and all your friends killed. Mission Command really should pay attention to what is going on in the galaxies. That man sitting between the Emperor and the General is the True Prince. It is said that he is destined to be the Prince of this Galaxy and possibly many others. He offers unity against these Followers which would solve a lot of problems and give us a fighting chance. He is commanding, I've met him, a good leader, a supreme strategist and genuine in his beliefs as far as I can tell. The only problem is that he is sitting beside the one person who covets that power and is in a position to get it. You my love have just given him a way he can do it easily. I think I have assumed quite rightly that you had no idea of the political situation. If you had any idea you wouldn't be here. I know your cover story. You obviously do not know their law. You are married to Kel, well you are to their knowledge. Should Kel die by accident or illness then you would be left a widow. As a widow you would be able to be claimed by the Emperor. It would be his duty to find you someone to support you and by Prima Matrimonia he would have first refusal as you are of noble blood. If he managed to do that and then eliminated the Prince he would be able to claim the Prince's forces who are so conveniently camped on his doorstep. Then all he has to do is see the Prince eliminated. He thinks that is already in hand. I am here for that contract when he commands me to carry it out. I am assuming that he intends that to happen in the next day or so."

Kyla looked up at him, she looked worried.

Joniel smiled. "I have a techno jammer running. Their cameras are now seeing and hearing a computer generated conversation between us full of diplomatic niceties and all the usual small talk. I will not eliminate the Prince. If I get it wrong that will leave me a renegade from my own people so I am going to join him. So we may be seeing a lot more of each other. If I get it right I may well join him anyway."

Kyla smiled and looked up at him. "We really do know how to mess up don't we?"

Joniel bent down and kissed her on the forehead. "It may not be all bad. If we can keep Kel alive then at least the Emperor will have shown his hand if I can play it right. That is what the Prince is gambling on, or I assume he is. He's no fool and I refuse to believe he hasn't realised the danger of the man he is sitting beside. He is a supreme strategist, I wouldn't put it past him to be playing the Emperor to get him to overstep his power. The Prince and I have spoken in the past. He already has a running contract against the person who puts a contract on him. All I have to do is take the Emperor out first and I'm released from my contract. So if I fail, I become a renegade, if I don't I can choose to join the Prince. But, be careful my love. Whatever happens, it could be very messy."

Kyla reached up and put her arms around his neck. Her eyes were slightly tearful. "Be careful. If we cannot be together I'd rather know you were out there somewhere..."

Joniel smiled. "You almost said safe there didn't you? I'll never be safe. I don't have a safe profession. Anyway, I'd get bored if I was safe. Be careful little one. You are wise and I trust your decisions. Don't let the orders from Mission Command get you killed." He bent down and cupped her chin in his hands looking into her face as if committing it to memory. He held her head in his hands and bent down his elegant neck and he kissed her passionately on the mouth. She responded and for a moment they put the world aside. Then he stepped away from her and the hologram that had been confusing the camera overlaid itself onto him. Hers did the same and he bowed. "I wish you a good night. I must return to my companions."

They entered the banqueting hall separately. Kyla went back to her seat and picked up her spoon and finished her dessert.

Kel leant closer to her. "Are you alright?" He looked worried.

There was a serving girl behind them, taking away the plates. Kyla leant back and let her reach over between them. The girl hesitated, sorting out the spoons on the plate as Kel looked as though he as going to speak again. Kyla watched her until she had finished what she was doing, ran out of excuses to stay there and was forced to move along to collect the next plates.

Kyla smiled, "I am well, this dress fits but there was a small problem."

The serving girl carried on with her duties and was now out of earshot.

Kel looked mystified. "And..."

Many in the room were beginning to get very loud and a small fight had broken out which was quickly dealt with by the servants. Kyla leant on his shoulder and he looked down, surprised. She turned and looked up at him. She whispered. "We have trouble. That honoured guest is supposedly the True Prince and the Emperor is trying to have him removed. If they kill you and make it look like an accident then the Emperor can claim me and then by right of blood he can claim the throne."

Kel put his arm around her and pulled her head back and leant down over her. Rennon looked stunned, Samson was watching the dancing girls. "We have right royally messed up this time haven't we?"

He bent to kiss Kyla but a loud explosion and the release of some doves distracted him. Kyla was able to pull away and look in amazement at the display. She cast a sideways glance and watched Joniel who had been covertly watching them before reaching for her goblet. She then reached over to Rennon and laughed at a joke that Rennon had not spoken. "Rennon, we've got trouble. The Emperor wants to kill his guest of honour."

Rennon took out his book and flicked through it. "No he won't, these banquets are legendary and it would be a disaster for him if anything happened to one of the guests at his table. My guess would be it would be either during the night or tomorrow."

Hours later the music still filled the hall, they had eaten their fill and drunk the excellent wine. The floor was beginning to spin when Kel helped Kyla to her feet and the four of them staggered their way back to their rooms.

Rennon leant forwards and kissed Kyla on the cheek before disappearing into his room, throwing his robes onto the floor and sinking into the comfortable bed.

Dr Samson stepped towards his door and missed it. Kyla opened it for him and Kel helped him inside, shutting the door while he put the staggering doctor to bed. This done he shut the door and joined Kyla in the corridor. She staggered slightly as they set off down the corridor. He opened the door and she stepped inside, he followed her.

The morning dawned bright, the sun streamed through the window and Kyla was already sitting at the dressing table brushing her hair. Kel was pulling his robe on. He walked to the window and looked down into the street below. "Everything looks pretty peaceful down there. You would never know. I think that must be it, they are attacked, they get over it."

Kyla stopped brushing her hair. "They get by, like we all do."

Kel smiled. "So what do we do now?"

Kyla smiled. "We go and see if we can trade what we have for what we want."

There was a sharp knock on the door and a Guard stood outside. "If you are ready I have been sent to escort you to your audience with the Emperor."

They fell in behind him and followed him down many corridors and through rooms until they came to an ornate metal door. It was guarded by two huge, ornately dressed guards who stepped aside to let their comrade and the guests past.

The guard knocked three times and opened the doors wide so that they could walk through into the opulent room. It was draped with purple velvet curtains and painted in a similar style to the banqueting hall. There was no visible desk. The Emperor they had seen the night before languished on a couch and chairs had been brought for them and set in front of him. Close up he was still a tiny man with pointed features. He almost disappeared in the mountain of his silk robes. He sat up as they entered and waved them inside. "Come in, sit, sit, we will talk. Now leave us." The guard scurried away, bowing.

All four of them were there and they sat on the chairs that were waiting. Kel looked at Kyla and turned as if to speak.

The Emperor pulled himself up to his full height and rearranged his robes. He wriggled slightly, making himself comfortable. "I must first thank you for your assistance yesterday evening, most impressive. You have indeed proven yourself as worthy allies. I am now willing to take that one stage further. There is someone I would like you to meet."

The door opened and the Prince strode in. He cut an impressive figure in his black well fitting leather armour and flowing black cape. He was without a helmet and his black hair was spiked, his beard neatly trimmed to a goatee.

The Emperor stood up and they followed suit. "I would like to present to you Prince Anathorn of the Northern Planets. He is born of the ancient dynasty of kings. He too carries the DNA. He flew in last night when he heard there was another of the dynasty present. I am indeed greatly honoured that he is staying as a guest on my planet."

Anathorn sat down casually on the proffered chair. "Please, be seated, it is indeed an honour to meet all of you. Your deeds and efforts towards the war have made a great difference and we all have a lot to thank you for. I must concur with what the Emperor so kindly said. It would be practical for the planets to form an alliance or come under one rule in order to present a united front against our most formidable enemies. For my part my credentials are well known throughout the planets in this system and I was happy to accept the invitation put to me by leaders such as His Excellency the Emperor. I am at your service." He bowed his head slightly, smiling kindly.

Kel grunted. "So you want to take over."

Anathorn smiled broadly. "Succinctly put. But not by force and I welcome only those who voluntarily wish to be part of the Union of Planets."

The Emperor coughed. "According to one of our legends a great leader will come to us in the time of our greatest need. Born of the blood, honourable of spirit, firm in resolve and destined to wear the quadruple crested crown on his brow."

Anathorn met Kyla's enquiring glance. "That may well be a long way off. There is so much to do and a long way to go before that happens. I intend to fight. Would you join me?" He was looking directly at Kyla. She blushed slightly and felt electricity running down her spine as he spoke. His voice was velvety, commanding, imploring her to agree with him. Her mouth opened and then closed again.

Kel stood up. "We work for Mission Command."

Anathorn smiled. "I know and how was Mission Command set up? By the money of an eccentric millionaire? Is that familiar?"

Kel and Kyla turned to Rennon and he nodded. "There was a bequest many hundreds of years ago which led to setting up a base camp in the stars and waiting for a coming threat."

Anathorn crossed his legs and relaxed. "Keriak thiantho leanthenon. I give for the future."

Rennon thought for a moment. "That is what is engraved on the foundation block. But anyone could know that."

Anathorn rested his hands on his lap and closed his eyes slowly and then opened them again. "Indeed. You will know the truth of it. It was my ancestor who set up bases in different galaxies, each to defend that galaxy. A gift to the planets he felt would be most likely to be the superpowers at a time when the galaxy needed them.

For your base he took great warriors and wise people from a planet in a closed galaxy known as Earth. He sought them out and they came by their own free will. They have since had children and grandchildren of their own but they still live on the base. Although my beginnings were humble since then I have dedicated my life to becoming the man that I need to be."

Kyla met his gaze and felt a warm feeling. "I can't begin to imagine what that must have been like." It was like there was nobody else in the room and he was speaking only to her.

The Prince smiled. "Your own history is known to me. Where is the difference? You were born to be Chieftain of a tribe. What is being born to duty other than following a path that is pre-ordained. That is the same for many people. That we can understand those that we seek to guide is all we can ask for. Whatever mistakes they make and however misguided they may be."

Kel grunted. "We all are born to duty. You want to be Prince and you can do the job then I'm sure that there will be some sort of diplomatic arrangement. If you mean with us then that is for the Base Commander and others to decide, not us. We're just an off base team on a mission and so far we haven't actually got very far with our actual directive."

Anathorn turned to him, his gaze intense, concerned. "Indeed. I would speak with your Commander. It is also true that you have not as yet been able to find your team member? I think we can dispense with the bartering here. You came to recover your team member who has been here since she was recovered from the wreckage of her Planet Hopper. You may have brought something to trade. Am I correct?"

Rennon looked confused. "That is correct. If she is here as a slave under your laws then we would like to buy her back. We believe we have something of suitable worth."

The Prince turned to the Emperor who looked a little sheepish. "Is this true? Do you have the person they are asking about on your planet?"

The Emperor took a deep breath. "I do indeed. She came here when we recovered her from the wreckage. She has been content to work in our Library and indeed she seems to enjoy her work. Her translation skills are second to none. It would take something very special to match her in value.

Do you have such a thing?"

Rennon looked the Emperor in the eye. "We would like to speak with her first."

Kel snapped. "Why was she not allowed to contact us?"

Anathorn was watching the Emperor out of the corner of his eye while appearing to be looking at Rennon and the others. "It couldn't hurt for them to speak with her. If she is content to stay then they may be content to leave her with you."

Kel spoke slowly, his voice measured. The obvious relief showing on his face. "That would be a good idea."

Anathorn looked to the Emperor.

The Emperor bowed his head slightly. "Yes my Prince, they may speak with her. I will arrange for them to be taken to her after our audience is completed."

Anathorn bowed his head. "I thank you." He turned to Kel. "Will that be acceptable?"

Dr Samson shifted in his seat. "She is a very emotional person and has been greatly distraught over these past few months after the death of what she believed was the last of her people. If she is in a situation where she also feels trapped I would not recommend it for her continuing health and stability."

The Emperor looked concerned. "I cannot comment on her mental stability. I can only suggest that her present circumstances will bring a stable and reliable aspect to her life. She has been provided with a comfortable residence in the Scholar's Quarter and of course employment. Keltar, our Chief Librarian is indeed a very level headed individual who has the respect of all who know him. He will make a most suitable mate for her." He looked over at Anathorn as if passing the lead on to him.

Anathorn met his gaze and took a deep breath. "It is one of my ambitions to attempt to protect some of the lost races and to promote their regeneration. It is early days but it may at least mean that one race will be saved. I am sure that the Emperor would also wish this. Whether they are in his possession or elsewhere in the galaxy they need to be protected." He looked directly at the Emperor. "There has to be a future, we have to focus on that and that is what we are fighting for. If one race can be brought back from the edges of extinction then that is a precious thing.

I have amassed an army and we have access to ships and people are joining us daily. There are many on different worlds who do not want to fall under the Follower's rule. They are flocking to us bringing with them technology, expertise and manpower. The army has grown, my Generals are some of the best in the galaxy or shall I say galaxies. We have many races amongst our army and they too have a great interest in ensuring that other races survive so that they can build again once this war is over.

I would return with you to your Mission Command if this can be arranged. I trust this will be acceptable to you." He smiled at Kyla who blushed slightly. She felt it again, that warm, tingling feeling. She couldn't take her eyes off of the Prince. Then she looked down at his wrist and recognised Joniel's hologram device. She smiled and bowed her head. "I am sure this will be acceptable."

Kel looked at Rennon, his expression quizzical. "Well if the Commander is willing to set up an audience who are we to stand in your way."

Anathorn looked suddenly serious. "We will make the arrangements to speak with your Commander. I will arrange a message to be delivered before the day is over. This will give you some time to speak with Shantara and to enjoy this beautiful city. After all, if we do not appreciate the beauty of what is around us and merely slip into a battle for that which is we will lose the passion we need to succeed. We are few, they are many but history has recorded many such situations. If the gods are willing, it will again. I must take my leave of you now." He turned to the Emperor. "I thank you for the opportunity to speak with your guests and I look forward to speaking with you again."

He turned to Kyla. "My lady, it has been delightful to meet you. I trust that we will be able to speak again soon."

He turned to Rennon. "Sir, it has been a pleasure."

He turned to Kel. "Sir, I trust we will meet again soon."

He turned to Samson. "It was a pleasure."

He stood up and strode out of the room leaving those present in silence.

The Emperor turned to his guests. "Now, I trust you found that a worthwhile meeting. There will be food available for you and you are welcome to enjoy our wonderful City. To speak with Shantara all you need to do is present yourself at the Great Library and you will be shown to where she works. Now I am afraid I must take my leave also, last night has left a lot of necessary work to do." He stood up and they followed his lead, standing up and leaving in silence.

Later that day Kyla and Kel made their way out into the City. It was teeming with people. Traders hawked their brightly coloured goods from handmade carts and their cries filled the air. Smells of cooking food, herbs, spices and animals created an indecipherable cacophony of scents that filled the senses. It was hard to move, people were pressed shoulder to shoulder as they passed along the main street. The smell of sweaty bodies and animal dung was overpowering.

Kyla leant close to Kel and he bent down to hear what she wanted to say. "You would think with all this technology and beautiful buildings that they would discover soap."

He smiled and put his arm around her as she was buffeted by the passing crowd. "Don't worry, we're nearly there. So, do you fancy doing any shopping or shall we join Rennon and Dr Samson at the Library. Do you think they have had enough time to speak to her yet?"

She looked up at him, her eyes bright with expectation. "Not yet, I'd like to look around a bit."

Kel looked down at her and smiled. He was a lot less tense than he had been for a long time. Then he tensed and she jumped slightly as he gripped her a little too tightly. She looked up at him trying to be casual but he could see the fear in her eyes. "We are being followed. I saw him in the Palace and I wasn't comfortable about him then."

Kyla wriggled slightly so that he loosened his grip. "Thank you. I would normally speculate that it was the Emperor keeping an eye on us but he said there are cameras. Then again there are politics here and that can always make things difficult. We are making alliances and there are going to be those who aren't happy about that. There are likely to be Followers amongst the people here. Let's see if we can get hold of that one and find out what he wants. Do you fancy a bit of shopping down that side road?"

Kel stepped back and laughed then pointed down the side road. Kyla looked where he was pointing and nodded then turned to face him almost walking backwards out of the street, laughing and trying to look light hearted and as if they were just playing. They ran down the street to a shop and ducked into the doorway.

The one who was tailing them followed them almost straight away. He stopped just before their doorway and looked at the goods displayed. He was a middle aged man, about five foot eight with sandy coloured hair and a worried expression on his face. Now he was nearer they could see that he wore Imperial Armour under his disguise. The angles of the plates made a distinctive shape under the loose material.

He cast the merest sideways glance when he spoke to them. "I needed an opportunity to speak with you. Things aren't how they seem. Look around you and you see opulence, well up there in the palace you do. Down here there are people forced into the army while other people starve. How many has he taken from the streets to fight in that Amphitheatre? He would declare himself a god again. He is petitioning the Senate to restore the old ways. If they do he will have supreme power. With the army he has amassed and if the Prince is out of the way he would have supreme command. If it was an accident when the Prince dies then he will step in to take his place, his army and his firepower."

Kel stared at him intently. "Why are you telling us this? What is your part in all this?"

The man bowed his head slightly. "I am Leitath De'Mari, right hand to Joniel. He, I and the rest of his men are in hiding. Earlier today My Lord was called to the Emperor. The Emperor ordered My Lord put to death on the spot claiming he was there to assassinate the Prince. Thankfully he still had one charge in his teleport for the day and we have him, he is safe. He was injured as he did take one blaster bolt before he could get away. He commanded me to warn you to leave this place as soon as you can. I must return to my lord now. Now that he can't be blamed Joniel fears that the Emperor will attempt to try something himself and put the blame on Kel. As a murderer that would be the same as you being a widow. To claim the Prince's position he would need someone of the blood. While you are here he could claim you by right of royalty. My lord cannot command you but he would ask that you leave, immediately." He smiled, turned and strode down the alleyway before disappearing into general populace moving up and down the street..

7

Kel and Kyla moved as quickly as they could through the crowds while trying not to arouse suspicion. Now they were ever more conscious that there were people following them. A few quick visits to random shops confirmed this. The same three people kept turning up.

Kel bent down and make it look like he was playing with Kyla's hair. "I don't know what we are worried about, we are expected to go to the Library. We might as well walk straight there."

Kyla grinned. "I know but I object to being followed." Then in a louder voice she added. "Kel, we'll have to stop messing about and get to see Shantara. Come on, we can shop another day or on the way back."

He smiled at her and they began pushing their way faster through the crowd, following the central flow up the middle of what looked like the main street. They couldn't read the signs but Kel had a fairly good idea where the Library was from looking at Rennon's city guide. He grabbed Kyla's arm after they were nearly separated for a second time and pulled her behind him. He then used his bulk to get through the crowd, gently manoeuvring around the others in the street.

Kyla was tiring. Her already white skin was drained of all colour and she stumbled occasionally as her leg could not hold her up. Kel slipped his arm around her and almost carried her as they made their way through the crowd.

Progress was slow but quicker than it had been. They followed the flow up the central arterial street which came directly to the central Plaza. Movement in the Plaza was even more difficult. It was surrounded by magnificent porticos, Council Buildings and one side of it was the Great Library. This was a feat of engineering in itself. It towered above all other buildings and its spires threw shadows over the crowd below. It was further raised up as it sat at the top of a huge flight of stone steps which were crowded.

The Plaza was full of people. Entertainers and street speakers had little circles of space in which to perform and the crowds around them formed a near impenetrable barrier. Kel and Kyla negotiated their way around these islands and pushed on through the crowd. They were nearing the steps when an enthusiastic juggler lost control of his flaming batons. The crowd stepped back to avoid the flaming brand and Kyla was caught in the ribs by the elbow of a young man who had lost his footing in the chaos. She gasped as the air was knocked out of her lungs and the searing pain rushed from her ribs to her back. Her legs gave out under her and Kel held her like a rag doll as she nearly hit the floor as the crowd closed in around them.

He almost carried her the last few hundred yards across the Plaza. She walked as much as she could but the pain was almost unbearable. Kel tried to hold her gently but with the buffeting crowd it was impossible to keep her safe from the elbows and bodies that crushed around them. He felt the first step by nearly tripping over it. The jolt made Kyla gasp. "I'm sorry, but we are at the steps, not far to go now and we'll be out of this crowd." He almost dragged her up the steps. Step by step they got closer but the crowd got thicker. By the time they almost got to the top of the stairs he was physically having to push his way through. Some objected, most saw the size of him and tried to give him space. Eventually he got to the top and the crowd was almost impenetrable. All he could do was try to shield Kyla from being hurt more than was necessary and push forwards. He stretched to his full height and tried to see over the crowd.

There was a cordon around the Library. The Emperor's Peacekeepers were keeping the crowd back and more of them marched about accompanying white robed official looking old men and women. The Peacekeeper's uniform was distinctive. Their breastplates bearing the Emperor's Eagle shone like glass, polished to perfection, matching scarlet capes fluttered in the wind. Their helmets were similarly well polished and adorned by a scarlet plume. They formed an impenetrable line and beyond that line the balcony outside the Library was almost empty.

Onlookers craned their necks to see what was going on. There was a man to his right, dressed in brown robes. He took a wrong step and elbowed Kel. "I'm sorry, please forgive me."

Kyla put a hand on Kel's chest. "Its quite alright, you cannot help it. What is going on?"

The man smiled. "I don't know the details but a couple of slaves have escaped. They were working at the Library until this morning. When the Librarian came to let them out both of their rooms were empty. This is an outrage. What if all our slaves got the same idea? Where would we be then? The guard are looking for them to make an example of them. Then again you can't trust these aliens can you? They say they had lilac skin and hair. Well that shouldn't be too difficult to find. It will be quite a spectacle when they do find them."

Kel grunted. "When?"

The man laughed. "Oh they always find them. All slaves are marked and tagged. If they step out of their controlled zone they will be located. If we are lucky they will be captured. If not then the guard with activate the chip in them and it will blow a major artery. Either way they won't last long. There is a long range on that transmitter. I know, my family have been making them for generations."

Kyla looked worried. "What happens if they are caught?"

The man smiled. "Then there will be a public gathering and they will be beheaded. That is the tradition. It hasn't changed for hundreds of years. You are new here are you?"

Kyla tensed up. "Traders, we thought there might be a market for our goods here. What is business like?"

The man looked serious. "Fair to middling, depends on what you have on offer. Luxury goods are hard to move at the moment as money is tight. Essentials on the other hand are commanding a very good price. It's a seller's market there. With so little money around people are concentrating on essentials. There's a lot to be made if you are careful. What do you trade in?"

Kyla smiled. "Unfortunately luxury goods so I think we may well be shipping out."

The man smiled back. "Very wise. Come back in a few months and no doubt it will all be different. Once this lull is over people will need to splash out and spend more. Get the elections over and we'll see."

Kyla looked puzzled. "Elections?"

The man's eyes brightened. "You haven't heard. The Emperor has called Elections next month. Every Government Official has to put in a petition for re-election. It should cause a huge shake up here. Out with the old, in with the new and we'll do better."

Kel felt someone pushing through the crowd behind him and looked over his shoulder, preparing to push the person away. He looked down on Rennon and Samson who had come through the crowd behind them. He turned slightly. "Good to see you two. We were just talking to this gentleman here about our trade arrangements. It seems that this is not the time for us to sell our luxury goods. May I suggest that we make a move out of here and return home."

Rennon looked tired. "A very wise decision I would think."

Kel pushed Kyla into the middle of them and they moved slowly down the stairway and joined the milling crowd below. Once in the anonymity of the crowd they made their way along the main street. Now more than ever they noticed the number of cameras that were set up. There was no chance of talking without someone seeing or hearing them.

Kel whispered in Kyla's ear. "I wish we had some of Joniel's technology now. Where does he get that stuff."

Kyla looked thoughtful and smiled as she whispered to him. "You really don't know who he is? Have you heard of the Rel'ha'asshin? Don't worry, the sound of the crowd will block out any chance of hearing what we say. Just don't look up. Remember the Emperor's lip readers."

Kel frowned. "I have no idea who he is. He's a tall enigmatic stranger with useful technology. The hit men? Who hasn't?"

Kyla smiled to herself. "He's not just one of them. He's their Father at the moment."

Kel looked stunned then smiled. "It explains why he has such good equipment. So what do we do now?"

Kyla thought and then smiled and looked up at him as if playfully reaching up to give him a kiss on the cheek. "You can take Rennon and Samson and get to the Hopper. I'm going to go to the Prince and tell him."

Kel caught her around the waist hard. "That is madness."

Kyla pulled her hand free. "Ouch. No, it isn't. While the Emperor thinks I'm going back to the Palace he's going to make sure I get there. Once I'm there he may make a move but I'm going straight to the Prince. You and the others would be safer on board ship. While you are safe and more importantly alive I am of no use to the Emperor."

Kyla pulled away from him and quietly said. "You have to know it makes sense. If we don't warn him someone else will kill him. Then Joniel's sacrifice will be worthless."

Kel looked puzzled. "Sacrifice, I thought he got away?"

Kyla reached up again. "The Emperor will have a price on his head by now and more importantly will have let it be known that he backed out of a contract. For the first time he's on the run, for something he didn't do, literally." Kyla backed away from them and pushed into the crowd speaking loudly and raising her head so the cameras could see her. "Come on, let's go shopping? Oh come on. If you don't want to then I'll go on my own. You can go and check those problems with the Hopper if you'd rather. I'll see you back at the Palace later."

Kel glared at her but she was out of reach and to grab her would draw attention to them. She disappeared off into the crowd as Kel and the others made their way to the docking port.

Kyla moved as fast as she could, dodging into the occasional shop and out again before moving swiftly back to the Palace. She was conscious of the two people who were following her. She managed to lose one in the crowd by diving down a side street, cutting around a back alley which was similarly crowded and coming out further down the street.

She got to the Palace and went in by the side entrance and the guards bowed as she passed by them. Their glances to each other were not lost on her. They didn't follow her as she moved as quickly as she could without arousing suspicion but she was now even more on her guard. She shut her eyes for a moment and mentally called up a map of the place as far as she knew it. Turn right, turn left, the stairway, the hallway and there they were, the Prince's personal guards. When she was sure of her route she followed it.

The Prince's guards moved to challenge her as she approached and crossed their swords in front of her. She cleared her throat, her mouth so dry she wondered if she would be able to speak. They were about Kel's height and well built. Each bore the Prince's phoenix insignia, their livery a dark gold and red. "I am Kyla, I come to seek audience with the Prince."

A disembodied voice came seemingly from nowhere. "Send her in, I grant her audience."

The Prince was standing by the window, silhouetted by the afternoon sun. He turned. "You may speak freely, there are no devices in this room." He indicated the pile of torn out wires and crushed microphones on a silver platter on the table.

Kyla took a deep breath. "You have to believe me and you aren't going to like this. The Emperor contracted Joniel to kill you. He has refused the contract." She said it all in one breath and then stopped abruptly as he turned and smiled.

He clasped his hands behind his back. "Won't be the first and certainly won't be the last. I thank you for bringing this information to me as that shows a loyalty and bravery that I appreciate." He turned around, his face slightly drawn but his smile still warm, his eyes kind. "It is dangerous on this planet now, for you and your friends. Joniel has already warned me, he has ways of sending messages and he had sworn his allegiance to me long ago. I appreciate what he has done and he is an unexpected asset. For your part, I thank you and this will not be forgotten.

Joniel is probably right in his assumption that the Emperor will try to claim someone of the blood. We are rare as we are from one family's bloodline which can be traced right back through the millennia. You aren't the only one but you are the only one here. You getting away will hamper his plans as he no doubt has it all worked out. So while you are safe, I am safe. That was why he double crossed Joniel or he may have realised he wasn't his man. He thought he'd win my trust by foiling an assassination attempt. If Joniel had succeeded it would have equally suited him. To take the throne he needs complete confidence from the army for them to follow him. He assumes they would just blindly follow him because he was Prince. That is not so."

Kyla was taking it all in. "So what are you going to do about the Emperor?"

The Prince smiled. "Absolutely nothing. If I am to bring peace to the galaxies then I need strong leaders. To attempt to do anything, albeit justified would weaken his power at the best. I cannot call him to task as I cannot call Joniel as a witness. I need his anonymity. If we take the Emperor out of the equation there would be a power struggle in the Senate here. That would unbalance this planet which is not good for this planet. I know where I stand with him and he has revealed his hand. My strength is that I know it, his weakness is that he assumes that I don't.

We need to get you all safely off planet and the easiest way to do that would be for me to invite you to a guided tour of my Flagship. I believe it is impressive enough to warrant it. Of course it would be more convenient if you took your own ship but that will not be possible. That was stolen earlier by Shantara and her companion. I took the liberty of aiding them in their escape and to throw suspicion away from you I have made it as inconvenient for you as possible. Your friends will no doubt have discovered the theft by now and I trust that they will express their anger and frustration in a suitably loud and impressive fashion.

As you are without a ship it would be wholly appropriate as my business here is concluded and I am ready to depart that I should offer to convey you to your home planet. So, if I and my guards accompany you now it would be totally politically correct. I have already said my official farewell's to the Emperor. He has the issue of two missing slaves to deal with. Here that is a major issue as their economy relies on the cheap workforce. As I took the liberty of disabling their device you can rest easy, Shantara and her friend are quite safe. Their escape may well put the idea into other slaves' minds and that is an issue that they will be debating long into the night.

We could use the teleport but I have no intention of arousing any suspicion or alerting anyone to the fact that I have one. If we take a gentle guided tour to my ship we can run into your incensed companions. I can then offer them the courtesy of a pleasure flight in my personal shuttle up to my ship. There will then be no suspicion raised.

We will undoubtedly be scanned so our discussion from the point we leave this room must be guarded. I have devices that could scramble their signal but again that would arouse suspicion. Once we are out of their scanner range I will arrange for you to be able to send a message on an open channel to your Mission Command and I would hope that they would summon you home. I intend to open negotiations with Mission Command and this would be the perfect opportunity to begin these.

I will make a point when we are on your ship of giving you a gift. This is a device that will deal with scanning problems in the future. I trust you can play your part in this?"

Kyla nodded.

He touched his collar. "I need an escort, full colours. Get the staff to pack and load, we are moving out." He let his hand fall. "Kyla, if you would come with me we will leave immediately."

Kyla was very unnerved as everyone's eyes were on them as they left the Palace. The Emperor's guards did not challenge them and they swept down the stairway to the open plaza. She was beginning to feel dizzy and stumbled slightly on the stairs. The Prince looked at her, concerned and stepped closer to her as they crossed the open empty Plaza. "This is the place where we are most vulnerable. If he is stupid enough to attempt anything it will be here. Be ready."

They crossed the Plaza without incident and the Prince's Hopper raised up from its underground parking in front of them. Rennon, Samson and Kel were in an animated discussion with a group of uniformed officials. Kel aggressively bending over one small man who looked terrified.

The Prince put a hand on Kyla's arm. "I think there is one poor soul there who needs a bit of a hand." He stepped away from her and realised that it was only his arm that was preventing her from falling. His strong arm swept around her waist and one of his guards stepped in to support her as the Prince strode over to Kel, his guards forming up around him to escort him, a retinue staying around Kyla. "Kel, what seems to be the problem?"

Kel was in full scream at the unfortunate man but he broke off and turned. "Your Majesty, it appears that these incompetent fools have allowed our ship to be stolen."

The Prince's face displayed a look of shock. "That is outrageous. That a guest here should have their property so carelessly treated. I trust that you will be making a full report." He glared at the official who nodded his head vigorously. "Well, this is not an end to the matter. You will no doubt be hearing from these good people about reimbursement for their loss. It seems you are left with an inconvenience and a lack of transport. May I be so bold as to offer you transport home?"

Kel's mouth was open and he looked like he had a dilemma. "I thank you." He stepped forwards towards the official who stepped back, looking up like a frightened rabbit.

The Prince turned on the official. "Go, now, immediately and make your report." The man looked relieved and scuttled off, accompanied by the other officials.

The Prince strode up into his shuttle, followed by his guards and the rest of his retinue.

Kyla smiled at Kel who was looking very confused. "It is good to see you well my husband. We will no doubt seek compensation for the loss of our ship. Your brother will no doubt loan us a vessel so that we may continue our business until this matter is settled." Kel looked at her dumbstruck. Rennon and Samson cast a sideways glance at each other and took their seats.

The Prince switched the radio on from the panel in the passenger hold. "Sirius 687 do we have a go for take off?"

There was a long silence and Kyla clenched her fists tightly, the air seemingly escaping from her lungs as her chest felt tight.

The Prince looked around them, slightly nervously. "Sirius 687 do we have a go?"

Still there was silence. The Prince stood up to his full height. "This is Prince Anathorn on board Sirius 687. I do not wish to be kept waiting. Do we have a go?" He looked around nervously at Rennon who was operating a hand held scanner. Rennon looked up and shook his head.

The intercom leapt into life. "Sirius 687 you are cleared for departure."

Anathorn stepped back. "Traskus, you have the comms. Take them home."

A disembodied voice came over the intercom. "Very good my lord."

Traskus lifted the Hopper smoothly off of the pad and they soared into the air, through the atmosphere and up into space. Once they were approaching the Prince's ship, the Prince reached into the pocket of his black velvet robe. "My dear, as a symbol of our new friendship I would like to give you a small token of my regard." He handed her a small gold clip in the shape of a flower. It was beautifully crafted.

Kel growled and went to stand up, his hand reaching involuntarily for his gun. He fell back into his seat when he came into contact with Kyla's stony stare.

She activated the device and it bleeped. Around the craft there were small detonations and wisps of smoke rose up into the air. "I thank you my Prince, the gift of privacy is always much appreciated."

Kel choked. "You mean…"

Prince Anathorn bowed his head slightly. "There are few places on that planet that are not covered by their intelligence network and they would not pass up the opportunity to bug this ship and probably your clothing. That device is a handy one to keep around. It will need to charge up again and that takes about a month but keep it safe. You never know when you are going to need it. We may talk freely now. I must thank you for your efforts and for the risks you have taken. It would not be wise to return to that planet for a while Kyla or to allow any of your people do to so."

There was a bleeping sound and the Prince pulled a small device from a concealed pocket in his sleeve. He placed it in his ear. His expression was grave as he listened. "Look, something has come up. Rennon, can you pilot this Hopper?"

Rennon nodded.

The Prince flicked a button on the earpiece. "We will be there immediately." He turned to the three. "Plans have changed. Please, take this ship for your return home. I would have been delighted to have offered you my hospitality and I trust that I will have the opportunity in the near future. For now I must bid you farewell."

He nodded to each of them in turn and pressed the button on his wrist as his Guard and retinue did the same. They disappeared in a blue flame and were gone.

Rennon opened the cockpit door and took the pilot's seat. He did a few checks then logged the home co-ordinates into the computer and was about to hit the return home button. Kyla caught his hand and spoke gently. "We would be best served not taking this ship back to Mission Command. I would suggest you radio ahead and arrange for us to be transferred to another ship to give time for this one to be fully checked out while in orbit. We are dealing with two men with definite agendas." Kyla met Rennon's steady stare. "He is a politician and Mission Command have not as yet agreed to meet or speak with him. I personally wouldn't leave an unknown quantity in our hanger bay."

Kel grunted. "I agree, I don't trust him."

Kyla smiled. "I'm not saying I don't trust him, what I'm saying is that we shouldn't put ourselves in a position to unnecessarily have to."

Later that day they were sitting in the cafeteria together. The room was full of people making the most of a break and one of the favourite meals on the menu, Shantilla's Surprise. The surprise being that it was very tasty and used a white meat instead of the usual brown with the addition of a fruit sauce.

Kel dug in with gusto. Rennon was most of the way through his and Kyla was daintily enjoying her portion. Samson was still in the Infirmary as he had a lot to do to catch up with being off base.

They all looked up when a group of uniformed strangers walked into the room. They looked around bemused and then filed over to where the food was being served. One by one they took a tray and started down the line.

They were attracting attention. They didn't look any different but there was something about them. In all there were four men, three were blonde haired, the fourth was brown haired. They all had identical haircuts and their camouflage uniforms were almost the same but the badges on the arm were different. They went along the line, helped themselves to the food, commenting to each other and taking a good look at each offering in turn.

Kyla dug Kel in the ribs. "Stop staring."

Kel looked defensive. "I wasn't, I mean, how can I help it. Who do you think that they are?"

Rennon piped up. "They are from Earth, they arrived this morning."

Kel looked surprised. "I thought that Earth was a closed world?"

Rennon thought a moment. "It was but the Followers have found their way to that galaxy and there is a fear that they will walk in there unopposed. That altered the status of the planet. They are in the same situation as we are now."

Kel took a mouthful. "How did they get here?"

Rennon looked down at his food. "Not long ago a group on their world discovered a device that had lain dormant for many years. It was a time and space travelling device used but Elias Shanti and his party of marauders. Something happened on Earth while he was there and the device went into stealth mode and rested for a number of years until its power cell almost ran out. That was a shock for the locals who had turned the chameleon room into a pub. Building and customers on the opening night were transported off world to the device's safe zone. I don't have the details but it appears that the whole network has now reinstated itself. So now we have our link to Earth without alerting the Followers."

The group sat down but the table was too far away for them to hear what was being said so they went back to eating their food.

Rennon looked up. "Kyla, you are quiet."

Kyla looked up. "Sorry, was I? I have a lot on my mind, don't worry, I'm fine."

Kel went to put his arm around her and she moved away. "What. I.."

Kyla looked surprised. "The mission is over, you aren't my husband now."

Kel opened his mouth then shut it again then muttered. "I'm sorry, was that just for the mission?"

Someone over the other side of the room dropped a tray and just about everyone jumped. Guns were pulled from holsters and scientists and ancillary staff jumped under tables. The poor woman who had dropped the tray looked mortified. She put her hands up slowly and backed away from the tray as the guns were put back in holsters and the room calmed down as she hurried to tidy up the mess.

Rennon checked his mission log. "The mission briefings and work schedules have just come in. Oh boy, I've a stack of paperwork waiting for me back in the Lab, the Commander wants a briefing tomorrow morning. How about you?"

Kel rummaged around in a belt pouch and finally pulled out his communicator. "I've got weapons training with the rookies this afternoon. Not so bad. How about you Kyla?"

Kyla looked down. "I'm not officially on the team."

Kel looked up from pressing different buttons. "You know I have no idea how this works. Look, you could change that, tell him you are staying."

Kyla looked surprised. "I don't know if I am."

Rennon put his cutlery on his tray. "That's me done. I'd better get back to the Lab. Look Kyla, we all want and need you here. You can do so much for your people by helping us to keep one step ahead of the Followers. Think about it, it is your choice of course but I hope you decide to stay."

Kel mumbled. "I hope so too. Look Kyla can we talk?"

Kyla smiled. "We are talking."

Kel sat up straight and the nerve in his neck was pulsing. "I mean can we talk alone."

Kyla's smile fell from her face. "Of course my friend, I'm happy to talk to you. Shall we take a walk to the Pavilion?"

The Pavilion was a huge glass observation room which was often used for relaxation. There was a music output in there which was playing random pieces of music which helped to add to the ambience. The room was fairly dark, lit only by subdued coloured lighting from around the room and from the ornamental fish pond at its centre. Coloured lights had also been embedded in the waterfall and under the fountain giving the room a very mystical air.

Sofas were scattered around the room in strategic places so that anyone sitting on one sofa could not hear what was being said on another. The cameras in the room were facing the door, anything that happened in the room was not under surveillance.

The door was open which meant free access. If anyone really wanted to they could type in their code, close the doors and have some private time for contemplation. Kel stepped aside and let Kyla walk in first. She wandered in and looked around the room, it was empty. Kel stepped inside and typed in his code, the doors shut and locked. Kyla jumped slightly and looked nervous.

They walked together to the nearest sofa and both sat down. Kyla looked around the room. "You wanted to talk?"

Kel muttered, mumbled but didn't say anything coherent. Then he took a deep breath, held it and let it out slowly. "On that last mission, was it just the cover? I mean did you only act the way you did because you wanted to maintain our cover?"

Kyla looked awkward. "It was a very sensitive mission. We all acted how we had to and it was a success. What do you mean?"

Kel looked frustrated. "I mean the way you were with me, was it just an act?"

Kyla smiled and he visibly relaxed. "If I had been your wife, that was how I would have acted in public."

Kel looked deflated and his whole body seemed to slump as if something had been taken away from him. "So it was just an act."

"It was an easy role to play and I enjoyed it very much. I trust that you didn't find it too onerous either."

"Eh?"

"Too difficult?"

"Oh, no, I enjoyed it."

"You didn't think that there was anything else going on did you?" Kyla's eyes bore deep into his.

Kel's expression hardened and the smile that had crept onto his face fell away. "Of course I didn't. Well, I have my answer now don't I? Perhaps we had better leave this place."

Kyla looked around at the stars through the glass dome. "Oh I don't know, I quite like it here, could we spend just a little time?"

Kel was looking away from her and he shifted awkwardly in his seat. "Sure, why not?"

Both of their communicators went off, making the low buzzing sound that heralded a new message. Both communicators were showing the words. "Report to Rennon's Laboratory, IMMEDIATELY."

They ran most of the way and arrived slightly out of breath. The doors opened wide as they arrived and the entered to see the Commander and Rennon looking down at a small machine that was humming away on the desk.

Rennon looked up as they came in. "Hello there, you are not going to believe this."

Kel looked around the Lab. It was small and crammed with bottles, pieces of equipment and terminals, all neatly stacked on shelves around the room. Rennon was standing by a table which had a black metal box on it. The box itself looked reasonably innocuous but by the way that the Commander was walking around it and Rennon was staring at it they knew it was somehow important.

The Commander smiled and sat on one of the lab stools. "This box was recovered on an off base mission about a week ago when one of our groups managed to take over a Followers vessel and recover their equipment. This is the first time we have managed to get anything like this. We have also retrieved a lot of information which makes matters a lot clearer. It seems the information we have already merely scratches the surface. We had thought that the Followers were a religious group who sprang from Fallow Earth. That is indeed quite possibly true. But there is an alien element to them as well. We have found connections to the Tresat. At the moment the connections are vague and eluded to but it's a break in giving us a direction to look in. We know nothing about this race other than its name. All references to it have been wiped out. I mean literally, documents deleted, books removed. There is nothing about them. That in itself means it would be a good idea to find out more.

You may have seen a group of visitors from Earth who arrived this morning. We brought them here to share this information. It seems that these entities were the ones who made Earth a closed system in the first place.

In truth we are not completely sure what we will achieve but it is hoped that by sending a mission to Earth we may be able to visit one of the places that is known to be "of the gods" and that the information there may not be as corrupted and influenced by the passing years as it may be in our galaxy.

The haste of calling you here is that I have the go ahead for the launch of missions to Earth. You have a "go" for tomorrow when you will be leaving on a joint mission with our guests from Earth.

It is a reconnaissance mission and we are not expecting much resistance unless the Followers have already infiltrated the planet. This is beneficial as you will not be permitted to visit that world armed with our more effective weapons.

The places of the gods you will be visiting are now tourist attractions. Access is free to all for a fee so we will make the most of this. You will be given side arms in keeping with the world you are visiting. Information about the world you will be visiting will be made available to you and I hope that you will take the time that you have to take a look at it."

.

8

The Commander sat in his room at his desk which was covered with personnel files. There was a knock on the door and he looked up and closed the file he had been looking at. "Enter."

Kyla stepped inside and shut the door behind her. She walked over to his desk as he smiled encouragingly.

He moved the file to the side of his desk and put his pen back in its place on the old fashioned ink well. "Thank you for coming. Please, sit down. As you know you have been with us for more than three months. There are of course rules and protocols that we must adhere to and one of them is that three months is the limit that a non-member can remain here. I have spoken to you about it before and although it has not been necessary for you to decide before, it is now. We are tightening up security as we do believe there could be infiltration. It is part of Article 27 that all personnel on base must be members when we raise our security status to Code Red. That is going to happen this afternoon. I trust you had sufficient time to make up your mind? You must understand this is purely protocol and no reflection on your work with us or your position within the team. Off the record I have seen you as an active team member for a long time. We must however adhere to the protocols so I must officially ask you."

Kyla cleared her throat and shifted somewhat uncomfortably in her chair. "I thank you. I have been very happy here for the past few months and I feel that what you are doing is a valuable contribution to the war against the Followers. I would like to stay and I accept your invitation. You are right, I have given it a great deal of consideration and I have done much soul searching."

"I am glad you have accepted. You have already been assigned most of the benefits afforded to staff members so little will change. There is one matter we must speak about though. I have received a directive from my senior officers that you are to be made available to work on secondment with Lord Joniel, now Prince Anathorn's right hand man. They have given the go ahead for this to be accepted. I would hear your thoughts on this matter. I trust you know Lord Joniel's history and are able to make this decision from a position of being well informed. I have read up on him myself and I would like to offer you the opportunity to refuse if you feel that you would be uncomfortable working with him. I understand that his occupation may well be contrary in ethics to your own calling."

Kyla smiled slightly. "I am very well informed about Lord Joniel's history and I would willingly assist him. Please convey my willingness to be seconded to his private staff."

The Commander smiled. "Very good, I am pleased to hear that. I have found Lord Joniel to be trustworthy in our dealings with him and our new found alliance with Prince Anathorn is proving to be mutually beneficial. Now, as to your first official mission with us I would like you to join with the others on the mission to Earth. I had to have your decision before this mission. Obviously it is a sensitive one and as you are a Non-Terra according to protocol you must be a member of this base. This automatically grants you the rights and permissions necessary. This is going to be a difficult mission as we do not know what you are going to be facing. Although we are proceeding with the co-operation of the British Government we feel that their ability to assist should there be a live fire situation would be severely limited. As a member of the team I can command you but I would prefer to ask you. I realise it is a long way from the planets you are used to."

Kyla stood to attention. "Sir, as a member of this team I accept all rank and command. I will happily take your orders. I have been reading up a little on Earth since our visitors arrived, it looks like an interesting place, not too dissimilar to some of our own planets."

The Commander opened a red folder on his desk. "That is one of the reasons why we feel it is important to send an expedition there. We believe that some of the religions and races common in our galaxy may have originated on Earth before it became a closed planet. At the very least they may have developed independently from outside influence. That could give us the opportunity to perhaps find out where the Followers came from. Information is confused here and much speculation and personal text has been added to the pure gospel that they may once have adhered to. It is hoped that we may fine the original text and be able to use this to break their control and at least throw doubt in the minds of their loyal worshipers. Also, amongst the information we retrieved there was also information about the Noble DNA. It seems that it is also present on Earth. It is something we feel is important to investigate as the mythology that seems to go with it involves leadership. Prince Anathorn believes that it may aid him in proving his right to rule. It seems that you may find more answers on Earth and there may be artefacts there like the ones here which you will be able to activate. Briefing is at 0800 hours, welcome to the team."

At 0800 hours Kel, Rennon and Kyla sat in the briefing room. Rennon had his notepad beside him and he was scribbling and doodling, Kel was sitting on one chair while having his feet on the next chair. Kyla sat bolt upright, her hair neatly brushed and her newly issued uniform pristinely clean, well pressed and smart. Her friendly "girl next door" smile reassured Rennon who had looked up nervously. Kel rapidly swivelled to drop his feet to the floor as the Commander entered, followed by the four Terran Emissaries.

The Commander took his seat at the head of the table and the Terran Emissaries sat opposite Kel, Rennon and Kyla. He put his red folder down and opened it at a page he had bookmarked. "Gentlemen and Lady, welcome to the briefing. May I first introduce you? On my left there is Captain David Rennon, our Science and Research Officer, to his left Kel Elyn, our weapons and ethnic tribes expert and our newest recruit, Kyla who joins us as our Combat Medic and Esoteric Expert. On my right I would like to introduce you to Connor Taylor who is an Astrophysicist and Weapons Expert, Damien Castle who specialises in Computers, Eric Lockhart who specialises in Extra Terrestrials and Daniel Carlton who is also a Weapons Expert. These are the representatives from Earth who will be taking part in this expedition. They are part of a team known as Red Rock which is concerned with Research and Development. You will have an opportunity to get to know each other later but for now I must continue with the mission briefing. We only have a short time to meet the window to get you to Earth.

We have been liaising with representatives from Earth for some time now and an ambassador visited us last month where it was agreed that increased liaison and a joint mission may be beneficial to all of us. Since then top people on Earth have been looking for a likely location to begin. Since then it has come to our attention that there is a foothold situation on Earth. The planet has been infiltrated and key officials who supported our cause have been eliminated either politically or physically. I received a report this morning and I will relay now what it contained.

It seems that the Earth Research Team have located an ancient scroll in a building known as The British Museum in the City of London, Britain, which has formed the basis of their research. There was a fair bit more in the scroll but the main bit they managed to translate was "To find the Isle of Hercules you need to seek the Sun in the Sacred Grove of the Kingdom of Heaven". In itself it sounds a pretty tall order but with a bit of cross referencing and their best people working on the case they have come up with a location.

Their investigations led them to take a look at an island in the Bristol Channel. This is a large river outlet on the West side of an Island known as the British Isles called Lundy. Lundy in its translation means Sacred Grove. It is also known as the Isle of Hercules. It is the only incursion of what they call Pre-Cambrian rock and is estimated to be 400 million years old.

As you know activation of certain artefacts involves an ancient bloodline. It is possible that this bloodline can also unlock certain places which may have been sealed for centuries. That bloodline was preserved through the centuries on Earth. This protection fell to the Knight's Templar organisation which still exists in modern Earth. It is mostly seen as a charitable organisation but its duty in history is far more martial. It was they who owned Lundy Island in the twelfth and thirteenth centuries. This connection could not be ignored either, as it is possible that there may be artefact based technology secreted on the island as well as information which may have been overlooked as irrelevant by the casual visitor. They protected the bloodline, they protected the island. It is not impossible that the two go together. There is a face like rock on the Island known as Templar Rock, we would like you to take a look at this among other things.

The Church on Lundy was built by the then owner, Reverend Heaven. The island was owned by the Heavens for a number of years and they were responsible for building many of the buildings that still stand today. We'd like you to take a look at the Church as it was not built in the tradition alignment for churches but in a more "pagan" alignment which fell in line with the Summer Solstice. The church is dedicated to St Helena who was the mother of the Emperor Constantine, a historic emperor from Earth's history. He is associated with being a follower of or having connection with a Sun God. It is similar to Chartres, in France and a separate delegation has been dispatched to investigate that location.

It is also said that Lundy was known as Gwair's Island, Gwair being a Celtic Sun God who was in legend imprisoned on Lundy. It is at least another sun connection.

Although nothing here would give us any indication that there was any alien influence there is one thing which may prove interesting. We have found information that two eight foot tall skeletons were found buried on the island in ten foot coffins. This in itself could be something worth investigating as according to the writings of Enoch, an ancient Earth writer, giants were supposed to be the children of an association between Angels who fell to Earth and mortal women. They were said to be giants who consumed the Earth because of their voracious appetites so they had to be eliminated which was the reasoning behind a great flood which is part of Earth's mythology and history.

An interesting sub text that the researchers also sent was about the bloodline. As you know Kyla here carries this bloodline which you may find very useful in your research. Members of this bloodline were known as "The Shining Ones" by various people on Earth. They have other names such as "El" was used to identify a "lofty one" which also meant shining in Mesopotamian Sumer. This became "Aelf" in Saxony and "Elf" in England.

The plural of "El" was "Elohim". In Gaelic Cornwall which is a county in Western England, the word "El" was the equivalent of the Anglo Saxon "engel" and the Old French "angele" which in English became "Angel". So it is possible there was some sort of association of these giants being the children of the Shining Ones, also known as "Heaven came to Earth" which may be some sort of "alien" connection.

It was a very tenuous link but sufficiently interesting for the researchers to want to make it known to you that they took a look at the location of Lundy. The Latitude is 51.166666 and Longitude 14.166666, that aroused some sort of suspicion with the mathematicians. Add the 5 and 1 you get 6. Add the 1 and 4 and 1 and you get 6. Then you have the 6 recurring. 666 is the circumference of the earth, it is also a "magical" number and associated with a magic square which is also associated with the sun.

Although there has been no factual information provided as yet to back this up it has also been pointed out that there are people on Earth known as Native Americans and they have ancient pictograms which depict future possibilities. On one of these pictograms there is the depiction of the Rising Sun being important at the end of days for the planet or at a time when the planet's people ascend into a different consciousness.

We believe that this association with the Sun is something specific and there are far too many connections for it to be mere coincidence.

So, I would like you to prepare for a trip to Lundy Island. As those of you from Earth know our transport methods are very limited as Earth is in a closed galaxy. The only place we are able to bring you to the planet is to a remote location in Wales. The Government has contacted us so we are acting officially but no doubt should anything go wrong they will accept plausible deniability for our presence on the planet. We have technology installed which will facilitate a smooth transition from this galaxy to the Milky Way which is the galaxy where Earth is located. It will also shield any energy signature caused by your arrival. It is one of our time, space and dimension travelling devices so it already has its shields active. We need to get you all in and out with the minimum amount of intervention and effect on the local population.

It may seem strange to you but you will be arriving on a smallholding in the Hill Country of Mid Wales which is a cover for one of the bases used by our new friends on Earth. You may have heard a little about it already. It has a good cover story. The area is used as a Live Roleplaying site. Players come and go and the locals think nothing of seeing strange machinery and other "props" that are used in the game. The players and referees themselves know nothing about the area's other use. As far as they know nothing changes but what actually happens is that the whole area swaps with a shadow area we have on another planet. So rather than travel you change places. When we need to get you back, we just swap you back. Nobody sees anything different if it is manipulated correctly as the swap occurs when nobody is likely to be looking. Now that we have ironed out some of the original glitches which involved an unfortunate set of guests being taken to an alien planet it is running smoothly.

Kel, I can see you are mystified by this. I was too when I first heard about it. There is a group of people on Earth who have a hobby which pretty much mirrors what we do for training here in the outer galaxies. They are given a persona or choose one and then they turn up for a weekend and act as that person for a weekend or longer. Where we are technically training people as themselves, which is reasonable when we are training soldiers, these people are actually training as if they are soldiers. The strange thing is that they actually choose locations and situations which mimic other galaxies. This has been used to Red Rock's advantage. They call themselves Roleplayers as they take on a role and they dress in a manner in keeping with the story they are investigating and carry replica weapons and other representations of the sort of things that we use on a regular basis. It was felt that having this sort of activity going on on the doorstep of a base where people are coming and going would be perfect. This base in Wales has been set up as one of these roleplaying locations. It suffices to provide an income for the operatives who look after it and also a cover so that our people can come and go freely and so that any technology that we bring in and move about does not arise any suspicion. So, you will be arriving under the guise of and during one of these gatherings.

When you arrive you will be met by a vehicle which will take you to a helicopter pad where you will be flown directly to the island.

You must under no circumstances draw any more attention to yourselves than is absolutely necessary. Also, don't let the roleplayers get their hands on any of your equipment as they will use it. Your arrival will be timed to hopefully ensure that all of those involved are a long way away investigating something on the other side of the valley but should there be a problem you will have to improvise. Please remember, your weaponry is real, theirs is not so please try to avoid any unfortunate incidents. If challenged you should rely on the owners of the house to deal with the situation. The host and hostess who own the building are very understanding and accommodating and we try to be as inconspicuous as possible. You arrive, you leave, let's hope it is that simple.

When you arrive on the island you will be staying in a building known as The Castle. Your booking has been made and they will be expecting you. You'll arrive after dark and it would be best to make your way to the Marisco Tavern which is amongst the main grouping of buildings. It is in the off season, the month there is late October and the majority of the visitors have now left so you will have plenty of chance to move about freely. Your cover has been arranged by our new friends on Earth. They are carrying on the roleplaying theme as apparently they find this a really useful way of moving around. Your cover is going to be as a group of organisers of one of these games as we believe that the island has been used to such games before so they will know what to expect. You will not arouse suspicion should anything be overheard but we would urge you to be cautious all the same. They won't take much notice of your equipment either.

Unfortunately there is a weight limit as you will be travelling by helicopter. We had thought of sending you via the Oldenburg boat from Bideford but that would take up vital hours and put you in contact with other people which we would like to avoid. I also have no idea how you will be after your trip to the galaxy so we'd rather not put you in contact with a possibility of seasickness. So you will only be able to take a very limited amount of equipment. It is essential that you take certain sensors so your personal equipment will be at a minimum. It is possible to cook and there is a well stocked shop on the island. Everything has to be brought on the boat so don't be surprised if the bread is sold out of the freezer. We will send a box of supplies with you but you will have to buy anything else the next day. We are expecting you to eat at the tavern. That is covered by expenses as are your drinks in the Tavern. It will give you an opportunity to question the locals. If you want to cook and that proves to be more convenient I understand that you have a supply of Earth currency. Castle nodded and patted his pocket. We will also provide you with civilian clothing and side arms." The Commander noticed the worried look on Damien's face. "Don't worry, these roleplayers have been on the island before and they carry replica weapons so the islanders are used to seeing such things and would not assume that they are real. Basic rules, keep them under your coats and concealed. The roleplayers do so they don't upset the islanders but what they don't realise is that the islanders are used to it and probably find the roleplayers quite amusing. Of course if anything does happen try to be as diplomatic as possible. We cannot get permission for the mission we are on and it is obviously not known that aliens, which is what you technically are, are present on Earth. I would say that the bottom line is do not get caught.

Do you have any questions?"

In turn they shook their heads.

The Commander smiled. "Very good, well if you have no more questions, you have a go. Good luck gentlemen and lady."

They stood up in silence and filed out of the room, following the Commander. He escorted them to the Hopper Bay. A tall thin man in a blue boiler suit was standing in the middle of the room making adjustments to various boxes of equipment. When he saw the Commander enter he stood up sharply, slapped his heels together and saluted.

The Commander smiled. "That won't be necessary son, as you were. We're ready to go. Are you ready Sanderson?"

The tall man relaxed. He ran his hand over his close cropped hair and looked worried. "As ready as we will ever be. All the systems are showing ready and I've run all the checks I possibly can. We are ready to go. Once we get this lot loaded you'll be able to leave."

The Commander looked around the room. "Thank you Sanderson. Well people, this is it. If you would step onto the metal plate one by one and when you are all on there we'll activate the machinery which has been kindly loaned to us by Lord Joniel."

There was the metal plate on the floor and in the middle of it there was a pile of bags and equipment boxes ready for them.

Kyla looked up at Kel and he smiled and stepped a little closer to her. Kel took a deep breath and stepped onto the plate. He looked around and then turned back to the rest. "Nothing, I don't feel anything so far." He held out a hand and Kyla joined him, taking his hand he reassured her. She then held her hand out and Rennon took it and stepped onto the plate.

One by one the others stepped onto the plate and waited.

Sanderson smiled. "Well, are you ready?"

They all looked at him and nodded. Kel piped up. "We're good to go Sanderson, don't be dramatic and draw this out, just get this over."

The Commander smiled. "You have a go Sanderson. Good luck."

Sanderson threw the switch and the room was filled with a bright yellow light, there was a sound of wind rushing and the light was gone, as were the travellers and their luggage. They appeared moments later in the passenger hold of a Hopper which was hovering above the base.

From there they flew to a planet some two hours away. They landed and unloaded the equipment into a small stone building which was a hollow shell. There were chalk marks on the floor which marked out tables and chairs. They carefully avoided these and then stood beside their equipment as they heard a metallic sound. The ceiling became a fluid blue, like water above them. Rennon was staring up in amazement. "That is the event horizon, how fascinating. How it can be on the ceiling I don't know."

Nothing seemed to move but lit candles, tables and chairs materialised around them. They were standing in what looked like a small bar. The stone walls were painted white and a candle chandelier hung above them. The ledge between the wall and the roof was decorated with plastic ivy and in the corner of the roof there was a rubber rat.

Kel jumped slightly and drew his weapon as he was faced by what he thought was a robot in a boiler suit. She was tall and thin. Next to her was another one, a male. The man was extremely tall, just a little taller than Kel.

Kel holstered his gun. "So what is so funny?"

The men tried to speak but they were incapable. Then Connor managed to regain his composure. "They are dummies, props used in the game. Let me introduce you to Mac, the MacKenzie Unit. She's a representation of a robot but they haven't found a face for her yet. This is James who is here as there isn't room for him anywhere else. Don't worry they are quite harmless."

Kel grunted. "Oh."

With a silent efficiency they grabbed the equipment and left the building not worrying about whose bag was supposed to be whose. It was pitch black outside and they could just about make out a house and a path going up a hill beside it. The road was behind a large farm gate and they could see a large black vehicle with its lights off waiting for them.

The driver of the four wheel drive vehicle spotted them and turned his lights on to illuminate the rough stone and soil drive. They headed for the vehicle and opened the boot which had been popped unlocked. When the equipment was safely stowed they jumped inside and the driver pulled away on dipped headlights. Two ponies, a handsome brown Cob and grey Welsh Mountain viewed them with some suspicion over their fence then went back to eating the grass.

They reached the helicopter port and grabbed the bags out of the back of the vehicle before the driver drove away. A helicopter was waiting for them on the pad and the paperwork had all been done. They were met on the tarmac and taken straight to it. They stowed their luggage away and as soon as they had their seatbelts on the pilot started the pre flight and within moments the blades began to rotate. They lifted into the air with hardly a jolt and glided swiftly forwards, ascending into the chilled night air. It was cloudless, the stars were bright pinpoints in the deep blue of space. Kyla couldn't help looking out in wonder and down on the lights of the buildings below. Soon enough they were over water and after a few miles they approached the tiny three mile long island of Lundy. At about four hundred feet above sea level it looked like a flat lump of rock sticking out of the sea. The island was mostly in darkness but there were pinpoints of light around a grouping of buildings on the southerly point and a lighthouse to the south.

The pilot brought the helicopter down to land with grace and precision. They disembarked and this time sorted out the bags so that they carried the ones with their own names on them. They shared the rest of the equipment between them. It was dark and hard to walk on the uneven grass, there were no street lights. Nobody had a torch they could reach so they had to make their way by starlight until they came into the golden glow provided by the windows of the Marisco Tavern and made their way past the outbuildings to the front door.

It was a two storey building made of old stone, painted white with a slate roof. There was one obvious door which opened into one end of the building.

They looked at each other and bunched up around the door. Kel was first through, followed by Kyla and then Rennon and the others. It was old wood and although painted it showed the marks of many harsh winters. The stone outside was in stark contrast to the well worn floorboards inside. The warm smell mixed with dust, paper and the smell of alcohol gave it a familiar warm tavern smell. Kel's boots made a heavy sound on the wooden floorboards. The room was well lit, bright after the darkness outside and that end of the tavern was empty. He took a sweeping look around. To his right there was a round table with four chairs around it which fitted into the area in front of the window beside the door. It was unoccupied. Further along the side wall was a recessed bookcase with books and games stacked higgledy pigeldy just beside the door in the back wall which led to another small room.

He could hear the bubble of conversation and the strumming of a guitar to his left so he turned that way. The others were following him past another small table on his left which was situated in front of the window. To the right was a bar which ran along the small room and into what looked like the main bar beyond where it swept around for a short distance before joining up with a wooden panelled wall.

They walked in silence through into the main bar. There was one long table along the middle of the room and tables beyond it set against the large glass windows which ran the full length of the room and across the far end of it. There were very few customers in the room. The most noticeable customer was an arty looking man with long white hair and a long white beard who was strumming the guitar thoughtfully in front of the fire which roared in the fireplace to the left and next to the staircase which led to the balcony which spanned the roof above them. There was a middle aged woman who dressed younger than her years who sat close to the musician, hanging on his every word. Her long hair was swept up in a pony tail and she in turn sat next to a grey haired man in neat walking clothes. They looked up as the visitors came in and the grey haired man raised a glass. "Welcome friends, welcome to Lundy." He smiled and the others raised their glasses as well.

Kyla stepped around Kel who seemed riveted to the spot. He relaxed. "Thank you, we're very pleased to be here. Is there someone serving at the bar?"

The white haired man looked up and stopped strumming. "He's just gone to sort something out upstairs. He'll be back in a minute. You arrive on that helicopter? I'm Nathan by the way."

Kyla nodded. "Pleased to meet you Nathan."

Nathan raised an eyebrow. "Didn't fancy the Oldenburg then?"

Kyla smiled. "I have a problem with sea travel."

A thin, dark haired man had appeared behind the bar. "Ah, you must be the party booked for the Castle. Your rooms are ready any time you'd like to go there. Here are your keys. Would you like a drink or to eat or would you rather go and settle down. I'll be serving food until 8pm so there's no rush."

Kyla looked at her watch that Rennon had bought her for her birthday, it was 6.30pm so they did have time. "We would like to settle into our rooms first. Thank you. I'm Kyla, this is Kel, Rennon, Connor, Damien, Eric and Daniel."

The barman smiled. "Good to meet you. I am Neil and my wife Jackie does the cooking. I'll get Samuel to help you with your bags and show you to the Castle. Do you have a torch? It can be a bit dark getting around. The main path is alright though."

Kyla smiled. "Thank you. We would appreciate someone to show us the way."

Samuel was a rotund chap dressed in a sweat shirt, faded jeans and army boots. He pulled an army parka over his shoulders and was fully wearing it by the time they stepped outside. "Follow me, its not too far. Do you need me to carry anything?"

Connor put a hand on his shoulder. "Don't worry lad, we have it covered."

Samuel forged on ahead and they walked away from the main grouping of old stone buildings and out onto the path. As they left the other buildings they came to the Church on their right. It was truly impressive for a small island, more of a cathedral. It was in darkness, the white stonework silhouetted by the dark night sky and a myriad of stars. They could see some sort of a statue up in the tower but any detail was lost in the darkness.

The path was well worn and the grass lush around them, well as much as they could see in the dark. "You'll like the Castle. It is an old building. It was built by Henry III in about 1250 and paid for by the sale of rabbits. It was a Royalist stronghold in the Civil War. It was also supposedly used to keep illegally transported slaves during the slave trade. It has been done up a lot since then and I'm sure you'll be really comfortable there. Is this your first visit?"

Eric was walking beside him. "Yes, first trip."

The castle was a square old grey stone building with well defined irregular natural stonework. It didn't seem to have a door but as they got closer it was possible to see that the entrance had a stone wall built around it to keep out the wind. It was more of a corridor in, closed off by a wrought iron gate.

They filed inside and down the steps to the courtyard. It was neatly kept and bare. Once inside it looked like three cottages facing each other each with its own set of door and windows.

Samuel had led the way. "Stay there, I'll go and get some lights on for you." He left them standing there and went to turn some lights on. The courtyard illuminated bit by bit and they were able to see when Samuel came back out.

Samuel turned his torch off as he left the building. "Do you need anything else or shall I leave you to settle in?"

Eric had just put his bag down. "Thank you. We'll be fine, see you later."

Samuel waved as he leapt up the stairs and disappeared off into the night.

Kel shut the gate behind him and went back to stand beside Kyla. He took her bag off of her and set it down. "Well, lets go and take a look around."

Kel went first, Kyla behind him and the others wandered on behind them. They took the right hand door first. There was a small lobby with stairs going up and an open door to the right which opened into a comfortably worn sitting room furnished with a sofa and two chairs. To the left was a neatly organised kitchen furnished with fitted kitchen units down the window wall and a country cottage style worn wooden table and chairs against the opposite wall. A light painted dresser held various useful kitchen utensils, plates and canisters. A door on the far wall led to the toilet and a small latticed glass window which opened to the outside of the Castle.

Kel walked through and opened the window and looked down, it was quite a drop down the outside of the building.

Connor stepped up and looked down as well. "Well I guess this place is fairly secure, that size of a window and with that drop I doubt anyone could get in through there. That's the only window to the outside I can see on this level. I might as well check out upstairs."

Up the stairs there were two bedrooms, one either side of the landing. Each had two neatly set up single beds. Their small latched windows opened onto the central courtyard.

Eric pushed down on the bed to test the springs. "Not bad, quite comfortable." He tried the other one. "This one isn't too bad either. I can't say that the view is that great though." He smiled and sat on the bed and bounced a bit.

Eric and Daniel were already half way down the stairs. The others followed them.

They filed back down the stairs and checked out the cottage the other side of the courtyard and it was almost the same except that there was only one bedroom upstairs also with two single beds. Daniel and Eric wandered into the bedroom. Daniel was looking out of the window into the courtyard. "Well I guess there's going to be a bit of room sharing going on. Lets see what the other building is like and we can sort out who goes where."

The end cottage was similar with a kitchen downstairs and a sitting room and bedroom with two single beds upstairs.

Connor wandered out into the courtyard and returned with a cardboard box. "Which house shall we use as our base of operations?"

Kyla took a look in the box. "Well the cottage on the right as we came in has a smaller sitting room but a fairly big kitchen and the toilets are downstairs. That would be the easiest. Shall we go there and then decide who gets what room?"

Connor grabbed the box, flapped in the cardboard lid and they moved into the kitchen of Castle Keep South. Connor put the box on the dresser behind the table in the kitchen and filled the kettle with water and set it to boil. They all took a seat and looked around. It was comfortable, very country kitchen and rural, the decorations chosen with care to fit in and feel comfortable. "I'll make the tea then, so what does everyone want? He pulled out a notepad and paper. I'll write down what everyone likes and then whoever is making the teas or coffees won't have to ask every time."

Kel looked up. "Hey, good idea. Mine's coffee, black with two. Kyla?"

Kyla was busy looking around the room. "Oh, white with no sugar."

Eric piped up. "Same as me."

Damien nodded. "Me too."

Rennon smiled. "And me."

Daniel shook his head. "Can't stand tea, I'm a coffee sort of guy. White with one."

The kettle clicked off and Connor took the mugs from the dresser and the provisions from the box and poured the drinks and soon they were seated around the table in quiet conversation.

Daniel took a mouthful of his coffee. "So, who wants what room? We're going to have to share so I would assume we'd want to stay in our own groups. So that would put Kel and Rennon sharing, unless either of you are with…"

Kel and Rennon shook their heads though Kel gave Kyla a very long and meaningful look.

Daniel put his cup down. "Well I would assume that if you're going to be in a room on your own you'd probably feel better and be safer if you have the room in the South Keep that is opposite them?"

Kyla nodded.

Daniel looked to Connor, Damien and Eric. "So that leaves us to decide who shares with who in the East and North Cottages. Any preferences or shall we flip for it?"

Connor looked up from his coffee. "I'd say lets think this one through. Its likely to be a quiet mission but just in case lets put one combat trained person in each room if we are going to split between cottages. So Daniel would you like to share with Eric or Damien?"

Daniel shrugged. "Who snores?"

Everyone bar Damien piped up. "Damien."

Daniel looked at Damien. "No offence mate but shall we flip for who gets Damien?"

Damien laughed and got a coin out of his pocket. "Sure, Heads or Tails Daniel?"

Daniel took a mouthful of his drink. "Heads."

Damien flipped. "Bad luck Connor."

Connor smiled. "Them's the breaks, don't worry about it mate, I've probably slept through worse, you didn't meet my ex wife did you? So, shall we get our stuff and get settled in."

Kel grabbed Kyla's bags as well as his own and headed off up the stairs. Rennon gave Kyla a very knowing look, she smiled and shrugged. Connor and Eric saw what was happening and gave each other a look and they both laughed, grabbed their bags and headed off for their rooms.

Kel put Kyla's bag on her bed and she followed him into the room. Rennon took his bag and went into his room across the landing and closed the door.

Kyla went to the window. "It's a lovely night, I hope the weather holds for tomorrow."

Kel stepped up behind her. She could feel the heat of him against her back and relaxed. "So you decided to stay, I'm glad. We're all glad."

Kyla turned to face him. "Thank you. It feels right for me."

Rennon was at the door. "Which bed do you want?"

Kel looked down at Kyla and she smiled at him and whispered. "You had better go. We can talk later."

Kel hesitated and looked surprised then he left the room. Kyla went to her bag and unzipped it. She then looked down at what she was wearing. She hadn't had much chance to think about it, she'd just thrown the clothes on and grabbed her bag to go. The jeans were comfortable, faded but decorated with a diamonte pattern on the pockets. The sweatshirt was comfortable and the hood looked warm and useful. The clothes in the bag were all fairly similar and felt soft and looked warm. Her ski jacket was practical and very warm, the lining was thick though it was lightweight. She threw it on the bed and left the bag on the other bed and unpacked a few things into the drawer before stowing the bag down beside the bed.

About half an hour later they were downstairs. The equipment had been moved into Castle Keep North and had been set up and Rennon and the two science specialists from Earth were connecting wires and taking readings, turning dials and noting the results.

Rennon stepped back. "Well, that was fairly conclusive. You will see from the readings on that module there that there is extensive EMP activity in this area, to be specific to the side of this castle. It may very well be that there is some sort of equipment located somewhere around here."

Kel grunted. "Well we'd better go and have a look. More chance we'll get the place to ourselves at night."

Eric nodded his head. "It would make sense, we might as well get the readings now. At worst we can then compare them to readings in the morning. My money is on the cave marked on the map. It would make sense to hide something down there. Shall we?" He indicated the door and they filed out and a few minutes later they were all down in the courtyard, coats on, side arms concealed and ready to go.

Eric and Rennon went in front as they left the keep, a small hand held detector held between them as they walked. Eric held the terminal, Rennon the wand like detector. The blue light of the terminal was clearly visible in the almost pitch blackness they faced when they left the interior of the Castle. Thick cloud cover had obscured the moon and stars.

Kel circled around them, Connor beside him, Kyla behind them and they took point, the rest took the six. Each in turn flipped down their night vision goggles and the world changed to a surreal green hue.

They turned left outside the castle and followed small sheep tracks where a track led to a slope. The track was quite wide but they stayed single file. They walked cautiously down the path as it was littered with stones. It was just possible to make out a huge stone lintel over the entrance in the darkness above a dark hole. Kel went ahead, he listened and sniffed the air. He then made his way carefully down the side of the cave and slipped inside, emerging moments later. "It's empty. It's a small mine shaft barely twenty feet deep."

They all moved inside, the detector first. It was crackling and beeping. Rennon looked up. "That is an amazing reading, we definitely have something here. By the reading I would say we have some sort of a dampener working here. What do you say Eric?"

Eric was staring at the box in his hand. "I agree, definitely something like that." He pressed a few buttons. "I've set it to do energy readings and to check out the type and source of the energy. Whatever is down there is generating a lot of energy, which is being partially hidden by a shield. It is only because we are so close and we have the right sensors that we can detect it at all."

Kyla went to step forwards but Kel caught her arm. "No, we find out what it is first before you go in there. If you touch it you might activate it which may be good or bad. It could be dangerous. It would be wise for us to find out exactly what we are dealing with."

He didn't see Kyla glare at him in the darkness. He let her arm fall and she stepped back behind him.

Eric was reading something on the hand held device. "Its definitely alien technology and it's a cloaking device. We may well be looking at something hidden here that we can't see because of the cloak. By what I can see it's a static reading which would indicate that it's a passive rather than an active device, protecting something rather than guarding an active entrance or something like that. I'd like to analyse these readings properly. That could take a while. May I suggest that we return, get a good night's sleep and take a look down here in the morning when its light?"

Connor took a look over his shoulder. "Well, its 7.30pm and if we want to eat tonight we could do with going to the Tavern."

Eric spluttered. "You have a point, unless we want a very hungry night we'd better get down there. I would suggest we stow this lot away, lock up and head out."

They returned to the Castle and put the equipment back in its boxes and hid it under and behind the sofas so anyone looking in through the window couldn't see anything. They then locked the doors and headed towards the Marisco Tavern, torches in hand.

Rennon was walking with Kyla, Kel and Connor wandered along discussing the benefits of different weapons and Eric and Damien were discussing the likelihood of finding alien technology on the island.

Rennon was first into the Tavern, followed by Kyla, then Kel and the rest. They filed into the main room. The white haired man had stopped playing his guitar and he was gone, the grey haired man was sitting by himself reading a paper. He looked up as they came in. "You're just about in time. Give a call and they'll get you something to eat."

The barman stepped around the bar. "Sure, the food is on the chalk board, let me know what you want. Make a list if it is easier. I've got instructions to run you up a tab, you can settle up when you leave."

Connor lifted a hand and smiled. "Thank you, we'll get settled and let you know."

They crossed the room and sat by the windows though they couldn't see anything outside. The tables were dark wood, the chairs spindle backed or pew like with high backs and comfortable with padded seats.

Connor put together a list of drinks and what they wanted to eat and took it to the bar and handed it over. He came back with a tray of drinks and passed them out. They sat around the table, drinks before them, in silence.

It looked like Kel was staring out into the darkness but in truth he was watching Kyla, or rather he was watching Connor watching Kyla. Rennon and Eric were in deep thought while the others were looking around the room at the collection of marine souvenirs like life buoys and name plates off of the many wrecks that had gone down around the island. There was a balcony above and a huge chandelier light which hung above them in the centre of the room.

The food arrived very quickly. The aroma and steam rising reminding them how hungry they were and they all tucked in eagerly. Again in silence as the room was too empty to feel comfortable talking when most of the things they needed or wanted to say were not for general hearing.

They eat their food and filed back to the Castle. They crossed the open grassland and were approaching the gate when Kel stopped them. "Something's wrong." They stepped aside and let him go first. "The gate is open."

Kel disappeared into the darkness. He felt his way carefully down the stone stairs, feeling the open metal gate and the cold stone of the wall either side of the stairs. There was very little light inside, just the starlight as the clouds had drifted off. He sniffed the air. It carried the chilled freshness of night but something else, the spicy aroma of something like aftershave. He sidestepped around the wall and into the courtyard and listened. He could hear vague movement to his left, someone was in the cottage and the door was open. He pulled his knife from its sheath and ducked down, moving silently along the wall under the window. He stepped cautiously up to the half open door and pushed it fully open and quietly stepped inside, shut the door and made his way quietly upstairs. He got to the top of the stairs and stepped into the bedroom when he was hit full in the chest by a huge hairy beast and he felt a burning pain as the claws dug deep into his chest. He felt its clawed hand on his shoulder as it threw him aside as if he weighed nothing and bounded down the stairs on four legs.

Kel rolled to his feet and bounded down the stairs after it. It had thrown the door open but when he got to the courtyard there was nothing there. The doors were all closed and as he tried them, they were locked. He ran outside and everyone leapt back stunned. "Did you see it? Did it come this way?"

Rennon grabbed his arm. "Nothing came this way. We heard a door slam back on its hinges and that was all."

Kel shook his head. "It was there. I know it was there."

Rennon looked concerned. "What was there? Kyla, he's been hurt."

Kel looked down, his shirt was torn and it was soaked with blood which was dripping from the open gash on his chest. "It was huge and hairy, moved on four legs and had claws. It was too dark to see anything else."

Kyla stepped forwards. "Go, check it out everyone. Kel, you are staying with me."

Rennon and Connor led the way cautiously down the stairs and one by one they checked the doors. They were still locked, on the left hand cottage had its door flung wide open. They checked it out, room by room, it was empty.

Rennon came back to Kel and Kyla. Kyla was holding a cloth to Kel's chest trying to stem the flow of blood. "Is it clear?"

Rennon took a deep breath. "Yes, do you want a hand getting him inside."

Kyla spoke gently. "No, I can manage. Lets get inside and set up some sort of defences for the night." She put her arm around Kel and led him down the stairs to the kitchen in the right hand cottage. He flopped into the chair at the table and she boiled a kettle while pulling out her medical kit from under the sink where she had put it earlier. She unbuckled it and opened it up, pulling out bandages and antiseptic. She also pulled out a handheld scanner. She ran it over him. She then took his finger, stabbed it gently with a needle and squeezed out some of the blood onto the end of the scanner.

Kel glared at her. "Isn't there enough blood going spare, did you have to take some more?"

She smiled and looked at the reader. "That blood is contaminated, I needed it straight from you before it touched the air. You are lucky, it doesn't look like there was any sort of an infection and I can't see any poison or other matter in your system. Come on, off with your shirt, well what's left of it."

She helped him off with his shirt. His chest had been raked, his muscles and six pack were cut across by the talons but the wound was not as deep as it had first appeared. Gently she dabbed on the disinfectant, washing off the blood before dressing the wounds and wrapping a bandage neatly around him. She then put the kettle on again.

Rennon came in. "The place seems clear, whatever it was seems to have gone. Nothing seems missing so we've no idea what it wanted or what it was. The readings are saying that there may be some sort of electromagnetic pulse that was associated with it. It could be that we have a gateway in the area and it came though and was just looking around. I've done readings on this place and there's nothing other than residual energy which would imply it isn't here anymore. We've set up detectors around the place and we'd better set guards. How's our wild beastie doing?"

Kyla looked up from pouring the drinks. "He's doing fine, it wasn't a deep wound but its going to hurt. It looks like there was no infection so he'll be ok."

She had finished pouring just as the others came in and sat around the table. Kyla folded her medical kit up and put it back in the cupboard and went and sat beside Kel, checking his bandages. "Well, so now we have an unwanted guest who didn't touch anything. As this is a tourist attraction and people stay here all the time I would assume that whatever it was it wasn't actually there to attack us or there would be reports of lost tourists."

Connor looked up. "We may have activated something when we went to the cave."

Rennon picked up the detector. "You have a point, I set the Arkhal Scanner to do an ongoing scan, there was a spike about half an hour ago and again when it disappeared, it looks like that thing came through then. That at least gives us the chance to sleep tonight. We can set it up to let us know if anything else comes through."

Connor took a long drink. "I'd also suggest we set a guard as well. Just to be safe. Kyla, can you keep an eye on Kel tonight. I know that the readings showed there was no infection but just to be safe, better not let him out of your sight."

Kyla nodded and Kel looked down and smiled. Nobody saw that but Rennon who smiled to himself as well.

It was 1.20am when they all made their way to their rooms. Kyla redressed Kel's wound and it had started to scab over. She sprayed it with antiseptic and re-bandaged it. As he was moving away Kel caught her hand. His look deep and there was something in his eyes that made her hesitate and then sit on the bed beside him. She could hear Rennon going to his room and then it was quiet. She got up and closed the door.

She turned back to Kel and sat on his bed. He reached up and stroked her cheek with his hand. "Are we ok?"

She looked surprised and a little confused. "What do you mean? Why shouldn't we be?"

He smiled. "After how everything started, after what I said. After."

She put a finger on his mouth. "It isn't you. I just like choices in my life."

He smiled. "You have choices."

Kyla smiled back. "I know that and I've made some. Now you need to get some sleep. We're ok, don't worry." She pulled the sheets up and made his pillow more comfortable. "Get some sleep."

Kyla went to the window and sat there for a while. Kel watched her then gradually drifted off into a fitful dream filled sleep.

Kyla watched the courtyard for most of the night then climbed into bed and drifted off as well.

Rennon sat in his room for a while staring at the scanner. The energy was steady, there were no spikes and nothing seemed to be moving. In the early hours he took the scanner and went downstairs, flipped the kettle on and made himself a cup of tea.

The night passed very peacefully. There was no sound in the still night air when those on watch did a patrol outside and there were no more strange creatures arriving to break their sleep. The dawn was crisp and bright, a slight sea fog rolled across the island.

They were assembled in the kitchen by 0900am drinking their morning coffee and getting ready to go out. By 0930am they were standing in the courtyard ready to head off. They had locked the doors and set up sensors and cameras about the place just to make sure.

The morning was bright and the sky blue. Birds flew about and the light wind blew the grasses and other plants gently. The path down to the cave was stark white where it had been worn down to the bare stone beneath what was left of the grass.

They filed down to the cave in silence and single file, Rennon in front with the sensor, Kel close beside him. In the morning light it looked far less intimidating. The stone lintel was dug into the sides of what now looked like a small mine shaft and they could see the back wall from the door. It was indeed only about twenty feet deep.

The inside of the shaft was a rectangular cut tunnel with a flat end where the mining or cutting had gone no further.

Kyla was standing behind Kel and keeping her hands well away from the sides.

Everyone but Kyla had a hand scanner and they were running them over the walls, the group information being assimilated and compared.

They ended up reading the back wall. Rennon looked at the scanner and looked up. "Whatever is going on is associated with this back wall. It feels solid but I'm wondering if it actually is." He took a small hammer and gave it a wallop. A chunk of stone fell away but there was no hollow thump. "Are we ready for Kyla to give it a go?"

Kel was about to speak but Connor jumped in first. "Kyla, what do you think? Are you ready to give it a go?"

Kyla swallowed hard and looked very nervous. "It is what I came for. What shall I do?"

Rennon ran the scanner over the wall. "It looks like this is the best place to try. The readings are at their strongest here. Just try touching it."

Kyla stepped forwards and Kel moved to stand almost in front of her. "If you feel anything, get back." He snapped.

She reached a hand forwards really carefully and felt the energy. She closed her eyes and images came into her mind. "I can see this cave but I am alone in it. The light is flooding in, much like it is now. There is a small stub of a lit white candle resting on a stone on the right hand side. I am me but I am not me, I am someone else, very like me. I feel her step forwards and place her hands on the wall and call up the energy. The wall fades to a transparent screen and the other side of the screen there are warriors waiting to come through. For some reason, no, hold on, I can feel it, the energy feels wrong. Something is imprisoned here, kept here.

I can feel what she felt. The planets were in alignment and it was Halloween, the veils between worlds were at their thinnest. She was reaching between worlds to bring back someone who had left the world a long time ago. She had waited for this person, no it is stronger for that, possibly a brother or lover or both. The ties between them go way back, dawn of time type stuff. But, when she felt the energy she knew it wasn't him. Whichever entity was there was trying to convince her that he was the one she was looking for. She was prepared to open the portal, that is what it is but she felt that he was coming with intent to destroy the world. She closed the portal and walked away. She had waited many thousands of years for the person but she just walked away because she had to. I've lost it. I can't get any more information. I can feel that there is a skin in front of the wall, a thin film of energy which is holding the machine in stasis. It is her energy that is keeping the portal shut and preventing the machine from opening it and allowing the prisoner free."

Rennon put a hand on her arm. "Spikes of energy, definitely spikes."

Kyla jumped back away from the wall.

Rennon was running his scanner over the wall. "It seems steady now. No sign of any clawed beasties. Did you see that? I saw something out of the corner of my eye."

They took up a defensive position, back to back, looking around the tunnel, weapons pulled out and safety lock's off. There was something in there with them, something they kept seeing out of the corner of their eye. Something that kept trying to get closer, its arms stretched out. It was small and spindly with huge teeth and as it made a leap for Kyla just about everyone shot at it. It hit the ground and melted into a black and sticky mess on the floor.

Kyla stared at the ground. "I guess that was what she didn't want to let out."

Rennon ran the scanner around and over it. Everyone else then followed suit. "No more spikes, the energy is back to normal. I would suggest we go back and rig up some way of putting a permanent cap over that portal to prevent anything else coming out that we don't want to visit."

They were in general agreement and filed back to the Castle. The Research and Development part of the team took over the kitchen table with their equipment and tools. They were intent on what they were doing, stopping only occasionally for tea and coffee. Rennon was getting on really well with the Earth representatives and as all of the Earth team had some sort of science training that left Kel and Kyla feeling a bit of a spare part.

Kyla was on her third cup of tea when she went to the sink, washed it up and turned to Kel. "Come on, we might as well go and take a look in the Church. It's pointless us standing around here waiting. What do the rest of you say? Shall we go and see what we can find out?"

Rennon looked up from screwing down a loose wire. "It would make sense but it is likely to be a place where there is going to be something you might activate. Without the scanners you might not know. Sorry Kyla, I think you and Kel are going to have to sit things out for a bit. Why don't you take a walk over to the shop and pick us up some supplies. Eating at the Tavern is fine but we're likely to do some late nights so having something in the cupboard will come in handy."

The shop was pretty much outside the Tavern, just a little way along the street. It was a small building that was stuffed full of the basics in life as well as a few luxuries like jam and spreads. There was also the stand of souvenirs the soft toys, maps and other pieces of information about the island.

They picked up a basket and started by the door. The bread was just as they had been told, in the freezer so Kel grabbed a loaf out and put it in the basket. Kyla was a little thrown as she hadn't really had a chance to think about it but he did look quite different in the clothes he had been given. His slim waist and well toned muscles set off the loose fitting white cotton shirt, faded jeans and trainers. His hair was neatly brushed and tied back at his neck and he did look quite a lot different. He was busy trying to decide what else they needed. Kyla reached across him and put some butter in the basket. Then they made their way around until the basket was brimming full of snacks and staples.

The woman behind the till was smiling at them. "Welcome to Lundy, is this your first visit?"

Kel put the basket on the counter and looked to Kyla for help. She pushed the handles of the basket down and smiled back at the lady. "Yes, we're staying at the Castle."

The woman started cashing up the goods. "Lets hope this weather holds and you should have a good time. Are you staying long?"

Kyla jumped a little as she didn't really know how long they were expecting to stay. "Oh I hope so. It all depends on Kel's job, he might get a phone call and we'll have to go."

She was turning a jar looking for the price. "That would be a pity. You came on the helicopter didn't you? I've always preferred that, much easier than the boat if you don't take well to that sort of thing. You are that group coming to look over the place for another roleplaying game aren't you? I'll never forget the one about ten years ago, that was quite an experience. You know they were doing a 1920 type game and someone even bought a bath chair. Then there was the one with the film quality props, something to do with a film I think. There was another one like that later. What era are you planning?"

Kyla took a deep breath and looked at Kel for some support but he was subtly looking at something on the display stand. "We thought modern day with a bit of an aliens twist."

The woman smiled broadly. "Well that sounds like fun. Make sure you get down to the cave near the castle and you'll do well to put one of your players at Admiralty Lookout, it's a spooky old place on occasion. There have been a few things going on there, especially when there are games going on. Then there seem to be various things that happen when there are games on that don't happen any other time."

Kyla took a step forwards and Kel started to pay more attention. "Really, any chance you could tell us about it. I'd like to be forewarned. What sort of happenings?"

The woman looked pleased with herself and settled down into a steady rhythm of putting the goods through the till. "Well, it started off fairly small. There have always been sightings of a lady in a blue dress but we had a psychic staying in the house a few years back and it all stopped when she left. My guess is that she dealt with the unquiet spirit. Then there were the faces at the window that someone saw on one event. The crew swore they were in the monster hut. They were using the camping barn across the way so it was quite a way from the building where it happened, "

Kyla tried to be as fascinated as she could manage. "And what about the Castle?"

The woman hesitated. "Well that place used to be open inside, the cottages are a recent addition in the grand scale of things. It used to be open to the elements and the Mariscos who used to live there, a bunch of pirates, used to keep their slaves in there before transporting them. They'd hide them from the customs men. Anyway, by all accounts many died and they left unquiet spirits around there. There was one report of a young psycic staying at the castle who was standing in the kitchen one day talking to someone in the living room. She felt someone behind her, a bony finger down her back and her bra strap was undone. Now that is about as physical as I have heard of something being but that would have terrified me."

Kyla looked up at Kel who smiled reassuringly.

The woman had finished running the goods through the till. "I wouldn't worry with a strong man like him here to protect you. You'll be quite safe. Now I've been told that you are putting everything on account and it will be settled at the Tavern, that is fine by me. Is there anything else you would like?"

Kyla reached out and put a couple of extra torches onto the counter. "Just to be sure."

Kel raised an eyebrow.

Kyla looked a bit sheepish. "I'd like one beside my bed and one as a spare."

Kel smiled and shook his head. "Scaring the tourists must be good for business. Go on, have the torches. It can't hurt."

They grabbed the bags, said goodbye to the woman and left the shop. They were just about to pass the Tavern when Kel turned to Kyla. "Would you like a coffee or something? I'd like a chance to have a chat and we're bound not to be needed for hours yet."

Kyla looked at the bags and thought through what they had bought in case anything would spoil. The only thing frozen was the bread and they needed that unfrozen anyway. "Sure, sounds like a good idea."

Kel went in first, followed by Kyla and they wandered down to the main bar. It was empty except for the barman. He was there wiping up cups and setting out cutlery that had come from the kitchen washed. "Good morning, can I help you?"

Kel stepped up to the counter. "Two coffees sound like a good idea. Kyla, would you like anything else?"

Kyla shook her head. The barman poured the coffees and handed them to Kel. He followed Kyla into the main room and they went upstairs onto the balcony.

Somehow the atmosphere was different up there, it felt much more rustic and maritime. The rail was a bit like that on a ship and the tables long wooden ones with chairs running along their length. They were lined up with the narrow end close to the rail, the chairs then arranged around them. There was a small single table near the window.

Kyla slid along the chairs and sat on the end one overlooking the balcony.

Kel sat opposite her and put her coffee down in front of her. He sat looking awkward.

Kyla smiled into her coffee and almost took a sip but it was too hot. "Kel, you don't need to feel awkward. Just say what is on your mind."

Kel looked down. "I still feel guilty about what happened when we met."

Kyla put her cup down. "If I say it a hundred times it isn't going to have any more effect than the first. What happened was not you, it was the drugs that were effecting you. There is violence in your nature, but I'm no dainty princess terrified of her own shadow. We are people who have come from worlds where we have to survive. I survived it, I healed."

Kel looked deep into her eyes. "But did you heal? I still see you feeling pain sometimes."

Kyla jumped slightly. "I didn't think anyone noticed. I have lots of old battle scars, you gave me one or two more but that was in our battle against the Followers. I forgave you a long time ago if that is what you are worried about."

Kel smiled slightly. "Well yes and no. I know you have forgiven me, I just haven't forgiven myself. I should have been stronger willed."

Kyla took his hand. "There was nothing you could have done against that drug, it was a complete mind overwrite with excessive violence. I bless the violence in your nature that you have tamed and use against our enemies. It is a part of who you are, you have embraced it and weald it like any other weapon. That doesn't stop you being a kind and gentle man as well. We all have darkness and deep down violence in our nature. That is how we are created and what we need to survive. It is in embracing all facets of our personality that we can become balanced and able to use those aspects when they are appropriate. It is that quality in you that I truly admire. You are a master of your art. That drug removed the balance and you can't punish yourself for that. You have protected me on countless occasions since that day. So, can we forget it? Actually, no, better than that, I have an idea. When we get back to Mission Command I want you to book the training room. I'm going to meet you on my own terms and see how you feel after I kick your butt."

Kel took a sip of his coffee and laughed. "I'd like to, hurting you haunts my dreams."

Kyla smiled wryly. "Well, believe me giving you a beating won't haunt mine. A fair fight is what you need. I never really thanked you for sorting the tribe out."

Kel hesitated. "Do you miss your people?"

Kyla looked sad. "Of course I do."

Kel contemplated his coffee. "If you had the opportunity, would you go back?"

Kyla smiled at him. "No, that is a stage of life that is over. I'd go back to visit but I don't belong there anymore. My home, my life and my family are on the base now."

Kel smiled broadly. "That is good to hear." He put his hand over her hand and their eyes met across the table. "This bloodline fascinates me. If we are of the same tribe I am wondering why I haven't got it?"

Kyla thought for a moment. "Well, there is one family which may have come to your planet and met someone there. Only their descendents would have the bloodline, not the whole population. It is supposed to be something "from the stars" but how it can be the same everywhere mystifies me. It must have started somewhere."

Kel was thinking too now. "So if we can find out where the bloodline originated it might help."

Kyla thought about that. "What worries me is that we may find their source."

Kel nodded. "The bone faced warriors worry me. That carapace is created and it is possible that has some influence from the entity or individual that they follow. That is a very chilling thought."

Kyla paused. "I thought that the bone faced warriors were mutated? So what if what we are looking for is through that portal?"

Kel smiled. "I was watching and listening enough to pick up that they are putting their own gate on the portal. That will mean that if we can activate it we can control who goes in and out."

He reached across the table, leaning forward and kissed her. He waited a moment, expecting a slap or for her to pull away but she didn't. He reached forwards and cupped her head with his hand, feeling the soft silkiness of her hair.

Someone clattered some cutlery downstairs and they both pulled away as if guilty. Kyla took a drink of coffee. "I, well, I. Look, it's a long story. I'll tell you one day."

Kel smiled. "Well I'm sure you'll tell me one day."

Kyla smiled back. "We'd better be getting back or they will be worrying."

They left the Tavern and headed back to the Castle.

9

Rennon sat in the cave, a laptop on his lap, a notebook on the dusty floor beside him. Damien sat beside him, he too had a laptop and they were both typing away franticly. Results sprang up simultaneously on both screens.

Damien looked at Rennon. "Well I never, Eion Particles. I wasn't expecting that."

Rennon looked just as surprised. "Last thing I expected. So, that means whatever technology they have here is the same as the drives we use to move through the corridors between the dimensions. You know what that means? We may well have a gateway here or at least some sort of gateway technology similar to that set up in Wales. You've heard about them I presume?"

Damien looked down at the scanner readout. "Eion Drives I have heard about but that's a technology of your world, not ours."

Rennon lay back against the cave wall. "Finding that Eion technology here means we are looking at what could be a gateway to a dimensional space. If its latent technology and what I mean by that is that it was left for many years just holding the gateway shut then it would be using the particles as they never run out as infinite dimensions collide at any one point so theoretically there is a constant supply of them. The machine wouldn't need to be manned or recharged. There has to be a device somewhere in this cave and my money is on this wall not being as solid as it looks. It is disappointing in a way as it could mean that whoever put that gateway there or at least locked it could be long gone."

Damien looked down at his results. "Shall we get Kyla in here? She may well be able to make it function and then we can locate where it is."

Rennon nodded. "The scanner doesn't seem to be able to pinpoint any technology so it might be our only option. Whatever is here has been hidden here for a very long time and no doubt countless tourists have been down here and touched the wall. Thank goodness none of them had the bloodline.

I'll go and get her, they should be back by now. You coming?"

Damien looked down at the readings. "No, I'll stay put here and see if I can get an idea of whether there is any sort of event horizon. It doesn't take two of us."

Rennon smiled. "So much for don't split the party. Ok, I'll be as quick as I can. Watch yourself." He set his laptop on the ground and left it monitoring. "I've set it to watch the Eion Particles and to look for any spikes. If you see anything, get out of here fast." He then walked out of the cave and ran up the path to the Castle not stopping until he got to the courtyard. Kel and Kyla were there chatting to Connor about the star constellations the night before.

They looked up as Rennon descended the stairs, two at a time. "Good, just the person I'm looking for. Kyla, we have detected Eion particles. Sorry, better explain, Eion Particles are what we use for a power source for IDT, sorry, Inter Dimensional Travel. We store them in imploded glass, they also power blasters and a lot of other things that need a power source. The type of Eion Particles down there are the same as we use in travel and they are harvested while travelling through the corridors so they do not occur naturally in any dimension. So there may be some sort of dimensional travelling device hidden in the cave. We can't find it with scanners so we were hoping you could activate it so that we could try to pinpoint where it is."

Kyla smiled. "Sure, where's Damien?"

Rennon turned to go. "He's still doing some tests and monitoring the cave so I don't want to be too long and leave him by himself just in case something happens."

Kyla sprang up the stairs and followed him to the cave. Kel stuck to her like glue and Connor wasn't far behind after calling to the others to join them.

Rennon was first into the cave and he skidded to a halt. The equipment was strewn about the floor and there was no sign of Damien. The laptop that had been on his lap was laying on its side like an open book. Rennon's laptop was still where it had been, showing its readings. Rennon went straight to it and tapped a few keys. "Looks like there were a couple of spikes really close together. I told him to run if he saw anything. I shouldn't have left him."

Kyla shook her head. "Get ready to do your detecting I'm going to see if I can't make this work." She stepped forwards.

Kel stepped in behind her, his pistol drawn, safety off. He put a hand on her shoulder and squeezed his fingers closed gently. "I'm right behind you, just be careful eh?"

Kyla rested her cheek on his fingers. "Sure, I'll be as careful as I can. I've no idea what I'm doing but I'll just try touching the wall to start with."

She reached forwards and touched the wall with her fingers. Immediately she felt a tingling which ran up her arm. "There's definitely energy coming from the wall but that may be the shield. I'm going to put my hand on it and try to make it open. I want anyone who isn't monitoring or involved in this outside the cave. You too Kel."

Kel looked down. "No way, I'm staying put."

Kyla shrugged. "Well you be careful then. Rennon, I want you monitoring but can you run the wires further away so you don't have to be as close."

Rennon looked up from typing. "Not really, I need to be able to move the device to detect precisely where the object or machine may be. I'm going to have to try to triangulate it by using my device and Damien's. I'm ready, how about you?"

Kyla took a deep breath. "I'm as ready as I'll ever be. I'm going to put both hands on the wall and then move about until I get some sort of energy signature. If you'd like to move the scanner with me hopefully we can get a reading fairly fast." Kyla put her hands on the wall in the centre and was pushed back by a rush of energy. Kel managed to catch her and to hold her up. She stepped forwards and put her hands on the wall again and this time it began to shimmer. A white light pentagram began to glow on top of it. "That's the shield, the protection that was put on it all those years ago. I'm going to go for reaching beyond that now. It isn't a complete shield, it seems to be specific and will only protect us from certain things. I'm going to reach beyond and try to touch the wall itself. Rennon, any readings?"

Rennon was moving the wand of the scanner over the wall. "I've got Star Energy mixed with Earth Energy, that must be the shield and I'm starting to get trace Eion Particles. Definitely getting stronger, oh boy, look at that, I think we're about to get a spike, heads up people."

Kyla felt the rush of energy and the stone giving way behind her hand. It was like rubber, she could push into it. Then it began to get transparent and she could see a corridor beyond. On the floor there was a metal plate and above it a similar plate so that it formed a type of gazebo with ornate pillars connecting the two plates. Kyla pushed and moved through the wall. Kel was right behind her, in contact with her so that when she was sucked through, he was as well.

Rennon made a grab for them but his hand closed around empty air.

Kyla fell forwards into the corridor, Kel holding her shoulder fell into the back of her but they kept their footing. Kyla turned around immediately and put her hand on the wall, grabbing hold of Kel's arm as she did it. They were pulled through the wall and ended up back where they started although Rennon had moved in to check out the wall and they bowled him over.

Rennon picked himself up and dusted his clothes off. "Boy am I glad to see you."

Kyla smiled, her face beaming. "I'm glad to be seen. Boy was that a worrying one. When we fell into that corridor I thought that was it. But it seems that it's a two way doorway, we can step backwards and forwards."

Rennon looked at Kel who was standing on the spot, his hand on Kyla's shoulder, looking stunned. "Well, what did you think of that?"

Kel smiled a little nervously. "Can't say I'd rate it as fun but she certainly reacts fast."

Rennon looked a little surprised. "What do you mean fast? You were gone nearly an hour."

Kyla looked at the readings. "No, I turned and came straight back out. There seems to be some sort of time dilation or manipulation"

Rennon ran the scanner over Kyla. "You are coated with Eion Particles. I would assume that was when you moved through IDS, the device is using the same technology as we use in our Star Drives. Any sign of Damien?"

Kyla's smile faded. "In truth I was so shocked at what had happened I could only think about trying to get back. We'd better try again and see where that corridor leads." She turned and faced the wall. "We'd better not all go, but best not to leave just one person behind. So, who is coming with me?"

Kel and Rennon stood behind Kyla, Connor behind them. She put her hands on the wall and pushed forwards. They moved through the wall and appeared in the corridor which was lit by burning torches that burnt with a purple flame.

Rennon stepped off of the metal plate and began scanning it, the walls and just about everything. "The place is loaded with particles. They become less and less as you move away from that wall so I would assume that this is some sort of transportation area."

A voice came from the wall. "And it is guarded."

Kel whipped around and pointed his pistol at the wall. There was nobody there but as they watched someone appeared. He was a man, about six feet tall, thin and with pale lilac hair. Kyla was forced to take a sharp intake of breath on seeing him and Kel growled when she did. He was truly handsome. He seemed shadowy, although very definitely there standing in front of them. He was dressed in clothing that mimicked the wall. "I wouldn't shoot at me unless you want to bring down the wrath of my people. You are visitors here, you can be guests or prisoners. That is your choice. You are in our land now and our ways are not your ways."

Kyla tried to smile but she could feel her lips trembling. "I'm Kyla, we would rather come as guests."

The local man smiled. "I'm glad to hear it. Now if you will follow me I had better tell you a few things about this land. We don't get visitors often and that closed portal should have stayed closed. That is nothing to do with you by the way. Perhaps it is time it was open again. You may have heard some tales of our people and others like them. Do you know the story of King Herla?" They looked confused. "Oh dear, we had hoped that during your research you had looked into such things. Had you no idea who lived beyond the gateways?"

Kyla shook her head. "We had assumed that they were gateways."

The man shrugged his shoulders. "Oh dear, well I'll tell you the story of King Herla as we walk as the corridor will suffice in distance for all that I need to say. Herla met a short man riding a goat one day, the man had the hooves of a goat and a big head. He was courteous and he said that in one year the king would marry and they would attend the wedding feast. They did and brought gifts, food and musicians and served them well. They asked nothing in return other than that the King and his men did a similar service when he married a year later. They did and the King was given a hound to help him get back to your world. The hound would jump from the saddle when it was safe to dismount. When he got back many hundreds of years had passed. Some of his knights tried to dismount but died of old age as soon as they hit the ground. In those days we were having some problems with the devices. It was unfortunate and these stories have become some of the most well known in your folklore. I would assure you that our technology is far more advanced now but if you are asked to do something, do it as there is always a reason. There are countless stories about our people coming through the gateways and of your people returning here or to other lands within our realm. Don't worry, we have no intention of returning you as withered old men and sorry my lady, I would not see your youth stolen away either. You will be safe with us. It seems we have a common enemy and the enemy of my enemy is my friend I think your people have said."

Kyla looked thoughtful. "Who are you?"

The local smiled. "You know your people very rarely ask that, most are interested in gold and treasures. I am Naiarlindris, King of the West Realm, forgive me for not introducing myself, we have very little contact with your realm since Christianity gained a foothold. Please, accept my hospitality and know that you are within my protection within the realm. You can call me Nai."

Kyla choked.

Nai laughed. "Yes I'm a faerie, one of the Fey Realm. You call my sort Sidhe." They came to a turn in the corridor and a door was immediately in front of them. It was huge, about twenty feet tall, solid oak and carved with leaves and vines. It stood within an ornate stone arch. Nai reached forwards, flipped one of the leaves open to reveal a keypad. He tapped in a sequence of numbers and the doors swung open. "Welcome." He stepped into the room.

The room was ornately painted with vines that ascended into the vaulted roof. There were tables set out in lines, each had a computer on it and sitting working away there were lines of tall thin individuals with green, purple or blue hair. There was a huge white write on board full of mathematical symbols and a metal device was set on a table and other scientists were wandering around it, their pale green coats stuffed with pens in pockets, notebooks and pieces of wire.

Nai let them take the room in. "This is our working room at the moment. I'm sorry we can't offer you our usual banquet but these are troubled times. We're working on similar problems to you I am led to believe. That there is a device we can't seem to get working."

Rennon coughed to get Nai's attention. Nai turned to him. "Young Kyla here seems to be able to activate certain artefacts, perhaps she can help."

Nai smiled politely. "I thank you and I do appreciate your offer but I doubt there is anyone in this room that wouldn't be able to activate it if it was the usual artefacts that you have been coming into contact with. The bloodline that gives you your gift is also ours. We have mixed and been a part of your realm for far longer than you would admit and we have a far greater part in it than you would expect. You are going to like this though, that is a Follower artefact."

Rennon looked stunned. "Their artefacts are different?"

Nai took a clipboard from a green haired scientist who had just strode over. "Very good, I'd try Lexiathiam, 30ml. Then scan it and if you don't get a reaction try Hexasilicate and if that has no effect, try heating it." The scientist looked down shyly and smiled at Kyla, blushed a darker shade of green and turned and strode off.

Nai smiled. "Please forgive my people, they rarely come into contact with travellers and they are shy. Yes, that is something you may not have discovered, we have a more secluded way of living and that can be very beneficial sometimes. We've been taking a good look at the Followers. I don't know how much you know but we found out that their conversion of your races is moving ahead at a frantic rate. They convert to start with but they have a sacrament which is very like your Christian one but the liquid that is used will actually alter the DNA of the person taking it. They are a created race, an experiment that went wrong I suppose you could say. It goes back to Earth history when various new races were being created. In the fertile crescent there was the Adama race, not far from there another race was being tried out. When they proved unsatisfactory they were wiped out but not completely. The survivors are the ones behind the Followers. The Followers are becoming them by some drug that seems to have appeared from nowhere. I have no idea what they are called in your tongue and I have found nothing in your texts and writings. For now we have had to focus on what they are doing and to try to find a way to combat them.

They have stolen a belief and made it a religion. That doesn't seem documented anywhere. I have found the original texts and the directives to protect the world. The organization was Fallow Earth and it started in Mid USA in the 1960s. I liked the 60s, the colours were so vibrant. Anyway, then

133

there is a jump in belief to this Fallow Earth Cult. This is where I believe these creatures infiltrated and started altering people. That's a hard one to fight. The actual DNA has been altered to actually be them. That's a mortal thing, I can't comprehend it so that's one for you to deal with. It does mean that you Kyla and anyone else with the blood cannot be converted. That is why your bloodline is so important. But it would put you all at the top of their most wanted list if they knew the truth."

He walked to a table set aside by the wall. On it were various metal items and boxes. "You may find this interesting." He picked up a bullet like object. "I'm assuming that you are thinking that it's a bullet, well it is in a way and it's the most terrifying innovation in their arsenal. They haven't started using them yet as its still in the experimental phase. I lost four good men trying to get this one. By what we have managed to find out it is a bullet and it carries the DNA so when it hits the victim they are converted. What we have to remember is that they are experimenting as well so things change. This could be a prototype, it could be a failed experiment, we have no way of knowing."

Rennon looked horrified. "My god! That is just outrageous."

Nai smiled and put the bullet down. "We're working on something to reverse the DNA conversion. By the way the DNA spiral works it is two lines of information twisted as you probably know. We're working on something that will reverse engineer the DNA back to its original pattern. That is proving difficult but I have my best people on it. As I said that is more something for you to understand as it's a mortal thing. Our way of thinking is too different. What I would suggest is that there could be something synthesized from your blood Kyla. Probably not a cure but certainly a temporary vaccination and I believe you mortals are very keen on your vaccinations."

Kel was studying the bullet. "Where is Damien?"

Nai turned swiftly. "Ah, I was wondering when you were going to remember him. He will be fine but I'm afraid he got in the way when the Hound got out. Mainanna, my daughter, was supposed to be watching him but she fell asleep. He found his way to the gate and your friend got in the way of his little scamper. The gate has been playing up since you arrived on the island my dear lady and it keeps opening. We've managed to keep most of our more unpleasant inhabitants away from the gate but we've had a couple of slip ups. What he met was a Cu Sith, pronounced "cooshee", he's the size of a small cow and very playful. Your friend will be fine but he's in our Infirmary at the moment in the capable hands of Miraim, our Medic."

Kel's look was like thunder. "He was attacked by a dog? Was that the creature I met last night?"

Nai looked down at his feet. "Ah, I was wondering when you were going to ask. I have to apologise for that. Narketra is a bit excitable and he didn't mean to claw you. Don't worry, there's no infection that will pass on to you and he does keep his claws very clean. He was very curious and I wanted to find out who you were so he thought he'd help out. He was taking a look around and you surprised him. Well done by the way, he's very good usually and only managed to cloak himself when he got to the courtyard. I did manage to call him back soon after that, he's very good at hanging around in bedrooms and I doubt you wanted him as a guest even though you wouldn't have known he was there."

A female scientist wandered past carrying a tray with metal tools on it. She smiled at Nai. "These have been repaired, Keslios did a very good job as always."

Nai smiled at her. "Thank you Trantalia, very good. I like the hair, that shade suits you."

The woman blushed and smiled. "Thank you my Lord." She then strode off, very pleased with herself.

Nai smiled at Kyla who was looking curious. "The fashion for coloured hair has been popular for a number of years. Naturally our hair is white so it takes dye well. It is one of our frivolous vanities I have to confess. Now we must attend to more serious matters. You now know that we exist and we would appreciate it if you didn't try to remove our device from the cave. Our exit on Lundy has proven to be one of our most effective for our water folk and we would like to keep it that way. We would also ask that you leave other devices around the world alone. We thought that directly telling you about the situation would be preferable to you wasting time and resources when you have such a dangerous enemy on your doorstep, and ours. We would of course like to open diplomatic channels though I know it is going to bog me down in incessant meetings and discussions for days. It has to happen as I am sure that you have protocols for this sort of thing." He looked towards Kel. "Don't worry, I'm not going to expect anything like that now. I'll talk to your appropriately trained personnel when the time is right."

Rennon was looking around like a hungry beast placed in front of the best steak. "The equipment you have here is truly magnificent."

Nai beamed a smile at him. "I know and you are going to want to trade for some of it I am sure. So I am sure that you will also wish to maintain our secrecy and if we can negotiate it use our transport system. All this may well be possible. For now I would like you to go back and report to your Mission Command and for you who came from Earth to report to your people."

Kyla was looking around. "Are you from Earth?"

Nai's smile fell from his face. "You know that is a very good question. We are not exactly from Earth, we came to Earth and many of our people in the past have created the myths and legends that used to keep people entertained on dark nights. We arrived on a ship many years ago when it ran out of power and was forced to land. We made Earth our home and its problems are now our problems. We used our advanced technology to connect with the one that humans inhabit but we have all the dimensions, not just your one. I am sure that you have worked it out by now by what you call Eion Particles around the gate that you are in another dimension, ours."

Kyla was still looking around. "Surely you could shut off the dimensional travel and be safe from the Followers?"

Nai smiled again. "We could if we wanted to but our existence has become interlinked, we would not yet abandon those who have lived alongside us, albeit unknowingly for so long. Your problems are our problems for the present. We will see what the future holds."

Kyla looked around the room. "What was the image I saw when I first came to the cave."

Nai smiled enigmatically. "Ah, the lost one. She came to the cave many years ago looking for he who was lost. He would not return to your world, he abandoned you all to your fate many years ago. She should have returned with him but she refused to. Over the millennia she has been reborn again and again. She lives her life and every time she carries on with what she believes is her mission. But over the years she has forgotten and re-learnt what that mission is so often that the memory is breaking down. She remembers she has lost someone, on occasion she does see him. When the veils are thin he sometimes visits her. Then she remembers for a while. He will not join her and be mortal again, she will not give up you mortals and return to him. But, while she is in your world he will protect it from the final vengeance. His ships are powerless as if he destroyed the Earth he would finally destroy her if she did not slip into spirit to join him first. What you saw was Desrinus, my son trying to lead her into setting him free when he had been trapped by my wife for actions against our people. She used the end of the tunnel for a while and he spent many years convincing the lost one that he was her lover."

Kyla looked at the floor. "What happened to him?"

Nai looked slightly sad. "He met with her true lover in spirit and he has never quite been the same again."

They walked back down the corridor towards the metal plate. "I don't know what you were hoping to find on Lundy but I hope that the alliance that we may be able to forge will be something positive you can take back to your superiors. I would trust in your discretion in what you talk about on the island and on your way back to your respective homes. The war is being fought on many levels and by many people of races you may never have heard of. The Followers are spreading through the dimensions, not just the galaxies and worlds. We could have walked away but we didn't, it may be too late for us already, it may not. For now, we will talk and we will see what the future holds. I would give you this." He handed them a small silver ring engraved with leaves. "Beware Faerie giving, this is a gift freely given. Never accept a gift from my people unless they say that it is given in that way or you will owe them a gift back. There are some very dark folk amongst my subjects, you would call them evil but evil and good has no meaning here. They have their ways of living and doing things that may well not agree with what you believe to be right. Now please enter the device and I will send you back to the cave."

Rennon turned to face him. "Thank you for what you have shown us. I hope that when you speak with our people that we will reach a mutually beneficial agreement. We do appreciate the gravity of what you have shown us."

Nai smiled and it was as if a warm glow had wrapped around them. "Farewell my new friends, I trust that we will one day meet again."

They were back in the cave, a little disorientated as it was night and pitch black. Their equipment was where they had left it and Rennon managed to pull out a torch from the side of his laptop bag. It was only a tiny pencil light but it gave them the opportunity to pack up and have a little bit of light as they made their way up the path to the Castle.

The courtyard was still and in darkness. Their feet echoed on the stone cobbles as they made their way in silence to the kitchen, comforted that the door was still locked.

Kyla put the kettle on. "So Rennon, how about you boot up your laptop and we can find out the date and time. I'd like to know if a hundred years has passed."

Rennon took out his laptop. "Under the circumstances that isn't funny. Thankfully only hours have passed, not years. Its now half eleven and the down side of that is that we've missed lunch and dinner in the Tavern. I hope that someone got to the shops today so we have something to eat tonight."

Kyla flipped the on switch. "Well you are in luck, Kel and I went earlier and there's a whole cupboard full of snacks, bread, cheese and other things. So, shall we put them on the table and help ourselves?"

Kel tipped back on his chair and clasped his hands over his stomach. "That would be great. I'm just wondering when Damien is going to join us. We didn't get to see him, for all we know they could have murdered him."

Rennon looked worried. "We did take rather a lot on trust. I'm going back to the cave."

Kyla turned to face him. "I wouldn't. Nai said that Damien had to heal, even with their technology that may take a while. I don't think they have him hostage."

There was a knock on the door and a muffled voice outside. "Thanks for waiting for me, that was a dark walk in my condition."

Rennon leapt to the door and opened it. "Damien, good to see you mate."

Damien stepped inside. He was dressed in a white shirt and black trousers and looked very healthy. "They looked after me well and I'm almost as good as new, few scars but can't complain. A very naughty doggie, did you see it, it was massive. I have no idea how that tiny girl controls it, then again she didn't, did she! Still, quite a place and the Infirmary, that was a real experience but I'm not sure what was the drugs and what was actually there. I guess I'll never know. But I'm back now, safe and sound."

Rennon was running a scanner over Damien. "Everything checks out but you seem different, certainly more chatty."

Damien had a wry smile on his face. "Just happy, I met a young lady while I was there, that was why it took me a bit longer to heal and leave the Infirmary. She was one of the nurses."

Rennon chuckled. "You old dog, good for you. A bit of Fairy skirt."

Damien went white. "Sorry, what did you say? Blimey so it wasn't the drugs, are you telling me she really did have hooves?"

Kyla set the drinks on the table and they were passed around. She picked hers up and took a mouthful. Then she started handing the contents of the cupboard to Rennon who put it on the table in the middle. Connor got the plates and gave everyone one and Eric got the cutlery. Very soon they were ripping chunks off the bread and buttering it with local butter and stacking it high with the cheese they had bought earlier. Kyla put a bottle of wine on the table and Kel got the opener, opened it and poured it into the glasses that Eric had put on the table.

Kel lifted his glasses. "To those of the Realm, may they prove the sort of allies that we really need to tip the balance in this war."

They all lifted their glasses. "To the Realm."

Kel then put his glass down and looked thoughtful.

Rennon caught his eye. "What is worrying you."

Kel smiled. "Well, I'm wondering how we're going to fill in the mission reports. I hope they can arrange a diplomatic meeting soon as reporting that we went into a cave, jumped dimensions and met a bunch of Faeries is not going to read well. Is it actually worth investigating the church and other places?"

Daniel looked up and put down his chunk of bread. "I was going to propose that we contact our respective superiors and report in and ask what they want us to do. I would suggest in the initial report we refrain from referring to our new found friends as fairies."

Kel took a big bite from his chunk of bread. "We can report in the morning. It has been a hard two years and if we can set an electronic guard let us have one night with the hope that things might turn a corner."

Daniel got up from the table and went to the window. He had seen a light at the window. It was still outside in the courtyard but he was sure he saw a tiny light floating off towards the stairway. "Looks like our new friends are still around."

Kyla spread some butter on a crust. "Well, it is the witching hour, that is supposedly their time by your folklore isn't it?"

Rennon got up and went to the window. "I would still like to set up the sensors so we have some advance warning if any of their dogs get out again. I'll be back, Damien, are you coming with me? We can get this place rigged up and then we can relax properly."

Damien took a bite, put his bread down and headed out of the door after Rennon, laptop under his arm.

.

10

The Commander stared blankly at the files in front of him. He slowly closed the one he had been looking at and put it carefully aside on a pile of others and straightened his pens. He picked up a notepad and flipped it open. He picked up his pen and thought for a while and then began to write. He thought and wrote for over two hours although at the end of it he hardly had anything written on the paper, but he had a lot of crossings out and enough words left without a line through them.

He turned to the intercom and pressed the "speak" button. It clicked and he took a deep breath. "People of Mission Command, this is your Commander speaking. This is a Code Red Information Bulletin, all channels. I am sorry to have to inform you that as of 0400 this morning we lost contact with all other Mission Commands in the other galaxies. Reports that we have received from our allies have informed us that these bases have been destroyed. I am also sorry to have to inform you that the Followers have now got major control in every galaxy, including this one. They have declared us as outlaws and I have to inform you that each one of us now has a price on our head.

It is not known how much information they have on specific members of staff other than our field operatives. Anyone who wishes to leave Mission Command should do so now. You will be provided with whatever equipment and transport we can spare.

I would like to send my sympathies to those of you who had family or friends on the other bases. Today has been designated a day of mourning and we have set up a wall of remembrance in the annex to the galley."

Kel, Rennon and Kyla were sitting by the window in their usual seat eating their breakfast. Kyla had been caught mid bite and she slowly put her fork down onto the plate and looked at the other two as she slowly chewed her bacon.

Rennon shook his head and looked down into his food. Kel was staring out of the window and clenched his fist so hard he bent the fork.

Rennon took a deep breath and let it out slowly. "That's it then. So what happens now?"

Kel unclenched his fist. "We carry on. We fight and we do what we can. It is probably going to be harder going and I suppose we may have to raid to get our equipment from now on but life goes on. I'm wondering if the Commander will move us all out of here. If the other MCs are destroyed I'd put money on this one being in the firing line soon enough."

They finished their meal in silence. The whole room had also fallen into an eerie silence other than the clatter of knives and forks. Many had walked out, their meals half eaten. Their meal done they walked out together. They hardly got to the door when their pagers went off. "Report to the Commander."

They went directly there, passing blank faced people walking in a dream. It all seemed surreal, nothing did seem real. It was the same corridor they had walked a thousand times but it looked different somehow, it smelt different and it certainly felt different. The feeling that nothing would ever be the same again was written on everyone's faces.

They hardly stopped at the Commander's door, just long enough to knock and for him to answer before they strode in and stood in a line in front of his desk. All of them stood, feet apart, hands behind their backs. The Commander tried to smile. He now had even more files in front of him. "I have called you here as you may have already realised things are going to have to change here. We cannot withstand a full scale attack by the Followers now that they have control of the fleets of all the galaxies they have conquered. I have decided that rather than sit here and wait to be destroyed we are going to take the base apart ourselves and fly out of here. Being able to skirmish fight and move quickly may be the only hope that we have of survival. I have contacted Baron Joniel of the Prince's Watch and King Naialindris and they have agreed to help us move our non-essential staff to places of safety.

King Naialindris has problems of his own. He has been forced to remove the devices from most of his gateways to prevent the Followers from entering his realm. The gateways that remain are very heavily guarded and he has warned us not to attempt to use them as the devices he has put in place are truly deadly. In his communiqué he was able to give us the location of a research establishment where the Followers are producing something new.

I've allocated you a combat class Zephyr with cloaking ability. It is in the hanger, fully fuelled and stocked with your share of provisions. Rennon you will take the Research and Development slot on the ship of course, Kyla you are going as the medic. Kel as weapons specialist but you are going to have to pick more crew than that if you are going to be effective. Do you have any suggestions or shall I allocate someone for you?"

Rennon shifted his feet. "Can we have some time to talk this over?"

The Commander smiled slightly. "Of course, but don't take too long, I've authorised the evacuation. Once evacuated King Naialindris' people are going to shift the base into a dimensional space where it will remain until we need it again. As he is shifting it out of phase and time nothing living would survive so we cannot leave anyone behind.

I would suggest that you do your thinking and discussing while packing up your things and moving to your ship. I am convening a final meeting in the Galley in three hours. I expect the ships to disembark as soon as possible after that. I have drawn up a list of possible names of people you might like on your team, take a look and get back to me. Thank you gentlemen and lady."

They left the room in silence and walked down the corridor which was now full of people carrying equipment and personal effects. They walked in single file, letting the people flow around them. Kel was in front and they went to his room first.

It was a small and plain room with very few furnishings, a bed, a bedside table, a wardrobe and a chest of drawers. There were no decorations or pictures. A stack of weapons by the door were swiftly thrust into a large bag and his clothes fitted into a barrel shaped kit bag which drawstring closed at the top. He slung it over his back and they moved on to Rennon's room.

Rennon's room was a light blue and decorated with prints he had acquired after his trip to Earth. He had almost a complete set of Waterhouse, Pre-Raphaelite Artworks, framed in ornate gold wood. They stacked easily on their sides in one of the cardboard boxes that had been left for him. He threw his clothes into one of the boxes and began stacking his equipment and scanners into a box. There was a note pinned to the inside of his door. It read "Don't worry about the contents of your laboratory. It has already been moved to the Zephyr." He read it, screwed it up and threw it into the wastepaper bin before continuing with stacking his personal possessions into boxes.

As he stacked he talked. "So who do we suggest?"

Kel looked up from helping him and stacking books. "Is there anyone specifically that anyone would like on the ship with us? "

Kyla was also stacking the books into the boxes. "I don't really know anyone, everyone I'd choose other than the doctor is in this room."

Rennon hesitated. "We could ask for Samson. I doubt we'd get him but we can try. Anyone else?"

Kyla smiled to Kel. "What about that nurse you were eyeing up?"

Rennon froze on the spot and nearly dropped the box he was carefully lifting into a packing case. "No point, I would expect she will be on the ship with her long term partner. She kept that one quiet."

Kyla's smile faded. "Oh, sorry, I didn't know."

Rennon smiled. "Not to worry. No, there's nobody I would choose, what do we need?"

Kel grunted. "More firepower is always useful."

Kyla thought for a moment. "A mechanic might be a good idea. If the ship breaks down there's nothing any of us could do about it."

Rennon nodded his approval. "Can you cook?" He was looking at Kyla.

Kyla thought about that one. "Well, I can manage the basics if I have to. How many crew does the ship need? Perhaps a dedicated pilot would be a good idea. What about Angus Larkin?"

Kel put the stack of books he was carrying into a box. "That sounds like a good idea. I know you can fly most things Rennon but we do need someone with specialist skills, I've heard those Zephyrs are hard to fly. The ship has twelve crew rooms so its up to the Commander how many he wants to send with us. Shall we leave it to him?"

Rennon picked up an ornament of a polar bear and wrapped it in a shirt. "Other than requesting Samson, why not?"

They finished packing Rennon's room and moved on to Kyla's. Her room was virtually empty of anything. She had the basic furniture and one or two pieces of clothing and washing accessories but other than that she had nothing personal to pack. They had left her a backpack and she filled it while the other two sat on her bed. She buckled the straps and threw it over her shoulder. "So, time to go then. Lets report back to the Commander and take a look at our new home."

Rennon flipped open his laptop and wrote a message to the Commander with the result of their discussion and then hit send.

They approached the Hanger Bay. The door was permanently open as people were coming and going and all security and quarantine protocols had been suspended. There were bits of rubbish strewn in the corridor that nobody seemed to be worrying about. Its usual pristine clinical tidiness was a thing of the past.

Their ship rose above them. Its silver shell had seen a few battles and was slightly pock marked but in general it was in a great condition and definitely space worthy. Rennon walked around it casting a critical eye over it and recalling its specifications on his handheld scanner and info dock. The entrance ramp was down and they were able to stride straight in. The ship seemed huge and clinically industrial inside. It was battle ready rather than a troop transport and had been built to be functional rather than comfortable. It had the basic rooms of Galley kitchen and dining area, a large communal area and separate private quarters entered by climbing down a ladder. They were all identical with a pull down bed and washing and toilet facilities, a wardrobe and places to store things.

Kyla looked around the room she had chosen and put her backpack down on the bed. Rennon slid down the ladder and landed beside her. She looked around and he watched her. She smiled and whispered to him. "Don't you think these dull silver metal walls are impersonal? It certainly has that military feel, you know that tidy precision that the base must have had once. I wonder how long it will take for this place to feel like home?"

Rennon shrugged. "I don't know, the base must have changed over the years and generations had made their mark. This room is a blank canvas, straight off the production line, just like mine. It is ready for you to make your mark."

Kyla took a deep breath. "That is the problem, what is my mark? My thoughts are running riot trying to sort that one out. Mere months ago I had known who I was and my life was pretty much planned out for me. Now it is an open road with no signposts." She sat on her bed and cupped her head in her hands.

Rennon sat beside her. "I've taken over two rooms, one for me, one as a laboratory. The laboratory is in one of the storage rooms. So how about you come and help me with the boxes and keep me company while I check over the controls and get ready with the pre-flight?"

Kyla looked down at her hands. "I'll come and find you in a bit. I'd like to spend a moment thinking if you don't mind. I'll be there later."

He put a hand on her arm and walked out of the door without looking back. As he left the room his pager flashed up. "Pilot arriving on board imminent. Rennon you may step down as pilot."

Kel prowled the corridors and rooms looking around. He'd thrown his box onto a bed in the room next to Kyla's but something was bothering him. He was trying to convince himself that he was not sentimental about leaving Mission Command. He was trying to convince himself of a lot of things.

As he walked he bumped into Dr Samson. He was carrying a box of medical supplies. "Few more boxes to get on board but it looks like I'm with you on this one. Seems the Commander thinks you might need my services."

Kel smiled. "Good to have you on board. Any idea who else is coming?"

Samson rested his box on a ridge in the corridor. "I'm not sure, its chaos out there, the protocols have gone to the four winds, sounds like there's an incoming battle cruiser and odds on it's a Follower vessel so we're in a hurry now."

Kel's smile faded. "Does Rennon know? He's doing the pre-flight."

Samson lifted the box back up. "He knows, he mumbled something about getting us off base as soon as he could but hoping for a pilot. We haven't got clearance to go yet so we'll have to wait a bit."

There was a clatter behind Samson. They turned as a dark haired man emerged carrying and impossibly large pile of boxes. He stuck his head around the pile and smiled with a really boyish grin. He was nearing middle aged, sported a short military haircut and an immaculately pressed black boiler suit with wings insignia on his mandarin collar. "Hello there, I'm Mac

Isaacson. I heard you needed a pilot, mind if I come on board?"

Kel shrugged. "Good to meet you. Better get your stuff stowed and up to the cockpit. I trust you have heard about the battle cruiser coming our way?"

Mac smiled. "I heard, hurried our packing and we're good to go, this is all of it. My wife has been stowing things in one of the crew rooms and I'll get us off base if there's nothing else you want to do. There are one or two more crew you will need to meet but there's time for that when we're safely off base. With that cruiser on its way it's going to be close. The Commander has ordered that we all just get away, he'll contact all of us later with our briefings and co-ordinates and the like. So, if you are ready, I'll cast off and we can get this boat out of here."

Kel looked at Samson. "I guess this is it. Have you got everything you need loaded?"

Samson looked a little down. "In truth I would have preferred to bring more but everything has been shared out and we didn't do too badly. I'm going to get this lot stowed away. I've already found the med bay so we're good to go. I brought a couple of my staff with me. How about you?"

Kel looked around the walls. "Nothing to leave behind I guess. Let's just get off base before there's trouble so they can get the base stowed away."

Mac pulled the ship smoothly out of the Bay and glided it into space so they could have a last look. Ships were flying off in all directions and they were the last but one. The Commander's ship followed them out and as they watched the base and the moon blinked out of existence and another moon blinked back into its place without the starfish shape of Mission Command.

Mac took a sharp intake of breath. "Blimey, that was cool. Look I've got the co-ordinates programmed into the computer. Do you want to do the honours?" Then they saw the battle cruiser rounding the planet and there was a scramble where both of them tried to hit the black button. The Eion Drive hummed into action and they flashed into the inter-dimensional corridor. The stars were gone, the cruiser was gone. In their place the elongated flashes of Eion Particles as they floated through the inter dimensional corridor.

Kel looked a little stunned when Mac got up and wandered away. Mac saw him looking and smiled. "Don't worry, once we are in IDC the Eion Drive pretty much looks after itself until we come out of the corridor again. It's a complicated procedure moving through the gap between the realities as it's not a straight line or consistent space. No pilot I know can fly the IDC manually, so there's no point sitting here and watching the auto drive doing its stuff. This ship is advanced enough to pretty much look after itself. The system will alert us if there's a problem and I'll be back if I'm needed."

Rennon had found the room that he had previously claimed and started moving his laboratory equipment into it. It had tables bolted to the ground and he began to set out his equipment. He stowed what he didn't need and laid out what he needed immediately. There were shelves and these were very quickly filled with his books and notebooks. The table was soon covered with all the things he had unpacked but which had not as yet found a home. He was just inspecting a hand held scanning device when a woman appeared at his door.

She was young, in her late teens he estimated, blonde, fragile and had fine features, her skin was like porcelain. "Are you Rennon? I came on board with Mac, I'm his daughter Eloise and I've been assigned to your Department. Here's my resume, I think you'll find I have the right qualifications." She didn't wait to be invited in, she walked into the room and started looking around. "Nice place, do you need a hand unpacking?"

Rennon smiled nervously. "You can start with that box there, the bioscanners are all on that shelf there and the spectrometers are just below them."

She set to her task with enthusiasm and in silence which brought a smile to Rennon's face.

Kel had gone to the galley and was making himself a drink, he sat down at the big table and drank it slowly, looking around and taking the place in. He heard someone coming and looked up. It was Kyla, she wandered in, poured herself a drink and sat down next to him. "So, what's up Kel?"

Kel took a long drink. "I hadn't realised how much Mission Command had been part of my life. Since they let me stay it has been home, then in almost half a day it is gone and there's no going back."

Kyla smiled. "Daunting isn't it? Well I wouldn't say no going back, its only in storage. Now if that isn't freaky enough?"

Kel smiled back. "Very. Daunting but exciting. Here we are with the whole expanse of space and other dimensions in front of us, we could go anywhere. Is it time to try the inter-ship communications yet?"

Kyla thought about it. "Not quite yet but we're not far off reaching the co-ordinates given for the first message. Have you sorted out your room?"

Kel turned the cup around in his hand. "I put my things in the room next to yours, is that alright?"

Kyla went silent and looked down.

Kel looked concerned. "Is there a problem?"

Kyla looked up. "No, no, nothing at all. It will be good to know you are there. So much has changed."

Kel put his arm around her. "Some things have changed but some things stay the same. We're a family now, you, me, Rennon and Samson. This is our home. Come on, give me a smile. We're big brave goddam heroes, we can handle anything can't we?"

Kyla looked up at him, tears in her eyes. She went to speak but she shut her mouth again. He put his other arm around her and hugged her just as

Rennon came in.

Rennon poured himself a cup of coffee and sat down. "I feel just the same sweet one. We've got about half an hour before the first message comes in from the Commander. I've met Mac and he has everything under control in the cockpit and Samson is settling in and setting up an infirmary. I apparently have an assistant now, Mac's daughter and she is quite happy unpacking. So, this is it, probably our only bit of quiet time for a while. I'd make the most of this bit of peace, my money's on the Commander giving us a mission straight away. It's been a lot in one go but we're all here and we're still together, after everything. Have you met any of the new crew yet?"

Kel sat back in is chair and relaxed back with his cup in hand. "Not yet. They are down in the crew rooms getting their things unpacked. I'm sure we'll all meet up later. Let's hope we all get on."

Rennon tried the coffee and pulled a face. "Not my favourite brand."

Kyla smiled. "We'll soon make this place a bit more like home. It is our home after all. We'll see what the Commander wants and then we'll put together a meal and celebrate getting our own place."

Half an hour later they filed out of the galley and went up into the cockpit. It was slightly crowded with them all in there. Rennon and Mac sat in the cockpit chairs and Samson and Kel sat in the two seats behind them with Kyla standing in the middle. Eloise was standing behind them with a tall, middle aged handsome blonde haired woman who they assumed was Mac's wife. There were four boiler suited men behind them, all of which talked amongst themselves and seemed to be ignoring everyone else. The five Marines who had accompanied Rennon when he had rescued Kel were also there. Mac flicked the radio to open channel and a red light began to flash. Rennon flicked a few more levers and the radio crackled into life.

The Commander's voice was clear, precise and warm. "I hope that you have had a chance to take a look around your new home. This is a solo channel so I will give you my message and then you will get a chance to answer. Intelligence has come our way that the Followers have a secret research base on Glasia Ventura, a small moon in the Rekarthis Galaxy. These are desperate times and any upper hand we can get could just make the difference. It would be beneficial for us to find out what is going on there and if it is useful to commandeer it. If it is useful to them then you have a go to destroy the base and leave nothing behind that they can find useful. From now on we will have to use guerrilla tactics, this will be your first mission and I would like to wish you every success. I will be closing this channel now so that you can respond. Following that I will transmit the co-ordinates of the research base."

The intercom crackled and went silent. They looked at each other and each one in turn nodded. Rennon flicked the comms switch and cleared his throat. "This is Rennon, we are agreeable, please transmit the location. We will acquire or destroy." He flipped the lever and sat back in his seat and they waited.

Moments later the screen showed that information was being transmitted and schematics, location and other information flashed on the screen in front of them. Rennon logged it away into the document files and everything fell silent. They were hanging in the velvety immense darkness of space, stars and planets all around them.

.

11

The galley was very like the rest of the ship, gunmetal grey and chrome, functional and new. It was now littered with cooking utensils, plates, bowls and other cooking paraphernalia that Mac's wife, Shannon had found and used and the table was set with the food she had prepared.

Shannon was in her late forties and neatly dressed. Her military upbringing and life was evident in her mannerisms and the way she went about things. The meal had been conjured up with military precision until Mac had appeared to help her. Then the utensils had suddenly got a will of their own and the place had become what she was still berating him for, a mess. They laughed and hugged each other and Mac started loading the utensils and now unnecessary bowls into the sink ready for the washing up later.

The rest of the crew began to wander in until everyone was assembled around the table. Each found a place they were comfortable with. Rennon sat at the head of the table, Kyla at the other. Kel sat to the left of Kyla. Eloise had come in with Rennon and sat beside him. Kyla and Kel smiled knowingly at each other as they noticed the totally obvious way in which Eloise looked up at Rennon in a very kiddish adoring fashion. The four boiler suits sat together opposite the five marines.

Rennon seemed happy, he was chatting with Eloise about their work and everyone was chatting generally and they began eating.

The food done Rennon tapped on the table with his spoon. "I must first thank Shannon, and Mac too of course for the meal, you did wonders with the rations. There is quite a bit we have to discuss but as we are nearing the planet I'll keep this brief. I was wondering if we should give our ship a name? As it was so new the powers that be hadn't yet got around to naming it. In case you are wondering it got shot up on its way to be delivered."

There was an explosion of conversation, arguments and raised voices for a while and then it fell quiet. Nothing had been agreed.

Rennon smiled. "Well that was productive. Shall we try again? Does anyone have any suggestions?"

Mac looked as though he was going to say something and his wife elbowed him. "Well, I was reading a book that had come from the Earth library that came over as part of our co-operation with that galaxy and I wondered if the Argo would be a good name. Its short and was the name of another ship that took its crew to great adventures and back again."

There seemed to be a general agreement and Rennon tapped on the table again. "Shall we vote?

Who is for the name "Argo"?"

Everyone's hand raised up in agreement.

Rennon smiled. "Well, that was relatively easy, welcome to the Argo."

The proximity alert rang out warning them that they were approaching the planet. Immediately they jumped up from the table and ran to the cockpit. Rennon and Mac leapt into the pilot and co-pilot's chair and the others slipped into the room behind them.

The planet was a ball of blue and green below them. Lush forests covered most of it, towering mountains and deep blue lakes. It stood serene in a sea of blackness and stars, its moons and sun hanging as if motionless and the other planets in its solar system set out like a huge model. From their vantage point it didn't look "real". As they looked down on the world most of it seemed to be unspoilt forests and rolling pastures. They circled the planet in stealth mode and Mac and Rennon set the scanners working.

As they rounded the planet on their first sweep they came to a huge city. Mac took them down a bit lower so that they could get a better look as he muttered. "Wow!"

Rennon was looking at the scanner too. "Neither do I. That's twice we've run it, shall we run it again?"

Mac was resetting the scanner to rescan. "Just once more, there has to be some sort of life here. Look at that place, there are absolutely no signs of any damage. They could be underground or shielded I suppose."

Rennon physically shivered. "I really don't like the feeling of this."

Mac tried to smile. "Neither do I, this is very, very wrong. Look at the place. The forest looks unspoilt and natural. Look at that lake, it's a beautiful colour but look at the signs, there are no animals, no fish, no birds and by the look of it, no people. That has to be wrong. We'll scan again."

They ran the scan again and then again. Rennon had the laptop on his lap now and he was typing furiously. "There's no error here, this place is totally devoid of any form of life. The atmosphere is ideal, there is no pollution and nothing that would cause this as far as I can see, well nothing now. The water is pure, drinkable and the buildings are undamaged. Something is very, very wrong. I've analysed the air, there doesn't seem to be any foreign agents it's pure and clear."

Kel looked at the scanner. "I wouldn't put money on this being a quiet walk in the park. Can you tell what this establishment was for?"

Mac looked up. "The scanners aren't that specific but somewhere in there is the research establishment and I'd put my money on something having gone wrong there. We can tell atmosphere and that sort of thing but as to what the machinery down there is for and everything else, the scanners aren't that specific. We'll have to go down and take a look."

Kel grunted. "Thought so."

Kel, Rennon, Kyla and two of the Marines, Jakeo and Arkarus were kitted up and in the shuttle which broke away from the Argo and glided down to the planet surface. There was a distinct landing pad and they brought it down on there.

The shuttle's scanners didn't show any change. Outside the sun shone down on the cream coloured concrete which glistened slightly in the sun. The air smelt warm and fresh, dry and mixed with the scent of grass and flowers. There was an eerie silence. Their boots rang out all the louder on the concrete as they moved in silence to what looked like a reception building.

They pushed the large glass doors and they opened, it was not locked. The floor was covered in a dark blue deep pile carpet. There was a long light wood desk that ran the length of the room separating the incoming traveller from what looked like an office. There were papers on the desk, and pens set out but as they got closer it was possible to see a thin layer of dust on everything where it hadn't been disturbed for a very long time. The terminals were switched off. Kyla went to a light switch and tried it, there was still power. Rennon was at one of the terminals, he touched the keypad, it was on sleep mode and leapt into life showing departure times and booking schedules. He opened a desk drawer and it was well stocked with pencils, pens and a small fluffy rabbit. A cup on the table had dried beyond being mouldy, the green powder on the bottom decayed with time.

To the right there was a large pair of double doors. Rennon gave them a push and they swung open to reveal a long corridor leading down the side of the office space. Kel took point, Rennon and Kyla behind him and the marines watching the back. They proceeded with caution but everything was still.

At the end of the corridor there was a large room furnished with comfortable sofas, a drinks machine, tables and magazines. They took a quick look around and then Kyla froze. "You'd better take a look at this."

The others came over and Rennon pulled out his scanner. "Dried blood, its been here a while but something must have happened. At last, its something at least. Heads up guys there may be something here."

It was only a small patch and that was all that seemed to be wrong with the room. They checked out the rest of it and moved on and out into the City.

The street was lined with parked vehicles. They were modern looking with smooth lines, aerodynamic and fuel saving, solar panels on the roofs. They were all neatly parked, their wheels pointing sideways so that they could drive out and then rotate the wheels to drive off. Rennon was fascinated and almost got left behind. They moved on down the street, scanners in hand. It was eerie, empty and echoed with a nothingness that seemed in itself intimidating and sinister.

Rennon held up his hand and they all stopped. "I've got an energy signature which might indicate where the research establishment is. Everything else is in shut down by the looks of things, except for that building over there. He pointed to an inconspicuous concrete building, single storey with very few windows.

They found a side door and tried the lock, it was securely bolted, as was the front door. Rennon tried the electronic decoder which could usually manage to open any electronically locked door but it had no effect. They were about to give up when an engine revved behind them, making them all jump. They got out of the way as Kel drove one of the cars into the door, smashing it open.

Once inside the entrance lobby they were met with a functional room with a security booth and what looked like bullet proof glass. The door was ajar and the corridor beyond it empty. As they moved along the corridor lights came on in front of them and switched off behind them. The corridor was a long silver tunnel, rounded at the edges and lined with doors. They took the first door on the right, it wasn't locked and inside there was a neat office, paperwork laid out, the terminal in sleep mode. A finger to a key brought it back up and the occupant had been mid letter, writing about the need for a rescheduling of the cleaning staff. Again the desk drawer was full of the usual office essentials and a couple of unused birthday cards.

At the end of the corridor there was a lift. Its doors slid open invitingly as they approached. It was lined with a plastic coating which Rennon immediately scanned. "Silicone, with some particles I can't identify. Shall we take the lift people or would you rather walk?"

Kyla looked inside. "Shall we find some stairs and do one level and see what we find?"

Kel grunted. "Seems like a plan."

There was a door beside the lift and they took it. Away from the public side of the building the stairwell was functional, concrete and had a basic metal handrail. The stairs were straight to a landing then dog legged back to another and again the lights came on in front of them, turned off behind. They went down one level and came to a door which was wedged slightly open. Kel pushed Kyla behind him and she glared at him. Rennon had his scanner out and was running it over what looked like what was left of an arm bone that was wedged in the doorway. He crouched down and pulled the door open.

The arm bone was clearly gnawed at one end and Rennon ran the scanner over it. "Heads up people, this bone has been chewed as you can see. The bite marks indicate that the teeth were possibly human."

Kel pulled his blaster and the others followed suit as they stepped out into the hallway. The doors were open and there were bones littered about the floor, some were almost complete skeletons but dismembered. Some still partially wore the lab coats and clothes they had worn in life.

Rennon and Kel move down the corridor followed by the others. The first open door was what looked like a mess hall. There were trays on the tables, the rotted food dried to the metal. The serving area was well stocked with rotted food, the heat lamps still keeping the blackened and decayed layer of rotted food warm. A drinks machine bubbled, the water inside being kept on the boil. Around the room there was evidence of a struggle. Tables were tipped over, benches and chairs lay on their sides and bones were strewn about.

Somewhere down the corridor there was a metallic sound. They all jumped and turned to face it but there was silence and the corridor was empty. They formed up in the corridor, everyone armed, ready for whatever might leap out at them. They moved along the corridor slowly, step by step, listening, watching and waiting. Step by step they came closer to the next room. Kel leapt across the doorway and stood on the other side of it, back to the wall, blaster ready. Kyla slipped along the wall to a position on the near side of the door and Rennon took a deep breath, scanner in one hand, blaster in the other and after scanning the room he relaxed a bit and took a step forwards.

The movement was swift, the rotting corpse that leapt out towards him was clumsy in its movements as it launched itself towards him. Kel fired first, blowing the body backwards and away from Rennon. It did not cry out as it flew back and hit the back wall. It slid down the wall, regained its feet and leapt forwards again, arms outstretched, mouth open, eyes wild in torn eye sockets. Rennon was firing, again and again the blasts ripped into the body but it still kept coming.

Kel was firing, his blaster knocking it back but it still kept coming, again and again. Most of the torso had been blown away but it still kept coming. Kyla began shooting at the legs until she got a direct hit on the bone and it fell face forwards to the ground and began crawling toward them. Still they kept firing and still it kept moving towards them. Kel pulled the pin on a grenade and shouted. "Fire in the hold". As one they backed away and dived back out of the blast radius.

The grenade exploded in a rose of fire and splintered wood and metal, bone and sinew. Its explosion cutting into the silence then it was quiet, deathly quiet.

The body lay in pieces on the floor some of it still burning. Bits of it still moved and as Kel stepped into the room he narrowly missed being grabbed by a hand which was crawling towards him. He shot it, the holes cut into the flesh but it kept moving.

The room was a laboratory, there were test tubes, liquid bubbled in glass bottles and the computer terminal leapt to life as Rennon landed in the seat and began to tap on the keyboard. "At last, a break, the password has already been entered and this terminal isn't damaged. I have entrance into the main computer people. Now hopefully we can get some answers. I'm going to download. There's probably no time for more investigation. My money is on there being more of those things."

He was tapping on the keyboard when they heard it, a dull moaning and a scraping sound of things being dragged. The marine in the corridor stepped back into the room and began firing, the others joined him. "Hurry up Rennon, we have company, lots of it and by the looks of it the locals are very hungry."

Rennon had already pulled a wire out of one of his handheld devices, a memory uploader, and pushed it into the USB port on the computer. He tapped a few more keys and then stood up, leaving it to do its job. "This won't take, good, done. Come on then people, let's get out of here. I've no intention of being food for the locals. I've taken a download of their information, we can read it later. Move out people." He grabbed the cable out of the port and slipped the MU into his pocket, picked up his blaster and joined them at the door.

The locals were shuffling slowly down the corridor, thankfully they were slowed down as they occasionally attacked each other and when Kyla blasted one of them and they saw the open wound there was a feeding frenzy, they leapt on the wounded lab technician and began ripping him to bits. That was their cue, they ran without looking back, retracing their steps until they were back in the shuttle and airborne.

From space the planet looked tranquil and peaceful. The forests were unspoilt and green, the water was blue, there were no life signs. Nothing had changed, nothing other than the group of shambling individuals who had gathered on the concrete, looking up and reaching up towards them. All was not well in paradise.

Back on the Argo Rennon had downloaded the information into his stand alone laptop and was looking through it. Eloise was helping him and they were deep in discussion.

Dr Samson was scanning everyone, rescanning and checking everyone for the slightest cut or graze.

It took Rennon a few hours to go though the data and information. He sat in silence for the most part, shaking his head and jotting down notes. "Eloise, could you get me a drink please?"

Eloise scampered off to the galley as Rennon pulled up the lab notes on the test subjects. The photographs that came up on the screen were what he had sent her away to avoid her seeing. They were truly horrific as they recorded the degradation of two test subjects, forced to share a room and infected with the prototype virus that made them hunger for each other's flesh. He watched as they ripped each other to pieces. He read the reports, the lab notes, the chemical reports and finally he logged out and sat in his chair, leaning back and staring at the blank wall.

Eloise came in with his coffee. He looked up and smiled at her. "Thank you. Could you get everyone together, I need to speak with them."

They gathered in the galley, everyone sitting around the table in the seats they usually sat in for their meal. Shannon had made drinks and they waited, in silence until Rennon looked up and spoke. "I can't convey what I saw on the recordings but believe me when I say it was truly horrific. What we have down there is a Follower Research Establishment and what they are researching is truly terrifying. What we have here is a virus which will turn all it touches into the ravening beast you saw down there. Its carrier is physical, any scratch and the virus will move from one to the next. I have read the reports and it was initially created for what they call their "Super Soldiers". Kel I think you saw first hand what some of their research was intending to do. They are creating an army of mindless drones who will do their bidding. This was the next step that anyone these drones come into contact with is infected with the virus and becomes like them. It had originally been intended that way but the virus got out of hand and one scientist developed what you saw down there. The planet has been abandoned and everyone was left to die as they found that it was uncontrollable.

There was some speculation in later reports that the virus was created for the worlds that the Followers are unable to convert. If they cannot convert they intended to destroy. The plan was to drop one or two of these infected people onto a planet and the planet would then be wiped out of all human life. Unfortunately it also spreads to other species, hence there being no life at all on the planet. Any contact with an infected entity spreads the virus. It seems that there was an accident in the laboratory and the virus began to spread, wiping out the scientists and everyone and everything else on the planet.

We will be safe as the virus can only spread through wounds and contact with an infected entity. Thankfully none of us were injured and the Doc there has managed to scan everyone, we're clear. Simply blowing up the

Research Establishment isn't going to destroy the virus. It may go airborne as it seems to be mutating. We do not have the firepower but I would suggest that we report to the Commander and he brings in one of the larger ships with the star drive cannons. It may be possible to knock the moon out of orbit and to use that to knock the planet into the sun. The heat from that should destroy the planet and burn up any virus that remains on there."

There was a stunned silence in the room. Kel leant back. "Well at least we don't have to go back down there. That place gives me the creeps. What is more worrying is what they are prepared to do."

Kyla looked down into her cup and thought for a moment. "Yes, but we have the recordings of what they are prepared to do. If we could somehow broadcast this to the planets we can show those who believe in the Followers what they are really like. Is that possible?"

Rennon thought a while. "Not from our ship but if we can get copies of this to the transmission arrays and break into news networks it may just be possible. The power of the media can't be underestimated. The Followers used it to good effect, perhaps we can use it to our advantage too. It would take breaking into the satellite stations and literally hijacking the system and then holding it long enough to broadcast. I would suggest we get to a RV point and transmit this information to the Commander. This is one precious cargo."

Mac leapt out of his chair. "I'll get us on course. Could this be a bit of a breakthrough?"

Kyla smiled. "If they believe it."

12

Kel looked out over the ocean from his vantage point on top of the shuttle. He was sitting cross legged, the sun beamed down on his bare back, his shirt lay behind him and he lay back onto it, jumping slightly as the hull was hot.

The sea was calm, the waves lapped lazily on the sandy beach as a seagull played in the thermals above. The shuttle was on an island, the palm trees hardly stirred in the light breeze and coconuts lay uncollected on the golden sand. Further down the beach a group of natives were fashioning a war canoe. They were hand carving the intricate wooden prow as most of the canoe was finished. Scantily clad women brought them drinks and helped out.

Suddenly there was a dull hum from somewhere above him. He opened his eyes and looked up in time to see a ground to space battle shuttle entering through the atmosphere. It descended so fast he could hardly get to his feet and shout a warning before it was raining fire down on the natives. They screamed and ran but fire engulfed them and gunfire rattled along the sand in lines, the bullets that missed thudded into the sand, sending grains in all directions. He saw the look on the faces and he recognised three of them, a woman and two children but he couldn't remember from where.

Kel screamed a warning and for them to come to his shuttle but they were running for the trees as if he wasn't there. Then a fireball hit them and they were engulfed in searing heat. He screamed in frustration and anger as he watched them die.

It was dark, the island was gone. He could feel the cold of a wall to his right, the softness of a mattress which was soaked in sweat. He sat bolt upright and looked around in the half light. He recognised his room and

Kyla who was climbing down the stairs. She walked over and sat on his bed. He mumbled. "It will never be alright again, never."

Kyla put her arms around him and stroked his damp hair. "It was a nightmare Kel, nothing more. It wasn't real. This is real, here and now. Its over, whatever you saw it was just a dream."

Kel took a deep breath. "Sure, just a nightmare. It just phased me a bit, it was so real."

Kyla ruffled his hair. "You'll be fine. Do you want me to stay?"

Kel pulled back from her. "Sure." He lent forward and kissed her and pulled her over onto the bed with him.

She wriggled further onto the narrow bed to save herself from falling off and stroked his hair. "Do you want to tell me about it?"

He looked up at the ceiling. "It was a perfect moment. I was on a tropical island, the sun was shining. A Followers ship arrived and killed them all in a fireball." His mind was racing, he didn't want to mention any more.

She rested her head on his shoulder and he relaxed and enjoyed the moment. He put his arm around her and they both fell asleep.

Rennon was in his laboratory. He was working with chemicals in a test tube, the tube turned blue. "Schrak, green, I need green, turn green damn you."

Eloise looked up from her terminal. "No success this time then?"

Rennon lifted the tube from its holder and tipped it into the waste chemical bin. "There has to be an answer."

Eloise looked at him long and hard. "What are you working on?"

Rennon picked up a new test tube. "I'm looking for an antidote to the drug they gave Kel. Its likely that is what they are giving to their Drone Warriors and if I can give them their free will back again I might be able to set them free of Follower control."

Eloise looked a little surprised. "So you think it's a chemical that makes people follow them? I thought it was a belief."

Rennon sat down on his stool and put his feet up on the bar between its legs. "Far from it." He went back to mixing chemicals and looking hard at the screen. "I need a break, will you be ok for a while?"

Eloise smiled sweetly. "I'll be fine, I'm a big girl now."

Rennon smiled and left the room.

As soon as he was gone she slipped off of her stool and closed the door carefully, checking that nobody was looking. She took the key and communicator that Rennon had in his jacket pocket, hanging by the door on a peg, and went to the cabinet where he kept the more sensitive drugs and samples. She unlocked the cabinet, opened the glass door and lifted out the tray of samples he had carefully labelled and took another vial from her pocket. It had a screw top stopper which she carefully unscrewed and then tipped a drop into each vial. For a moment the liquids steamed as they met and then went back to looking normal again. She put the vial into the waste chemical box and then put the tray very carefully back onto the shelf.

She went to Rennon's terminal and smiled widely as she saw that he had not logged off, his research was all there in front of her. She took a disc from her pocket and downloaded the contents of his laptop onto it, then slipped it into her bag. She then uploaded the contents of another disc marked with a red cross onto Rennon's laptop. She then removed the disc and placed it in a glass bowl, took a glass bottle from the cupboard and poured the concentrated acid over the disc before tipping the contents into the used chemical bin. There was a loud "pop" from the bin and it jumped a bit.

She then turned to the thermostat on the wall. She keyed in her code and raised the temperature. She then opened up the terminal and took out the contacts behind the buttons. She then disabled the intercom and shut off the air conditioning unit and melted the controls.

Eloise looked around the room and checked that everything was back to how it had been before Rennon had left then went back to her chair and carried on with her work.

Rennon came back about a quarter of an hour later with a coffee and one for her. "Milk no sugar, is that right?"

Eloise smiled at him. "Perfect, thank you." She took a sip but it was too hot so she put it down beside her terminal.

Rennon coughed and she started a little then smiled and moved the cup to a table a safe distance away. "Sorry, I forgot."

Rennon sat down and carried on typing. He ran a diagnostic and then raised an eyebrow and smiled. "Well, well, now Eloise this looks promising." He reached into his pocket and took the key out and went to the cabinet.

Eloise slipped down off of her stool calmly. "I need to go to the ladies room. I'll be back in a short while."

Rennon smiled. "Of course, no problem. I'll run a test or two and then we can pack up before dinner. Kyla is cooking, that should be a treat."

Eloise walked out of the room and shut the door. She keyed in her code and silently locked the door then opened up the panel. She took out a vial and poured it over the buttons so that they melted. She replaced the cap, shut the cover on the keypad and wandered off down the corridor.

Rennon took the vials from the cabinet and carefully set them down on the table. He took the third one in and looked at it and his brow furrowed a little. He held it up to the light and then he reached for a scanner and ran it over the vial. He carefully put the vial down into its tray.

Something was wrong in the room, he could tell there was but he couldn't see what. Everything looked normal. He ran his finger around his collar, was it his imagination or was it getting hotter? He went to the thermostat, it was ridiculously high. He pressed buttons but he could get no response and the numbers just kept rising.

As he turned he noticed that the vials were smoking. He ran his scanner over them again and ran a second scan. He ran to his jacket and found his communicator was missing. He turned in time to see the smoke rising from the vials, it had turned a thick yellow colour. "Oh my God, heat, the heat is going to set them off. Dequathoraxine, I can't believe I didn't detect that before."

The intercom was dead. The expected crackle as he opened a channel just wasn't there. He looked at the air conditioning, it was shut off. The air wasn't circulating. He ran to the door and keyed in his code, it wouldn't open. He leapt to his laptop and began tapping keys but they seemed dead. The keypad had been disconnected, it was performing its own routines and there was no way of knowing what they were. Symbols had appeared on the screen, none that he recognised.

He picked the laptop up and took the bottom off of it and ripped out the back up battery and the main battery and unplugged it from the mains. Immediately the wireless connection was cut as the laptop screen went black, the laptop was switched off.

Rennon didn't have long to relax as the liquid in the vials was bubbling violently. As the vials exploded Rennon just had time to leap under a table. The table shielded him from the exploding vials. They lacerated everything they touched and everything they had lacerated was then sprayed with the liquid the vials had contained. Rennon was on his back when the table vibrated, jumped in the air because of the pressure of the explosion and landed, the legs broke and the table came down on him hard.

The table had been next to the wall which on the Zephyr was the outer shell. The blast penetrated the shell and the room began to depressurise. The suction lifted the table and forced it up against the hole, sealing it off.

Rennon lay on the floor like a rag doll. The sensors were working again now that the laptop was turned off and was no longer controlling them. They immediately sensed the burning debris and activated the sprinklers and set off a warning which flashed around the ship.

Eloise was in the ladies room and she smiled to herself when she heard it. From the privacy of her cubicle she pulled out her hand held transmitter and typed out a message. "Mission successful" and hit send.

In the cockpit Mac was monitoring frequencies which he did often to make sure that there were no Follower craft in the area. He was just in the process of alerting the crew to the emergency in Rennon's lab when he detected the outgoing message and with lightning reflexes intercepted it and diverted it to a storage device.

Mac's voice was commanding and monosyllabic. "Crew, this is an alert. There is a fire in Rennon's laboratory, all available hands are to attend." He shut off the intercom and then opened the relay he had intercepted.

Kel and Kyla got to Rennon's laboratory first and it took mere moments for them to realise that something was seriously wrong. Kyla flipped open the keypad and saw the melted keys. Kel saw them too and pulled out his blaster when he saw Rennon laying prone on the floor of the lab through the toughened glass window in the door. He was about to fire when Kyla caught his arm and stopped him.

Kyla looked serious. "Look, Kel, the wall, the skin is broken. If we open this door then what will it do to the pressure?"

Kel looked at the table hanging as if in mid air over the hole in the wall. He looked at Rennon on the floor. "I would say that the pressure would stay the same, it is sucking out, not in."

Kyla smiled. "Very smart, well I hope so, so go on then, lets do this."

Kel levelled his blaster at the lock and fired, blowing a hole in the door where the lock was so that they were able to slide it open. Kyla ran to Rennon and checked him over. "I'd say he's got broken ribs and he's unconscious." She ran a scanner over him. "He's broken three ribs and he took a heavy crack on the head but it's unlikely to be more than concussion. He'll have the mother of all headaches but he should be fine with some rest. Help me get him out of here."

Kel helped her to lift him and they moved him out of the room. Kel mostly carried him, Kyla helped and they managed to get him to the Infirmary where Samson was waiting. He acted swiftly and got him on a bed, scanned him and began with an intravenous drip.

Jack looked concerned. "He's fine but what the hell happened?"

Kyla put a hand on Rennon's shoulder. "I do not know. When we got there the door had been sabotaged, the key pad had been corroded with acid or something. Something had exploded in the room as well but we probably won't know until he comes around. If he's going to be alright we had better get back. The outer hull has been breached and its blocked up by a table."

Jack looked even more concerned. "A table?"

Kel smiled. "A very strong lab table."

Jack didn't look much relieved. "Oh, well that's the thing isn't it."

Kel and Kyla ran back to Rennon's laboratory where the marines were busily welding the table to the wall.

Kel leant on the intercom outside the Laboratory and keyed in the cockpit's code. "Mac, we need to put down as soon as possible for repairs. We have a slight problem."

Mac's voice came over the intercom. "The problem is greater than you think. Can you join me outside the ladies toilets on level two?"

They looked at each other and ran. They arrived about the same time as Mac did. He was armed and he kicked the door in and rushed inside. He was met by Eloise, transmitter in hand uploading from a hand held scanner.

Mac almost screamed at her. "What do you think you are doing?"

Eloise smiled her sweetest smile. "What do you think I am doing daddy

161

dearest, I'm doing my duty. I will be revered for ever more for what I've done here. The Followers now have the whole contents of Rennon's hard drive. What do you think of that? Are you going to ground me? Are you going to talk down to me? Not any more I don't think." She pulled a blaster out from her pretty flower decorated bag and pointed it at him. "Don't think I won't use it. They told me I might have to do this and I'm fully trained and prepared. You are no longer my father, I have a new family now."

Her father laughed at her. "You stupid fool. I intercepted your first message and that one is going to exactly the same place, the storage device in the flight deck."

Eloise screamed with anger. The blaster in her hand erupted with a blue light which hit Mac full in the chest as he fired just that fraction of a second later. His blaster bolt hit her in the chest too, knocking her backwards. Kyla fell to her knees beside Mac and she began CPR. She pulled her mini med bag that she always carried on her belt and pulled out a pre-drawn injection and slammed it into his chest, pushed the plunger and carried on pumping his chest. She tried again, and again, and again while Kel stood over them helpless. He began to pace. Kyla looked up at him for a second. "Check Mac's blaster, is she stunned or dead? Also, stop that transmitter uploading. Just in case. He could have been bluffing."

Kel leapt on the linked scanner and pulled the connection so the screen went blank. He then grabbed the blaster on the floor and checked the dial. "Set to kill, he wasn't messing around. I don't understand, that was his daughter, what is going on?"

Kyla was still pumping Mac's chest. "She's a convert, without the implant as she chose to follow them. How he must have felt when he saw it was his daughter sending the message. I can't imagine. But, he has to fight now and it will probably be hard to get him back because he doesn't want to come back. But he's going to, he has no choice, we need a pilot." She was pumping frantically, keeping to the rhythm. She pulled out a second syringe and jabbed it into his artery. "Come on Mac, live, we need you."

Mac choked back to life, he took in a big, deep breath and then screamed. It was a pitiful, pained, hurt wild animal sound that tore the heartstrings of all who heard it. He fell back into Kyla's arms and she lay him down gently on the cold floor and stroked his head. "Welcome back. Take it easy and we'll get you to the Infirmary."

Mac was choking. "I intercepted the message, its on a loop and is only downloading into our mainframe buffer. The Followers got nothing. Is she?"

Kyla felt for a pulse. She shook her head. "I'm sorry, she's dead."

Mac gasped for breath. "I pretty much knew. There was no coming back from that. She wasn't drugged, she… oh my god, help me." He began to go into convulsions and Kyla slid to the ground, cradling his head on her lap and trying to pull him into the recovery position.

Kyla looked up at Kel, helpless. "Kel, is there anything different about that blaster."

Kel picked it up and turned it over in his hand. "There's an attachment, its well hidden but its there, on the side."

Kyla looked at it while holding Mac who was foaming at the mouth. His eyes were wide and dilated then he became suddenly calm and looked at her with eyes had lost their focus. He reached up and grasped her neck before she could react. Kel was faster, he blasted Mac who fell back onto Kyla's lap.

Kel grabbed him and dragged him off of her lap. "I'd say that was another of their innovations. He isn't Mac anymore, look at him. I'm sorry, I didn't have time to set my blaster to stun."

Kyla leapt on Mac and tried to restart CPR.

Kel caught her arm and pulled her away. "There's no point, he isn't Mac anymore."

Kyla fell back against his legs, exhausted and looking lost. "I don't know what to do, how can we fight this when our own people are turning against us?"

Kel put a hand on her shoulder. She grabbed his arm and leant her head against it, tears flowing down her face. "This is crazy, how can we?"

Kel squeezed her shoulder gently. "We can go on but we'll have to be more careful and we need to let the Commander know, there could be other operatives aboard other ships. I'm also going to go and check the cockpit. Come on."

Kyla got up and went over to Eloise's prone body. "Just a minute. I want to see what she is downloading from. If Rennon's laptop got caught in that blast it may be the only copy of his notes." She detached the disc from the scanner and placed it on the wash stand.

Kel took his blaster out of his holster again and blasted Eloise in the head. "You just don't know. She may have had some of that drug in her system. I'm not taking any chances." He turned and blasted Mac in the head as well.

By the time they got to the cockpit, Shannon was already there and she had ripped out most of the control consol and was in the process of shredding wires. As they opened the door she turned her blaster and fired on them. They both fired back, catching her on the chest. She fell to the floor but so did Kyla who careered backwards into the wall. Kel turned and was too late to catch her. She crumpled to the ground in a heap. He immediately grabbed Shannon's blaster, turning it over in a mad blind panic to check for the additional hardware. It was an ordinary blaster and he recognised it as the one that they had kept under the control panel in case of emergencies.

He scooped Kyla up and ran full pelt to the Infirmary. The doors hardly swished open as he dashed through them and put her down carefully on a spare bed. Jack Samson was already crossing the room and he moved like lightning. He began CPR while his assistant doctor applied a drip and offered him a pre-prepared injection of adrenaline.

Kyla screamed as she came back to consciousness. Kel took a step forwards but Samson's assistant stopped him.

Jack stepped in front of him. "Kel, I've got to carry on, she's not out of the woods and there's still a way to go. What happened?"

Kel stepped aside. "Eloise is dead, Mac's dead, Shannon's dead and she wrecked the control panel before we took her down."

Jack Samson looked at his assistant. "So we're held back from imminent death by a table and there's no controls to drive this boat or a pilot to fly it. Pass me that syringe. I'm just not going to worry, if we're crashing, there's not a lot we can do about it. Kel, why don't you go to the cockpit and see if you can come up with a small miracle."

Kel ran to the cockpit. Shannon lay dead on the floor and wires hung out of control panels, screens were smashed and buttons were pulled from the panel. Kel looked out of the window at the blackness of space, the tiny pinpoints of light twinkling in the blackness. The Argo hung lifeless in the darkness unable to move, unable to control where it went, floating motionless.

13

The Argo floated helplessly in space. The tiny pinhead lights of its windows the only sign that it was not a piece of space debris. Inside was a flurry of action.

Kel looked at the blank consoles in the cockpit hopelessly. The wires were a mess. Some were cut, others ripped out and some hung down with the piece they had been attached to still suspended at their end. He had tried the intercom, the comms for long distance space contact and other systems were all dead. Shannon had done a good job of rendering them useless.

Kel picked up the manual he had been trying to use off of the floor and put it on the pilot's chair. He stormed out. The door swung shut behind him as he strode off down the corridor to the infirmary.

Jack Samson was over straight away as soon as Kel burst through the doors. He put a hand on Kel's shoulder. "Look Kel, don't disturb her. She's in a bad way. She's crashed a few times but she's stable now."

Kel gave Jack a look that made him back off as he strode over to the gurney where the doctor had been working on her. She was sleeping, a breathing tube out of her mouth and wires attached to her. He then bent down and kissed the sleeping woman on the forehead. "Sleep and be well. I'll not leave you."

Jack glared. "I don't want you here cluttering up my Infirmary. Move her to a side room, you can sit with her there. If there is anything out of the ordinary, call me. I'll rig the monitor to a wake up alarm and emergency. You know the difference?"

Kel nodded and he and one of the assistants pushed Kyla's bed into a side room and closed the door. He sat down beside her on a chair and watched her for a while. After about half an hour she opened her eyes a bit and moaned and the wake up alarm went off. He reached forwards and took her hand. "Do you want me to get painkillers from the Doc?"

She focused on him and smiled. "No, I'll be fine, just catch the truck that ran over me would you?"

Kel laughed. "We did, don't worry, Shannon is dead. We wiped out a complete family today. Eloise and Shannon were both Follower converts. Rennon is still with us. Samson's working on him. He'll be fine though, thanks to your speedy actions."

Kyla smiled. "All in a day's work. I heard something about controls being damaged?"

Kel's smile faded. "A bit of an understatement. The controls have been ripped apart by Shannon. She did a real number on the control panel and communication system so we need to wait until Rennon is up on his feet to get it fixed. I had a look at the manual but there's no hope of me understanding it. Are you any good with that sort of thing? Good job you recovered that disc. We do at least have Rennon's laptop contents and on there is the information we got from that last planet. So close to losing it eh?"

Kyla smiled, and then winced. "Not as far as I know. We're getting careless Kel, I didn't see that coming. Rennon will be on his feet soon enough and he'll sort it out. For now we'll have to hang in space and hope that we aren't found by a Follower vessel. Look on the bright side they left us floating. My only worry is that Shannon took out the comms before it could block what Eloise was sending."

Dr Samson put his head around the door. "Rennon is conscious. He is in a foul mood but his injuries are fairly minor in the grand scale of things. He has gone with some help to try to put the control consol back together again. If you are feeling like some verbal abuse you could always go and give him a hand and let me get on here. Morning Kyla, good to see you awake. I'll be with you in a while."

Kel smiled. "How bad can it be?"

Kyla smiled enigmatically, closed her eyes and drifted off to sleep as Kel left the room.

As Kel got to the door he was met by Rennon swearing and throwing things around. Wires hung everywhere, the soldering iron was hot and balanced precariously on the command console and Rennon was under the control panel. He realised Kel was there and got up too quickly, bashed his head and swore some more. "This is impossible, hopeless, how can I be expected to cope with this sort of damage."

Kel caught his arm and pulled him into the pilot's seat and sat beside him in the co-pilot's chair. "What's up mate?"

Rennon smiled ironically. "Plenty, I can't believe she did what she did. I really thought I'd found a soul mate there, someone I could work with. Then the bitch uploads a drone program into my laptop, steals a copy of our hard drive and rigs the only samples we have to explode and nearly takes the ship with it. Just a few things. I can't believe I've lost it all, and the info we found."

Kel looked at the wrecked console. "Like mother like daughter I guess. We didn't. Kyla got a disc off of her that she was uploading to the Followers. Seems she downloaded the contents of your laptop before she put the drone in. Its in the security locker, safe."

Rennon visibly relaxed. "That is at least some good news. There was a lot on there. Yep, you said it, what a pair, but they didn't have to take our pilot with them. He was a good man and an excellent pilot."

Kel put the box he had been carrying on the console. "Brought you some wiring, thought it might be useful."

Rennon smiled. "I could use it, she has wrecked miles of the stuff."

Kel smiled back. "Women eh."

Rennon looked down. "They aren't all like that, how's it going with Kyla?"

Kel looked out of the window. "CPR for over an hour, three injections and she crashed twice."

Rennon looked at him. "Look here mate. If you want that woman you'd better make a serious move soon while she's still with us. If you don't I will."

Kel looked shocked. He opened his mouth to speak and then shut it again. He thought for a while. "There's more to her than she's telling us. She won't tell me. Do you have any idea?"

Rennon smiled. "I'm not kidding, a woman like that doesn't come along every day. You know me, I'm oblivious to most things when it comes to relationships. There could be a hundred and one reasons. We've all lived, loved and been hurt. Perhaps its something like that? Andralon asked for her on her home planet, perhaps she wanted to be with him? We don't know, you could try asking her."

Kel sat down in the co pilot's chair. "She said she'd tell me one day."

Rennon looked up and took the screwdriver out of his mouth. "Then she will. Now, lets get on with fixing this wiring." He grabbed the box off the table and crouched down under the console moaning slightly and grasping his ribs. He pulled out wire after wire, cut out the old wire and spliced and soldered in the new. Kel helped him, handing him the coloured wires as he called for them. They worked in silence, both lost in their own thoughts.

It took many hours but finally Rennon stood up, holding his injured ribs and rubbing them. "Now that hurt. But the job's done in part and we should at least be back in control now. Thankfully she didn't really know what she was doing and pulled out wires in clumps. I've managed to reattach them. Let's see what sort of a job I've done shall we?" He flicked on the console and lights flashed and the screen of the command module sprang into life.

"You beauty, spot on, just what we need. Oh hell, look at that?" He was pointing at the proximity scanner. "We have company coming our way, lots of it and I bet it's not for a party."

He grabbed the intercom and switched it on. "We have company, we have ships on their way. I'm receiving a hail."

Dr Samson responded. "You'll have to handle it, Kyla crashed again and I've got her sedated."

Kel swore. "Oh well Rennon you had better take the hail."

Rennon was opening a channel and they waited.

"This is Captain Hortios Abenath of the Command Ship Quesenth. You are within our territory and have not hailed us to announce your presence. Your ship is unfamiliar, announce yourself."

"This is Captain Rennon of the Argo. We are in need of repairs and our communications array has only just been repaired."

Abenath responded, his voice measured and calm. "State your purpose."

Rennon took a deep breath. "We are exiles from our home, our ship has just been damaged by a saboteur and we seek to set down somewhere to effect repairs."

Abernath responded immediately. "Our galaxy is a closed system. Our scanners indicated that what you have said is true. You may not set down here but we will escort you to our borders and you may be able to set down on Kealaros. It is our law, none may visit uninvited. These are troubled times. Go, with our blessing but know this we will be scanning you and at the first sign that you wish us ill intent we will blow you out of existence. We will assist you with our tractor beams. Will you accept our assistance?" The intercom clicked off.

Rennon sat down in the pilot's chair. He looked at Kel who nodded. He clicked the external intercom switch. "We would be grateful for your assistance." He flicked the intercom off. "Well that was over quickly. We've got control at least. We'll limp there but we can get out of this galaxy. We don't have the Eion drive but we have normal thrusters, I'll fire them up."

Kel looked at the repaired command console. "It looks much better than it did."

Rennon smiled. "All part of the service. It's a fairly good repair, the communications are back on, we could use the Eion drive at a push but I want to run some tests first. She's a good ship, she'll hold together. It is only a small hole and the marines did a good job welding it. If we can set down without any trouble we should be fine. I'll log in the co-ordinates and we can all settle down and get some rest."

Kel slipped into the co-pilot's seat. "That would be good, we could all do with it. Rennon had you better get yourself back to the Infirmary? You aren't looking so good."

Rennon rubbed his side. "It hurts like hell and the doc will catch up with me if I don't go back. I'll set up the autopilot, that seems to be running ok and I'll get back to the Infirmary." He choked slightly and a trickle of blood ran down from the side of his mouth.

Kel leapt from his seat and caught him as Rennon almost passed out.

Rennon put a hand on his arm. "I've got to get that autopilot sorted out. Give me a moment then I'd really appreciate some help getting back to the Infirmary." He leant forwards, his face showing the agony he was feeling and began switching levers and keying in co-ordinates. "There done, now if you would be so kind." He stood up and Kel stepped forwards and half carried him to the Infirmary.

Kel returned to the cockpit and sat down in the pilot's chair and looked out through the window at the stars. He rubbed both of his hands over his face, feeling the roughness of his palms and fingers and ran his fingers through his hair as he leant back in the chair. "Boy have I got to do something." He got up and left the cockpit, closed the door and strode off down the corridor.

Rennon laid back on the Infirmary bed and Jack ran his scanner over him. "Well done, you've undone most of my good work and now I've got to spend more of my valuable time fixing you. Relax, this may take a while."

Rennon moaned as the doctor felt around his injured ribs. His assistant was sitting with Kyla in the separate room watching her intently. Kel came in and the assistant looked relieved. "You can watch her now and I can get on with my duties for the day. She's fine. Watch her breathing though. At the first sign of trouble call Dr Samson."

Dr Samson came into the room in about an hour. Kel looked exhausted but he kept his vigil. Jack smiled at him and put a hand on his shoulder. "She's going to be fine. It was a tough one but as long as she stays put for a bit she'll be fine. Look I've spoken to Rennon and its going to take us nearly a month to get through this galaxy." He attached a pad to her chest. "Look, that alarm will go off if there's a problem. If you want to go back to your room you can or I'll get one of the assistants to run a bed in here. Which?"

Kel looked up at him, raising an eyebrow. "In here."

The bed arrived and Dr Samson pulled the shutters closed leaving Kel to roll onto the bed and close his eyes.

Kel sat in the chair, the bed was not in the room. Kyla smiled at him in a reassuring sort of a way. "Just say it, you know you can say anything to me." She was sitting on the edge of her bed holding his hand.

Kel took a deep breath. "I know, but this is different. You know, put a blaster or a sword in my hand and I don't have a problem, at the moment I'm terrified as hell. It's not like I'm some teenager asking his first date out. It's not as if I can take you anywhere but, how do I put it. Anything that I think I should say just sounds lame. Will you go out with me is so teenager Earth. On our world we wouldn't have this problem. The Aunts were always a good idea. They do the asking and the arranging. I don't have one of those so I'll just have to ask. If I was to take you somewhere romantic with a view to us being more than friends, what should I do?"

Kyla smiled. "I never thought you'd ask. Well, we could start with a walk together after dinner, a bottle of wine and some time watching the stars. It's about the best we can do for now."

Kel smiled, he looked relieved. "And after?"

Kyla blushed. "That is a question you just can't ask. We'll see how the evening goes. For now I really need a shower too." She saw his enquiring expression. "Alone." She smiled as he blushed too. "I'll see you later." She got up and climbed up the stairs of his room.

Kel woke up. The machine was bleeping slightly and Dr Samson had rushed into the room. He pulled back the covers and grabbed a pre drawn syringe which was on the metal tray beside the bed. He injected her and began administering CPR.

Kel grabbed his arm but he ignored him. Blood was running out of the side of Kyla's mouth and soaking the sheets. It ran down onto the floor and pooled at his feet as the machine began to scream. Dr Samson put the paddles down. "Declared. 11.22pm Eion Standard Time. I'm sorry Kel. She's dead."

The machine was screaming and Kel awoke to find Dr Samson in the room turning a dial to turn the volume down. "Welcome back little one. You had us worried there for a while. Kel, what's the matter you look white as a sheet."

Kel sat up. "Just a nightmare."

Kyla turned her head to look at him. "Again, are you sure there's nothing on you?"

Kel looked puzzled. "What do you mean?"

Dr Samson raised an eyebrow and picked up a scanner. He ran it over Kel and then ran it over him again. "Hold on a minute, there is something. I'm detecting something in your blood. It could be an after effect of that drug they gave you."

Kel swore. "Great, so now I'm going to get nightmares as well. All part of the devoted Follower service I suppose."

Samson looked at the scanner. "We'll get Rennon onto it as soon as we can. I'm going to sedate you both so that you can recover and so that you Kel can get some good non-nightmare disturbed sleep."

When he was sure that Kel was asleep the doc left him to work on Rennon who lay there moaning. "Will you shut up, I can't give you any more painkillers and I've got to move those ribs back where you've moved them out of line again. Well did you manage to talk to Kel?"

Rennon gave him a knowing smile. "I was going to try what we said, you know making out I was after her but I think they've spoken. Its more complicated than we first thought. She's hiding something, or at least not talking about something. Then again we all have a past don't we?"

The doc looked concerned. "Kel's going to take something like that hard. He's very black and white about things. We've got another problem there. There are after effects of that drug. I'm going to need you to work on one of the bio-scanners using the new information we have. He's having nightmares, no doubt he'll be getting paranoid and her being evasive on top of that is going to play on his mind."

Rennon moaned and held his side. "Get me out of here and I'll get on it. We can't make her tell but you could talk to her. Kel not only sees things in black and white, he's a potential loose cannon if he's upset. We don't need that."

The doc smiled. "Now relax, that's it done. The ribs are straight again and you are strapped up. The pain should ease off in a minute or two. Relax and it will make it easier. Look I'm going to put you out for an hour or two, it will help the bones set, these first few hours are essential."

Rennon looked up at him with a strained expression. "Ok, makes sense."

The doc ran the scanner over him and drew off the right amount of clear liquid from a bottle he had taken from the cabinet, injected him and Rennon drifted off into a dreamless sleep.

The Argo sped through space, the auto pilot compensating for planets and asteroids that got in the way. They were followed until they came to the edge of the territory and then the ship turned back and left them to it. The ship sped on for a month until it came into the orbit of a small green and blue planet and the proximity alarm went off to alert the passengers that they had arrived.

Rennon, Kel and Kyla made their way to the cockpit. Kel sat in the pilot's chair, Kyla in the co-pilots and they waited to be hailed. Nothing came. After about an hour Kel adjusted the intercom, still nothing. They looked at each other and activated the off ship scanner and waited.

The figures flashed up on the screen. There were life signs but there was no technology. It was a totally technology free planet.

Kel sat back into his chair. "Ok, so now what do we do? If we land there we could cause an absolute panic."

Kyla thought for a moment. "I doubt we're the first to arrive but we don't actually need to land. There's a moon over there, if we land on the far side of that we can probably manage to do the repairs using the gravity suits. It is a basic weld. Hold on, a weld, we need oxygen for that or do we have one of those bubble units, I can't remember what they are called. You know, the ones that form around the worker and make a bubble of breathable air to work in outside."

Kel tapped some buttons. "Hold on, I'll check the stock list for the hold. Yes, I think we do. Good idea, at least it's a chance to fix the hull. I'll take us down, hold on."

Kel took the ship off of autopilot and engaged the cloaking device. He then took the ship around the moon and took it down to land very gently. He barely kissed the moon's surface, the lock down clamps held them and they were landed.

Kyla smiled. "Well done, that was a beautiful landing."

Kel smiled back. "Well thank you, one of my better ones. We're locked down so I'll go and get that suit on. Could you hold the fort here? I would like someone watching the controls if I'm going outside, just in case."

Kyla looked nervous and caught his arm as he was getting up. "Be careful. Are you going to take any of the Marines with you?"

Kel smiled. "I always am careful. No, its not a combat mission and it might be easier to do it on my own. See you in a while." He left the cockpit without looking back and the door swished closed behind him. He strode down the corridor, trying to ignore the fluttery nervous feeling he had inside. He hadn't wanted to admit it to Kyla but he hadn't done a space walk before and doing one on his own for the first time was not the ideal way to go about it.

The hold was neatly laid out with everything on shelves and well labelled. He was able to locate the suit fairly quickly. He took it out of its packaging and carefully climbed into it, checking all the pipes and running the checks that he could. He took a deep breath and walked to the airlock. He stepped inside and closed the door behind him. He activated the gravity unit on the suit and stood in front of the door leading out into space and tried to concentrate on what he had to do next. He took his safety line and clipped it onto the hook just beside the door. He then pressed the door open button. The air hissed as it escaped when the outer door slipped silently open and he stepped out onto the moon surface. The grey soil was dusty and he left a deep imprint as he walked. The gravity suit kept him pinned to the moon's surface as if there was gravity on the planet. He was carrying the portable bubble as Kyla had called it and his welding tools, all carefully strapped together and he walked around the ship for a short distance until he came to the hole.

It looked much worse from the outside. The metal was peeled back like a skin and he could see the back of the table pressed up against the hole. They had been lucky as it barely fitted over the blast hole.

He could just about reach so he clamped a second safety line to the hull of the ship and took out the bubble. It had a black control box and was like a large tent when inflated but he had to get it that way first. He took it out of its bag, the bag itself began to float away and he only just caught it and tied it to his belt. He then held onto one edge of the bubble and the rest of it floated out into space. It had black sensors around its edge and when he activated it, wherever the sensors touched they stuck. That meant they stuck to him, the ship, the floor, his equipment and he had to turn it off and start all over again. He had better luck the next time and managed to seal the bubble tent around himself and the atmosphere ran thorough it so he was able to work.

The welding tool flared brightly in the darkness of space. The lights on his helmet were dull in comparison. It took a moment for his eyes to adjust and for the visor of his helm to blacken until it was shielded enough for him to carry on but soon enough he was welding the sheets of metal that had peeled away back where they belonged. He then put the patch on, a cunning device which measured the hole and poured liquid metal over it which sealed like a skin, impenetrable and secure.

He was just finishing the welding when something hit the bubble from behind him. The air hissed out immediately as the bubble tore under the pressure of the gas inside which now had an escape route. As the gas escaped the bubble collapsed around him. A second missile hit him on the back of the head, hard.

Thankfully his helmet had taken the brunt of the blow but he couldn't see what had hit him or who. The opaque bubble was now completely wrapped around him and he lost his balance. As he fell the gravity suit tried to compensate and malfunctioned so he was flung out into space. The safety rope pulled taut but held and he was able to grab it through the cloth and pull himself back upright. The gravity suit compensated again and he was standing on the moon surface, tied to the ship, wrapped in the bubble again. He was beginning to panic, his breathing was rapid and he could feel the adrenaline rushing through his system making his thoughts irrational. He tried to tell himself they were irrational, he had air, he was linked to the ship and the airlock. All he had to do was to unwrap himself and he needed to be calm to do that. The more the panic set in the more he wrapped himself up in the cloth.

He stood for a moment and let the cloth settle. The lack of gravity made it float away from him and the calmer he was the more he was able to let it do that. Finally he saw a gap in the cloth, grabbed it and managed to pull the cloth down over him and to stand on it even though it was still caught around his safety rope. He wasn't taking any chances, he bundled it up and tucked it under his arm, grabbed the pack of tools and turned off the welding tool which snaked around him. Fortunately it had a safety cut out so it was only lit while he was holding it, as soon as he had let go the flame had been extinguished.

He took a deep breath, calmed himself and unclipped the safety rope from the ship. As it floated away from the loop he had used he didn't wait. He strode as quickly as he could to the airlock, leapt inside and hit the door closed button, just managing to pull the cloth out of the way of the closing door. The airlock re-pressurised and the air was pumped back in. He hit the internal door open key and leapt inside. He didn't wait to get back to the storeroom in the hold, he tore the suit off of himself where he stood and left it in a pile on the floor. He leant against the closed airlock door and shut his eyes. He looked down at his hands, he was physically shaking and his head was pounding.

It took a while for his breathing to go back to normal and for him to calm down. When he was able he scooped up the equipment and returned to the hold and stashed it away. He then almost ran back to the cockpit where Kyla was waiting, her eyes were wild, her hair messed up where she had been running her hands through it.

She didn't give him a chance to speak, she leapt towards him and hugged him so tightly he thought she was going to push the air out of his lungs. Then it hit him, he was alive, he had survived. "Hey you little one. Come on, don't worry, I'm fine." He cradled the back of her head with his hand and as she stepped away he bent down and kissed her hard on the mouth.

Kyla took a deep breath as he backed away. "I'm glad you are alive. We're locked down for the night out there now. I've put the shields up and we should be ok. You got hit by a small meteor storm. The gravity on your suit must have attracted it. You were lucky, if the rocks had been any bigger you might have had your helmet cracked."

Kel smiled back. "I just got lucky. We'll leave it at that. Rennon suggested that we went and took a look at that planet tomorrow."

Kyla laughed. "You just can't leave a planet alone can you?"

The next morning the shuttle hovered slightly and went into stealth mode as it left the ship. Rennon and Kel were in the control seats, Kyla sat behind them. They circled the planet and hovered as closely as they could without risking being heard or the effects of them being there being noticeable.

They hovered over a small town. The sun bleached wooden buildings looked dusty though the women were out with their brooms in brightly coloured long full skirted dresses and bonnets. The school house was brimming with life, there were children playing around it, the church was neatly kept as was a small graveyard to the back of it. The main street was a corridor of shops, a saloon, whore house and livery stable with a corral at the back, as well as many other shops. Each shop had its own veranda and there were people sitting on chairs outside watching the passers by.

Kyla put a hand on Rennon's shoulder. "Now that can't be right, look over there at that water tower. You would expect something like that but look at what it's made of. That is stainless steel, they haven't even made any attempt to hide it. It just looks out of place."

Rennon began tapping keys on his scanner and then he waited. "As you have guessed, there is a pulse coming to that tower and a pulse of a different frequency leaving it and covering the whole town. It seems to be something sonic, too high pitched for us to hear but it is analysing as something on a par with brainwaves."

The only transport seemed to be horse and cart or horseback and the street was busy. Carts carrying goods pulled by farm horses trotted up and down the street until they pulled up at the store or went to the warehouse. An elegant lady was just alighting from a well kept, polished black landau. She had a driver and a footman on the back, the footman jumped down, lifted down a step for her and helped her down onto the veranda and she disappeared into the Bank.

People seemed to know each other, they waved in a friendly way and there were groups of women deep in conversation.

Just outside town they spotted something in a clearing. It was surrounded by a small coniferous woodland. It was a covered wagon which had just pulled up in the centre of the clearing. It wasn't the wagon as such that was interesting. It was the antennae array on the roof. Anyone from the ground wouldn't have spotted it but from above it was clearly visible. Rennon had spotted it and was hovering overhead so that they could watch what was going on. The driver got down and began to unbuckle the harness. He hobbled his horse and went back to the wagon.

Rennon was tapping keys. "I'm getting a vague reading from that wagon, there's technology in there alright. I can't tell what type but there is a low residual reading and the occasional stronger pulse which links up with that tower in town. I'm analysing the output and it looks as though it is the same. So we have our source and its destination, now all we need to do is work out what it is doing."

Kel strained in his seat. "If he'd just pull back that door we might be able to get a look inside. If we can find out what sort of equipment it is and possibly sabotage it then we may be able to break their control here if this is a controlled planet."

Rennon was working on the magnification on the lower camera. "I don't think so, not at the angle we'd be able to get to and the trees that are in the way."

Kyla was standing behind them out of her seat trying to get a good view. "Well, I'm for going down there and taking a good look. We don't know what sort of equipment it is and we don't have to assume that its something detrimental. It is low development around here, we are into territory that the Followers haven't taken over yet. You said that yourself. Ok, I'd guess that he's a Follower or something like that. If he's not then we don't need to worry about it or bother him."

Rennon flicked a switch. "Now I see, take a look at that. He's what they used to call a snake oil salesman. He's put out his board, look there and on the back of the wagon, he's got out his bottles. That is cunning, come in selling medicines, which isn't going to be hard on a back water planet like this and put the drug in the medicine."

Kel sat back in his chair. "Definitely worth a look but we'll have to do this carefully. Can we sort out a place to land?"

Rennon flipped some buttons on the console. "I can but we'll have to look to what we're wearing first. We can't just walk in there as we are."

Kyla looked down at her boiler suit. "You have a good point there, let's get back to the Argo and get something from the costume locker."

Back on the ship they walked down the lines of outfits neatly covered in clear plastic dust covers. They were hung on rails in lines up to the ceiling controlled by a keypad which would bring down the rail of the era or planet or type the enquirer was looking for. Kyla keyed in "Cowboy Earth, Mid West" and the bars began to rotate.

Rennon looked along the row of the men's outfits and ran his fingers over uniforms, suits, shirts and trousers. "So who are we going to be then? I'd say something low key, farm hands perhaps? Maybe we should think about being prospectors? Hold on." He pulled his laptop out and keyed in their location and pulled up what information they had on the planet. "I should have done this first. Alright, so we have a low technology planet, the main trade is grain and lumber, silver is the main currency and most of it has been milled into coins. We have silver coins but they are minted for other planets, we don't have any currency for this one. That planet is Xathuron. We're in the Oberarth Galaxy just past the Exinian Nebular. It's part of the Retorian Confederation, a group of planets colonised from Earth in the early 1800s. I'll check the history as that seems a bit strange, oh no, wait a minute, no its not. There was a group of Founding Fathers who were on a ship bound out of Northampton England. Their ship got caught on a Eion storm when a pleasure cruiser piloted by a bunch of drunken teenagers broke the time and space treaty and dropped out of the time corridor above them. As the cruiser had been seen and the vortex it created was sinking the ship the crew were taken on board with beaming technology and stowed in the hold. The crew beamed them down here with all their equipment, tools and possessions and left them believing they had found the New World, which they had of course, but not in the way they meant. Apparently it caused quite a stink on the cortex and was one of the instances cited when it was made illegal to use the time corridors for anything other than essential travel. That brought on the research into Eion Star Drives and using the gaps between the dimensions rather than the Eastioninian Drives which used travelling faster than the speed of light to trigger the Drive. Eion Star Drives are more controlled than the more haphazard Eastioninian Drives."

Kel looked as though he'd lost the plot. "So, they could have technology but they have chosen not to or they haven't developed it yet?"

Rennon tapped more keys. "No, they are under the protection of the Retorians who keep this group of planets protected. If we go down there it will be in direct violation of about a gazillion laws but if we leave it, well if that is a Follower then they have a problem."

Kel smiled. "Then why don't we just blast him now. A quick pinpointed bolt would vaporise him, the village folk would know nothing."

Rennon glared at him. "No, for one thing we may be able to pick up something useful from that wagon, who knows what he's got in there."

Kel's smile faded and he shrugged. "Come on then, what can we get away with?"

Rennon tapped his keyboard and some pictures came up.

Kel smiled, "Well my choice isn't hard, Kyla, looks like you are in for an uncomfortable time, look at those corsets. Rennon your choice might be more difficult, how about a suit?"

They wandered down the rails, pulling clothing off, holding the costumes up against themselves in front of the mirror and then moving on. Finally all three had made their mind up with a lot of comparing, decision changing and general trying on of clothing.

Rennon was indeed dressed smartly in a black, slim fitting slightly thread bare suit with a bowler hat. Kyla was plainly dressed in a brown faded cotton dress with matching bonnet that had seen better days but looked cared for. Kel looked comfortable in buckskin, it wasn't much different to his usual mode of dress but his hair was straightened and he had gained his feathers back.

They cloaked the Hopper and landed in a clearing about a mile from town. There were no human tracks anywhere near it so they locked up and carefully wandered off to town.

The sun was blazing and almost directly above them and it was early afternoon when they walked into town, each carrying a bag. They aroused a fair amount of interest but in a friendly way as the locals waved and they got the occasional "Welcome stranger."

They hadn't taken into account how difficult it would be to actually move about the town. They were constantly jostled, they had to jump out of the way of wagons and they generally had to pick their way very carefully along the road. Kel pointed towards a store and they all headed that way. When they got there Kel went in first, he pushed the door open and a brass bell rang.

The store was well stocked with all manner of vegetables, material and other goods all carefully displayed. The place was pristinely neat and tidy. The inside had been freshly painted white and the goods were well dusted. The floorboards were well worn but they had obviously been scrubbed as clean as was possible and swept regularly. By the counter there was a table of freshly baked cakes and bread which immediately caught Rennon's interest.

The woman behind the counter was in her early twenties, her dark brown hair immaculately curled under her bonnet. Her skin was remarkably milky white and her steely blue eyes took every part of them in as they walked through the door. Kel stepped up to the counter. "Do you trade?"

The woman looked him in the eye which was difficult as she was about two feet shorter than him. She was delicately built, almost bird like but she pulled herself up to her full height and put her hands on the counter to balance. "I do if you have something worth trading."

Kel pulled a bag from his pocket and laid out various pieces of tribal silver jewellery he had taken from the costume store. He smiled as the woman's face lit up. "So, what would you give me for these?"

The woman picked the pieces up and turned them over in her hand then laid them out in front of herself so she could look at them together. "I'll give you five silver for them."

Kel smiled. "I'd need at least ten. That is fine workmanship."

The woman picked one piece up. "It is indeed fine workmanship, I'll give you seven."

Kel's smile faded and he made to pick the pieces up.

The woman looked a little nervous and shifted her weight. "Alright, I'll give you ten but that could be more than they are worth. I like them and you have an honest face." She took a small key that was hanging on a chain around her neck and unlocked the big wooden box that was firmly bolted to a table behind her. She counted out the silver and placed it in Kel's hand which she cupped in her other hand and closed his hand on the money. He made to move away but she had put her other hand over the top of his. "We don't get strangers in town often, I hope you will have an enjoyable stay and if there is anything I can do to make it a bit more comfortable, just let me know." She patted his hand and then let his hand slip from hers. She looked up at him and he saw fear in her eyes. In hesitating for a moment he noticed a reflection in a well polished cooking pot. There was a man behind the screen to his left. He wasn't able to see details as the curve of the pot distorted the image.

Kel opened his hand and looked at the coinage, counting quickly, there were ten coins there. "Thank you, I'll keep that in mind. You have a lovely store here madam."

The woman beamed a smile that said it all. "Why thank you, I try my best."

Kel looked around. "Not that you have any competition, well except for the wagon that pulled up outside the town."

The smile faded from the woman's face again. "That would be Nathan the Medicine Man. He visits here regularly." He saw the fear in her eyes and the man behind the screen shifted his weight. She cast a nervous sideways glance at the screen.

Kel's brow furrowed. "Thank you for the trade. If I get any more I will be sure to bring them to you."

178

Once outside Rennon stepped up beside Kel. "That was tidy. I liked the link."

Kel looked down at him. "I'm not comfortable about any of that. She is hiding something."

Kyla looked stunned. "How do you know?"

Kel kept walking. "Because she wasn't on her own in that room, there was a man behind the screen. She was nervous and she paid me way over the odds for those trinkets. The clasping of the hands meant that she was hopeful of some help. Her body language was nervous, she is frightened of something. I also smelt aftershave. Looking around that place she does not sell anything like that. It's a branded type from the Centurion Moons of Elakor. I know it specifically as I had a bottle of it once." Sadness came into his eyes as he remembered the day his wife had given him the small box carefully wrapped with shiny silver paper. It had been their first anniversary and their first child was on the way. He had associated that smell with the happy days that followed and smelling it again brought back that memory.

Kel handed Rennon the money. "Other places may not be so accommodating with my sort. If they are anything like the people they became when they landed on their new world on Earth. Trappers are probably welcome at the store but in the Saloon they probably prefer more genteel types. Rennon, you'd better handle the finances."

Rennon took the silver and looked at the coins. "You could be right. But you know I just took all that on face value, I'd have walked out happy with a good trade. If there is more going on here then we'd better take a look around. Shall we visit the Saloon and then take a walk out to visit that travelling salesman?"

The saloon bar was virtually empty. There was an old be-bearded scruffy looking prospector type sitting in one corner with a glass of whiskey in front of him looking very contented. Three well dressed be-suited gentlemen looked up from their card game. The piano was closed up, a small vase of flowers placed on top of it. A group of five farm labourers were sitting by the window, plates of food in front of them and the bartender was washing his glasses in a bucket of water on the bar.

The saloon itself was dusty, the floor was covered in a layer of dust from the road mixed with grubby sawdust and the tables were covered in stains of spilled beer. There was a huge glass mirror behind the bar but the shelves which showed up the dust marks of bottles that had been removed were almost empty. Two bottles of whiskey sat on the bottom shelf and a row of dust harbouring empty bottles had been placed randomly along the top shelf. The walls had been painted red but they had seen better days and the stairs going up sported a threadbare red carpet which had suspicious brown stains on it.

The three pushed the swinging half doors open. The main storm doors were wide open and fixed back on the outside. Rennon stepped in first, then Kel who took a quick look back to make sure that Kyla was following him inside. As the bar was so quiet they caught everyone's attention. The farm hands watched them while chewing their mouthfuls of food. The barman tucked the cloth he had been wiping glasses with into the belt around his slightly grubby once white apron and put the bucket on the floor.

The barman smiled as they approached. "Welcome to my humble establishment."

Rennon put on a smile. "Thank you, we'd like drinks."

The barman set up two glasses on the bar. When they looked surprised he smiled. "You are new here, women are forbidden to drink, it's virtually a hanging offence if the Temperance League catch you. Its difficult enough for us men. My last shipment never arrived, they found the wagon just outside town and the farmer who was bringing the cases in was found in a gulley about half a mile away with his skull cracked open. Since then I've had real trouble finding someone to fetch it."

Rennon smiled sympathetically. "I can see why. What do I owe you sir?"

The barman put the bottle back on the shelf. "That would be two silver."

Rennon paid him and took a sip of the whiskey which was very rough. "As you say we're new here. Is there anything else we need to know?"

The barman smiled and leant on the bar, his pleasure at being asked very obvious. "Well, it's a quiet place and unnecessary violence is frowned upon. We have about a hanging a week but that is mostly farm hands coming in and getting leery and causing trouble. The Sheriff is hard on any sort of crime, most are punishable by hanging or a good long time in the lock up which can end up as the same thing. As you can imagine we don't have much crime here. The biggest crime around here used to be not going to see the padre on a Sunday, now that the new religion has come that's no longer a crime but just about everything else is." He looked nervous and froze on the spot when he noticed one of the gentlemen in the card game listening far too intently to what he was saying. "Anyway, if you keep your noses clean, go about your business and don't trouble anyone none, you'll be fine."

Rennon had noticed his nervous sideways glance towards the card player and could see him through his reflection in the mirror. "Well, thank you, we're peaceable folk just fixing to spend a while then be on our way." He picked up his glass, Kel followed suit and then went to a table by the window after giving each other a nervous knowing look.

Kyla joined him sitting by the window. "How about we see if we can hire some horses from the Livery and take a ride around? I haven't been riding in years."

Rennon cast a worried look at Kel. Kel smiled. "A bit of a look around sounds good to me. The scenery is spectacular."

The street was busy outside and they had to dodge their way between carts, riders and people walking. The Livery Stable was at the end of the street. Rennon went in first and took a look around. There were quite a few horses in there and as he knew nothing about horses they all looked fine to him. The Livery owner was mucking out and he saw them coming in. He leant on his broom and tipped his Stetson hat at them. "Afternoon gentlemen and lady. Are you bringing horses in or would you like to borrow some?"

Rennon smiled at him. "Afternoon, we'd like to borrow some if you have something quiet. We'd like to ride around the area as the lady here would like to see the scenery on horseback."

They rode out on the horses and they were quiet as promised. They did what they were told and the three trotted down the street and out of town. Once out of town Rennon scanned them. "We're clear. We can talk. Well, it looks like the Followers have a foothold here."

Kyla was looking at the scenery. "I just had a nasty thought. You've already had some whiskey here, how do you feel?"

Kel looked worried. "I hadn't thought about that but I would assume that if the Followers don't want the whiskey in town they wouldn't supply it so they couldn't tamper with it. I feel fine and I still think that they are the scum of the planets."

Kyla's brow furrowed.

Kel smiled. "Come on, what are you thinking about?"

Kyla smiled and relaxed. "I was just thinking that I wonder what the effects of alcohol are on the drug if they are using it? I know it could be a religious belief that they don't like people drinking but alcohol makes people more "liberated", perhaps there is something in it?"

Rennon thought for a moment. "You could have something there, I'll work on that one."

They pulled the horses together in a line and looked out over a river valley. The village was behind them and in front of them were wide open spaces. They were in a river valley, the river was way down and very little water flowed down the wide river cutting which meandered in huge loops along the valley floor which rolled away until it met the mountains. The grass was dry and slightly yellow the bushes looked drought starved.

Rennon steadied his horse. "Shall we go and take a look at what Nathan the snake oil salesman is getting up to? We might be able to get some sort of an idea of what is really going on."

Kel turned his horse. "Sounds like a plan." He tilted his Stetson hat forward and kicked his horse on into a gallop. The black paint pony mare jumped forwards at his first touch, put her head up and galloped away. Her nostrils flared and she pranced and bucked slightly.

Rennon turned his horse to follow. His black gelding was reluctant but soon caught up with Kel. Kyla turned her bay gelding and he hardly needed telling, he was happy to be off after the others.

Nathan was sitting on a chair outside his caravan, feet on a stool, hat pulled down over his face. His stubble was more than a week in the growing and a cigarette hung out of the side of his mouth. His greasy black hair had more than a smattering of grey. His brown duster coat hung on the door of the wagon as his grimy white shirt and brown waistcoat was more than enough in the heat. A fly landed on him and he moved his hand to bat it away then he leant back and closed his eyes again, coughing slightly. He opened his eyes a slit and looked around, the fly was back and annoying him.

He had put his sales board out advertising "Dr Jones' Wonder Elixir, just one silver a bottle. You can't put a price on good health". His horse was quietly grazing as he began to set his store out. There was the platform on the front of his wagon.

Kel circled around the back of the wagon. The back door was slightly ajar and he was able to get to the stairs unnoticed. The horse looked at him, its ears went back but he continued eating, twisting the long grass around his tongue and pulling it into his mouth and biting it off before chewing contentedly. The stairs looked as though they would creak so Kel opened the door slightly with his knife blade, controlling the swing so that it made no sound. It opened without any problem and he was able to see inside.

To the right there was a control panel which was high tech, it had a communications array and something else that he couldn't recognise. Clothes were strewn everywhere and the place smelt of unwashed clothing, cigarette smoke, rotten wood and a distinctive herbal spicy smell.

As Kel turned the salesman woke up. He was on his feet in a flash and had his gun drawn. Kyla reacted with similar speed and before Nathan could get a shot off she had a knife to his throat and was pushing him back down into his chair. "Pleased to meet you Nathan. Now drop it." Nathan let his gun drop onto the floor and Kyla kicked it away. "There's a good boy now just a few questions if you don't mind and I'm sure you won't if you like breathing."

Nathan opened his mouth his rotten teeth blackened and yellow stained from the cigarettes. His eyes were wide with terror. Rennon leapt from where he had been hiding and wandered over. The man's eyes moved from one to the next. "What do you want to know?"

Kyla nearly gagged, the man smelt of body odour and cigarettes. "Where did you come from?"

Nathan looked bemused. "I came from Dogwood, it's about ten miles from here." He smiled as if he thought he was being smart.

Kyla moved the knife on his throat. "I'm not used to questioning and I could lose my temper, or slip so I would advise you to try to interpret what I'm asking in the most favourable way for me to get the answers I want. Then we can end this amicably and you can go on your way. Let's put it another way, where do you get your medicine and what is that equipment in your wagon for?"

Nathan's smile faded. "Well little lady." Kyla glared at him and he swallowed nervously. "Sorry, force of habit. I pick up my boxes from a drop ship just south of Reahaven and I follow a route which covers the towns in this sector. I was doing pretty poorly until I found this new supplier. Now the people can't get enough of it. It flies out of the boxes and I then go back, get more and off I go again. The equipment in my wagon was part of the deal. I can't work it but I make sure the lights are all flashing and use the switch at the end to tell them if there is a problem. It has been working just fine, well until now. They didn't tell me what it was for."

Rennon was already in the back of the wagon taking a look at the equipment. He called out. "I think he may be telling the truth, this equipment is all set on auto run, it doesn't need any input to keep it going."

Nathan smiled and his eyes brightened up a bit. "Yes, they check it when they give me the delivery and they said I was doing a good job."

Kyla smiled and moved the knife off of his throat, keeping it within sight. "I wouldn't like a nasty accident. Now, you are going to be...". She didn't finish her sentence as Nathan made a lunge for her and instinct took over, she cut his throat in a smooth movement and he fell back into his chair, holding his throat and choking as his blood flowed down his shirt and his eyes went blank.

Kyla wiped her knife on his shirt. "Damn it, I thought he was co-operating."

Rennon stuck his head out of the wagon. "He was but he wasn't altogether telling the truth. I found these in his wardrobe." Rennon pulled out a Follower Priest's cassock. "It seems old Nathan there is living a double life. I'd check his wrist if I were you."

Kyla undid his cuff and pulled his sleeve up. Strapped to his arm was a control panel with a stunner attached. "Good job I got him then, that is a contact stunner, if he'd touched me things would have been very different. So what do we do now?"

Kel was checking under the wagon and Rennon was franticly typing on the keypad. "Its rigged to blow, there's a failsafe attached to the life signs scanner. If I can just override it, it would be very useful to have this equipment, we could learn a lot. There you go and five seconds to go, the man's a genius." He stepped out of the wagon and beamed a smile at Kyla. "Now we have ourselves a transmitter and hopefully some interesting information on the hard drive and if we are lucky and I analyse this" he held up a Medicine Bottle "we might just have something here. I say that we use the hoist on the Hopper to take this whole wagon back to the Argo, we can dismantle it there. We'll lose matey boy along the way but I don't know what to do about the horse."

Kyla went over to the black horse which was quietly eating grass. He looked up when she came over, one ear forwards, curious. "Are there any facilities for keeping animals on the ship? We seem to come to these low tech planets often enough."

Rennon laughed. "You want to keep him don't you? Well we have room in the cargo hold and we hit dirtside enough times to pickup hay and feed. It all depends on how he takes to space travel."

Kel wandered over. "Why not, if he kicks the hell out of the Hopper on the way up we'll know he's not going to be a good crew member but you can clear up the mess. What's this, little girl wanted a pony?"

Kyla smiled. "No, not really, part way practical as we've got to make this man disappear and I'm not sure where the horse would go if we set him loose. I do like him and having our own low tech transport would make sense. If we're taking the wagon with us why not make the most of it. Lets face it if we come to other towns like this and have to stay a while we can't stay in the Saloons."

Kel looked quizzical. "What do you mean?"

Kyla smiled. "Because if they are putting something in the food and water that means that we can't eat or drink in any place that we stop. So having our own wagon means we don't have to."

Kel smiled broadly. "Alright, the horse can stay but you can get him into the Hopper. Get that horse and we'll hook him up. Rennon give me a hand getting the body inside and packing his things up."

They picked the prone body up and put it inside the wagon, picked up the sign and packed that inside as well. Kyla had managed to get the horse and was holding it in front of the shafts. She stood at his head, holding both of the reins to keep him steady. The men then pushed the carriage forward until Kyla was able to run the harness onto it and once hooked on Rennon jumped up and took the reins.

Kel leapt up beside him. "Take the wagon there, onto the stony ground. When we're on solid ground we can pick it up from there."

Rennon returned to the Hopper, jumped on board, and started the pre flight. As he brought the cloaked hopper down, Kyla calmed the rather stunned horse. The Hopper uncloaked and she led the calm horse up the ramp into the crew hold of the Hopper and tied him to one of the bars at the end. He seemed curious rather than afraid but stamped a little as the ramp raised behind him. She stroked his nose and he calmed down. They took off and hovered and Rennon let down the clamps, hovered over the wagon and clasped it securely with them. To be sure Kel took some chains and strapped the wagon to the clamps. He had to climb up the wagon and the clamp and around the side of the Hopper.

Kel climbed down and while Kyla and Rennon flew the cloaked hopper and its cargo off back to the Argo he removed all sign of what had happened

184

while leaving the wagon tracks heading off until they disappeared onto stony ground.

14

Kel had begun to pace the clearing. He had gone through it all in his mind over and over, he'd been trying to plan what was going to happen next but somehow he couldn't focus. Then it had started to rain. It had been a real torrential downpour and he had nothing with him to build a makeshift shelter. All he had was his cotton duster coat and what little shelter the trees provided. He had watched the storm clouds come over from the East, slowly rolling across the open plain towards him and then it arrived. The rain was at least warm but by the time he saw a slight disturbance in the clouds above and realised the others were back he was soaked to the skin. His buckskins hung heavy on him, clinging and very uncomfortable. His feathers hung limply, tangled with his bedraggled hair.

Rennon flew through the storm, it effected the electrics in the Hopper slightly but not enough to make a real difference. The rain lashed against the front screen making it hard to see but he was patient, bided his time and waited until he was absolutely certain both by what he saw and what the readouts were saying. Then he glided the Hopper down and landed it smoothly in the clearing. He scanned immediately on landing even though the scanners had been doing their job all the way down and when they landed he knew exactly where Kel was and was able to drop the ramp so that Kel could run inside out of the rain.

Kel stood in the Hopper bay, dripping on the floor. Kyla threw him a towel and he began drying himself off. She smiled. "I wouldn't worry too much about drying off here, we've got to get those horses back pretty soon and we'll be riding through that storm to get there. So, what are we going to do? Do we ride into town, drop the horses off and leave or are we planning to stay?"

Kel grunted and dried his hair. "I'd say we should take a better look around the town and if we disappear now they might start asking questions when Nathan disappears as well. Why not go back to town, get rooms and see what we can find out. With Nathan gone there is going to be a gap in the supply. Shall we find out what happens next?" He took his coat off and shook it.

Kyla took a step back. "I'd like to take a better look around the town too. The Followers obviously have a foothold but if we can break it now it is going to be a lot easier than when they get more established."

Rennon looked thoughtful. "OK, well we could give it a look. We do have to take the horses back. So what is the story going to be this time? We didn't have to introduce ourselves much last time and if we are staying the night we'll have to be more specific."

Kel raised an eyebrow.

Rennon smiled wryly. "Well, for one thing I would expect they have very definite views on couples who are not married sharing rooms."

Kel coughed.

Rennon smiled at him. "Well I had to say it. There's no point us getting into the Saloon and then there is a problem. We've got to get our stories straight. Are you going in there as husband and wife again or Kyla would you like me to step in this time." He gave Kel a very knowing smile, his eyes glinting with mischief.

Kel growled. "Well it worked well last time." He looked at the floor. "I noticed that the woman in the shop wore a wedding ring so that is traditional here too."

Kyla looked from one to another. "I have no jewellery."

Kel's expression went blank. He reached around his neck and pulled a small buckskin pouch that had been hanging down inside his shirt. He opened the pouch and tipped out two gold bands, one slightly larger than the other. Kel looked at them and clasped them in his fist. He looked at her, his eyes had a lost look. He slipped the larger ring on his finger, it was a perfect fit, and took the other one. "Give me your hand."

She held out her hand left hand and he slipped the ring onto her finger. He wrapped his hand around hers and she looked up at him. He coughed. "She would understand." He smiled and Kyla relaxed. "So, shall we be husband and wife again?"

Kyla grinned. "Why not?"

He put an arm around her. "So, Rennon are you going to be her brother or mine?"

Rennon smiled wickedly. "I'll be hers, then I can get at you disapprovingly if you treat her badly."

Kel grinned. "I won't ."

Rennon winked at him. "You'd better not or you will have me to answer to. Come on then bro in law, lets get this ship locked down, get mounted up and back into town. The sooner we get that ride over the better. Where are the horses?"

Kel turned to go. "I tethered them just behind those trees. They seemed alright about the ship leaving so they should be alright now."

The horses were waiting quietly, eating what they could reach of the grass. Kel untied his and leapt up, the other two followed.

Rennon took point, Kyla beside him and Kel rode behind as they faced the storm. The rain had not let up, it was now getting colder and they were all soaked to the skin by the time they got to the town. They rode straight to the Livery Stable and rode in through the doors.

The owner was waiting for them and he took the horses from them and began drying them off and rubbing them down. "I'd get yourself to the Saloon and dried off if I were you. You don't want to get sick."

Kyla smiled at him. "Thank you, we will. They are good horses."

He patted the one he was drying off on the back. "I know they are, glad you were pleased with them."

Kyla stepped forward again and stroked the horse's nose. "The Saloon is alright then?"

He rubbed the horse down with a dry cloth. "The Saloon is just fine, basic but it is kept well and you will get clean sheets. But, be careful if you are staying in town any length of time. You will probably have already realised that you can't drink in the public bar. It is frowned on for you to be in the Saloon anyway. If you want a drink then your husband will have to take it up to the room for you. If you would like to buy horses to travel on your way I do have three for sale, not these three, I raised these myself but I have three that are fairly quiet and would do you well. For now, have a good night."

Kyla rubbed the horse between his ears and turned and left, the other two went with her.

When they got to the Saloon Rennon went in first. Kel stayed behind him with Kyla close to him. The bar was much more crowded now and they had to push their way to the bar. The barman moved to serve them when it was their turn.

He put two glasses on the bar. "Same as before?"

Rennon nodded. "And a room for me and one for my sister and brother in law."

The barman smiled at Kyla who looked nervous. "My wife takes pride in her rooms, I'm sure you will be comfortable. If you would like your husband to take you upstairs now you may find that more acceptable. It can be very rowdy here at night and a woman in the bar may cause more trouble than any of us would want. You are welcome to buy a bottle." He was looking at Rennon and Kel.

Rennon reached into his pocket. "What do I owe you for a bottle and a night's board? We may want to stay longer but we're not sure at the moment."

The barman was watching a group up the end of the bar. "Five silver would cover it. Rooms six and seven. I would show you to your rooms but I think I'd better keep an eye on what is going on here."

Rennon smiled. "We'll be just fine. I think we'll make our way upstairs now."

The barman put an open bottle and two glasses on the table and palmed a third to Rennon who raised his eyebrow. "Thank you."

The barman nodded and wandered off up the bar to where the farm hands were getting very loud as Rennon backed away from the bar. His space was rapidly filled by other customers and he took Kyla's arm and escorted her to the stairs. They went up straight away without looking back and turned right at the top of the stairs. When they realised they had gone the wrong way they came back and tried left. That was more successful and they found the rooms.

Rennon sat in a chair next to a small table and next to the large bed. The room was indeed very clean and scrubbed until the wood was worn. Kel sat on the bed and Kyla was looking out of the window. Rennon pulled a scanner out of his pocket and scanned the room under the cover of his coat. He looked up. "All clear, no bugs or listening channels."

Kel smiled. "That is good to hear. So we can talk."

Rennon poured three glasses of the whisky. Kyla wandered back to the table and sat on the other chair. She took a glass, the other two took theirs and they clinked their glasses together.

Kel went to the window. "It all looks pretty peaceful out there. There are far less people about now though. It will be dusk soon." He leant against the window frame and looked the other way down the street. "All seems pretty quiet. People are going off to their homes and the shops are shutting. The store is shut now and the Livery Stable is closing its doors."

There was a knock on the door. Kel stepped over and opened the door carefully, his gun drawn and kept just out of sight. Rennon shifted Kyla's glass off the table and put it on the window sill out of sight. As the door swung back it revealed a tiny, slimly built woman. Her hair was tightly pulled back in a bun under her crisp white bonnet. Her apron was starched stiff and pristinely white. She carried a pile of towels.

She waited on the threshold for Kel to invite her in and then she put the towels down on the bed. "Good evening gentleman and lady. Here are some clean towels for you. If there is anything you need, just let me know. I am Martha, you met my husband in the bar. I trust he got you everything that you need."

Rennon stood up. "Thank you, he did."

Martha smiled knowingly. "But I would say he didn't tell you it all. This is going to sound very unusual but we have a strict lock up policy. We lock up at dusk and we do not open up again until dawn. We would also suggest that you keep your windows closed. It should be a cool night after the rain so you won't get too stifling hot. Whatever you do, do not go out at night. We will lock you out and there are some strange folk about the village at the moment."

Kel's interest had been piqued. "What sort of strange folk?"

Martha looked nervous. "They are the sort who would kill you if they catch you outside. Look after your wife as a few women have gone missing in the village. Two or three people a month have disappeared. We lock up our doors at night now. Be careful and good night to you all."

Kyla walked over to the woman and took her arms in her hands. "Thank you for the warning. Was it always like this?"

Martha looked down at her hands, they had become awkward. She was clasping one hand with the other and then she folded her arms and looked straight at Kyla. "It started about a year ago. But thankfully help came and our town is a lot safer now. We have a lot to thank the priests for. There is still some trouble at night but nothing like it was just after a young boy from this village awoke the creatures."

Kyla saw how nervous she was. "Did the boy survive?"

Martha smiled. "I think so."

Kyla smiled at her but there was an intensity. "Haven't you seen him to know if he is alright? Surely this is a small town and everyone seems to know the others and be fairly friendly."

Martha's brow furrowed. "You know, now you come to mention it I haven't seen the boy lately. His family arrived in the town a few months before the troubles happened. My sister has a boy at the school but she didn't mention that he knew this child. I suppose his parents must have moved on. But, that is odd, as we have the Saloon we usually get to hear most gossip. Very odd. Then with the disappearances I suppose we had enough to think about. I had better be getting downstairs as I have the evening meals to start cooking."

Kyla relaxed a little. "Can we have food up here?"

Martha smiled. "Of course dear."

Kel was standing by the window looking out into the street. He grunted and sat down at the table. Rennon was watching the woman intently. She noticed and he smiled. She smiled back and looked away shyly.

Martha turned and left the room. Kyla closed the door behind her and leant against it, listening to make sure that she had gone back downstairs. When she was fairly sure, which was difficult as the sound of conversation from downstairs was quite loud, she opened the door and took a look out into the corridor, it was empty. She closed the door, locked it and turned to the others.

Kel tipped his chair back and put his feet on the table. "Well, it doesn't take a genius to work out what has happened here. Cunning though, very cunning. But what do we do about it?"

Kyla smiled. "Well I think we've made a good start. That little lady is more than likely the village gossip. The seeds of doubt have been sewn. Its not all guns and killing Kel, a bit of subtlety can go a long way."

Kel smiled. "Oh I don't know, I bet it will end up with a shootout."

Rennon smiled back. "I have no doubts that it will. Don't worry about the food, I can scan it to make sure there's nothing in it. So, are we going out tonight to see what those things are?"

Kel took a look out of the window. "Need you ask? We will have a better idea of what is going on if we know what we are up against."

Kyla went and sat on the bed. "Well we're sitting targets here. The balcony out there would give direct access into this room and those windows wouldn't hold anyone out who really wanted to get in. I say we get out of here and onto the street and see if we can hunt the hunter."

Kel smiled and stood up. "Now you are talking."

Rennon stood up. "Unanimous then, we'll wait until it is dark enough to cover us getting out then we'll take a look around. Shall we eat first?"

Kel looked at Rennon. "You know me, I'm always hungry."

Rennon went to the door. "I'll go down and get us something. You can stay here Kel, I don't want trouble."

Kel put on a very fake hurt look. "I don't know what you mean." He closed the door after Rennon had gone out and turned the key. He then turned and leant on the door and looked over at Kyla who was sitting on the bed. "Come here."

Kyla stood up and slowly walked across the room. Kel slipped his arm around her waist and almost lifted her up as he wrapped his other arm around her, bent down and tried to kiss her but she pulled back smiling. He looked disappointed by smiled. "You two had me worried today. I don't like waiting."

Kyla smiled up at him. "I've noticed. We had some trouble getting the horse out of the Hopper and finding somewhere to put it. Rennon wanted to download the information he had as well. You know him. He's easily distracted when there's a terminal around."

Kel smiled back. "Well there was me, stuck in the rain while he played with his terminal, nice."

Kyla smiled. "Well you got a chance to be closer to nature after being cooped up on the space base for so long."

Kel frowned. "Could have been dryer." He went to the window. "Well at least the rain has stopped. We'd better get out of these wet things before we catch something. Would you like a hand."

Kyla turned to glare at him then remembered the dress. "Oh, er, yes thanks."

Kel smiled and opened up the bags and began hanging up clothes for them while Kyla got out of her soaked dress. "It is still a marvel to me how you managed to ride that horse with that on."

Kyla smiled. "It's a wonder to me too but I managed. Probably not how you are supposed to but they'll put that down to us being foreigners and all." She hung the soggy dress over the wardrobe door and pulled off the petticoat.

Kel walked over and began to unlace the corset underneath. "Whoever thought of these things must have had a real wicked streak. That can't be comfortable. How do you breathe?"

Kyla breathed a sign of relief as Kel loosened the strings. "These are the invention of a man who wanted to make sure that women couldn't do much. Still, gives you a great waist."

Kel bent down and bit her neck. "Your waist is just fine."

Kyla froze and stepped back as if something had pushed her. She put a hand on his chest and pushed him away. "Don't, just don't." There were tears in her eyes.

Kel looked surprised. "What have I done? What's the matter Kyla, come on you have to tell me now. Hold on… biting your neck… was that it? Was that what upset you?" He turned away from her and took a deep breath. "Ok, I'll back off. I didn't know you were spoken for."

Kyla flashed a quick sarcastic smile. "I'm not." She shook her head, her curls falling down over her shift. "Some things just cannot be."

Kel turned and grabbed her arm. "Don't play games with me. Tell me straight."

Kyla relaxed and looked up at him, her eyes slightly stony. "Some loves cannot be, some unions cannot be. However both parties may want it otherwise. I've told nobody about this as there's no point. That is the end of it. Baron Joniel has his duty. I have mine. He is a servant of the Dark Lord, I follow the White Lady. He is a Darklaskion, a life sucker. If we were to spend but one night together and if he were to touch me he would not be able to control his true nature and he would not be able to stop himself killing me. Enough reasons?"

Kel looked down at her kindly. "Enough reasons. But you can't be alone forever."

Kyla smiled. "I'm never alone."

Kel looked at her quizzically. "What do you mean?"

Kyla looked up at him. "Before he loved me he bound me to serve him on his ship. That is a life binding. I was just an apprentice then on my first pilgrimage. But then his base was attacked and he was at the point of death. I could and should have left him there but I brought him back and then everything changed. I changed him. I brought him back as I let him drink my blood willingly. As a servant of the White Lady that had an effect on him. The binding he used then cannot be broken and it mutated as our emotions changed. It was created out of something dark, love changed it to something else. That was how I managed to call him when I was at Mission Command.

That is the secret I must keep and now you must also. That is why he walked away from that contract and why he now serves The Prince where in all his thousands of years of life he has never served any man."

Kel put his arms around her and pulled her into a hug. "I understand."

Rennon knocked at the door and Kyla slipped behind the screen taking the dry clothes with her. Kel opened the door and Rennon came in with a tray and three plates of food. "I didn't disturb anything did I?" Kel glared at him and Rennon smiled back cheekily, went to the table and put the tray down.

When they were all in dry clothes they sat around the small table. Rennon had brought in a chair from his room so he didn't have to sit on the bed and they tucked in after he had analysed the food and pronounced it safe to eat. They piled the plates on the tray and left them on the table.

Kel opened the window and slipped out onto the now dark balcony while Rennon moved the lamp to the other side of the room and left it burning on the dresser. Kyla followed Kel out and Rennon stepped out and closed the window. He used Temhold Gum to hold the window shut before joining the others down the balcony. Most of the rooms were in darkness so it wasn't too hard to get to the end of the balcony. Kel climbed over the wooden wall and shinned down the supporting post. Kyla followed him, much relieved to now be wearing trousers and a shirt. Rennon kept watch and then he shinned down as well and joined the others in the shadows around the corner behind a water barrel.

The street was quiet other than the noise coming from the Saloon. The piano player was in full swing and the sound of conversation spilled out onto the street. The door was shut and the curtains were pulled across. There were a few cracks that the light got through but other than that the front of the Saloon was in darkness.

Kel spotted something, across the street and down a side alleyway. Something was moving in the shadows. He had only noticed it as it had moved across a white sign board that was illuminated by the next door house's window. Kel grabbed Rennon's arm. He jumped and only just managed to keep a hold on his weapon. "There's something over there in the shadows, moving towards the street." Kel was off across the street before either of them could stop him. He sprinted across the dusty road, leapt in the air and landed on the shadow and rolled it backwards into the dirt.

The two were locked together in hand to hand combat when Kyla and Rennon got there. The figure was dressed in rags and as Rennon turned his torch on them they saw its face was covered in what looked like a mask. It seemed impossibly strong and Kel was thrown back against the wall and as he recovered his feet and Kyla and Rennon made a dive at him the figure turned with a remarkable turn of speed and disappeared off down the alleyway. Kel had found his feet again and was running, the other two very close behind.

The creature reached the corner of the house and ran around the back, closely followed by the three of them. The alleyway was wider along the back. The residential houses had been built in no particular order and many encroached on what would have been the road. They had to really sprint to keep up with the creature, then when turning a corner they were faced with four more. Now outnumbered Kel slowed a little and let the others catch up and they faced the five in a line.

The creature that had been running stopped just past the other four and turned to join them. Then the four of them rushed forwards. There seemed to be no organisation to their fighting, they were just violent, there was no control. Kel was having a little difficulty as he had ended up with three, Rennon and Kyla had one each.

Kyla got a lucky strike on her one. He flew back into the wall and fell to the ground unconscious. She leapt on him and tied his hands and feet with a cable tie. She then leapt across to help Kel, catching a blow that was aimed at his head with her dagger and almost taking the hand off the creature which screamed but kept fighting, spraying blood onto the dusty ground. Kel had put one of his down, his sword had easily taken its head clean off. The second had been caught on the backswing and was now holding its throat. He then turned and lashed out at the one that Kyla had been helping with. He caught that one across the chest with his sword and it stepped back, winded. This was enough to give Kyla the chance to cut its throat. As it fell to the ground Kel finished off the other one.

It was quiet in the alley. Rennon pulled out his torch. "Well, let's have a look at what these things look like." He felt under the creature's chin and grabbed a hold on the mask. He pulled it firmly upwards and it started to peel off then stopped. The mask was grafted onto the skin and wouldn't go any further. There were tendrils coming from the mask and burrowed into the skin so it looked fibrous. "That is disgusting. That mask has grown onto the face."

Kyla looked away and checked out the alley and all around. Kel knelt down and took out his knife. He began to cut through the threads. A white liquid flowed over the face and splattered onto the floor. He jumped back in time so that he didn't get any over him.

Rennon took out a box from his pocket and started getting samples into the tubes inside. He took skin, blood and the white liquid and the tendrils. He labelled them up and put them into the box and shut it. "Ok, I'm done. I can scan all this when we get back to the room. All we need to do now is get rid of the bodies."

Kel went from one to the next, checking and making sure they were dead. He cut the throat of the cable tied one. Kyla was watching out and was able to warn them when she saw more of these things coming out from the shadows. There were at least twenty of them and they were moving towards them at a frantic rate. Kel and Rennon sprang to their feet and pulled out their blasters. Kyla had her blaster out, set to silent and her red beam of energy cut into one after the other as they closed the gap. By the time what was left of the creatures reached them there were only four left. Kel cut one almost in half as it got to him, badly wounding a second. Kyla sliced her one's head off. Rennon engaged in a frantic exchange of blows before Kel sliced its head off. With a backswing Kel finished the injured one off. They backed away back down the alleyway they had come down and ran across the road. Kel gave Kyla a leg up onto the support to get up onto the balcony. She then lent down and gave Rennon a hand up, she grabbed his arm and helped him up. Kel stepped back and took a run at it, launching himself off of the lower balcony he caught the top balcony and swung himself up.

When they were inside they shut the windows and moved the wardrobe in front of them. It moved easily with all three of them pushing and pulling. They moved it just in time as they heard the glass breaking behind the wardrobe and the sound of something scratching at the back of it. Sharp claw like nails dug into the splintering wood, the wardrobe rocking as the onslaught continued.

The scratching stopped but they didn't relax. They looked at each other and had their blasters ready. The let up wasn't for long as the wardrobe fell forwards and the creatures crashed into the room en masse. The three began franticly firing and the bodies started piling up on the balcony. The creatures seemed to be unthinking, they just kept coming. They climbed over the ones that had already fallen. Then they stopped, it went quiet and the three were left standing there. They stood there for almost half an hour and then moved to the window together and looked out. Everything was still.

They waited but nothing happened. The hours went by but still nothing. Kel got up. "Now we have to tell the owners. Keep vigilant. I'm going downstairs." He went to the door and went outside. The corridor was empty and he then walked down the stairs. The downstairs room was still full of people so he pushed his way through and went to the bar. The barman came over, all smiles, but his smile left his face when he saw Kel's serious look. "You had better come upstairs. There is something you should see."

The bartender followed him upstairs and into the room. He stopped in his tracks, mouth open. When he had recovered his composure he stepped forwards and took a look at the bodies. "I can't believe this. That is Jake, I have seen that jacket a thousand times before he disappeared. All these people, they were the ones that disappeared. What is happening here?"

Kyla stepped forwards and put her hand on his arm and as the bartender collapsed into tears Kyla put her arms around him. "They aren't themselves any more. There is a group of people out there called The Followers and now they have come here. They are your Priests. Where they can't convert people they drug them. Your people have been drugged and turned into these creatures. The Followers have then stepped in to sort out the problem so that you think that they are your saviours."

The barman started walking around the bodies. "I'm going to bring people up here to see this. People need to know. You must come downstairs and speak with them. Will you do that?"

Rennon stepped forwards. "We will. You had better go down first and say what you have seen. We will then come down and explain."

The bartender took a long last look at the bodies on the floor and left the room. The three of them filed out behind him and down the stairs. The bartender stopped on the stairs and shouted. "People, people, you must listen to me. We are being deceived. Our people are being taken and being turned into the creatures that hunt us on the streets. These people have killed some of the creatures, they are upstairs. They were our neighbours and our friends. I have asked our guests to explain what they know."

The bartender looked over to Rennon. "Please, if you would now explain what you told me."

Rennon cleared his throat. "The creatures that hunt your alleyways are indeed your friends and neighbours who went missing. The bartender here has recognised some of them. We are not from this place, we have travelled many lands and seen what these people have done. Wherever they go they seek to convert all they meet. Those who will not convert either disappear or are dealt with harshly. You are seeing here what they do. They have come, turned some of your people into the creatures you will see upstairs. Then they have arrived as your saviours, keeping you safe by keeping you inside at night and keeping you under their control. Go upstairs and see what has been done to your friends and neighbours."

There was a rush to get upstairs and the four of them had to move quickly to get out of the way. The mob rushed into their room and there was a general outcry when they saw the bodies. A voice inside the room raised higher than others. "We cannot allow this to continue, we must stop it, now. Who is with me? We must go to the place where the Followers are staying and we must rid our town of them. Who will come with me?"

Everyone filed out of the room and ran down the stairs. Kel, Kyla and Rennon went back inside and a man looked up. "I am Ewan, the undertaker. It looks like I'm going to have a busy few days."

Rennon sat on the bed and took out his scanner and began to scan the test tubes. "Not that busy. I would suggest that these bodies are burnt. Those face masks are made of a living tissue. Be careful what you touch."

The undertaker stood up. "Well, I'd better get them moved and I'll see if I can't get the minister out of the jail. He is going to be one relieved man." He went down the stairs and they watched him cross the street to the Town Jail.

The mob was on its way down the street and they disappeared around a corner. Kel looked at the other two. "We'd better go help them out. Those Followers may have other weapons in that place."

They ran down the stairs, through the nearly empty bar. The bartender's wife was there along with the Saloon Girls and the elderly pianist. They watched them go past and raised a glass.

Outside the night air was chilled and fresh. The moon was full so the street was well lit. As they rounded the corner the townspeople were pulling the Followers out into the street and tying them up. The bartender was with them. "We will give them a fair trial and a fair hanging if that is the right thing to do."

Kel caught something out of the corner of his eye. The symbols hanging around the Followers necks had started to glow. "Run everyone, there is going to be an explosion."

Most people heard what he screamed and backed away from the bound Followers leaving them in the open square. The fireball caused by the cumulative explosion was ferociously hot and when it died down there was nothing left of the Priests or their building but ash.

It took many days to clear up the debris and Kel and the others stayed to help with the clear up. When they left there was an empty space where the building had been and plenty of plans for what to build in its place.

15

There was a light breeze and the sun was shining down with hardly a cloud in the sky as Kel, Rennon and Kyla galloped their horses across the plain towards the town in the distance. They had dropped their Hopper off in a forest a few miles to the south and had continued on horseback. They were approaching Endar, a surprisingly high technologically advanced world considering the look of the place. With all the advancements the world had remained in a style that was rural and rustic.

From a distance the outer defence walls glimmering white in the sunlight. This was due to the high quartz content in the rocks which had also allowed such advances without the industrialisation that had caused pollution on so many other worlds. It was this advancement that Mission Command were interested in learning more about. Rennon was managing to balance his hand held scanner as well as control his rather feisty horse. The scanner gave off the occasional bleep that was barely audible above the thud of the horses' hooves and their occasional snorting.

Kyla was using all her concentration to hold onto the saddle as she was definitely not used to riding side saddle. With the heavy long dress that was the custom to wear there was no opportunity to ride any other way.

Kel was smiling broadly, he had chosen a white linen loose fitting shirt which was worn outside his trousers and tied with a belt and a black woollen cloak which was rolled up on the back of his horse. Their swords were in keeping with the style of the planet but they had left their blasters behind on the Argo. Guns of any sort were not permitted on Endar and they didn't have any of the pulse emitting crossbows which were the only hand held energy emitting weapons allowable. This was supposed to be a diplomatic mission to speak about technology so they didn't expect much trouble, but then again, trouble did always seem to find them.

Inside the outer walls they could see spires and minarets of the stone houses with slate roofs. There was a large moat around the town which seemed to be full of something that moved as they got closer. There were people on the walls and they were throwing what looked like food down to be snapped up by the hungry mouths poking up from the waters below.

As they approached a party of five mounted guards came out to meet them. They were smartly dressed in a red and black livery with tabards that were emblazoned with the rearing horse symbol of their King and Queen. A similar emblem was emblazoned on the flag which flew on the turret.

The guards rode four abreast towards them, their horses perfectly matched in time, colour and livery. As they neared three stopped and the fourth rode forwards. He smiled and bowed his head. "I am Tristinian, welcome to Camlan. The High Magus is expecting you. My lady." He bowed his head deeply.

The guards broke formation, Tristinian and another rode in front and three cut around to ride behind them as they were escorted across the drawbridge and into the town.

The gatehouse was an impressive structure. It was made of the same quartz as the rest of the wall and like the rest of the wall it was smooth, there were no cracks where the bricks were put together and no sign that it was plastered. The gatehouse looked like it was made of one solid piece of quartz. The gatehouse entrance was arched. Inside the ceiling had been painted with a rich oil painting depicting knights jousting. The quartz above allowed light to penetrate so the painting had the appearance of a stained glass window. To the left and right there were doors which were closed.

They passed under a portcullis which was drawn fully up at the beginning and end of the gatehouse and there was evidence that the floor below them was a trapdoor as there was a very visible crack down the centre.

Tristinian was smiling at them as they looked around. "Its quite a structure isn't it? Passing through this gatehouse is by appointment so you won't find any of the townsfolk here at this time. If you pass through it without permission then there is a stasis field which will hold you in suspended animation until you can be collected. I thought I'd point it out now to save any awkward embarrassing moments later. You will of course be permitted to wander about the town once you have met with the Magus. It is quite safe. We do not have crime here as it definitely does not pay." There was a twinkle in his eye as he turned and rode onwards into the main market square.

The square was bustling with life. Brightly coloured stalls were laid out with all manner of goods and food. The stalls were made of painted wood with a painted wood roof which sheltered the goods from rain and sun. The market stall holders were shouting about their wares and others walked about with tall sticks with ribbons and small dolls and other brightly coloured toys tied to them.

Tristinian led them down the centre of the Market Square. He turned in his saddle slightly. "You are lucky that you have arrived on both market day and the day of our weekly joust. Will you be partaking? All are welcome to try their skills at tourney."

Kel looked interested but then thought about it. "No thank you but we'd be very interested to watch."

Tristinian smiled. "A wise decision, the knights are very skilled and if you have not been brought up to it you may benefit from a few lessons before you take to the field. No doubt the Magus will have an invitation for you all."

It was beginning to get difficult for the people to move aside to let them through so they dropped to single file as they entered a street of shops. These were immaculately painted in bright colours which contrasted with the white quartz stonework. Each had a large window display which appeared to be open to the elements but they noticed a small boy who was pressing his face up against what was actually a force field that did the job of glass. He left a smeared imprint of his face and was chased off by the shop owner who took a cloth and wiped it off.

There was a real mix of peasants in basic brown linens and wool and those who wore bright velvets and brocade which definitely looked like more expensive fabric. Everyone was mixing and talking to everyone else and as far as they could see there was indeed no crime. The stallholders left their stalls and wandered off and chatted to each other and customers wandered along perusing the stock and shopping. If nobody was there they threw the money into a honesty box and took their goods.

Kyla kicked her horse up behind Tristinian. "How do you manage to keep so little crime with so much on display that would be so easy to take?"

Tristinian smiled. "Well each stall has its own force field. When goods are moved too far away from it without being paid for the stall will emit a targeted high pitched sonic stun which is directed at the thief and renders him or her unconscious. The Town Guard are also summoned and the miscreant would be taken away to be dealt with. We haven't had any theft now for many years. We do have minor crimes which are generally dealt with by an hour or two in the stocks which keeps everyone happy as it is a good opportunity to use up any rotting fruit and vegetables and the stallholders make good money selling it."

Kyla looked puzzled. "I thought you said there was no crime."

Tristinian beamed at her broadly. "The stocks are mostly full of children who have not obeyed their parents."

Kyla laughed. "I like that."

Tristinian turned in his saddle to face her. "So do the parents and we find that our young people soon learn right from wrong."

They rode up the central market street until they came to another moat which was edged with weeping willow and aspen. All along the bank lilies were growing in a profusion of colour. The drawbridge was lowered so they rode across, disturbing the swans that had been feeding beside the bridge. Three black swans glided gracefully away around the moat. Large fish were swimming in the moat and people from the town were sitting along the bank either resting or eating food they had bought from the market.

They entered another gatehouse which was similar to the first and the other side of it there was a large open courtyard around which there seemed to be many doors. Tristinian stopped and another guard stepped out of the side door to the gatehouse. "Eloitos, these are the Magus' guests, if you would escort them to see him and get their horses tended to."

Eloitos bowed deeply. "Of course my Lord."

Tristinian turned to them. "Eloitos here will see to your every need. I must apologise for not taking you further but our jurisdiction ends at this gatehouse and the Inner Court Guard take over from here on. I trust you will have a good meeting with the Magus and I look forward to seeing you again later." He bowed deeply and rode away.

Eloitos clapped his hands and two young squires dressed in tunics and trousers in the same livery colours as the guards ran out of the other door. "I would like you to tend to these horses."

One of the squires took the head of Kyla's horse. "My Lady, I will lead you to the dismounting block, you will find dismounting there a lot easier." He had just caught her as she was about to try jumping down. The horse looked at him and sniffed him. He stroked its nose and walked them over to a large block where Kyla was able to slide almost gracefully down and then walk down the steps. The boy smiled broadly, bowed and led her horse away.

The other squire was holding Kel and Rennon's horses while they dismounted. He then led the horses away.

Eloitos waited until they were ready. "I will take you to the Magus now unless you wish to refresh yourselves first?"

Rennon looked at Kel and Kyla. "We will be fine, please take us to the Magus. Can you tell me why there are so many doors?"

Eloitos looked around the courtyard. "This is the inner defence of the town. If we are in a siege situation the townsfolk move in here and those are the rooms that they are able to share until it is safe to return home. We have never been in a siege situation but it was all part of the design when the town was built."

Eloitos led them to the base of a tower and opened the door. Inside there was a spiral staircase circling the outer wall of the tower which went up nearly a hundred feet. Kyla looked at the stairs with dismay. Eloitos almost laughed. "My Lady, do not fear, you will not be expected to walk up those stairs. They are there in case there is a problem with the lifting system. Please, allow me." He held his hand out and the air shimmered slightly.

"Now if you would all step through I will close the force field and you will be safe."

Kel stepped forward and noticed that there was a clearly defined square crack in the floor. He put his hand out and turned to Eloitos who nodded. He felt the air resist him above the crack and as he moved his hand forwards he met resistance. He was able to step through and once inside he could feel a stronger force field wall around the perimeter. When they were all standing in the square it began to rise. There was a slight cranking sound and up they went.

They passed many levels, the spiral staircase snaking around them as they went up and up until finally the lift stopped at a black oak door with ornate silver hinges and a large ring. Eloitos touched a silver panel in the shape of a goat's head and spoke. "My Lord Magus, your guests have arrived."

The door swung open away from them and revealed a corridor heading away. The corridor was made of the same smooth quartz and flickering torches lit their way. Kel stopped to look at one of them. "Is that flame?"

Eloitos stepped back beside him. "It is a hologram of a flame, we found that the smoke was distasteful and tended to cause dust and a black mark on the ceiling. It is quite safe to touch and there is less of a fire risk."

There was a large arched doorway at the end of the corridor and many doors before then on the left and right. They were led to the big door at the end which swung open as they approached.

The room inside was plain. The stonework was arched to the ceiling. Along the far wall there were seven windows, arched and leaded with a crisscross design. Two central pillars held up the roof and the Magus was sitting on a large chair in front of them. He was a well built man, bearded and with a thick mop of black hair. He wore purple velvet robes which seemed to shimmer. Three chairs were set out in front of him and he stood up as they entered and walked to meet them. "Thank you Eloitos, that will be all. I am Drakus, High Magus to King Artis and Queen Martana. Would you like some refreshments? I have good wine from Meridina, hot Estinian brew or the presses of flowers."

Rennon stepped forwards. "Thank you, I would like some of the Meridinan wine." He looked to the other two and they nodded. "The same for my companions."

Drakus smiled. "Good choice. I will definitely join you for that." He poured them each a generous measure in large tall engraved silver goblets. "Now, please sit. You have been sent to speak with me about our advancements. I am not one for diplomacy and playing games so please, I am sure you will be relieved, just speak your mind and state what you are looking for."

They sat down. Rennon took a sip of the rich and fruity liquid. Its bouquet was flowery and it warmed him to the core. "As you know we are now fragmented across many galaxies. That has put us at a great disadvantage when it comes to fighting the Followers. We are looking for anything that will help us and we heard about your quartz power storage. Being able to store power more efficiently would mean we could travel further and faster."

The Magus smiled. "We have such technology and that is no secret and we have it in abundance. I can see no reason not to assist you as our contribution to the war against the Followers. I have consulted with my King and Queen and they feel that any help we can give you will help to keep the Followers from our door. So, we are prepared to give you the technology you wish for. I have scanned your ship, she is a good vessel and we have suitable technology you can add to her. We would also give you a Star Base. We have many in orbit around this planet. These move like ships so you should have no trouble keeping them from interception by the Followers if you are cautious. That will give you a base from which to launch your operations. I will download the information about how to operate and repair the base into your hand held device. As you know our ships are grown from quartz and the energy storage is in the structure of the vessel. This gives unlimited power storage and does not compromise on space. The whole ship can pick up the Eion particles as you travel through the corridors making it relatively easy to recharge. Also, we have Eion blasters installed which you may also find a valuable tool against the Followers. The Star Base has many short range fighters on board and I will also give you the manuals on those.

What we ask in return is that you continue with your fight against the Followers. We wholeheartedly support The Prince in his endeavours and our alliance with him has been long and profitable to all parties. The forthcoming marriage of our Princess to The Prince will ensure a continued friendship.

You have arrived on the day of our weekly joust and I have been asked by the King and Queen to invite you to attend as our guests. We trust you will find it an entertaining and colourful affair. You are also very welcome to attend the banquet afterwards. We can make rooms available should you wish to remain with us until morning."

Rennon smiled, looked at the others who nodded agreement. "We thank you for your generosity and we would be delighted to join you for your joust and banquet."

The Magus smiled. "I am delighted and we will look forward to seeing you there. Please enjoy our hospitality. Rooms will be prepared for you and you are welcome to take a look around our town." He indicated the windows. "Eloitos, come in here please." His voice was raised and commanding.

Eloitos rushed in through the door bowing as he entered. "My Lord Magus."

The Magus sat down regally. "Eloitos, you will show our guests around the town and arrange for the best rooms to be prepared for them. They will be attending the joust this afternoon and the banquet afterwards. Please arrange for their every need."

Eloitos bowed deeply and waited for the three to join him. Rennon took the lead, stood up and the other two followed him after turning and bowing to the High Magus.

Eloitos headed off down the corridor and onto the platform at the end of the corridor. They followed him and down they went. Once at the bottom they stepped out into the courtyard. "So, where would you like me to take you?"

Kel took a look around. "What do you think we should see?"

Eloitos smiled. "Well isn't that the question, what you should see or what it is right for you to see?"

Kyla stepped up beside him and spoke quietly. "What we should see?"

Eloitos looked very serious. "Well, if you are sure. There is plenty you should see."

Kyla smiled. "Are you man enough to show us?"

Eloitos smiled. "I am but you must walk with me and do not comment or act on anything that you see. Do you agree?"

All three nodded.

Eloitos walked ahead of them. "Then follow me. I will take you through the market."

They walked down the market street but half way down the street they took a detour down a side street. Away from the pristine market street the stonework didn't look any different. They turned a corner and another and it all looked very similar. Then they came to a doorway. Eloitos opened the door and behind it there was a wide open space. Lines of crops grew in neat rows and farmers tended them. They moved on and travelled past fields full of animals. It was spring and there were lambs and kid goats springing about with their mothers. Further on there were lines upon lines of polytunnels all growing food using a mixture of soil and hydroponics. The plants seemed to be thriving and they all looked well cared for.

Eloitos turned and smiled at them. "This is what the Magus would not have had me show you. We are a hard working people and everything you see here has been earned by the toil of our backs. The Magus would have it that their technology does everything. That is not true. The King and Queen are very interested in all that we do and they are always very supportive. They do not always get the support or loyalty that they deserve from the High Magus as he believes that he rules this land. He most definitely does not but he would like to especially now that they have brokered a deal whereby the princess is going to marry the True Prince. That will seal their position in the politics of the Universe for years to come.

I showed an unknown guest to see the Magus only yesterday. He came here very quietly and the Magus commanded me not to tell the King and Queen. I didn't get a look at the man's face but there was something very shifty about him.

Kel spoke quietly. "So do you think that the Magus is doing a deal with the Followers?"

Eloitos was staring at the floor. "I don't know but it was a bit strange. I'll give you the official guided tour now if you would like. Follow me."

They said very little for the rest of the tour and it ended in the castle where they were shown around the battlements and the fantastic view and the state rooms and then it finished at their rooms.

Eloitos bowed. "Well, I will leave you here. Make yourself comfortable and I will look forward to seeing you at the joust."

Once they were in their rooms they shut the doors and as soon as Eloitos had gone Kel and Rennon went to Kyla's room.

Kel was the last one in, he shut the door and locked it and leant against it. "When will we go somewhere and it isn't complicated. What should we do about what we know?"

Kyla smiled at him. "For now I'd say nothing. Lets keep vigilant at the joust and see what happens. There's nothing diplomatically we can do without making things very difficult. Anyway the Magus had a guest who was a bit shifty, so what? It could have been anyone. Come on, lets be careful but there's no point in acting before we know the truth of the situation."

Rennon nodded. "I agree. If we charge in with accusations with no proof we'll destroy all that we've set up so far. We'll wait."

Kel smiled. "I agree."

16

The banners fluttered in the wind around the arena. Everyone was seated. The knights were parading in the arena and the crowd was roaring. One by one the knights rode up before the King and Queen and tipped their lances. Then they rode in a big circle around the arena so that everyone could see them.

Each wore their own colours, a tabard and ribbons on their helmet. Each had their shield emblazoned with their family crest, all but one. His shield was black. One by one they stopped in front of a lady in the crowd and took a favour. The ladies had ribbons tied to their arm just for this purpose and they all looked hopeful as their favourite rode past. Their knight took the ribbon on the lance and rode off and back into the circle. The black knight had done two revolutions and he still had no favour. He rode to join the others and they all lined up. Half went one way, half the other and they lined up facing each other.

A squire rode along with a box and the knights put a disc with their colours into the box. He then rode along the other line and pulled out a disc at a time, giving it to the next knight along so they knew who they were going to joust against. This done they rode out of the ring leaving two behind, the first two to ride against each other in the joust.

A blue knight and a yellow knight squared up and the king stood up and dropped the small flag. The two knights charged at each other and the blue knight unseated the yellow and rode victorious back to his end of the field. Squires rushed to help the fallen knight back onto his horse and he rode back to his end of the field. The king dropped the flag again and they charged and again the yellow knight unseated the blue knight.

The squires rushed to help the blue knight and once seated on his horse he left the field to tumultuous applause. The yellow knight rode out of another exit as the red and green knights rode in. They repeated the process again and again until only two knights were left, the black knight and the red knight.

They faced each other and they charged. They collided and neither was unseated though both of them took a glancing blow on the chest. They galloped around the arena and returned to their end of the field and lined up again. They charged and the red knight unseated the black. Again they lined up and this time the black knight unseated the red. It was all down to the last charge. They lined up and everyone was out of their seats. They charged and the black knight unseated the red knight. He hit the ground and rolled. The squires rushed out and helped him back onto his horse and he rode up to the King and Queen who congratulated him and gave him a blue ribbon.

The black knight rode up to the King and Queen and stopped his horse in front of them. He bowed his head and as he looked up the Queen spoke. "Sir, I would ask you to remove your helmet and to reveal your identity to us." Her voice was commanding and enhanced so that everyone could hear it.

The black knight bowed his head and stabbed his lance into the ground so that he had both hands free. He grasped the helmet and pulled it off. The Queen and King smiled. "My Prince, we are honoured to welcome you to our Planet."

The Prince smiled and bowed his head. He grasped his lance and tipped the end of it to their daughter, a delicate blonde haired waif of a girl who sat by the queen's side. She was smiling broadly. "My Lady, you would never have accepted a stranger's lance and given him your favour, would you honour me by giving me your favour now so that I may be your champion?"

The woman beside Kyla was watching, mouth open. She turned to her friend. "Now that is how a man should act." Kyla smiled.

The princess took off her veil and tied it to the end of his lance. "Of course, it is a great honour to meet you at last."

The Prince bowed his head. "My Lady, I would not attend our wedding without having met you first. I hope that I will be invited to the banquet tonight and that I will have the chance to speak with you."

The King stood up. "My Lord, we would be greatly honoured if you would be our guest of honour tonight."

The crowd were standing and applauding as the Black Knight galloped around the arena. He saw Kel, Rennon and Kyla and stopped his horse causing a dust cloud. "My friends, I did not realise you were here also. I trust we will have an opportunity to speak later?"

Kel shouted over the noise of the crowd. "I hope so."

The Prince finished his circuit and galloped out of the arena. The crowd fell silent and the King, Queen and Princess stood up and left. Once they had gone everyone else started leaving the arena as well.

As they left the arena Kel whispered to Rennon. "Good job we didn't say anything about the unknown visitor. Accusing the Magus could have got us thrown out."

Later they were in Kyla's room and sitting chatting when there was a knock on the door. Kel opened the door and the Prince stepped inside.

He smiled and shut the door behind him. "I hope I'm not disturbing you."

Kyla smiled. "Not at all, you are very welcome. It is good to see you again."

The Prince smiled back. "It is good to see all of you, particularly today. I came here to take a look at my bride to be and I've just spent half an hour in her company. She is a very pleasant young lady. I am sure she will make a wonderful wife."

Kyla frowned. "Well you helped us out of a difficult situation once, would you like us to get you out now?"

The Prince looked worried. "No, don't get me wrong, she's a lovely girl. I came to speak with you on another matter. About a month ago Shantara went missing. After she flew off in your ship I monitored her for a while and after a considerable amount of convincing she came to work on a research moon of ours. Then one day she disappeared. We didn't think anything of it at the time. She had had a row with the man she was with and then went missing. I wasn't told straight away and I only found out just before I left to come here. I've got my people onto it now but I thought I'd find out if you knew anything. I'm also here because you are all going to need an alibi."

Kel looked concerned and frowned. "Why are we going to need an alibi? I'm just glad that Rennon has already scanned the room and shielded us."

The Prince smiled coyly. "You don't think I haven't already thought of that? We are safe to talk or I wouldn't have said that. I made sure that I was plainly seen by various of the staff as well as the King himself coming this way. I told him I was coming here as you were old friends and I wanted some time alone with you before the banquet as we hadn't had much chance with the war effort. You are going to need an alibi, much as it is much more convenient that I have one too."

Kel growled. "What is going to happen?"

The Prince smiled. "I think dinner may be cancelled and Joneil is here. Does that say enough?"

Kyla stepped closer to the Prince. "Why?"

The Prince took out a scroll of paper. "The High Magus had a meeting with a high ranking Follower member yesterday and the Follower took this away with him. Baron Joniel and I have been in town about three weeks now and we have had a good scout around and found out plenty.

It seems that the High Magus has been locked in a power struggle with the King. The Queen had to intercede in an argument which almost cost the King his life. It was smoothed over as the political consequences of the High

Magus being declared disloyal would have been catastrophic. To appoint a High Magus is no easy feat. It takes months of deliberation between all the Magi and they then have to come to a unanimous decision. As they all probably want the position the planet would be thrown into turmoil which is exactly what we all wanted to avoid. This has now been avoided as the Tower of the Magi has been warned about the High Magus' deception and was watching when he had his little visit. He had got too confident and believed he was above the Law of the Magi which states that no mage is beyond the law or above the King. As the King had declared the Followers outlaws and traitors to the galaxy he was making a deliberate attempt to undermine the King's power. That automatically gets him thrown off the high tower.

The Magi have secretly already held their vote and they have their unanimous replacement. Someone I wholeheartedly support and who will be a real asset to the Kingdom.

But, to avoid unpleasantness and to make sure that the King has a free hand to hunt for any Followers who are hiding in the town they need a reason. Our dear Joneil is going to give them that reason tonight when he removes the High Magus and plants enough evidence to implicate all the people they want to remove. We already have quite a list and we think it is pretty exhaustive. Once they are removed it will be a lot safer in this Kingdom. So, as you can see, it is going to be a busy night. So I would suggest that we sit a while and chat. I took the liberty of bringing this. It is a rather fine bottle of Mendurian Brandy and I had these glasses hand cut from the finest crystal.

So, my friends shall we catch up on some old times?" He put five glasses on the table and poured out four of them.

Kyla took the proffered glass. "I thank you and I wish you well in your endeavours. But, why five glasses, are we toasting absent friends?"

The Prince smiled. "No my dear, I have every confidence that Joneil will be joining us very shortly if not right away." He was about to put the cork back in the brandy when he hesitated. "Alright Joniel, you can transport now, the room is clear."

There was a slight crackling noise and Joniel appeared, hand on wrist and dressed in a long black robe with a deep hood. "Evening, I'm glad you put me out a glass, I haven't missed anything have I?"

The Prince raised an eyebrow. "I certainly hope not." They both laughed at this.

Joneil took his glass. "No, I had plenty of time to do the job calmly. So now you owe me my Prince."

The Prince smiled. "I'll pay up, I always do."

Joniel took a sip of the brandy. "Hmm, nice, you always get the best. Excuse my manners to the lady present. Kyla, it is a delight as always to be in your presence." He took a step towards her and took her hand. Instantly he shuddered and looked confused. His ever unreadable features melted to something like a smile. His eyes were bright and glistening. "Something is different about you?"

Kyla looked confused. "I don't think so."

Joniel lifted her hand and kissed it. "We will possibly speak later on this matter." His eyes flashed a vibrant blue. He turned to Anathorn. "So, what is she like, your wife to be?"

The Prince took a sip of brandy. "She is a charming and educated young lady."

Joniel raised an eyebrow. "Well that should make for an interesting marriage. It's a good job I dealt with the High Mage when I did. In his shoes I would probably have been looking to have either you or the princess removed. Your alliance would have been extremely inconvenient to him."

The Prince looked to the others. "Well, all irrelevant now. My new father in law to be should be safely on his throne and his major threat has been eliminated. Our chance to get our hands on their technology is now assured."

As he finished speaking there was a loud explosion from outside the window. The hologram forcefield window vibrated, its stained glass effect distorted momentarily. Ordinary glass would have shattered with the force of the blast. They were all on their feet in moments and leapt to the window to look out.

The Prince was first there. "By heaven, that is a Kerillian Cruiser. How the hell did that get through the planet's defences?" As he spoke a second bolt of energy hit the city, obliterating one of the towers. "Joneil, can you get them to safety?"

Joniel thought for a split second. "I can't locate them well enough to be able to go directly to them but if we find them I can take them with me, yes, of course but first I'm getting you out."

The Prince didn't get a chance to argue. Joneil calibrated his wrist band and grabbed him and they were gone.

The tower that had been hit was burning and masonry fell on the buildings below, crashing through roofs and falling into the street, blocking it and hindering those who were rushing around carrying buckets and helping the injured. A jet of water streamed down over the tower extinguishing the flames as a third bolt hit from the cruiser. Then there was a bright light in the sky and the cruiser exploded. Tiny white hot fragments of it rained down on the town below as people screamed and ran for cover. Anything that could ignite did ignite and all around the town jets of water were activated to put out the flames.

Kyla was half way out of the door, Kel caught her but he saw the determined look on her face and followed her out. Rennon was just following them when Joneil turned up again. He followed them out of the door, securing the stopper and pocketing the brandy as he went.

The corridor was in chaos, people ran about and women were screaming. As they ran down into the main hall they could see why, there were bodies everywhere. It was where they had brought all those who had been caught in the explosion. They were lined up, covered in sheets and it looked like the casualties had run into the hundreds. War had come to the planet.

A guard had been stationed by the bodies and Kyla ran to him. "Have you seen the King and Queen?"

The guard looked down at her, his face was streaked with smoke where he had been helping with the fire. "They are over there." He pointed to the corner of the room. The King and Queen were there, comforting a family. The Queen's robes were stained with blood and soot and her immaculate make up was now streaked by tears. The King was beside her with his arm around her and they were both clasping the hand of an elderly woman who was standing in front of one of the covered bodies.

It seemed quiet outside now but more bodies were coming in and being stacked in neat lines on the floor. Joneil looked wildly about. "I'm sorry, I'm going to have to take my leave of you. I'll check about outside but I can't stay in here with all this blood." He put his hand on Kyla's arm, squeezed it and turned away. "I won't be far away and if there's more trouble I will get you out of here my dear."

Kel caught Kyla's other arm. "Come on, lets go out with him and see what we can do." They followed Joneil out into the courtyard and then outside the castle. It was hard to move as there were lots of hysterical people milling about. Some were looking at the skies, some were looking at the blasted buildings, others just walked with their heads down and looked shocked.

Kyla heard a baby crying, she was sitting by the side of the road with her fingers in her mouth. She scooped her up. "Where is your mummy little one?" The child looked at her, her blue eyes watery as she took her wet hand out of her mouth and pointed to the alleyway. Kyla handed the girl to Kel who held her like she was a bomb about to explode and stepped into the alley. There was a body on the floor, it had been mostly blown to bits but it was recognisable as a woman. There was a little boy dead beside her. Kyla pulled the woman's cloak out from under her and laid it over them and went back to the street. "Come on little one, I'm going to take you to the castle and they will look after you there."

Kel handed the girl over as Kyla looked at him and shook her head. He put a hand on the little girl's head and ruffled her curls. "We'll take you there and someone will look after you."

Rennon was helping a man to stand up. His leg had been shattered but it had been bound and he was able to walk. He had been knocked over by the crowd and was finding it difficult to get his footing without someone else knocking him over. He leant on Rennon's arm, his other hand on a stick someone had given him and they all made their way back to the castle.

They made many more trips out to the town and back with survivors and every time they got back the body count was growing and the bodies on the floor were now piling up two high. The King and Queen had retired to their rooms to tidy themselves up ready to talk to the people and the guards were rallying people to bring them to the main square ready for the Royal Proclamation.

About half an hour later the crowd in the square fell silent as the King and Queen stepped out onto the balcony. The King looked around at the people below and cleared his throat. "My People, this has been a sad night for our town and for our Kingdom. Good souls have left us tonight and our town will be the lesser for their passing. But, those of us who remain must carry on. We must rebuild and we must bring vengeance down upon our enemies. Where we have been content to sit back and let others do our work for us, now it is our time to take to the skies. It is our decision to join with the allies to stand against the Followers who were the perpetrators of this foul act.

Tonight has also seen other foul acts. Our High Magus has been murdered by Follower spies who have been active in our town. But, he did not die in vain as we have evidence now of who they are. They have been arrested and will now be brought out in front of you."

The guards came out on a lower balcony, pushing five men in front of them.

The King looked down on them. "These murderers cannot be allowed to live within our walls. Tonight I have consulted with the Magi and it has been decided that our laws must change. These men are guilty of treason as well as murder and the punishment for this shall be death. Captain of the Guard will you execute these men for me."

The Captain of the Guard stepped forwards as the men looked about them in horror. He pulled out his blaster and went along the line, shooting each one in turn, in the head, at close range. One by one they fell forwards until they were all laying dead. The crowd roared its approval.

The King then raised his hand and there was silence. "We are living in exceptional times and when the murder was discovered a Council of the Magi was called to elect a new High Magus so that there can be a continuity. For the first time in our history there was a unanimous decision on the first vote. I am pleased to announce that Gerdan Menias has been elected as the new High Magus. If he would kindly step out onto the balcony so that you may meet him."

A tall thin man dressed in long purple velvet robes stepped out onto the balcony beneath the one the King stood on. He bowed to the people and then stepped back.

The King held his hand up to silence the loud applause. "Order will come out of this chaos but for tonight we must survive as best we can and take our rest where we can. We rest much safer in our beds tonight now that these traitors have been eliminated. They were also the perpetrators of this attack as the Terrinial Shield was turned off. We have footage that it was one of their number who did this act. It has now been reinstated so please my people, find rest where you can and tomorrow we will begin to rebuild our town."

The King and Queen stood together on the balcony as the crowd applauded and cheered. They then turned and went inside.

Kel slipped his arm around Kyla's waist and she looked up at him. She smiled and whispered. "I'd better get inside and see if I can help any of the injured."

Kel kissed her on the forehead. "I'll come in with you and see what I can do to help. Rennon, how about you?"

Rennon was looking about in disbelief. "I can't believe how fast and furious that attack was. They didn't stand a chance if that thing came in cloaked but I'm just amazed that the shield was all that protected them. They are supposed to have star bases up there."

Kel thought a minute. "Well if they weren't looking or they didn't have the scanner on at the time. I've had a bad thought, what if there are spies on the bases?" Just as he said that there were flashes of light in the sky which lit up the square. Followed by another, and another. Six in all then everything fell silent. Kel dragged Kyla inside and Rennon followed. "I would hazard a guess that those explosions were the star bases going up. If they have saboteurs on board the Followers could have done that. If they did then its possible there is going to be another cruiser attack."

They all nearly jumped out of their skin when Joneil appeared beside them and grabbed Kyla around the waist. "I'm taking her back to your ship. Stay here and I'll be back for you. This place is about to come under attack by four Kerillian Cruisers." Kyla opened her mouth but the words were lost.

Joneil appeared with Kyla in the Hopper and put her down and was gone again. He returned with Kel and then with Rennon and then sat down himself. His robe was stained with soot. Kyla moved to sit next to him. "Can I take a look?" She said quietly as she saw the wet blood on his hands.

Joneil looked at her a little bit stunned. "Yes, er, thank you."

She opened the front of his robe. His chest was a mass of burns and embedded shrapnel. "How did you get this?"

He looked down and winced. "I got the King and Queen out but I couldn't save their daughter, she was trapped under falling masonry. We were in that tower that exploded. I shielded them from the explosion."

Kyla got the medical kit out from the Hopper storage compartment as Rennon started the pre flight checks. She pulled out a large pair of tweezers and began to gently remove the broken metal shards that were stuck in

Joneil's chest. As she watched he was visibly looking tired and he had begun to go grey. She pulled out a blood bag from the medical chilled cabinet and poured him a beaker full. He drank it down. It helped a little. Then she carried on with pulling out the pieces. She pushed him back so that he laid down on the bench which made her job a lot easier. When she was sure she had got all the pieces out she disinfected the skin and put a dressing over the whole of his chest. He made to get up but she put a hand on his shoulder and pushed him back down again. "Now its Rennon's turn to get us all out of here. How are we doing?"

Rennon was just lifting the Hopper off and he already had it in stealth mode. "We're doing just fine. I bet you are glad we didn't bring our own horses or we'd be doing a rescue mission at the moment to get them out."

Kyla smiled. "I'm very glad, we were lucky to get ourselves out. Joneil, how do you feel."

Joneil looked up at her, his eyes tired and strained. "I feel like I've just had a building fall on top of me. I need living blood my darling, that was helpful but it won't allow me to heal those wounds."

Kyla got up and shut the connecting door between the cockpit and the main bay. She helped Joneil to sit up as he was struggling and sat down beside him. She offered him her wrist but he pushed it down gently. He brushed her hair back with his hand so very gently and leant forwards. He brushed his lips over her cheek and then ran his mouth down her neck. He held her hand, his other hand clasped around the back of her head as he bit into her neck. She tensed as she felt the first flush of the pain but the bite numbed it and she felt nothing other than his skin against hers. He forced himself to let go and he fell back against the wall, his eyes wild and blood red, his pupils elongated to cat like slits, his extended fangs still had not retracted and tiny drops of blood hung on their tips. He licked them and they retracted back into his jaw. His eyes were back to normal and the colour had returned to his cheeks. "You died?" He caught her hand.

She tilted her head on its side. "Technically I died three times. I got shot. How did you know?"

Joneil smiled and took a deep breath. "Because the binding is broken, you are no longer bound to me." He looked down.

Kyla smiled back at him. "And?"

Joneil looked lost. "And now you are free to do as you wish, then you have been for a long time."

She bent forwards, put her arms around him and kissed him. "Indeed. And I have thoughts on our other problem too. I have shared our secret with Kel, as I had to. I would share it with Rennon too if you would give me your permission."

Joneil looked confused. "Why my love would I need to give you my permission?"

215

Kyla smiled thoughtfully. "Because it could change everything."

Joniel looked away. "In what way." He made to stand up but she pushed him back. He was too weak to resist.

Kyla looked down, she looked somehow serene despite the smoke marks on her face and her tangled hair. "I cannot go on living like this, not any more. I want to ask Rennon to find a way… But, I need to know, how do you feel?"

Joniel looked back at her. "For so long now I haven't known how I feel. I'm not a man of feelings so my answer to you is simple. I feel and that says it all. Do what you can. If you can find an answer come to me, be with me. If you can't we'll find a way to survive. We have for so long. Is that enough of an answer for you? You changed me Kyla, you made me who I never thought I could be. It hurts."

Kyla smiled. "I know."

Joniel choked. "No I mean it hurts, physically, now. Help me…" He choked again and blood gushed out of his mouth.

Kyla pushed him back onto the seat and ripped the dressing off of his chest. She pulled out the medical bag and scanner. It bleeped and flashed as she turned it on. Joniel was convulsing on the seat. "No you don't, I'm not going to lose you. None of the holes were big enough for a shard to have passed through. I don't understand." She ran the scanner over him. "Got you!" She pulled on gloves and grabbed a scalpel from the medical box and cut a slit big enough to get her hand inside. She poured disinfectant over her hands and reached inside. Her fingers touched something hard and sharp, she grabbed it between thumb and first finger and pulled gently but firmly and pulled out a needle shaped lump of metal. She then poured disinfectant over the wound and dressed it.

Joniel was choking, his eyes had rolled back. She took the scalpel and cut across her wrist, dripping the fresh blood into his mouth. He was convulsing so much that the blood sprayed around the cabin. She pinned his shoulders down with her knees and held his head steady with one hand while forcing her wrist over his mouth. The blood flowed fast from the severed artery until he stopped convulsing and lay still. She climbed off of his shoulders and sat on the floor beside him, her wrist still pouring blood into his mouth until she passed out.

Joniel came around moments later and saw her on the floor and instantly realised what she had done. "No, I can't have this, I can't do this." He lifted her from the floor and bound her wrist. Immediately a red rose of blood flowered on the bandage. He laid her back onto the bench and tipped her head back. She was barely breathing. He bit deeply into his own wrist and let the blood drip into her mouth. A gag reflex made her swallow.

Kel's voice came over the intercom. "Is everything alright in there?"

Joniel didn't hear him, he could only hear one thing, Kyla's heartbeat getting stronger. "There has always been an answer my love, I just never wanted to give you the choice."

Kyla came round almost instantly and tasted the blood in her mouth. "What have you done?"

Joniel looked guilty. "I had no choice."

Kyla's eyes reflected her anger. "All these years! All these lonely years you could have done this, you could have let us be together?"

Joniel's face was without expression. "You aren't angry with me?"

Kyla almost screamed. "Of course I'm angry with you. You could have done this years ago." Kyla moved along the bench to where she could reach the door and opened it. Joniel relaxed and she guided him gently down so he laid on the bench, his head on her lap. She stroked his hair as he fell asleep and they glided through the darkness of space on their way back home as the wound on her wrist closed up.

17

They were barely out of planetary orbit when the next star base exploded. It was close to them and the shock wave knocked them sideways. Rennon had to think really fast on his feet to keep them from crashing. All the systems went down and they were blown off course. He compensated for the knock on effect and managed to get them back on track.

Down on the planet flowers of fire from the explosions blossomed as the Star Bases started firing on their own planet and also on the Hopper. Rennon got the shields up in time but they were buffeted and knocked about as the blaster beams hit against their shield damaging it. The shields were holding but barely.

Joniel sat up, clutching his chest which Kyla had now re-bandaged. "Well it looks like its going to be a bumpy ride." He stood up and staggered a little into the cockpit. "Rennon, you are a good pilot but it's not a speciality of yours. Would you like a hand?"

Rennon was concentrating hard and beginning to panic. "You would be welcome."

Kel got up and Joniel painfully climbed into his seat and began flicking switches and pushing buttons. "She's a good craft, just compensate for the blasts, bring her gently back to where she was and let the momentum drift her back on track and very, very carefully tip the thrusters and you will be back where you should be. There you go and we should be just outside the range of those blasters now. What they really need are". He paused and seemed to be looking around for something. "Ah yes, a little late but not bad." He smiled.

He looked up and pointed to a huge battleship that had just appeared above them. It was almost as big as the planet and arrived all guns blazing, firing green bolts at the star bases. Joniel smiled. "Stun blasts. A very cunning creation as they stun everyone on board so we can then go and find out who we need to punish and who is innocent. Lovely shooting, not a blast wasted. May I invite you to visit my flagship?" He waited for an answer but there was silence as they watched the ship stun each star base in turn.

Kyla leant on the back of Joniel's chair. "Well, that is impressive."

Joniel raised an eyebrow. "I am rather pleased with her. That should solve the problem and the people down there should be suitably grateful so you might just still get all those things they promised you. No, you can't have one of those, that is the only one at the moment and I'm not going to tell you what I had to do to get her. The silver lining here is that anyone with Follower allegiances has now shown their hand and can be dealt with." He altered their direction and flew them up underneath the ship after sending his personal code. The bay doors opened, they glided inside and the doors closed as Joniel guided the Hopper up to dock. He clicked on the radio and keyed in the frequency.

A silky male voice filled the cockpit. "Welcome home Sir."

Joniel smiled. "Thank you Jaz. Get the guest rooms ready and let's crack out some of the good stuff tonight. Is the Prince comfortable?"

Jaz's voice sounded like he was laughing. "The Prince is making our life a misery but he seems quite happy now."

The Prince chipped in. "Just glad to get back here and do something."

Joniel smiled. "I told you not to worry, when will you listen to me? I trust that Jaz has treated you well."

The Prince had humour in his voice. "Your son is as charming as ever."

Joniel looked around at the three and put the mike on silent. "He's no doubt been winding the Prince up, they don't exactly see eye to eye since Jaz took a fancy to a dancing girl that the Prince was a bit keen on. That was back in the days when he knew nothing of his status and was free to do that sort of thing." He flicked the mike back on. "I'm glad to hear it. How is it going, we can't see much from here?"

Jaz's voice came back over the intercom. "The star bases are all neutralised and there are shuttles going up to them as we speak. I've received a transcript message from the planet surface. They have managed to isolate the Follower contingency in town and they have been dealt with. All that remains is to eliminate those on the star bases and they should have a fairly clean kingdom. I think we can count that as a bit of a success, despite all the losses. I understand that they have been heavy. You have clearance to enter the corridors. I'll see you shortly." The intercom fell silent.

Joniel got up and strode to the back of the cockpit. "I would like you to be my honoured guests and we can see about some dinner. I don't know about you but I'm feeling a little peckish." He looked meaningfully at Kyla who glared at him.

Kyla got up and followed him. "You have had quite enough from me for one day. I'm sure you have your own supply."

Joniel looked hurt. "And I thought we were getting on so well. Now I've got to go and be mean and moody with my people. Please, follow my lead and be careful. Kyla, I know, I have some explaining to do."

Joniel alighted the Hopper first and showed them to an airlock which was brushed chrome. The door swished open to reveal a sumptuously decorated corridor. The carpet was deep pile and a rich burgundy colour and matching drapes hung in swathes along the wall. Dark and moody oil paintings lined the corridor and at the end the door was wooden, or looked wooden, arched and swung open with a sinister creak when they approached.

On the other side of the door there was a large living room area. The huge black marble fireplace was filled with a roaring fire. Candlesticks on the mantle burnt with an orange glow and the room was luxuriously decorated with heavy flock wallpaper, more of the deep burgundy carpet, ebony furniture and lit by pewter candlesticks. There was a large table, red velvet sofas and small tables. The room was well populated with men and women dressed in elaborate velvet evening wear, sitting in groups. The men wore lace jabots under velvet suits and the women slinky black velvet evening gowns.

There was an air of nervousness in the room as they entered. All eyes were on them. The room was reasonably well lit and they could see a sweeping staircase ascending at the back of the room.

The inhabitants fell silent as they walked through the room and they looked at each other within the groups nervously. Joniel looked about them regally, his face stony cold. They had not seen this side of him before. He seemed taller, broader and definitely moodier.

A well dressed liveried servant stepped forwards and held out a silver tray on which there was a cut glass decanter full of a red liquid. Joniel took a glass and the butler poured him a generous measure. The butler offered the tray to the others but Joniel shook his head slightly and the butler took his lead, bowed and backed away. Joniel took a large sip of the red liquid and they saw his complexion visibly become more healthy. He smiled slightly at Kera who was looking very nervous and strode across the room. The three kept very close behind him. When they got to the staircase Joniel turned to face the room. "We have struck a blow today to ensure the safety of this planet, which is in our interests. Our alliance with the people of this planet will bring us riches and new technology. I trust all has been well while I have been away?"

Various occupants of the room looked down at the floor and others looked accusingly at them.

Joniel glared. "I can see that the usual differences of opinion have been playing out while I have been absent. It does not become you, we are in a time of war and our very race could be threatened if the Followers get a firm foothold. I do not have to remind you that they are fanatical and our people are considered an affront to their beliefs. Your internal wars are nothing in comparison to the danger we face." He turned and seemed to glide up the stairs. The three followed him in silence.

The stairs opened up into what looked like a huge ballroom. There were four intricately carved crystal chandeliers on the ceiling, the candles flickering with a warming glow. The floor was a polished wood, worn slightly by countless dancing feet. The carpet covered the distance from the dance floor to the wall and tables were set out around it. Joniel didn't stop, as he glided across the polished dance floor. "I had this brought from our palace on Septa Transverra along with many of the other decorations in this place. The planet was ransacked by the Followers shortly afterwards but they found very little that we had left behind other than the traps we set for them. We are now also a nomadic people." He strode to the door the other side without stopping. He threw it open and strode on through the corridor beyond. It was all they could do to keep up. Kel closed the door behind him and had to almost run to keep up with them. They turned a corner and entered a lift system which took them to what looked like the Command Room. It was bustling with people going about their duties. It was noisy too with individuals calling out readings and reporting the status of the planet below.

Jaz and the Prince were standing beside a panel covered in switches and buttons. Jaz was staring with an intensity at the console and occasionally he pushed a button or flicked a switch. The Prince was looking over his shoulder and seemed to be commenting occasionally and flicking a few switches of his own. They both turned simultaneously and Jaz stood up.

Jaz was a tall thin individual who did bear a striking resemblance to Joniel. He was definitely younger and a lot thinner, he lacked his father's broad shoulders and confident demeanour. Joniel stepped forward. "Well done. You did a good job, very neat and tidy, exactly the right decision. "

Jaz looked at the floor, he had not and didn't seem to want to meet his father's gaze. "Thank you sir. I can only take part of the credit, it was grandmother's plan. She has asked me to tell you that she is pleased with what you are achieving and the way you have command of the houses on this ship. You can expect a visit from her in the next few weeks. You are expected to present yourself before the High King and mother is already on his battleship."

Joniel looked around the room at the assembled crew. "Good, everything is in order so I will retire to my rooms. My Lord, if you would like to join me." He smiled at the Prince. "I think we have much to discuss. Kel, Kyla, Rennon, would you like to accompany me also? Jaz, can I leave you in command?"

Jaz smiled. "Thank you father."

They left the command room and after many corridors they came to a suite of rooms, similarly luxurious and decorated with the same dark and broody paintings, this time of pale faced men and women in elegant attire. Joniel saw them looking around the paintings. "My family are always with me, even though some of them are no longer physically with us."

Kyla was looking at a beautiful dark haired woman who smiled down on her from the heavy gold frame. Joniel stepped up behind her and put a hand on her shoulder. "You have now met my wife Marikana, a dear sweet lady, a ferocious fighter and a loving mother to our seventeen children. She was a shrewd warlord and commander of the Northern Fleet. She departed this world many years ago. Sadly we lost my father in a Follower raid on our home planet before we realised the seriousness of their incursion." He indicated a stately looking gentleman who hung in pride of place over the white marble mantelpiece. Next to him was a blonde haired woman, her hair intricately curled around her elfin like face. "And that is his mother, Ariansa." He strode across the room to the far wall where a large landscape painting depicting a river valley was hanging. "This is my home world, now sadly ransacked but we will reclaim it when the Followers are gone." He pressed the side of the frame and it opened away from the wall like a door. Behind it there was a recess. "Would you like a hot drink. I have Mendurian Coffee which is very good if you like the taste. Tea from Perusia is also very palatable. Or I have other drinks if you so wish."

Kel had been looking around in wonder and silence since they had got to the ship. He was currently standing in front of a sombre looking elderly lady with a kindly smile who seemed to watch him wherever he stood. He stepped left and right and then stood still looking at the painting carefully. "Coffee sounds good. Who is this?"

Joniel turned and smiled. "That is my great grandmother, Ketariana. You may meet her one day. She is considered venerable even by our years but has not yet succumbed to the frailty. She is a formidable strategist. I spent much of my younger years with her and she taught me my trade."

Kel looked thoughtful. "So that sweet old lady is an assassin too?"

Joniel laughed. "I suppose you could say that she is. But she would never dirty her hands with taking contracts like I do. They all look down a bit on my profession. I was the youngest of the sons, so my position within the hierarchy was not so defined as my brothers and sisters. Where I have got I have got by my own hand. Which is why I can make my own choices." He smiled meaningfully at Kyla.

Rennon was looking at a delicate glass candlestick. "So what is your position? I did wonder."

Joniel was pouring coffee for them all. "I am commander of this ship but as I have other affairs the day to day running of it usually falls to my son Jazrael and his wife Keeta. That leaves me free to handle other business. I've never been one for politics, I have my own way of dealing with problems but family protocol states that I must conform in certain ways and it suits me well." He set the coffees down on an ornate gold leafed table and pulled up some similarly gold leaf design high backed chairs.

Rennon took a seat. "You mentioned the houses?"

Joniel smiled. "A constant battle between different families and clans for status is a way of life for us. It almost destroyed our people a few thousand years ago when it led to the Clan Wars. Out of that my family rose victorious and to prevent the war happening again laws were past and agreed to unanimously that our family will be the ruling clan throughout the generations. That doesn't stop the other clans fighting but it does leave us able to concentrate on other matters."

Kel took a sip of his coffee. "Aren't you challenged?"

Joniel drank some of his coffee too. "No, it is the law and our laws set down by the ancestors may not be challenged."

Kyla was still looking around. "Do you marry within your own clan?"

Joniel smiled. "Not always. Any marriage outside the clan has to be agreed by the High Council and has to have the majority of votes from the elders of each of the other clans. The other clans of course can marry who they choose." A visible sadness came onto his face as he spoke and his eyes involuntarily wandered to a painting above a gold half moon table on the wall by the door. The painting was of a beautiful raven haired woman with bright green eyes. "My sister, Kyrianath. She was a rare beauty and a vicious warrior. She died by her own hand as her love was forbidden. But, lets talk of other things. That planet should be able to sort out its problems now and hopefully you'll still get whatever they have promised you. My Prince, I don't know how to put this but I'll be blunt as there is very little I can do to dress it up. Sadly the princess was lost in the battle."

The Prince looked as though he had been shot. The colour drained form his face and he stared at Joniel as if he didn't believe him. "How did it happen?"

Joniel looked him in the eye. "She was with her parents in the Royal Tower when it was hit by a blast from the first Star Base to be taken over. It was a well planned strike and there was no chance for anyone to get away from it. By the time I had gone in there she was already dead as a block of masonry had landed on her. The only comfort I may be able to give is that it was quick, she wouldn't have known anything about it. I managed to get her parents out as they were in a different room which had been shielded by the structure of the building so the ceiling held up a little longer. I was only just in time to get them out. The tower was hit again and the explosion took the wall out. After that the tower collapsed and I believe all remaining lives were lost."

The Prince looked down. "She was a lovely lady, her loss will be deeply felt in their kingdom. I spent but a brief time with her but even in that short time I know she would have made a fine wife and mother to my children. Sadly it was not to be."

Rennon put his cup down. "We were all saddened to hear of your loss."

The Prince smiled slightly. "Thank you. We have all lost so many people in this war already but I hope that it never gets to the stage that we have lost enough that it doesn't matter anymore. It will have to make me fight harder now won't it."

Joniel looked serious then seemed to lighten up. "And now you'll have to go through all those fathers trying to convince you to marry their daughters again."

The Prince frowned. "Indeed."

Joniel pushed his empty cup away. "So, what next?"

The Prince pushed his empty cup away too. "Now we have to start formulating a plan. We know more about the Followers now and sorting out this incursion has given us a big morale boost and hopefully given them something to think about. I have prepared a compilation of the information we have which I would be pleased if you would convey to your people Rennon. I'm going to make it available to any planet that wishes it. I think spreading the information about what the Followers are really like could be our only way of fighting them. We've won the battle and we should celebrate that but winning the war is a long way off. Sadly we will lose many more people before the Followers are gone. That is the problem with fighting a belief, it is hard to kill and whether it is right or wrong, if people believe it to be a just cause they will fight for it. In their eyes that puts us in the wrong."

Kyla looked into her empty cup. "But surely losing free will and being drugged into believing in something is wrong."

Joniel choked. Kyla looked awkward and smiled nervously. Joniel raised an eyebrow.

The Prince smiled. "As with politics nothing is ever as clear cut as that. There are many who believe that the Followers offer a just and righteous option to the regime that has been offered to them in the past. Those are the planets where we will have the greatest difficulty. There are some tyrants out there who actually needed dealing with as they treat their people abysmally and their living conditions are close on impossible. What we do have to get them to understand is that we would deal with the tyrants as much as the Followers will and that we will offer them the freedom of a better life. The more I travel and see planets I realise that there is another way if we can get them to accept it. The Followers filled a void and fulfilled a need. That was the secret of their success."

Kel smiled. "Well that made no sense to me so could you explain it a bit clearer."

The Prince looked around the room and thought for a few moments. "Every planet is different and has a different level of technology. So their needs are different. In some societies certain things work and everyone benefits, in others there needs to be a different way of sorting things out. Mostly over the years this has evolved naturally and the people are content, well they are never content, but they are best off with what they have. There are places where this has not happened because individuals have stepped in for their own gain without considering the long term plan. There are certain basics that have to be addressed. The first is that people need to eat and breathe. That by its very nature should secure a firm agricultural base for each planet that needs oxygen as its breathable gas. Some races do not breathe oxygen so their planets are very different. I am also firmly of the belief that to provide a firm base for growth each planet where there is a single ruler should be self sufficient. It is possible that with the technology we have, if we share it, that each individual area can achieve this. I'm talking about the basics here, what is needed to feed the people on a day to day basis. Anything that is only provided by an individual continent or country should then provide the basis for trade.

I can see why the Followers have such appeal to certain planets. They offer a coherent rule which has never been seen between the planets and galaxies before. They offer a basic level of technology which will limit some and bring others up to the same level and they offer a controlled food supply so that nobody goes hungry. It's what they also offer that is our problem. They wish to enforce this regime whether it is wanted or not.

As you will have already seen, the planets are very diverse and have developed their own level of technology. If the Followers are allowed to take over then there will be an uniformity between the galaxies and culture and the vitality that makes the planets individual will be lost. The truth of it is that if we had all looked to the problems of our own needy earlier they would not have been able to gain a foothold so fast. I am firmly of the belief that there should be a change in any case. We shouldn't have to enforce it, but we should be able to suggest it. A fair day's pay for a fair day's work."

Joniel smiled. "And I suppose you have a plan for that?"

The Prince smiled. "Each planet is different but what I have seen is the more we develop certain technologies the worse it gets for certain people. What I'm saying is not all progress is good progress and that looking to the need for people to be able to earn a living and to have pride in feeding their families should be more important than rationalisation and providing goods and services with a limited workforce. We have the intelligence to automate everything but do we have the wisdom to know that by doing that we are taking away the purpose in life? There is a fine balance and an energy that needs to flow. If that flow is disrupted then it is like a disease and it is self defeating as the governing entities have to deal with those who can no longer work so they have to provide the money to do so. To do that they have to create taxes to pay for it. So in the end the only difference is that certain people are left without the pride and purpose of having their place in society."

Rennon was thinking hard. "So how do we achieve this?"

The Prince frowned. "The theory is easy, putting it into practice now that is the hard part as on many planets the advancements are already there. Firstly I think by protecting the planets that are working from those who would change them. We have a vast galaxy and if there are individuals who want an automated society, they should be allowed this. We have planets that are uninhabitable because there is no atmosphere. Those would be ideal for colonisation by those who would be happy to live in a fully automated and synthetic environment. I would advocate developing them and allowing those who thrive in such an environment to relocate there where they can find their peace of mind. Places like the planet we have just visited should be preserved. You have seen their level of technological advancement, it is quite remarkable but they have found their balance. They are still an agricultural based society and much of their work on the land has returned to being done by hand. The seasons matter to them again and they are happy to go out and do the fruit and vegetable picking. It has become part of their social calendar and the money it brings to the population gives them that extra income that makes their life comfortable. I have been there at harvesting time. I have also seen the benefits of the forcefield biodomes that they have developed. Crops are protected from the weather but rain is allowed through when it is needed and the picking is done in the dry. You didn't get to see the factories but they are there and they are extremely efficient. The parts that are dangerous or unpleasant to assemble or create is automated totally, the manual assembly of safe materials is be done by real living people on production lines.

Small businesses and crafts are encouraged and the market is a vibrant part of the town life. Rents are low and cover maintenance and that allows the stall keepers and shop owners to flourish. If they flourish they can pay their taxes and the town prospers. You have seen the condition of the place. That is due to the guilds. They run an apprenticeship scheme and children go from education into these guilds. They start with simple tasks like road sweeping and general maintenance and then progress to stonemasonry and the other more complicated tasks like the electronics of the forcefield windows and other aspects of the town."

Joniel stood up. "More coffee anyone? I think this discussion is going to go on for a while. If you would excuse me I must go and get a report on how things are going on the planet. Kyla, if you would like to accompany me." He bowed slightly and offered her his hand. She took it and he escorted her out of the room.

18

The stars twinkled in the cloudless sky. A heavy muggy heat hung about bringing a musky dry aroma out of the buildings along the sides of the canals. Long thin boats drifted along them, propelled by young men in elaborate jackets and flowing cloaks pushing them with poles which penetrated deep into the water to meet the sea bed or pushed against the stone of the side of the canal. Some carried cargoes, some carried people. Each one was decorated elaborately in gold and black with a stripe of colour running from prow to bow and an elaborate statuette on its prow. Houses rose up from the canals and walkways, tall elegant constructions built with balconies, walkways and minarets. Each house was painted around the leaded windows in gold and above each residence and workplace a flag hung limp on this breezeless night.

As their boat entered the central canal, Kel, Rennon and Kyla were amazed by the huge stone plaza that faced them. It was a truly awesome construction that rose up out of the sea as if it had been created beneath it and then born. The whole structure was very organic, the sweeping stairway that rose up out of the sea was festooned with carved seaweed. The flat wall where boats tied up was stone carved as wood. Giant sea horses rose up out of the plaza floor, the stone waves rising around them.

The centre piece to the plaza around which everything else radiated was a huge statue of a muscular man, his bare chest bore an impressive six pack, his long hair and curly beard rugged around the broad features of his face. In his right hand he bore a trident, his left he held out flat, palm upwards. His torso ended in a huge fish's tail which curled around him. Four sea horses arose from the carved waves around his tail, their nostrils flaring as their hooves were represented as splashing up stone water. The plinth was ornately carved with waves and water ran down along the ridges these created into the huge pool below. Around the pool the restraining wall was also ornately carved. Its stone fish swam in an eternal circle clockwise around its base and the top was carved as waves out of polished marble.

The plaza itself was lit by posts with lights on the top. Each light was carved in the shape of a clam shell. The cobbles were also carved as shells from stones of many different colours all sealed under a clear impenetrable resin. It was impossible to see but the fountain as well was coated with an invisible force field which kept it immaculately clean despite the intricate carving and countless crevices which would have been impossible to maintain.

Around the plaza there were alleyways made of countless stalls selling goods or food. Street entertainers walked about plying their trade, young boys and girls with them holding a pot for passers by to throw money into.

Across the back of the plaza there was a huge multi storey stone building. From the bottom layer to the eighth each floor sported a long balcony along the entire length which was intricately carved and painted with gold. Either side of the entrance on the ground floor balcony an orchestra was playing. The music filled the plaza.

To the left and right there were five buildings a side. Each carved in the same intricate fashion and to the same design. Each was different in its own way and each bore a flag on its top which matched the colours they had seen on the boats.

Kyla was looking around in wonder. "Rennon, have you read up about this place?"

Rennon smiled and sat back against the soft velvet cushion in their boat. "This is the Plaza Del Elatonia. That building at the back is the Guild Hall where all the guilds and traders have their offices. The ground floor is where all the administration is done. The upper floors are where the merchants have their meeting rooms where they can meet clients and where trade which goes to all the planets in this alliance is done. The ten houses you can see around the plaza each belong to a different ruling family. The people on this world are all descended from these ten families

The ruler of this place, the Dojet resides in a palace to the right of this plaza with his entourage of servants and the High Council, ten good men, one from each of the families. The Dojet is chosen from those "of the blood" as only they can operate the artefacts that keep this place safe. Unfortunately our business is in a far less fine place but I wanted to take a look at the Plaza while we were here."

The oarsman propelled them on past the Plaza and down a side canal which passed by other ornate buildings and under intricately carved closed in bridges that spanned the canal from the upper floors of the buildings which towered above them.

Rennon was looking at a map on his hand held scanner. "All of these buildings are connected at roof level by these bridges making a network that runs throughout the whole city. We'll soon get to the poorer areas, these are not connected other than by the canals."

They passed the ornate buildings which came to an abrupt end at a huge stone wall. There was a gatehouse in the wall which spanned the canal. Above its parapet the gate guards were looking down at them, the door was just finishing its sweeping movement and had reached full open position, the water was still swirling where it had been moved. The guards above them were each dressed in a similar livery and held spear blasters, they seemed fairly relaxed about the boat passing underneath and were only paying it casual attention.

Kel grunted. "How did they know to let us through?"

Rennon tapped something into his scanner. "The oar is a propulsion device but it also holds a communicator. Our information was keyed in when we got on board so the gate guards would have got our signature in advance."

As they glided away from the gatehouse the doors swung shut with a metallic clang. Behind them was the ornate splendour of the ruling quarter, in front of them the poverty of the rest of the city. Stone buildings were replaced by a shanty town of buildings clinging to poles driven into the sea bed below. Bridges were tied together and precariously clung to the side of these structures. As they passed side canals washing was hung out on semi circle metal rods. The oarsman sped up and they narrowly missed the contents of a chamber pot being emptied out of an upstairs window.

The canal reeked of effluent, mouldy material and rotten wood. Dead rats floated in the water, some half eaten by the fish that occasionally came up to the surface and swam around the boat.

There were lights but as they got further away from the Plaza these got less and less until the oarsman put the boat's lights on so that they could see where they were going in the darkness caused by the overhanging buildings. They met another boat coming in the opposite direction, they saw its lights first and then its prow coming out of the gloom. The oarsman shouted a greeting in a language they didn't understand and received one back as they passed by each other.

Rennon had been looking nervous. "You have to be careful of pirates around here. The canals are rife with them. There is access from this city to the southern seas and that is where most of the pirates hold up as it is a popular trade route."

They passed down many canals until the boat docked at a small jetty beside a wooden building. Rennon got up to get off and the others followed suit while the oarsman steadied the boat.

Kel knocked on the door and it opened almost immediately. They were met by an elderly woman. Her apron was pristinely clean and neatly pressed and in stark contrast to her dark blue dress, her bonnet neatly tied around her grey curls. She was waif thin and her face looked drawn and bony but her smile lit up her face as she stepped aside and invited them inside. "Welcome to our home. I am Estrath and you must be Kel. Ah, Kyla, a pleasure to meet you my dear and of course you must be Rennon. My son is expecting you all, please do come in. Don't worry about your shoes, the floor will be cleaned later. The kettle is on the boil. Destral, good to see you again. If you'd like to visit Elatinia I could send you a message when my guests are leaving."

The oarsman smiled broadly and touched his flat round hat with his hand in salute. He was illuminated by the light from the doorway, his waistcoat was a work of art, neatly decorated with countless pearl buttons and his long cloak was edged in a similar fashion. His trousers were skin fitting and his crisp white shirt was fixed into them with a burgundy velvet cummerbund. He smiled and navigated off down the canal.

Estrath closed the door behind them and pulled across a locking bar. She keyed her code into the pad beside the door and the door flashed momentarily with a blue light as the force field came on. "There, that's better. Now if you'd follow me." She pushed past them in the narrow corridor and led them up some stairs which opened into a large space. The majority of the room was wooden with floorboards that were polished and well dusted. The cooking area stood on a stone platform. Around the cooking area, on the edge of the stone platform there was a low brick wall which extended on three sides up into the ceiling. To the right of the kitchen area was a seating area where comfortable but threadbare sofas welcomed them. A low table in the centre was piled high with wires and equipment and behind this there was a man in his early thirties who was screwing together an interface and pulling bits of wires out of the mound in front of him. "I do wish you'd keep your bits and pieces in your room Eland, you knew we were having guests."

Eland looked up. "Sorry mother, I'll move it if you would like me to."

Elstrath smiled. "I'm sure our guests won't mind. After all its Rath you have come to see isn't it?"

Rennon looked surprised.

Estrath put a hand on his shoulder and gave him a kind smile. "It didn't take a huge amount of working out when we get visitors that there would be a reason and the only reason I can think is that my son has the skills you are looking for. I'll pour the tea, he'll be down in a while. Please take a seat." She indicated towards the sofas.

They sat and looked around the shabby but clean room. Eland kept casting them a nervous look as he put together the wires and screwed bits together. "Sorry about the mess but I got started and it got a bit out of hand. There was a loose connection but that shorted out the central core so I've had to replace some bits. She should work fine now."

Watching him gave them something to do. He gradually pieced together the multi armed robot, wired the circuitry and put it all back together. He then stood it up and switched it on. Immediately there was a loud bang from inside the robot's chest and it fell back onto the sofa, its spider like arms rigid, its legs in the air. Eland looked mortified.

A deep voice came from the stairway. "Bad luck Eland, you'd better go back to basics on that one. The Epsinian Coil is shot, if you don't find a replacement for that you'll have the same problem again and again."

Eland looked deflated and a little angry. "Yes brother." He picked up the robot and bowed to their guests. "If you will excuse me I will take this to my room."

Rennon bowed his head and Eland crossed the room passing Rath on his way. Rath went and sat down as his mother brought a tray of tea over to the table and passed the cups around. "So, speak your piece and let's get this over with."

His mother looked at him in horror and cuffed him around the back of the head. "What have I told you about being rude? These are our guests. You should allow them to speak their piece in their own time."

Rath rubbed his sore head. "Sorry mother. I must apologise."

Kel grunted. "I like direct, it makes it a lot easier. You have the skills that we need and we want you to join us. You know that, we know that, so what will it take to convince you?"

Rath glared at his mother who smiled back, her hands in her apron pockets. "Well, the option is to live my life here doing household chores or step out into the wider universe and return to a life of imminent danger and personal fulfilment."

His mother looked horrified. "But I thought you had your fill of the military life when you'd done your term and come home."

Rath smiled, looking down at his lily white hands and manicured nails. "So did I but things change mother and the Followers are a threat, not to us here yet but they will be if they aren't dealt with. You need an Engineer and Pilot, I'm happy to oblige. There now that wasn't as hard as you thought it would be was it? Its amazing what four years of washing up and scrubbing floors can do to take the edge off of the determination of a military man who had seen enough fighting."

His mother looked down. "I suppose I knew it would happen one day soon. You aren't like your brother, he's content to play with his electronics and has a good job here. He'll be marrying Tennal soon and that will be his life. You, you would never settle. Poor Renak has tried with you for so long perhaps it is better to put the poor girl out of her misery. She can then find someone who will give her the attention she needs."

Rath looked suitably chastised. "She is a lovely girl but there is no spark there, it would just be a convenience and that isn't fair on her or me really. It wouldn't last, I've told you that before. My brother will give you the grandchildren you need, and you don't know I may find someone some day.

But for now if we don't solve the Follower problem before it comes here there won't be a future for anyone."

Elstrath offered around a plate of her home made biscuits. "I suppose you don't need a cook on your space ship do you?"

Rath looked at the others and they looked at each other. Rennon tried the biscuit and smiled, raising his eyebrows. "Well, we don't actually have a cook." He looked to see the reaction on Rath's face. He was smirking. "What is that smirk for?"

Rath looked into his cup. "I'm keeping out of this and I'll let my mother explain. I wouldn't know where to begin."

Elstrath smiled. "Well how about having a granny on board to look after all your cooking and laundry needs? It makes sense."

Kyla smiled kindly, trying not to be patronising. "But what if we were attacked? What if something or someone got on board?"

Elstrath looked very serious. "Well then dearie, I'd like to see the entity who could come in and disturb my kitchen."

Kel grunted.

Elstrath glared at him. "Don't be rude young man. You might have the muscles but do you have the skill?"

Kel raised an eyebrow and looked at the tiny lady who met his gaze with a steel grey stare. "So, what are you, combat granny?"

Elstrath smiled. "As my son so kindly pointed out earlier, I'm not a granny, yet." She gave Rath a meaningful stare.

Rath signed. "Ok, I give in. Mother is just mother now but she used to be Lieutenant Colonel Elstrath of the Kerlarinian Special Force. In truth she'd probably give me a run for my money any day in a straight fight and in stealth and covert opps I couldn't match her for experience or skill. She is also a good cook and takes a pride in laundry. But, who would look after this place?"

Elstrath looked about at her neatly presented though age worn home. "You mean this wonderful palace that we call home? I think that if your brother was faced with having to look after the day to day running of this place he may take his romance a little more seriously."

Rennon frowned. "I hadn't actually thought of it but in truth we could do with someone." He looked at the others and they nodded.

Rath smiled. "Well, I've only done a few opps with mother but I don't think you will be disappointed though after you've met the wrong end of her frying pan a few times you may wish you'd left her behind."

Rennon smiled cheekily, working out that he was well out of range. "Well we can always reconsider."

Elstrath got up. "Fine, I'll go and pack. Rath, I expect you have a bag packed already, I noticed some of your things had started going missing from the laundry pile. You'll find fresh underwear, go on then, get yourself packed.

I don't expect these good people want to hang around here. There's a universe to save." She got up and wandered over to the kitchen and began opening cupboards. "Now, I'll leave the basics here but there are a few things I'd like to take with me. So, this ship of yours, what's she like?"

Rennon looked a little bemused. "Well she's brand new off the production line. Fairly spacious and with a good galley. The controls are state of the art for her type."

Elstrath picked out a good frying pan. "No sonnie, I meant make and version."

Rennon shook his head in disbelief. "She's a Firebird 3100 Combat Class."

Elstrath was looking through her spice rack. "Not bad, not bad. Would have preferred the earlier model myself, I'm very much for if it isn't broken don't fix it but I'm sure she'll be good when it comes to it. There, that is about all I need from here, I wouldn't want to leave without my favourites. I'll just go pack a bag and we'll be ready. Oh, you might like to be taking a look through my old collection. Some of the girls are a bit out of date now but they are all functional and kept in tip top condition." She went to a cupboard near the door and opened it. The shelf unit inside was well stocked with basic household needs but she wasn't interested in those. She flipped a small wooden panel on the side of the cupboard, behind a can of beans and keyed in a code on the keypad within. The shelf unit swung forward to reveal a rather impressive arsenal of blasters, stun guns and ground to air launchers. "So what do you think of this little lot?"

Kel was on his feet and over there. "Very nice, how do you find this one. May I?"

Elstrath smiled. "Of course. She's a good model, fires slightly to the right but that was because the barrel took a hit in her early days but if you compensate she still aims true. A bit slow to recharge but I've found that one good blast from her tends to take most things down. Those ground to air missiles tend to pack a heck of a punch. I remember the last time I used her, it was on one of those Etathian Darts, a rebel group were planning a coup and thought to take out the Embassy on Solinos so it was a low level run ready to drop their payload so she had to be quick and accurate. She did the job a treat and the damage was minimal as there wasn't enough of the vessel to do any structural damage when it came down."

The blaster was a fire from the shoulder tube which looked big in Kel's hands and he took a sideways glance at the tiny lady beside him. Somehow she didn't seem so small and fragile now. Her eyes were bright and sharp and he just knew she was evaluating him and how he held the weapon. "It's a weighty old beast."

Elstrath was leaning on the shelf. "Its more your prepared mission weapon than a carry in case. It has a tripod as well if you have time to set it up. A fairly useful multipurpose tool really and its range can be up to half a mile."

Kel raised an eyebrow. "Impressive. So, are you planning to bring these with you?"

Elstragh looked at the assembled weaponry and ran her wizened fingers over the grey and silver metal of her collection. "Well, if there's room I'd like to. They may come in handy. How about while I pack a bag you pack some of these for me. There's a few kit bags folded in the bottom and the ammo is in the shelf above for the really old stuff. I kept some on that fire the old style bullets. Some of that old stuff can get through personal shields you know."

She bustled off and up the stairs while Kel and the others got busy packing the blasters and ammunition.

19

The planet hung in space like a giant blue ball on one side of it there was the sun on the other the moon. A slightly orange haze hung about the moon giving it a halo as the sun reflected off of the reflective particles that made up its surface.

Kel, Rennon, Kyla and Rath, one of the Marines were in the cockpit, Rath flying, Rennon co-piloting.

Their approach was calculated and Kyla was lost in wonder as she looked out of the window down onto the cacophony of towers and spires, landing pads and precarious looking bridges that spanned the gap between buildings. The air was filled with craft of all sizes. Some flew in lines and Rath had just got his permission to join one of these queues to land. They flew into formation with all the others and began a slow and laborious descent to wait their turn.

Kyla was still fascinated, watching the different craft weave their way through the slightly orange glow of the sunset. "So Rennon, what can you tell us about this world."

Rennon smiled and got out his handheld computer. "This is Aronicus Prime, First Planet in the Kerithian Planetary Alliance and home to the Government of Ar and the High Elders. The buildings you see below you are hundreds of years old and built by a previous civilisation that inhabited this planet. There are many myths and legends about this place, mostly associated with the surprising disappearance of its inhabitants. I can't say I don't find that more than a little disturbing myself.

For those of you who missed the brief." He looked at Kyla and Kel. "I will tell you the gist of what was said. It was basically along the lines that we have been invited here to meet with the Prince. These days he's too tied up with the trappings of power to be able to travel so it is the only way he can get to see us. Our acceptances have been sent on our behalf and we have an audience as soon as we land.

The trade here is basically technology, software products, information and spyware. It is well known that there is a data base here and a filter through which most of the electronically submitted material is scanned, sifted and stored if appropriate.

It has a standing army of over two million and most of the population are armed and ready to be called up at short notice. They have also all trained in some way or the other so picking a fight around here is not a good idea." He looked directly at Kel who smiled, shook his head and leant back in his chair.

"I don't think we're going to see much of the planet but there isn't really much to see as it is almost totally covered by this city. We will be landing at the Central Hub, a terminal which has access directly to the ministerial buildings and the building they are now converting to the Royal Palace. The buildings are built on foundations that go down to the bedrock under the surface of the water. Beneath there are caverns which stretch down through the bedrock using natural caves and watercourses. It is said to be quite amazing but very few have actually seen these caves and tunnels. All the manufacturing is done down there.

The City is so cosmopolitan now that there is no real native race living here. It was built by a race who left long ago and others have migrated into it to make it the place it is now."

The Hopper glided effortlessly down onto the landing pad. Rath flipped the landing switches and looked around at them. "Gentlemen and lady, we have arrived."

Rennon smiled. "Thanks Rath, nicely done."

Rath keyed in the code they had been given and a docking tunnel expanded to meet them. "Well here goes, prepare for a whole stack of etiquette and bureaucracy." He stood up and smoothed down his black suit.

Kel looked rather uncomfortable in his but Kyla couldn't keep her eyes off of him and was trying not to laugh. Kyla herself was wearing a smart black dress and neat shoes. Rennon as always looked totally comfortable in his smoothly fitting pinstripe suit.

Rennon took the lead. "Well, here goes."

They strode down a long corridor and were met by an elderly robed man. His long grey hair was neatly tied at the nape of his neck and his beard was neatly trimmed although it was long and hung down his front. As he bowed it nearly touched the ground. "Greetings and welcome." He stood up. "The Prince is expecting you. Would you like some refreshments or shall I show you directly to see his Majesty?"

Rennon bowed. "If you would be kind enough to take us directly to the Prince that would be very gracious of you."

The elderly man relaxed. "Please follow me."

At the end of the corridor there was a sliding door which led to a lift which took them down many floors. It opened to a sumptuously black carpeted hallway lit by neon tubes. The walls were a silvery iridescent blue which shimmered as they walked along to the large metal doors at the end. Two guards stood at ease but smartly, each wore silver boiler suits and carried a light assault rifle. Machine pistols were strapped to their respective belts. They looked up as the lift door opened but seeing the elderly gentleman they stood to attention and saluted. The elderly gentleman snapped his heels together in a very military fashion and saluted back. "Stand down gentlemen, these are personal guests of the Prince." The two guards relaxed to stand with their feet slightly apart, their rifles, stock down, barrel in hand by their sides.

The right hand guard turned and keyed his code into the access panel and the door slid open to reveal a small lobby. They stepped inside and the door closed behind them. The gentleman smiled. "You will now be scanned. I hope you will forgive the personal intrusion but security is of the essence." He smiled kindly and they saw a red light go on above them followed by a green light. "Very good, now you may proceed."

The wall in front of them slid aside and they were able to step into a corridor. The elderly gentleman walked ahead of them and keyed his code into the third door on the right hand side. It slid open and he stepped inside. "Please follow me in and I will announce you." He stepped into the green and gold room. "Your Majesty I am pleased to announce that your guests have arrived." He bowed deeply and stepped to the left so that they could step into the room.

Rennon went in first, followed by Kel, Kyla and then Rath. Rennon bowed and the others followed his lead.

The Prince laughed and made a mock bow himself. "My friends, please, come in and take a seat. Thank you Justice, could you arrange some food for us all later?"

Justice bowed. "Yes my Lord." He left the room and the door slid closed behind him.

They sat on sofas which were arranged in a triangle. The Prince was dressed in a formal plain black business suit, jacket, pale blue shirt and dark blue tie with a tiny gold embroidered motifs of a phoenix. His black patent shoes were immaculately shiny and he looked very comfortable in the whole outfit. He sat with them, taking a seat on the empty sofa and pulling his trousers so that the knees didn't pull. "As you can see things have changed somewhat and my life is drastically different. I was accepted very easily into the hierarchy as some ancient texts were presented that apparently foretold my arrival so we are managing to organise our troops and the resistance now. We've had quite a few resounding victories lately with the aid of our allies and we are starting to make a move on some of the outer planets to try to regain control. This should begin to loosen their stranglehold on the galaxies.

But, I'm sure you know all that. I have been following your careers with a personal interest and I must apologise for summoning you here but as you can imagine making private visits turn out to be real affairs of state these days.

Would you like something to drink?" He looked around and at their agreeing nods he got up and went to a panel on the wall. It opened to a bar. "There are all sorts here as well as hot drinks. The coffee is quite remarkable, they bring it in from Teka. The Tekan Special Blend is quite something."

Rennon piped up. "I'd like to try some of that." The others nodded approval.

The Prince spooned out the black granules into the mugs he had lifted down from the shelf above. "Tekan all round then."

When the kettle had boiled he smiled and poured mugs of it, put them on a tray and brought them over with a milk jug and bowl of sugar. He placed the tray on the table and placed a mug in front of each person before sitting down. "I don't believe I have had the pleasure of being introduced but I have read your file, very impressive. May I call you Rath?"

Rath looked a little stunned. "Er, of course your majesty."

The Prince smiled. "Thank you but you can drop the formalities in here. I get enough of that all day. Well, it is lovely to see you but I do have a reason for calling you here. I won't beat around the bush, I need your help on a mission. As you know myself and Kyla here share the DNA which allows us to use certain artefacts. That is basically why I asked you to come. We have come across intelligence that there is just such an artefact which will allow me to not only identify the Followers but in some way to loosen the control that the entities that the Followers follow have over them. Of course it is in a place where only those with the DNA can safely get to and of course it could be a trap but it could be something that would swing the war in our favour.

Being able to present the information you found regarding the experimentation has helped. It is tipping the balance but getting it broadcast on some planets has proven difficult. If we can expose those who are opposing it as Followers we may then be able to get it broadcast on public channels. It is of course multiplying like a very welcome virus on the private and social networks around the galaxies to the point that certain of them have now been shut down by the Followers.

We are greatly hindered by having to be cautious about Follower spies and we know that they have those with the DNA under their control. That is a whole story in itself that I won't bore you with now. It seems that we 'of the blood' are immune to their drugs but they have prisoners they can bring in if they need to activate artefacts so they would be able to use such a device should they obtain it. And of course they would be denying it to us. We now have agents within their ranks and we do not want them discovered. An artefact that proves someone is a Follower would also prove that someone isn't. So, I've called you here to ask if you would be prepared to come on a small secret mission with me. I am calculating that the last thing anyone would expect would be for me to undertake a mission and sidestep the protocols around here. So, Kyla are you willing to come with me? Would the rest of you be prepared to get us there?"

Kyla took a sip of the now slightly cooled coffee. "Of course my Prince." She smiled. "Good coffee."

The Prince nodded and smiled.

Kel looked over. "Of course you can count me in. Rennon, Rath, are you in too?" They both nodded. "Well it looks like you have got your team. When do we go?"

The Prince drank some coffee. "I would like to go almost immediately, the longer we leave it the more chance the Followers will have to find out about it. It seems that an opportunity has presented itself for me to slip away undetected. There is to be an official dinner tonight and I have a double who can stand in for me. It does happen often and my closest aides will think nothing of it. It is a high protocol affair so he wouldn't be expected to speak with anyone other than those sitting with him. They will expect me to be here pouring over the many financial papers and documents they have piled up for me. The last thing they would expect would be for me to be elsewhere. That will be the perfect opportunity for us to leave with the minimum amount of people around to witness our departure. I have taken the liberty of having equipment and clothing set out for you in case you agreed and there is a small Hopper prepared and ready for us."

Rennon looked around the room. Other than the sofas they were sitting on, the rest of the room was very high tech. The table was a sheet of glass which seemed to be suspended in mid air above a plain black box. The chairs around it looked like they were made of glass at a first glance but longer inspection revealed that they were actually a form of resin. The silver grey carpet matched the walls and ceiling and other than that there wasn't any other furniture in the room. "Well I think you knew pretty well that we'd agree. So, how has it been?"

The Prince smiled. "It has been a whole run of politics and planning. Getting through the red tape to actually be able to do something has proven a nightmare. To organise the mission we are going on would take months if I put it through the ordinary channels. So, this is much easier."

Kyla smiled as she saw the worried look on the Prince's face. "But, is it not a big risk to do this? What if something happens to you?"

The Prince smiled back. "A necessary one. I can't tell who is a Follower around me at the moment. It is hoped that this artefact will be able to tell me so I not only want to get hold of it, I want to get hold of it without my own people knowing I've got it. That is why I've asked you to help me. It is something I need as there have already been four assassination attempts and the constant worry is detracting from my real work and using resources that could best be placed elsewhere. That is also why I suspect a trap but I can't let my well founded paranoia stand between us and retrieving this, if it does do what they claim it does. The information came from a very sound source."

They finished their coffee and followed the Prince out into the corridor and along to another door. This door led to corridor after corridor which eventually led into a small room where clothing and equipment had been laid out. They got changed in silence into the grey military style outfits and strapped on the side arms. They then followed the Prince out into the hangar which was empty. The Prince whispered. "I've called a staff meeting to discuss pay and conditions, as you can imagine everyone wanted to attend. I've had that Hopper over there prepared by a crew I thoroughly trust but Rennon if you'd like to scan it just to make sure."

Rennon pulled out his hand held scanner and ran it over the vessel from a distance. "All clear on this but I'm picking up a tracking device. Shall I neutralise it?"

The Prince smiled. "I'm thinking no, lets take it off and install it on this one. Its due to be taken out by a drone on a reconnaissance mission. You haven't met our drones yet have you? Artificial humanoids who are programmed to undertake a specific task. Quite creepy really but very useful for saving quite a few lives."

Rennon strode over to the Hopper they were taking out and located the beacon. He carefully removed it and carried it to the new vessel and installed it in a similar position. "There, the two vessels are close enough at the moment that they won't detect it has been moved."

They climbed aboard the Hopper and the rear hatch closed. Rath and Rennon took the pilot's seats and the rest of them sat in the back. It as another A Class Hopper with access to the cockpit so they could leave the door open and still communicate.

The Hopper took off and hovered slightly before gliding out of the hanger. The Prince keyed in a code which allowed them to depart safely and they were soon up in the vast expanse of space and jumping into the inter-dimensional corridor.

An hour later they jumped out of the IDC and flew through the blackness of space until they came to a small green and blue planet which was part of a system of seven others and a sun.

The Prince stood behind Rennon and Rath. "That is Elak, home to the Elakians who are best known for their wood sculpture. What we are looking for is in a cave on their sacred mountain so we are going to have to come in cloaked and avoid detection or this could be a major diplomatic incident. They are allies and trading partners and we don't want to offend or upset them. To ask permission would take days and it may alert them to what they have. I cannot guarantee that some of them haven't fallen into Follower control so it is less complicated just to make this a covert mission."

Kel laughed. "You mean steal it."

The Prince nodded thoughtfully. "I mean borrow it without permission. I have no intention of permanently depriving them of their artefact and when this is all over I will return it."

Kyla smiled. "The Prince would never be such a rogue as to steal it now would he?"

The Prince looked thoughtful. "So you've done your homework. Some of my earlier exploits did involve me relocating certain equipment that belonged to my enemies."

Rennon looked up for a moment from the calculations he was making. "Did you expect anything else? We wanted to know a bit about you."

The Prince smiled to himself. "Of course. I wouldn't have expected anything less. Of course you could have just asked. I make no secret of it. I had the good fortune to have a romantic start in life by being orphaned and adopted and then I lived a colourful life before finally reclaiming my true inheritance. Which roughly translates to me being a street urchin who was adopted by a family who didn't mind encouraging my less law abiding attributes before my true lineage was discovered."

Rennon set his scanner aside. "I've completed the calculations and I can bring us down directly above the location you gave me. There is a small goat path that runs down to a cave."

The Prince looked in earnest at Kyla. "When we go into the cave we have to go in alone. Only those with the DNA will be safe which is what I'm counting on to give us the advantage. If you keep the ship on weapons standby just in case and we'll get in and out as quickly as we can."

The Hopper touched down and they negotiated the goat track, viewed by several goats who had taken up positions on rocky outcrops above them. The Prince had one of Rennon's scanners and scanned the entrance. "For a cave entrance that looks so natural I have never seen so much technology. We have already been scanned and then the activity stopped. So hopefully that means that it has recognised our bloodline and we are now safe to enter. Please follow me, I think we had better dispense with ladies first." He stepped over the threshold and into the darkness of the cave beyond. Kyla followed him and stood behind him as he clicked on his hand held torch which illuminated part of the cave.

The cave opened out into a large expanse about thirty feet across. The air was chilled and smelt of vegetation and damp. The floor was slightly damp and the rock was coated with centuries of debris which had rotted down into soil. Although fairly smoothly hollowed out rocky outcrops stuck out into the room. The walls of the cave were decorated with ideograms. These were mostly stick men who danced around camp fires. Bears and wolves leapt across the landscape and a bird rose above them. It was a simplistic representation of a bird with a zig zag base, body rising from this and flowing into two outstretched wings and the beak pointing to the left as they looked at it. Kyla walked over to it and was about to touch it when the Prince caught her arm gently.

He smiled at her, his face mere inches from hers. "It is safe but we don't want to leave any residue of our being here. Scanners could pick up our presence so it's best not to touch anything. There's just that one tunnel so I suppose that is the one we take."

A tunnel led off from the cave and the two followed it. It opened into an alcove on the right hand side which contained a stone coffin which almost filled it. The alcove was of a different stone, it was sandy coloured and carved to look like smooth stone blocks. The floor had also been covered with the same stonework as had the ceiling. The coffin itself was made of the same stone, carved smooth. The coffin lid was shut and it took both of their combined strength to rotate it open. Inside there was a body wrapped neatly in bandages. The bandages looked clean and showed no sign of decay. The Prince frowned and scanned the area. "I'm picking up residual EMP on the coffin but nothing on the body." As he stepped closer a hologram of a robed figure appeared in the corridor. Its hood was pulled up over its head but as they stepped around the coffin to get a closer look its hood fell back to reveal the head of an Ibis. The figure moved and became more solid. The Prince pushed Kyla behind him and took a step forwards to stand in front of the figure. In its hand it had a large black metal ankh which it offered to the Prince.

The Prince scanned it again and again, each time the figure was becoming more solid until it was fully in the room. The figure bowed and spoke in a language they didn't understand. The Prince activated the scanner and words appeared on the screen which read. "Welcome to the tomb of Thoth, Architect of the Universes. Within our walls you will find what you desire or you will find death." The figure then placed the ankh on the body.

The Prince swung round and began scanning the body. "I'm picking up life signs. Kyla watch out, that thing is coming to life."

The body sat up slowly and raised its hands to pull the bandages away from its face. It then climbed out of the coffin and headed straight for Kyla. The Prince got in the way and it stopped and looked at him. Beneath the bandages there were watery brown eyes that darted about. It stepped to the left, it was blocked. To the right, it was blocked. Then with lightning speed it grabbed the Prince and threw him across the room. He hit the wall, his head contacting the rock and slumped to the floor. Kyla was backing away and had pulled out her blaster. The mummy was still advancing as she pointed the blaster at it and fired making a huge hole in its chest. It looked down mystified and fell over backwards and was still.

The Ibis headed creature looked on in amusement and spoke in its own language.

Kyla ran to the Prince who was just coming around and rubbing his head. She checked him over for signs of concussion but as he seemed to be alright she helped him up. He dusted himself off and scanned the body on the floor. "Well Kyla, that was a bit unexpected. Come on, better get this done and get out of here." He then noticed the words on his scanner. "Your fear brings haste and rash actions."

The figure bowed and faded back into the wall. The mummy lay on the floor, blood flowing from the chest wound.

Kyla went over to it. The Prince tried to stop her but his hand missed her arm. She knelt down beside the body and felt for a pulse. There was one, it was weak. She rolled him over and she could see now that the bandages were wrapped over the man's clothes. She pulled out her own bandages, sprayed the injured area with disinfectant and marvelled as the wound began to close. As it closed she caught sight of something silver inside and wires. Tiny lights flickered red, green and blue before they were obscured by the skin which was growing over them. She scanned again, there was definitely life there but there was also something else, there was an EMP.

The creature sat up and clasped its chest and rubbed it slightly as it was almost healed. It then spoke in a similar language to the Ibis headed man. The scanner translated. "Thank you for your assistance guests to the Temple of Thoth. Please speak a few words so that I may place your language."

The Prince stepped up next to Kyla. "We are travellers."

The creature thought for a moment. "You are welcome in the Temple as the Keeper has already sanctioned your passing. I will accompany you."

Kyla looked at the Prince who shrugged. "Well I suppose if you wanted to kill us you would try again now. What is your name?"

The creature looked at the Prince, his bandages almost completely fallen from his face. His watery brown eyes looked a little sad. His long dark hair apparently hung down his back but that was still wrapped in bandages. His hair was flattened to his face where it had recently been wrapped. He pulled at the bandages and removed some of them. His skin was slightly tanned and flawless. "I have no name but I am referred to as Intendi."

The Prince smiled. "Well Intendi if you would like to join us you would be welcome and I'm sorry about shooting you earlier."

Intendi looked at the Prince blankly. "It was what you chose to do out of the choices you were given. All choices were perfectly valid."

The corridor went on for another thirty feet and turned right. There were many cobwebs and spider webs along the ceiling and the floor was littered with debris from them. The Prince went first and kept Kyla close behind him. Intendi followed on behind. Kyla and the Prince had torches attached to their guns and they pointed them up and down the corridor, stopping occasionally to listen.

It was quiet, there was the sound of dripping water in the distance and however carefully they walked the sound still echoed up and down the corridor and it was almost impossible to avoid the debris on the floor.

The corridor went on for about a mile and they soon realised that the floor was gently sloping downwards. It was hardly detectable until the scanner started giving depth readings. The slabs on the floor were becoming more distinct and then quite abruptly the tunnel ended in a steep stairway dipping downwards into the darkness. They both came to the top of the stairs and they looked down with both torches. The stairs were swept or at least there was no dust on them. They were also cut from a different stone, a dark grey with a vein of black running through it.

The Prince pulled out his scanner and pointed it down the stairs. This is illogical and completely wrong. Why build a tunnel that slopes down to end abruptly in a staircase. Intendi, do you know anything about this place?"

Intendi thought for a moment. "Please define know."

The Prince considered his words. "Have you been along this corridor before?"

Intendi looked at the corridor. "No."

The Prince waited as the readout appeared on the screen and then he showed Kyla. "Well, it looks clear. No mechanisms detected, no explosives, according to the scanner it is just a staircase. There are no apparent hidden passageways or rooms that the scanner can detect. This is a corridor ending in stairs going down. It has to be a trap but I can't work out what. There's not a lot more we can do than to walk down there as carefully as we can. Are you alright with that?"

Kyla looked at the stairway and smelt the musty air. "It looks like the only thing we can do."

The Prince put a foot on the first step, nothing happened so he started off down the stairs. He was careful, keeping one hand on the wall and taking it slowly, step by step. Kyla stayed close behind him and followed him down. Intendi wandered along behind.

The stairs descended for a quarter of a mile until it opened into a cavern. The Prince stopped at the entrance and let Kyla step beside him so that she could see the cavern as well. It was a huge and rough hewn from the rock to form a space about a couple of hundred feet across. On the far side of the cavern there was a stairway up to a raised level. On the raised level there were two thrones. In front of them the room was huge and in each quarter of the room a pyramid rose up out of the floor. The Prince looked at Kyla and she shrugged. He held out the scanner and lights began to flash and figures and words started flashing across the screen.

Kyla pulled out her scanner too and began to point it around the room and viewed the scanner in surprise. "I'm getting a lot of readings from this

244

room. There is an immense amount of energy being generated from here and it seems to be centred on those pyramids. The one on the left has a particular energy signature." She pointed to the pyramid closest to the raised platform on the left hand side. "It is pulsing with Eion energy and moving in and out of phase or dimension. Intendi, do you know what this place is for."

Intendi's face showed no emotion. "At last you ask a valid question. This place generates energy which maintains the energy field around this planet which protects it from those who would harm it. The pyramids are transformers which protect the planet from the many sun storms which occur here. The sun's energy would destroy any technology so such precautions had to be set in place in order to allow the machine to continue its function."

The Prince looked surprised. "So why isn't this place better guarded?"

Intendi bowed. "Thank you. The structure itself was built by an ancient race who believed that it was better to keep your enemies out than to defend once they are within their walls. If you had been travelling to this planet with the intent of destroying it or harming its people you would have been dealt with. As there was no need to defend against you the defences were shut down. Had you not carried the DNA the situation would have been very different."

Kyla looked puzzled. "Why would the DNA ensure that we didn't mean harm to this planet?"

Intendi bowed to her. "It doesn't but your radio communication and discussion in your shuttle informed us that you were travelling here seeking help to define your enemies. As that was your mission there was no need to defend against you."

The Prince looked thoughtful. "Alright Intendi, would you tell us where we can find the artefact that we seek if you already know our intent and have heard our discussion."

Intendi bowed. "I have not personally heard your discussion but yes I would tell you."

The Prince looked a little annoyed. "I said would you tell me."

Intendi bowed. "And I replied, yes I would tell you."

The Prince looked at his shoes and smiled. "Alright Intendi, before I get annoyed. Where is the artefact?"

Intendi bowed. "Right here."

The Prince took a step forward and then calmed himself. "Alright Intendi. What question should I ask so that I can get the artefact to take back to my people?"

Intendi bowed. "There is no valid question in this circumstance."

The Prince looked even more annoyed then glared at Kyla as she laughed. She took a step towards Intendi. "Intendi, are you the artefact?"

245

Intendi bowed. "Yes mistress."

Kyla smiled at the Prince who looked a little sheepish. She then turned back to Intendi. "So what are you? What can you do? How can you detect the Followers and why did you let us continue?"

Intendi stood up straight. "I am a standard information model D221456719, D Class. I am programmed for etiquette and general information. Information can be uploaded into my systems. My sub routine which allows me to detect the most minute amount of any trace drug in a human or humanoid system and neural programming is what allows me to be able to detect the Followers. You did not ask me any questions so I did what I was permitted to do."

The Prince smiled at Kyla. "Well done. So Intendi, will you accompany me and join my entourage? In this role will you be able to inform me if those around me are Follower spies? Do you think for yourself or do I have to tell you absolutely everything?"

Intendi bowed. "I will accompany you and join your entourage. I will be able to inform you of anyone in your court under the influence of another if that is what you wish of me. I am here to perform tasks initiated by your orders. If you wish to download anything into my memory banks I am programmed to listen for as long as you wish to speak to me. No necessity is implied in my programming."

The Prince smiled. "I think I am going to have to be very careful about how I word any questions or orders I may give you."

Intendi bowed.

Kyla was looking about. "Intendi, why are there two thrones on that platform?"

Intendi bowed. "They are there to be sat on."

Kyla smiled and looked a little frustrated. "Who is supposed to sit on them and what do they do while they are sitting on them? Can you give me any information about the thrones relevant to us?"

Intendi bowed. "They were built for the Lord Osiris and the Lady Isis. They would carry out the goings on of the court while on those thrones. The thrones are a communication and control device which gives the one seated on them the ability to control the planet's extra defence mechanisms. They also control the finer details of the planet's environmental and physical defences. They are artefacts keyed to the DNA you carry and you would be able to use them to perform all the functions that they were designed to carry out. They have many thousands of sub routines which I will list."

A worried look flickered over Kyla's face. "That will not be necessary."

Intendi bowed. "Very good mistress."

The Prince turned to face them. "Why do you call her mistress?"

Intendi bowed. "I have had the opportunity to read her genetic code and she has initiated my systems by physical contact. I am thus programmed to address her in that way."

The Prince put his hand out and touched Intendi's.

Intendi bowed. "Master."

The Prince thought for a moment. "Are you programmed to follow the commands of those you touch or is this an initiating program? Can I command you to only follow my commands or will you follow anyone's commands?"

Intendi bowed. "I am programmed to follow the commands of those I touch during this reboot and initiating program. You may not. I will only follow your commands."

The Prince took a deep breath. "Kyla, help me out here."

Kyla smiled. "Alright. Intendi. Is this a start up protocol where you are initiating your systems and defining those who may command you?"

Intendi bowed. "Yes."

Kyla looked around the room as she thought. "Is the start up phase complete? Can one or other of us command you not to accept any more controllers?"

Intendi bowed. "Yes. Yes."

Kyla took a deep breath. "Can we later command you to accept more controllers?"

Intendi bowed. "Yes."

Kyla smiled. "Can you only answer direct questions? Does your programming allow for independent thought? If not, why not? "

Intendi bowed. "Yes. No. Earlier models were supplied with an active learning facility. The resulting artificial intelligence was found to be unsuitable and difficult to control."

Kyla frowned. "Would you like an active learning facility?"

Intendi bowed. "I have no function that complies with like."

The Prince looked thoughtful. "May we leave this facility unchallenged and in safety."

Intendi bowed. "No."

The Prince opened his mouth and then looked at Kyla. "Go on, you seem very good at this."

Kyla looked worried. "Who is going to challenge us and what threatens our safety?"

Intendi bowed. "Your craft is under attack from a Follower battle cruiser and its presence would ultimately affect your safety."

Kyla looked horrified. "Can we use the thrones to destroy the battle cruiser? If so, we are in a hurry can you tell us how or can you undertake this task for us?"

Intendi bowed. "Yes. I can tell you how or I can undertake the task for you."

Kyla stared at the thrones. "With the greatest haste please would you destroy the battle cruiser?"

Intendi moved with lightning speed and took a seat on the throne. He lifted a panel on the arm of it and began pressing buttons. A hologram screen appeared in front of him and he touched a brightly shining dot on it. There was a slight rumble which shook the room and the dot disappeared from the screen. Intendi then pressed more buttons, the screen vanished and he stood up and returned to them. "Your command has been carried out. The battle cruiser has been destroyed."

Kyla and the Prince both looked relieved. "Are we still in danger? If so, who from?"

Intendi bowed. "Yes. You are in danger from your enemies. I have no specific information as to the names of them all."

The Prince looked at Kyla who gave him a wry smile. "Alright Intendi is there anything else we should do here before we go? Can we leave this facility safely? Will you be accompanying us? Do you need to bring anything along with you?"

Intendi bowed. "There is nothing that you should do. Yes. Yes. I need to bring my emergency battery pack and my repair kit with me."

The Prince smiled. "Can we leave now?"

Intendi bowed. "You can leave now."

A flash of inspiration seemed to come across Kyla and she smiled broadly. "Do you have an inbuilt operating manual which can be downloaded onto the Prince's laptop? Do you have a function to respond to anything other than direct questions? If so, what is it? Do you have any other programming or inbuilt programs that could be activated?"

Intendi bowed. "Yes. Yes. I have an etiquette sub routine. Yes."

The Prince took a final look around the room. "Kyla, we had better get out of here. That battle cruiser may have transmitted that it had encountered us in this quadrant. If so, I had better get clear before there is a diplomatic incident. We have what we came for. Time to go I think."

Once back on board they initiated the drive and sped off into the IDC.

20

The Erlik Landspeeder Mark II swept across the uneven terrain and skipped over the watery swamp and quicksand that made up nearly half of the planet of Kisrexian. It had long been their defence as it was hard to form any kind of tactics in such a harsh terrain.

They were lucky, it was a good day. The normal monsoons and hurricane speed winds were conspicuous by their absence and Rath was enjoying a gentle skip along the planet's surface. They had visited one settlement and they were well on their way to the second when they spotted a black shape bearing down on them.

Rath took evasive manoeuvres and just managed to move the ELM sideways before the talons and giant beak bore down on its previous location. The bird was immense. The ELM was easily overshadowed by it.

The bird swooped and glided effortlessly up into the gentle thermals. Its forked tail splayed as it flew above them, matching their course. It was clearly watching them and clearly intent on another attempt at them. It folded its wings and down it came at an impossible speed. Rath swore under his breath and again managed to move the ELM before the bird could get its huge talons onto it. Then the bird jolted slightly and flew upwards making its own evasive turns to get away from a huge reptilian bird which had got hold of its tail. The new assailant was huge, nearly twice the size of the first. It resembled a giant flying lizard, its scale like skin slightly red in colour. It snapped at the tail again but the bird took the opportunity to exercise an amazing and frantic turn of speed and was able to get away.

Rath took the ELM into the trees and hovered over the flooded ground. The trees were covered in a thick hanging vine which fell from the branches and covered the ship, concealing it from even the reptile's keen eyesight.

Rennon relaxed slightly, his knuckles were white where he'd been gripping the arm of his chair just that little bit too tight. Kyla turned to smile at Kel who was clasping his blaster tightly and looking around nervously.

Rath switched on the cloak and relaxed back into the chair. "Well I think I'll let that little one have a chance to fly away a bit." Just as he finished speaking a warning light came up on the screen. The proximity alert light was flashing on and off indicating that they had company.

Looking out of the window they could see very little as the moss had fallen from the trees and completely covered them. It too would be invisible to anyone looking. Rath bent forwards and flicked a couple of switches and the external intercom sparked into life. Rennon leaned forwards and flicked another switch before pulling down a laptop and opening it up so they could see the screen. On the screen they could see the relay from the external cameras. Most of them were now covered in moss but the port and starboard fore cameras were giving them a clear picture of what was out there.

It was very dark under the moss laden trees. Their black twisted trunks eerily reflected what little light there was and the moss hung down ominously, glowing slightly green in the dim light. They were surrounded by water but there was a small raised path to their right. It looked manmade, the stones were regular and cemented together to form a causeway which snaked its way around the trees.

A man with a donkey were walking along the path. He looked very on edge, he was looking anxiously from side to side. His donkey had obviously noticed something which had spooked it as it jumped sideways, threatening to fall off the path at any moment so he was also having to spend a good deal of his concentration keeping the beast calm and on the path.

Around him things splashed in the swamp. Tendrils broke the surface then were swallowed up by the black liquid again. Occasionally there was the dull splash as a fish like creature jumped from the water, snatched an insect from the air and re-entered the water leaving its circular ripples to fan out over the water surface. The place was teeming with life. Insects, bugs and flying creatures of all sizes went about their daily business.

The traveller was covered head to foot in a long robe. The hood was pulled up over his face but what glimpse they did catch of him revealed that his face looked like it was bandaged.

Rennon had his handheld scanner out and he was taking readings. He keyed in the planet's name and a stream of information ran across the screen. "He's a traveller alright. They wander the swamp lands doing odd jobs and moving from place to place by appointment. The bandages you see are just that. The biting insects are so prevalent around here at this time of year that bandaging the face in material soaked in a repellent and antihistamine is the only way to move around. He'll be bandaged over most of his body. We are in the Retasinian Swamps, about a mile from our destination and my guess is

250

that he is travelling that way too. We can't offer him a lift as opening the airlock would let in the insects so we'll have to let him walk I'm afraid.

The town we are going to is encased in a force field which keeps the insects out. The inhabitants can go about their daily lives quite safely during the day. There is a curfew at night as the power supply cannot cover a full day. They then retreat to their houses and lock themselves in.

This is all basically the result of the powers that be realising that their use of the natural resources and tampering with the environment would have a bad effect. It didn't have the effect they expected. They predicted floods and mass starvation due to climate change. They got climate change alright, the lands did flood and this provided the perfect breeding ground for anything that enjoyed that habitat. A water world is fine but when you add to that a warm and humid atmosphere you are going to encourage things that bite.

We are going now to Cyber City. It is a technologically advanced place. That donkey down there, its not real, it's a replica of a real donkey, programmed to react in the same way as a real one would. They lost most of the real animals long ago, they just couldn't survive the biting insects and in those first years of chaos the animal life was the last thing they thought of preserving. Now it would cost too much to feed anything like that. By the way, don't expect any gourmet dinners while you are there. They live on reconstituted protein most of the time, supplemented by the occasional delivery of fresh food. Here we are far away from any of the trading belts.

You wouldn't believe this used to be a thriving plant and a real hub of commerce. How things can change. Here, well it was the eco terrorists. They wanted to make a point and broke into a research establishment. What they set free should never have been allowed outside a restricted area. So, to compound their biting insect problem they have huge predatory beasts that are happily reproducing in the warm swamp there is out there. Truly a lovely place to live."

Kel looked up. "So why do they?"

Rennon smiled. "In truth, because it is their home and mostly because they can't leave. Take a look around, do you see any airborne vessels? They are rare here. The Corporation rules the planet and they won't let anyone gain access to anything like that. They keep the population pretty much on what used to be called the bread line. That is they pay a minimum wage, provide the accommodation, provide the food, clothing and just about everything else. So what the people do earn goes straight back into their pockets."

Kel grunted. "So why doesn't someone do something?"

Rennon looked down at his scanner. "Why should they? They have food on their tables, a roof over their head, zero unemployment and a comfortable life. Those who do choose to argue against it are free to leave. But few survive long outside the force field dome. Some have set up communities, some have survived by being driven so insane by being bitten that they no longer care. Be careful of them, they will attack without provocation and general prowl the swamps in bands attacking anyone they find."

Kel leant back and put his feet up. "So a controlled place with a few vagrants living free but in abject poverty. Sounds a lovely place!"

Rennon smiled to himself. "On the face of it, it is. They have little to complain about as everything is controlled for them. After so many generations they are used to it. They had rebellions at the start. The rebels have become the foundation of the workforce in various mines and factories sited a long way away from decent civilisation. They are now into their third and fourth generation and the people there know no different. They live in controlled domes but the set up is very different. You'll see on the horizon, this place is the height of good taste, impossible architecture and controlled civilisation. So no doubt we're going to be in trouble the minute you and Rath step off the shuttle.

Try to tone it down boys. We don't want to be leaving you behind. This is one of the few planets that fought off Follower intervention successfully. As far as we know they haven't been infiltrated and are keen to be allies. Leave it to Kyla here, I'm sure she can secure a diplomatic agreement for us."

The dome was now clearly visible amongst the swamp and vegetation. It appeared like a shimmering bubble rising out of the green quagmire below. Occasionally it shimmered and a silver or black ship spewed forth into the cloudy skies above.

The screen fizzed slightly as the lasers burnt off the accumulated insect bodies and they could see clearly again.

The dome was slightly cloudy but it was just possible to see through it. Buildings towered to impossible heights and the contrast between the high technology of the city and the green swamp around it was remarkable. It was as if the bubble held the technology back, or was it the other way around?

A streamlined dart like plane was now flying alongside them and they were being requested to provide identification or a security code. Kyla bent forwards and typed in a code she had been given by the Prince.

There was a moment's hesitation where they all held their breath but it was unfounded as a deep husky voice sounded over the intercom. "You have clearance to land on Pier 7. On behalf of our people we welcome you and hope you enjoy your stay with us."

The dart like ship veered off to the right and left them to fly through the dome barrier. It parted like water and they were able to pass through as it flowed over them. The ship juddered slightly and veered a little to the right but it kept on course. Rath made the necessary adjustments and they were flying true again.

Rath cleared his throat. "So does anyone have any idea where Pier 7 is then?"

There was silence.

Rath smiled. "Ok, well I'd better call this one in." He thought for a moment and took a deep breath. "This is the Shuttle Obsidian, requesting directions to Pier 7."

The husky voice was back. "We apologise for our omission, a pilot will be with you shortly. Please hold your current course."

Rath clicked the intercom off. "Well that should sort it and I got to hear that delicious voice again. Now if we could get an onboard computer with voice delivery that would really make my day."

Rennon turned to him. "That is easily arranged. Most of the vessels have the technology but it is usually turned off as it is too damned annoying. I'll activate it for the return journey if you'd like me to."

Rath looked very pleased with himself. "Sure would, I'll keep you to that. That voice certainly does it for me."

A silver dart was now flying alongside them and then it took up the lead just in front of them and wound its way past the tower blocks and pinnacles that made up the skyline. Now that they were following someone it did make perfect sense. There was a web of crossing pathways above the buildings that made a grid.

There was little time to wonder at the architecture but the general view was of an immaculately and pristinely planned and executed construction. Everything seemed to fit in with the building next to it and it was as if the whole place was built at the same time. Each building dovetailing with the next to give an ergonomic dream of efficiency were they could feel the thermals and updrafts buoying the ship up.

Rennon grabbed for his hand held scanner and tapped on the keys. "As I thought, the city was built in one go, planned, designed and executed. The updrafts we are experiencing are from the ventilation systems. The hot air rises from the buildings and it is cooled in the atmosphere and then sinks around the outside of the dome to be pumped back through the cooling system which runs through the whole city. Each building is built on a skeletal infrastructure where each building supports and strengthens the next. It's all quite smart really and saved them nearly thirty percent on building materials.

The building materials are manufactured from waste products reclaimed from landfills which were created as part of their old existence. They have taken all those never degrading plastics and used them to their best advantage in making the buildings and vehicles we are seeing. They use solar and wind energy to generate the power to run the city. The geo-thermals from the buildings and from vents dug deep into the earth provide a heating source which in turn provides more thermals to run turbines between the buildings which are turned by the rising heated air. They are hard to see as they are delicate and activated by the slightest breeze. There is no weather here so no danger of damage by a freak storm. It's quite a place. Of course now that we're going to scratch the surface we'll see more we may not like."

Kel gave his usual wry smile. "Then let's land somewhere where we can see what is really happening them."

Rennon caught his arm as he was about to alter the course. "No Kel, not this time. These are allies and the war isn't going well enough that we can afford to make enemies on our own side. We may get a chance but for now, let's just do what we're told and keep them happy. This trade agreement and protection through their sector of space is essential."

Kyla was looking down on the city below. "It is totally amazing but even from here I can see that down there is very different to the high rise buildings above. Look down there. It's almost a shanty town." He hit the magnify button for the ship's windows and got herself a clearer view.

In the depths between the buildings it was very dark. It seemed as if it was raining as the condensation from the building's air conditioning was condensing and dripping off of every available point. It fell on streets where the less fortunate lived. Down there it looked like a shanty town of shops, traders and people trying to scratch a living. Neon shop signs lit the street, their colours reflected back in pools of water that had accumulated there. Bright coloured umbrellas floated around everywhere like demented butterflies as they flitted from shop to shop and made their way through the crowds below.

They were all now fascinated by what they were seeing. By any standards the technology these people walked around with was out of date and basic. It didn't take long for Rennon to open his mouth and point at a piece of equipment. He was about to speak when the intercom sparked into life. "You will be landing shortly. Please approach slowly and with caution."

Rennon flicked on the intercom. "Thank you and thank you for your assistance."

The voice responded immediately. "It was a pleasure." The dart broke away and flew off to join the lines of sky traffic making their way across the airways above.

Rath took over control. "Well I guess I'd better bring this little lady down good and slow then. Strap yourselves in, you never know."

The shuttle glided down and landed effortlessly on the allotted pier. The pier was just that, it protruded from the top of a high tower block out into the sky beyond stopping abruptly in a landing pad which they had just deftly landed on. Rath flicked the switches to standby and landed mode and smiled contentedly. "Another smooth landing by yours truly." The smile was wiped from his face as the tower block to the right of the one they were attached to exploded in a ball of flame.

Rath was most of the way through the take off procedure by the time a reassuring voice came over the intercom. "We are sorry about the disruption.

It seems that Likatel Industries is having certain problems with its employees currently. Do not worry, this will have little effect on the building your pier is attached to."

Rath looked at Rennon. "Pretty words but I've seen how those buildings are put together they are interconnected. What happens to one has to harm the rest."

Rennon looked about the scene and then at Kyla, giving her a reassuring smile. "Yes, but their structure is very cunningly worked out that it gives strength to the next building but does now rely on it. We should be fine. I'm more interested in why the employees felt they had to take such drastic action."

Kyla looked worried. "I would say we're not really in a position to go delving too deeply into their affairs. But they can't stop what we see and what we may see. I say we take whatever is offered and keep our eyes open. Now, I expect they are scanning us so I would suggest that we made this ship secure and go and visit our new allies."

Rath was already switching switches and pressing buttons. "I've set the autopilot to take off if it detects any trouble, to hover away from any detected trouble and to return to pick us up. It's a good system but I really wish we had a Mackenzie Unit."

Rennon looked confused. "A Mackenzie Unit? I don't think I've heard of one of those."

Rath was just finishing his switching process. "I doubt you have, it was all very hush, hush. A Mackenzie Unit is an autopilot with a difference. They are cyborgs built to fly all manner of different planes. I had the opportunity to fly with one once, chatty fellow though his topics of conversation were limited to flying. They resemble humans, some have synthetic skin grafts to make them look more human. On many they just plain don't bother. It's a bit unnerving as they have a solid metal endoskeleton which looks like a metal skull with red LED eyes. Of course when they get the full skin job they look just as human as you or I."

Kyla looked interested. "What are they like though?"

Rath thought a moment. "Well the one I met was just a regular Joe. He got into the pilot's chair and flew the plane, finished his shift and got out. He talked a bit and you'd not really know that he wasn't human other than he had no real emotion. He took everything on face value which was both refreshing and difficult. But, I heard a rumour of a new Mackenzie Model. It could be just a rumour though but some say that they have upgraded the Units and added a personality, even making one an Artificial Intelligence. A bit dangerous if you ask me but then, it is just a rumour.

Well they fly well as they can be programmed and can run through simulations faster than we can think. I like them personally but I only met Matrix 221, an early version."

Kyla shuddered. "Actually it all sounds a bit creepy. I've never been comfortable with the idea of cyborgs."

Rath was logging his hours and information in his small notebook. "That's why they were kept as military models. They were useful for flying into dead zones and some of the less hopeful missions. It's harder to mourn a person than a piece of kit. I did once catch a glimpse of the store room. Now that was creepy. They just stand in a line, some that are out of service hooked up on the wall. I kid you not. They finish their day, walk in there and are put away for the night. Economical I suppose."

Kel looked up from his quiet contemplation of his hands, the fingers of which were interlocked. "Well, what about this super cyborg, did they hang that one up at night as well."

Rath looked at him trying to work out if he was serious or taking the rise out of him. "Well no, I don't think they did in the end. To start with perhaps but I heard that they gave her a room."

Kel raised an eyebrow. "It was a she?"

Rath smiled. "Yes she was a She and by all accounts had quite a figure. Shame they never got around to fixing up her face. I heard that was the one thing that really upset her. Then all this hit and the unit was lost when the ship downed over enemy territory. All lifesigns were lost and they don't go looking for lost equipment and lose more lives. But, as I say, that is most likely a rumour or a bedtime story told by some drunken soul or the other."

Out on the landing pad six soldiers, each dressed in a shiny black carapace, were marching towards them. They marched in unison, visors down, hand swinging synchronised with their marching steps. The crossed the landing pad and formed up in a line in front of the Hopper.

The crew went down to meet them. Kyla stepped forward as one of the soldiers took a step forward to stand about three metres away from her. His visor became clear plastic and she could see his face behind the slightly reflective surface. He snapped his heels to attention.

His voice was slightly metallic, synthesised as he spoke, his lips moving in sync with what he was saying. "Welcome to our planet. Please follow me."

He turned on his heels and the crew followed him. Rennon turned and the Hopper door closed and locked behind them. He fell in with the rest, the residue of the retinue fell in behind him. They moved swiftly across the landing pad and through a large double door into the room beyond.

It was similar to most reception rooms they had seen in their visits to other planets. A fairly bare room, sparsely decorated, a reception desk and someone there with a terminal waiting to take their details and put them through their immigration controls. Rennon stepped forward to give the necessary details and processing was swift as they were official visitors so most of the protocols had already been completed.

Kel looked bored and had started to shuffle his feet. Kyla elbowed him discreetly and he raised his eyes to the ceiling and stood still.

Their processing done the guards took them down a side corridor. Everything was white and chrome, the lighting came from clusters of LED lights in the ceiling and the hard plastic floor made a dull sound as they marched along it.

The walls were panelled, each panel ending in a chrome metal strip. The holes in the panels which reflected slightly red as they passed were not lost on them either. At the end of the corridor the door swished open and they were led out onto a balcony. The safety wall was clear plastic, the floor the same opaque white plastic. They looked down on what looked like a factory floor combined with offices. Machines worked, people assembled things and office workers sat at their desks.

They were led along a balcony corridor which overlooked the workforce and past many doors until they came to one which opened and they were led inside.

The room was sparsely furnished. A clear plastic table, a plastic chair behind it and chairs set out for them opposite the elderly dignitary who sat behind the desk.

He got up as they entered the room and stepped towards them. He was dressed in a white robe with a single simple silver amulet around his neck which flashed slightly red. "Welcome, please take a seat. May I offer you some refreshments?"

Rennon sat down first. "Thank you for your hospitality but no thank you."

They all sat and the dignitary returned to his seat. I am High Chancellor Utiah of the Ocatonian High Council and I speak with the authority of High Council behind me. Would you forgive me if I dispense with some of the protocol here? The Prince has informed me that such etiquette is not necessary in your presence."

Kel smiled. "That would be welcome."

Utiah smiled back. "Good, then I will continue with the more important things that I have to say to you today. Thank you for coming so fast. Our discovery has been both a blessing and a curse. As you may have seen while landing, some of our more, how shall I put it, rebellious I suppose, elements have been stirred up by our discoveries. They mostly comprise our youth and it is to be expected. We are keeping a careful watch on it and the culprits are being dealt with firmly and fairly. After all, they will probably be our leaders of the future. But youth aside there are serious issues here. We have found documentation in an old abandoned city here which has changed our outlook on the world. We too have been troubled by these Followers and the documents we have found relate directly to them. Or more precisely where they came from, or should I say where they didn't come from.

We have in our possession a notebook which was found in a box in a

257

ruined building in part of the old city. As with anything we find of the old ways we brought it here for our librarians to scan it, publish it and preserve it. Information is always made available to our population whether it is detrimental or beneficial and they make their own mind up.

We have been worried for some time that many of our younger elements have been charmed by the writings and teachings of the Followers. Their texts are indeed a good model for what we could say was an utopian society. If carried out to the letter of the original text it would provide a world where everyone lived in harmony with nature and used the worlds resources practically and effectively. But, as with all good ideas there were people to exploit it. I don't need to tell you about this, you deal with the outcome every day.

The notebook belonged to Erasmus Bolt who lived on this planet until he moved to one of the border rim planets near Estran'Ka'Nelanos. This was long before this city was built and before the older cities became abandoned. He was a youth then, barely a teenager and this is his diary with all his hopes and dreams for this world. It has long been speculated that he was the father of the organisation which became known as Fallow Earth. But in his writings it clearly states that all men should be free to make their own decisions.

This is what is igniting the fires within our youth. They rebel against our ways. They want to see more control of the population and the information that is generally available. The building you saw them destroy was our Library. It was a needless act, all the files were backed up and are part of the network. They'd have to destroy the whole city to destroy the information. We will rebuild. But it is the intent that disturbs me. That our people should wish to have such control."

Kel coughed. "If I might be so bold. The people who live in poverty at the base of your fine buildings don't seem so free and informed."

Utiah smiled. "First impressions can be deceiving. You were looking down on our entertainment district. Other than clinically flying through the countryside outside in shuttles and airbuses our people have little by way of physical recreation. Down there they can live out their fantasies. They take on personas unlike their own and are able to play out the games physically that they play within the computer during the rest of their lives. What you see down there is real but it also is not. The Larping Foundation was established many years ago and is one of our most profitable companies. Its shares on the Exchange have rocketed of late. People enjoy being able to escape and to be someone else in a controlled environment where they can't actually die. They may die as their persona but when they leave the game they are healthy and well, if a little tired and have got any aggression out of their system. Before the Larping Foundation we were spending a fortune in maintenance and cleaning to keep those alleyways clear. Leasing them out has turned this land into an asset."

Kel smiled. "Well I never would have thought."

Utiah smiled back. "It may seem very alien to you. You live an exciting life. For the rest of us who are tied to the mundane of work and living, we need our escapes and to be able to develop our imagination. But, I digress, not that you are unwelcome to ask. I welcome it. The notebook proves that the origin of the Followers was unlike what they are now. This coupled with the footage you have been able to provide us with has almost completed the package. We are able to provide them with the reasoning and back it up with the evidence of what this organisation has become. That is but a start. What we need to do is find out why there was such a dramatic change. I refuse to believe that it was just greed and the need for control and power by certain individuals. It was too dramatic a change and too quickly. Also, the martial state of the Followers is totally contradictory to the gentle and humanitarian approach of its founder. We have the beginning, we have the end. Now all we have to do is find out why. I have provided the Prince with a full scan of the notebook. You may ask why I invited you here when I have already sent the information on ahead. I invited you here because we may well have found something on this planet. We cannot investigate it."

Kyla looked shocked. "Why not?"

Utiah smiled. "Because anything we find must be publicised to the populace. Those are our beliefs. The High Council have suggested that we do not get involved with this. What we do not know we cannot tell." He pushed a small piece of paper which was water stained and folded in quarters across the table. "Take this and leave. Do not speak further to me about it. I have told you all we know and I would not discuss it further. Do you understand me?"

Kyla took the piece of paper and slipped it into her pocket. "Completely." She smiled and took a small black rod out of her pocket. She placed it on the table. "The Prince's office will send you the information that goes with this. I trust our trading meeting has been beneficial?"

Utiah bowed his head. "I hope so."

21

The Argo floated meaningfully through the emptiness of space. A multi coloured nebula swirled behind it like a halo of colour and stars and planets dotted the infinite velvet blackness of the Renisinnian Galaxy.

Kyla rolled over after waking from a fitful sleep. She reached out and switched on the bedside light which illuminated the room. The normal shadows in the room seemed wrong, there was a dark patch she didn't remember.

As she reached for her pistol, concealed under her pillow, Joniel stepped from the shadows smiling. "No need to shoot me my love. I'm just here for some time with you."

Kyla smiled. "So why just stand there, why didn't you wake me?" Out of the corner of her eye she noticed the drawer of her cabinet beside where he had been standing was slightly open. "I could have looked forward to your visit if you had let me know you were coming."

Joniel smiled. "Can't a lover come and make love to his woman on a whim."

Kyla pulled out the pistol and shot him in the chest. He barely flinched and moved towards her with lightning speed. She shot him again and again as he bore down on her.

Kel was in his room. Dr Samson bent over him and was just withdrawing an empty syringe from his bare arm. "Kel, listen to me. I am your friend Dr Samson. You have to go to Kyla tonight, she needs you. She has been drugged by Joniel and that is why she will not come to you and be with you. You know it is only right that she should be with you. Put that right. If you do not do this tonight there will be no hope for your people. Go to her, take her and break the bond and ties that he has over her. Go to her room now.

Nobody must stop you. Kill them if they do."

Kel got out of bed as if in a dream, threw his clothes on and grabbed his blaster. He climbed the ladder out of his room and stepped out into the empty corridor and went to Kyla's room next door. He could hear shots. He opened the door which wasn't locked and jumped down the ladder. He saw Joniel bearing down on Kyla. In a swift motion he shot him in the back which blew him forwards onto the bed, pinning Kyla down.

In a couple of paces he was across the room and pulled the prone body off of the bed.

Kyla looked up at him, visibly shaken. "Thank you. I don't know…" Kel grabbed her and pinned her arms to the bed. He tried to kiss her but her knee came up under the blankets and all he could do was cough and splutter as she managed to use his momentum towards her to throw him over the other side of the bed.

She reached over and hit the alarm button as Kel leapt cat like onto the bed. She was out from under the covers, thankful that she had chosen that night to wear at least a silky night gown. She backed away as Kel rushed at her, his eyes wild. She balanced herself for his impact and then used his speed against him. She grabbed his shirt and pushed him past her so that he careered into the wall. He hit his head and slid down as she reached over and hit a nerve centre, rendering him unconscious. She then slid to the floor next to Joniel's prone body, taking his head onto her lap as the tears started to fall.

Rennon climbed down the ladder and looked about. He bent down and was about to check for a pulse on Joniel's neck when he moaned slightly and opened his eyes. Rennon took in the wounds all over him. There was very little blood but Joniel looked near to death. Joniel coughed slightly and came around fully. "It was Kel. He attacked me. Kyla are you alright?"

Kyla looked at him with eyes that did not see. She opened her mouth and screamed until Joniel wrapped his arms around her. Then she fell silent.

Rennon was taking it all in. "Kyla, what happened?"

Joniel looked up at him, his eyes flashing with anger. "I told you, Kel came in and attacked me. Then he attacked her. He will never accept that she is not his woman."

Rennon reached down to Kel. "There's a pulse, a weak one." He flipped up his communicator. "Dr Samson to Kyla's room immediately. Kel has been hurt."

Joniel was trying to comfort Kyla. Out of view of Rennon he had his hand over her mouth. He looked up at Rennon. "I am taking her out of this." He threw a small communication device to Rennon. You can contact us via this, keep it safe. I'll speak to you later."

Rennon looked down at him. "Can't we help with your injuries?"

Joniel looked down at his chest. The wound was barely bleeding now. "Don't worry, you concentrate on things that matter. Like getting your shield back up. It was too easy for me to walk in here, you must have a spy on the base. Get Kel dealt with. I'll bring her back. I'm going to take her out of this dimension so only that device will be able to communicate with us. I want time with her and time is something we do not have here. Give me the location and time of your next mission and I'll have her back with you by then."

Rennon pocketed the communicator. "Look after her and I'll deal with things here. Just a minute." He pulled his scanner out and scanned Kel. What Joniel didn't see was that the scanner was actually pointed at him. He turned as Joniel was bending down over Kyla, pulling his blaster in a smooth movement he shot Joniel in the head. He took the communicator out of his pocket and put it on the floor and blasted it to pieces. The shaped charge inside it blew a hole in the plastic flooring.

Dr Samson arrived and rushed to Kel and began administering to his wounds. Rennon scanned him as he came in without him noticing. In a smooth motion he brought his blaster around and shot him in the back of the head just as the real Dr Samson came in. The body fell to the ground on top of Kel.

Samson looked at the carnage. "So who is the patient?"

Rennon pointed to Kel. "I'd hazard a guess at him. That isn't Joniel and that isn't you."

Samson began dealing with Kel. "The last bit I'm certain about. As to the rest of it what happened here?"

Rennon was scanning. "Our shields are down so we must have another Follower agent on board. These two must have got in somehow." As he finished his sentence he saw a wisp of smoke coming from Joniel's head. "Tell me it isn't what I think it is." Rennon parted Joniel's hair. Circuitry was shorting out. "Well at least the unit is dead now, if dead is the right word for it. Well Samson, I think we just met our first MacKenzie Units. I'm going to call in Joniel. I mean the real one. I don't know what happened here but if they are able to send Units we are going to need him."

Samson was straightening Kel's twisted leg. "Good idea. Actually, not much damage here. Kel is going to have a mighty headache in the morning though."

Rennon sat down beside Kyla and put an arm around her. With his other hand he pulled a small box out of his pocket. Inside of it there was an ornate round transmitter that looked like a pocket watch. He flipped it open and put it on his lap. He pressed a button and a hologram keyboard appeared in the air. He typed. "Joniel 4265397802 Rennon Argo." He waited.

The hologram flashed to a blue screen above the keys. A message flashed up on the screen. "Message Accepted. Baron Joniel." It crackled slightly and Joniel's voice emitted from the communication device. "Rennon, what's up?"

Rennon looked at Kyla, tears were streaming down her face. "Kyla needs you." The connection went dead, the hologram disappeared and he shut the cover of the device.

There was a crackle of electricity in the air and a slight popping sound and Joniel appeared. He looked around, taking it all in, especially his replica on the floor. "This alters things. You were right to call. Kyla?"

Rennon got up and let Joniel take his place. She was staring wide eyed at Joneil's replica on the floor then looked up at the real Joniel. "I think I've hurt Kel. He tried to attack me. Joniel, you, that isn't you."

Joniel got up and pulled Kyla up onto her feet. "Is there anywhere I can take her? Somewhere private?"

Rennon had just finished scanning him. "Yes my Lord, there is a room down the corridor."

Joniel looked at him a bit strangely. "Why "My Lord"? Have we not been friends long enough to dispense with the formalities?"

Rennon smiled, the softness in Joniel's expression throwing him. "Had I better scan you again? What happened to the stand offish Joniel we all know?"

Joniel smiled. "She happened."

Rennon helped Joniel up the ladder with Kyla and took them to an empty room at the end of the corridor. He was about to close the door when he hesitated. "Don't worry, I've scanned the ship and restored the shields." He turned to go.

Joniel looked up. "I know." As Rennon shut the door Joniel laid Kyla on the bed.

She sat up and put her arms around him as he was about to stand up. "It's the real you?"

Joniel smiled down at her, his eyes sad, his expression concerned. "Rennon has scanned me, I'm definitely me. So what happened?" He sat back down again.

Kyla thought for a moment. "He was in my room hiding in the shadows like you always do. I noticed he'd been through my drawer which I assume you never do."

Joniel looked concerned. "How did you know it wasn't me? He looked pretty like me."

Kyla smiled enigmatically. "When they programmed him they must have automatically assumed that as we are lovers we make love."

Joniel kissed her. "If the world was fair we should. I still would not risk killing you but it doesn't mean that I don't want to and it's getting harder to resist." He kissed her on her forehead.

She thought for a moment. "Joniel, the blood is taking a hold on me. I do feel different now, I can hear things, see things I couldn't hear and see before."

He smiled. "That is how it will be."

Kyla smiled back and he dried her tears with a handkerchief he pulled from an inside pocket. She looked at him in the neon glow of the room. His hair was neatly brushed, his tie fastened with a phoenix pin and tucked precisely into his suit. "So much has changed. Have I changed enough?"

Joniel looked nervous. "I don't know. I want you to have changed enough. I want this waiting to be over. It has been unbearable over the years that others have been with you and all these years I could not."

Kyla smiled coyly. "Been with me, in what way?"

Joniel looked away. "You know in what way."

Kyla managed a weak laugh. "Says the father to seventeen children."

Joniel turned to face her. "I had to do my duty by my family and they were all before I met you."

Kyla smiled and put a finger on his lips. "Who says that I was with anyone else? Who says that I have ever been with anyone else? I was an initiate of the White Lady. Such things are forbidden until I achieved Master."

Joniel looked stunned. "I never thought about it."

Kyla looked down. "I would have been an old woman by now if I had not attained Mastery. Was that not one of your fears?"

Joniel looked at her and raised an eyebrow and mentally did the calculations in his head. "You mean?"

Kyla smiled. "For someone so bright sometimes you can be completely dim. Didn't you ever wonder how Maran managed to be hundreds of years old while her people lived to three score years and ten? Mastery has brought me more than the healing arts and the sight."

Joniel smiled. "So you achieved Mastery? I thought you were on a pilgrimage to attain mastery when the Followers captured you?"

Kyla shook her head. "I attained Mastery of the Art of the White Lady nearly fifty years ago. The pilgrimage was to get the "True Light" which is a healing art only given to Masters of the High Order."

The smile fell from Joniel's face. "Kyla, you call me the dim one. Your mastery would have protected you from me years ago." He got up and began climbing the ladder.

Kyla looked at him in horror. "Where are you going?"

Joniel looked down at her. "Where do you think? I'm going to lock the door." He turned with a broad smile on his face.

Rennon had helped Samson to take Kel to the medical bay. They had scanned the Units and they were inert so the Marines were taking them to Rennon's laboratory where his assistants were getting ready to start analysing them. Everyone on the ship was awake now.

The mugs were laid out neatly on the table by the time they all arrived at the galley. Biscuits were on the plate and their "Ma" was busying herself with filling pots of tea and coffee with boiling water. "Sit down now my dears you have had a long night. Is everyone here? Where are Kyla and Kel?"

Rennon poured himself a mug of hot coffee. "Kel is in the Infirmary. Kyla is with Joniel."

Ma smiled. "Good on the last part. They make such a sweet couple don't they?"

Samson choked on his biscuit. "The assassin and the barbarian healer, a very sweet couple." The emphasis was on sweet. "Have you ever taken that woman on in a sparring match. She kicked my ass half way to Endalox Tyrrian."

Rennon smiled. "And she kicked Kel's ass tonight but we'd better be careful about joking about that one." He cast a glance at the Marines who were all in stitches laughing. "Ok, which of you hasn't had their butt kicked by her then?" They fell silent. "I thought so."

There was a crackle of electricity and a slight pop and Intendi appeared in the room, backed up by two of the Prince's Guards dressed in black business suits. Their black ties were neatly tucked into their suits and they also wore phoenix tie pins. Intendi bowed. "Intendi is pleased to see you all. The Prince has sent Intendi on the request of My Lord the Baron Joniel. Intendi would like to tell you that Teraskis there is a Follower spy."

As he finished speaking Teraskis tried to leave the table but he fell over backwards in his chair as the two guards opened up on him with their machine pistols.

Intendi bowed. "I must apologise for the disturbance at your table Ma. It is probably quite unforgiveable but these are difficult times."

Ma already had a mop and bucket in her hand. "You are forgiven Intendi. Now would you three like to pull up a chair or do you have to report back immediately?"

Intendi bowed. "The Prince has asked me to stay here as long as is required. He is in Council at the moment and will not be needing my assistance for an hour or so. I believe my counterparts here would wish to partake of your hospitality." He cast a sideways glance at the expressionless guards as a flash of a smile flickered across their lips. "I think I can confirm their wishes to be able to sample your hospitality."

Ma was mopping up as the Marines carried their fallen ex comrade away to the morgue. "Very good, take a seat. I've got some scones baking, they will be ready shortly. Tea and scones, always good for any shock I always think."

When the four Marines returned and everyone was seated at the table eating scones and drinking tea and coffee Ma sat down with them. "So my dears, what are we going to do now?"

Rennon looked up from contemplating his plate. "We'll carry on with the mission."

Ma smiled. "I don't want to interfere."

Rennon smiled. "Ma with your experience I wouldn't call it interference. What do you have to say?"

Ma looked serious. "If I was a Follower leader and I had a secret or at least a weakness I would assume that someone at some point is going to discover it. I would put a good deal of protection around it. Also, if I felt that a small force was beginning to be successful I would use that secret as the bait to eliminate it. It would be a risky action but not if they have committed a considerable force to protecting it. Don't you think you came upon that information far too easily? I took the liberty of scanning that planet while you were on your mission. They claim that the youth were rebelling. I have uploaded CCTV footage which proves it was men and women of all ages who were rebelling and that building was not the Library.

I didn't want to speak out of turn but I felt it is my duty to point this out to you. This is the first meeting you have had on the subject and I have prepared a full report. Its in the second drawer down, under the clean tea towels."

Rennon looked shocked. "I didn't think?"

Ma smiled kindly. "Don't worry dear, you haven't had time to think. It was only this afternoon that you got back from that planet and we have only just submitted our reports to Mission Command. That they waited to show their hand until now means that we are on to something. But I feel in my humble opinion that we should expect a trap. They are expecting you to go in there as you always do, just this small group. If they are using their secret or weakness as bait perhaps we should go in there heavy handed and take it by force. The stakes are too high to take any risks."

Rennon interlocked his fingers and rested his hands around his mug. "Alternatively it could be a strategy to get us to commit our forces in one place so that they can wipe us out."

Ma nodded her head. "As you can see, both are viable options and options are what we should be considering. I was told of the situation by Samson earlier. They are using your weaknesses against you. Divide and conquer is a legitimate military strategy. They knew Kel's weakness for Kyla. They knew Kyla would most likely let Joniel get close to her and that could have eliminated her and that communication device would have eliminated you Rennon. Samson no doubt would have walked into one part of that trap at some point and that would have left us severely weakened."

Rennon frowned. "I can't see the reasoning behind what they did?"

Ma smiled back at him. "Samson, would you like to brief everyone on what you have got from Kel now that he is conscious?"

Samson put down his coffee mug. "Ma, thank you. Kel is in a state of shock obviously. I have managed to neutralise the drug in his system as much as I can and he is getting a certain amount of recall. MacSamson used his state to play on his internal fears that Joniel was taking Kyla from him and

266

that losing her to him would be the end of his people. He was sent in there with one purpose, to rape Kyla. I can hazard a guess about what that action was intended to achieve. Kyla would be unbalanced by that. Kel would be guilt ridden and it would be reasonable for Joniel to kill him. For some reason they don't want Kyla dead. At their facility she was left alive when the rest of the people they had taken had been experimented on and killed."

Rennon looked up. "She would have been killed. They tied her up for Kel to kill her."

Samson smiled. "That may possibly be true or they may have intended to get him out of there before he killed her. We can't know that. At that time they were not as powerful and may have feared offending the White Lady. That may have protected her. If Kel killed her then that would have put the blame onto him."

Ma put a fresh pot of tea on the table. "I think they did discover what they wanted to know, or rather didn't want to know when they had Kyla prisoner. Those with the noble DNA are immune to the Follower drug. When they knew this they needed to dispose of her and using Kel was the best way of doing it in an economic fashion. To see how he responded to the drug. Their testing on him would have revealed their racial links. They weren't to know that Kyla didn't know her ancestry. They were probably assuming that with her lack of contact with a man that she was not attached to anyone and with Kel's obvious good looks assumed that she would be attracted to him."

Rennon and the Marines were mumbling between themselves.

Ma smiled. "Samson I think you'll confirm what I say. I'm not speaking out of turn here."

Samson nodded. "Rennon, shut your mouth before flies get in. It is usual for an initiate of the White Lady to avoid such physical contact. It is now known that she had a loyalty to a forbidden love so it was unlikely that she would have given her favours elsewhere. According to Kel, Kyla had attempted to kill MacJoniel before he arrived in the room so she must have discovered he was not the real one."

Rennon took a deep breath. "Now that's a turn up, I assumed that Kel had killed him."

Samson smiled. "Apparently he did. He finished the job."

Arkarus looked up from his coffee. "Sir, could you explain what happened exactly?"

Rennon looked around their expectant faces. "We can only assume what they were attempting to achieve. Firstly they wanted to put doubt in our minds and make us distrust each other. Until now the existence of Intendi here has been a closely guarded secret for just this eventuality. Secondly they wanted to eliminate Kel. They guessed that either Kyla would kill him for attempting to attack her again or they had MacJoniel there with a good reason to kill him with jealousy as the motive. I can only assume that they were going to leave sufficient evidence to blame Joniel for Kel's death and possibly Kyla's. That would leave us with doubt about who is loyal, having lost two key personnel and driven a rift between us and Joniel.

I can only assume from this that Joniel's part in the mission would be expected and that it is something they fear. I hadn't intended to invite him along but after this I would say that it is essential."

Ma smiled. "I am so proud of you all. It isn't all guns and blasting you know."

Rennon smiled. "And now I have two MacKenzie Units to reprogram and evaluate. Their CPU may have vital information about the Follower base or at least where they came from. The reports have been filed, Kel is on the mend, Kyla is in very good hands." One of the Marines sniggered and got elbowed in the ribs. "So I say we relax and wait for orders from Mission Command."

Ma put another pot of coffee on the table. "I'm going to bed now. I'll clear up in the morning. Just leave your cups in the sink." She turned and left the room with a warm smile on her face as she turned and looked back at them all.

22

The Prince sat at the head of the meeting table. His head was in his hand and he was jotting down notes as the dignitaries and officials went over and over the same ground. Joniel stood behind him. He shifted his weight from one foot to the other but never lost concentration. He watched everyone like a hawk. Occasionally one or the other would give him a nervous look and shift in their seat. There was almost a flicker of a smile that came over his face every time that happened.

One by one the crew of the Argo had been called to give evidence as had other crews from ships around the galaxies. They had trailed in, said their words and been questioned and now it was time for the talking. That had gone on for hours.

The Prince stood up and everyone jumped. He put his pencil down and rested his fingers on the table in front of him. "Gentlemen, I have listened to your discussion for these past hours and it is now time for you to start drawing your speculations to a close. You are elected men, representing your constituents. It is now time for you to speak up for those you represent. This is not a time for idle gossip and to enjoy being the people in the know about what is happening." There was a horrified look on most of the participants' faces. "You are here to make decisions and while you are discussing people are being killed."

One portly official whose suit was made of the finest cloth looked incensed and started to go very red. Joniel took a step forward and the official tried to look into his vibrant blue eyes. He was about to stand up but he sat back down again.

The Prince turned to him. "Marcus, your careful consideration of situations and exacting attention to detail is always welcome. You have listened to the evidence and the speculation. What is your evaluation of the situation?"

Marcus spluttered as all eyes were on him. "I, I mean I, well…" He composed himself. "According to the intelligence we been presented with there are various options. What we need to evaluate is what the Followers will expect us to do or more importantly what they want us to do."

The Prince looked frustrated. "Yes, that is what has been said for the past two hours. What is your evaluation of the situation and what do you suggest as a possible response?"

Marcus had started to go very red. "Sir, I am a politician not a military strategist."

The Prince smiled. "That is quite correct. Who is in agreement with Marcus here? You may vote on whether you feel this should be a military handled matter and outside the jurisdiction of the High Council."

Every member at the Council Table looked relieved. They reached for their voting pads and pressed the "yes" button. The Prince watched the unanimous vote come up on the hologram in the middle of the table. "Very well, then we have a decision. Thank you gentlemen, lunch will now be served in the atrium."

The Committee Members got up and walked out chattering between themselves. When they were gone the Prince turned to Joniel. "We can expect another assassination attempt I would assume."

Joniel smiled. "My men are ready."

The Prince smiled back. "I have no doubt. It would be a brave would be assassin who would take on the masters of your art."

Joniel smiled enigmatically. "Indeed."

The Prince sat down. "So, what do we do now? I'm assuming that I'll have to call the Generals together and come up with a military solution."

He indicated a chair and Joniel sat beside him. "Thank you. It would seem the next likely step. But will it hold things up?"

The Prince lifted an eyebrow. "Not really, I've already issued orders to move certain key personnel into position. The discussions here are a formality that needs to be adhered to. It complies with the laws and the protocols. I spoke with the Generals for most of last night and they are in agreement. All they needed was a free hand to act."

Joniel smiled. "You old dog, you knew what would happen?"

The Prince smiled. "I knew what wouldn't happen? Alright there was no way the Council would accept responsibility for this one. They don't want blood on their hands and if they can palm it off onto the Generals they will. It's the Generals who have their careers on the line. But as they have their lives on the line as well it should be their decision. The key skills in this room were totally inappropriate for the decision to be made."

Joniel looked around the table at the debris. "Another meeting over."

The Prince looked at him, concerned. "What is troubling you my old friend?"

Joniel suddenly looked very tired. "Too much talking, not enough action."

The Prince smiled. "I hear you have been getting quite enough action lately."

Joniel jumped slightly and looked awkward.

The Prince's eyes sparkled mischievously. "With moving your ships into orbit and keeping your people under control is what I meant. How do you manage it?"

Joniel looked relieved. "The same way as you do. I play politics and try to stay one step ahead."

The Prince suddenly looked serious. "When this is over I've drawn up a document that gives you a full pardon for the murders you have committed. Your family lands are to be restored to you on Ceraksa Ventrusk but I have taken the liberty of also transferring a small planet in the Dernasinian Cortex into your name. It will be a good place for you and Kyla to live once this is over."

Joniel looked awkward.

The Prince smiled. "Its no big secret, I have my spies too. Well I was talking to Ma and she told me. I'm really pleased for you. It was a long time coming. So, will you be giving up bachelorhood again?"

Joniel looked at the notepad on the table. "I'd settle for seeing her alive at the end of all this for now. What happens after I do not dare to hope for."

The Prince looked down. "Quite right, quite right. I won't command you on this one. We're going to go in with as much as we can spare of the fleets. I know you have put forward your flagship and command on this one and I appreciate it. I am also going to send in the crew of the Argo. The fleet is just a decoy which may give them the chance that they need to get in there, find out what is happening and get out again. Jaz is a good strategist would you leave him with your fleet to command?"

Joniel gave the Prince a knowing smile. "My Lord, I am extremely proud of my son and his skills are without question. But I would ask why?"

The Prince smiled. "Because however much I may want you to command that fleet I also want you to go with the crew of the Argo. Nothing will stop Kyla going and I feel that the crew will stand a better chance of surviving if you are with them. Kel is injured and we cannot count on him because of the drug. Rennon is a good fighter but he's a pilot and a scientist. Samson is no combat medic so I've moved him back to the Command Ship to run the Infirmary. I feel that you, Kel, Kyla and Rennon would make an effective strike force. Is that a low enough number to use your teleport?"

Joniel looked relieved. "It is. I would want this. You can command me if you like, it would be my choice."

The Prince smiled. "Then I'd get back to the Argo if I were you and get involved in the preparations. They are nearing the Dresnik Planetary System and there is barely a day before they come into orbit around the planet. I have committed what I can spare of the fleet and it will be arriving shortly. I assume you will similarly command your son to bring your fleet into line. I have left sufficient vessels around the strategic locations to ensure our survival should it be a Follower plot to leave our resources undefended. You have a go."

The Prince stood up as did Joniel and he was about to key his wrist pad when he looked over at the Prince. They took a step towards each other and hugged. Joniel stepped away and pressed the key pad and disappeared.

The Prince pressed his key pad and similarly disappeared. As he did so an explosion rang through the building and smoke billowed from the next room. A second explosion erupted from underneath the table where a briefcase had been left.

Joneil arrived on the Argo just moments before the Prince. Joniel turned to look at him quizzically. "I thought you were going back to the Palace?"

The Prince smiled. "I did, well a MacPrince did. With Rennon's help we have loaded my biosignature into our own unit and he with his trusty friend and loyal subject Joniel are now on route to the Palace in a shuttle." There was a bleep from the Prince's communicator. "Here, you might as well see this. It's a relay from the Unit.

A hologram appeared above the Prince's wrist which appeared to be the front window of a shuttle. The Prince spoke slowly and clearly. "Testing PA76894, respond when appropriate."

The Prince's voice came back through the intercom on is wrist. "PA76894 responding. I am reporting on activity in the Council Chambers post your departure. The Chamber was completely destroyed by an incendiary bomb located in the Council Chambers. A secondary device supposedly located within one of the Council members detonated almost simultaneously. All Council members are deceased."

The Prince looked horrified. "No survivors?"

The image moved from side to side. "No survivors. Explosions were reported within moments at sixteen locations around the galaxies equating to the sixteen locations of our official rooms. I as your decoy am still functional although I did have to diffuse a bomb which I found located in the aft cargo hold. I have retained it for inspection. We are requested to issue a statement on the hour. I am awaiting your instructions."

The Prince switched off the transmitter. He shut his eyes. "I have known those people for so many years. I can't believe they are all gone. They might have been a right royal pain in the butt but they had to be, it was their job."

Joniel looked down on the Prince and smiled. "You are doing your duty. You are still alive and we have hope. Lets hope that this is an indication as to how important this information or whatever it is going to be is. By the way, what are you doing here?"

The Prince brightened up. "Did I forget to mention I'm on the mission as well? Oh, must have been an oversight. I can fulfil my official function through the Mac Unit, I'll be of more use here. I'm a soldier, not a diplomat."

Rennon came into the galley where they were standing talking. "Oh, you've arrived. My Prince I have arranged a room for you in the crew quarters. We have no finer rooms I'm afraid. Joniel, I believe you will make your own arrangements." He smiled knowingly and Joniel gave him a playful glare. "News has reached us about the bombings. It is a great relief that you are still with us. It must have been a close thing?"

The Prince shook his head thoughtfully. "Very close. Still, the show must go on. I assume we are on course and everything is in order."

Rennon smiled, clicked his heels together and saluted. "Yes My Prince."

The Prince furrowed his brow. "Are you being insolent?"

Rennon laughed. "No, I just like the sound of it. My Prince."

The Prince shook his head. "Even in the darkest of moments you can lift the spirits. Still, better get on. Apparently I have a speech to record. I can record it, make mistakes and then upload the finished version to MacPrince. If I survive this I might just keep him on. Then he can do all my official engagements for me, well the boring ones anyway. What is our E.T.A. at the planet?"

Rennon looked down at his handheld terminal. "Two hours, fifteen minutes and thirty three seconds. We'll be in orbit in a little under that time but there is a moon which we will have to navigate around to avoid being seen. I've scanned the planet with long range scanners. The planet seems to be devoid of much in the way of any kind of technology. The technology is all around it. It is surrounded by cloaked Follower craft."

The Prince shrugged. "So we have choices. We can go in and fight them all or we can teleport down to the planet's surface and hope they don't blow the planet out from under us."

Rennon looked worried, put his terminal down and started clicking keys. "That is feasibly possible. It is not an eventuality I had logged into the outcome module. I will recalibrate it and see what comes up." There was a pause while he clicked more keys. "Oh, well that can't be good. There is a fifty percent chance that this is their preferred plan as they have a battle cruiser capable of the sort of firepower necessary to do that. So, what do we do?"

The Prince thought for a moment. "Can they read through our cloak?"

Rennon thought about it. "Possibly."

The Prince sat down. "So, how close can we get without being detected on their scanners?"

Rennon clicked buttons. "Close enough for what?" There was no answer so he carried on clicking buttons.

The Prince looked up. "Can a cloaked cruiser get close enough to blow that thing out of space before it realises we are there?"

Rennon looked at the screen. "It could but not without alerting the rest of the cruisers to our presence."

The Prince smiled. "I am assuming that. Do you still have that Dr Samson Mac Unit on board?"

Rennon looked worried. "I do."

The Prince looked around the room. "Don't worry, I'm not bringing this ship that close in. I know how attached you are to her. I've brought a fireship along. She's a D Class Battle Cruiser with retro shift and Eion Drive capability. I am proposing that we drop her out of the Eionisphere, blow the cruiser to pieces and she then jumps back out again. She may be destroyed, she may survive but the only pilot we would need would be the Mac Unit if you can reprogram it. If we lose the ship, we lose the ship. It will give them something to think about while we teleport down to the planet and see what we can find out. We can bring in the fleet to engage the cruisers that are positioned on the outer rim. By the looks of it they have committed their biggest cruisers to the centre. A good move, just what I would have done. If the little guys can't take us out we would be damaged when we got to the bigger cruisers behind."

Joniel took a deep breath. "Your plan is what precisely?"

The Prince looked around them. "I plan to jump in the fireship and take out the planet buster. That ensures that we can't lose the planet in one go and end up standing in mid space. Then I plan to bring in the attack force to keep the rest of the ships occupied. They will hopefully not realise why we took out the planet buster. It is after all the biggest ship with the greatest firepower and the only one that can get the range to hit our fleet while it is engaging the outer cruisers. While the fleet is engaged we'll teleport down onto the planet and hopefully find what we are supposed to. Have you scanned the planet for lifeforms?"

Rennon looked gravely at the Prince. "I have, there is only one."

The Prince looked confused. "Do we have the range to find out anything about this individual?"

Rennon looked down at his feet. "I have managed a long range bioscan utilising a divisional relay teleported onto a nearby moon."

The Prince looked worried. "So, what is the problem? Who is it?"

Rennon was looking at his screen. He took a deep breath and then faced the Prince. "This is about as accurate a scan as you can get considering the distances we are covering. Normally we would be unable to effect such a feat of engineering but in this case he is the only signature on the planet so it was a lot easier to pinpoint him. It also eliminates any possibility that we were scanning the wrong person."

The Prince glared at him. "You are waffling which means that I'm not going to like what you are going to say. Who is he?"

Rennon swallowed hard. "I have run the biosignature through the computer and the data base. There is no doubt and the computer is ninety nine percent certain that the individual on that planet is your father. Also known as Erasimus Deck, the Founder of the Fallow Earth Organisation."

The Prince looked wildly at Joniel as if for assistance. "My father, you have to be kidding me. Holy crap now I've got a problem. I'm sure the galaxies are going to love this little family reunion."

Rennon smiled. "Not so fast. What has brought us here is Erasimus' diary. His intent was pure and the writings of the Fallow Earth Organisation were very far removed from what we are seeing today. I think the opposite. I think this is what they are looking to cover up."

The Prince thought for a moment. "Why not just kill him?"

Rennon clicked on the terminal. "Because there is one commandment they rarely mention. It is a corruption of the original creed of not corrupting the mother earth. In their text it has been translated as not corrupting the "lifegiver". I would assume they means their "Father" in a more literal sense. He is down there and by the looks of it he is without any form of communication. I have checked the archives now that I know what to look for. He disappeared about two and a half years ago. One day he was there, next he was eradicated from the records. I'm tracking him by the space he has left, not what I can find. There is a deletion which went through the whole computer system on exactly the same moment on exactly the same day. I can find his omission by the computer trail it left. They took him out of existence and probably brought him here as they could not kill him."

The Prince looked at the screen. "So if we take him from the island or interfere in any way they will probably try to get us to kill him."

Rennon looked surprised. "Why do you think that?"

The Prince smiled. "Oh, only a hunch but if they can manage to eliminate him they eliminate their only threat. He can command them, he is their "Father". They cannot corrupt the Father so what he says must be incorrupt. They can't kill him but they can fire at us and if he or the planet gets caught in the cross fire then they have adhered to their rules. If we speak to him they may well consider him corrupt and that may invalidate the clause that is keeping him alive."

Joniel breathed out swiftly. "I've got it. The word of the father, the gift of the father is the son. You are his son, his blood. Rennon, how many children did he have?"

Rennon tapped into the archives. "Only the one."

Joniel looked relieved. "You are his heir. If anything happens to him do you think that you would inherit his position?"

The Prince smiled. "Lets go down there and ask him shall we?"

Joniel went more white than he already was. "You have to be kidding me. You are going to risk them using that planet buster on you?"

The Prince raised an eyebrow. "No I'm going to continue with the original plan and send the fireship in to take out the planet buster. I'm then going to take the rest of the fleet in to keep their ships occupied. I'm also going to bring the Mac Prince in on my flagship to act as a decoy. I would put money on them throwing their full arsenal at it to try to eliminate me before I get to my dear father. That leaves us free to go down to the planet and speak to him."

Joniel gasped. "You really do know how to come up with them don't you? So I suppose I have some equipment to relocate for you."

The Prince smiled. "If you would be so kind to put that into effect after I've delivered a rousing speech. I suppose none of you are good at writing rousing speeches are you?"

Rennon laughed. "We'll fight for you, we'll probably end up dyeing for you but please do not ask us to write your speeches for you. That is one demand too many."

The Prince laughed too. "I thought as much but you can't blame me for trying. Now, Joniel, you had better go and find Kyla as she won't be best pleased if I send you off before you've had a chance to meet up. Rennon, I believe you have some programming to do. I've got a speech to write."

The door opened and Ma walked in. The Prince looked down at his shoes. "As if that isn't enough now I'm going to get a lecture. I just know I am. It is good to see you again."

Ma smiled and crossed the room swiftly. She straightened his tie and dusted particles off of his shoulders. "Now what have I told you about being smart. Look at you Prince and all. I remember you when you were just a squaddie. This little one came into my troop really wet behind the ears. We soon knocked you into shape."

The Prince winced as she pulled a stray hair off of his jacket. "Knocked me out don't you mean?"

Ma smiled. "Only the once and you did deserve it. He was a right urchin. A child fresh out of the orphanage sent to us as punishment for crimes sufficiently unlimited. Look at my boy now though." Ma looked around at the stunned faces. "Oh, I'm sorry, My Prince. Have I offended you?"

The Prince smiled. "You have. Where is my hug? You saved my life enough times to be excused any form of official protocol and I wouldn't dare try to enforce it on you anyway. Not now that you are retired."

Ma smiled. "Who said I was retired? If I'm retired where's my pension? I've been on active service right through, covert ops mostly. After all, who would suspect a sweet little old lady? I wouldn't tell me the plan, I'm not taking part but you could tell me what time to get dinner ready and don't you dare be late."

The Prince looked down and smiled. "I wouldn't dare."

The Renaissance appeared just within range of the Follower ship with planet buster capability. The Mac Unit that looked like Dr Samson was at the helm, the rest of the ship was on autopilot. His piloting capability was fully activated and his circuitry was more than capable of flying the entire ship without any assistance.

He stood on the flight deck, a lone figure, standing stock still with cables and wires plugged into ports on his neck, arms and hands. His eyes were shut, his personal motor functions shut down. All he could do was fly the ship at the command of Rennon who was in control of his operating system. Rennon was monitoring all functions of the ship. From the hologram of the crew to intercepting the Follower scanning device and projecting back the vital signs of a whole crew. His fingers flew over the keyboard, his eyes darting from left to right, taking it all in on the twenty or so screens he had open. He flicked from one to the next.

As soon as the ship materialised he initiated the weapons array. Beams of light flared from the ports and the Eion Cannons blasted into the ship which had been completely caught unawares. Joniel's adaptation of the drive capability had allowed it to jump to its location from a distance and a speed far greater than any scanner could have picked up.

The battle cruiser with planet busting capability erupted in flowers of flame and fell out of orbit. It crashed into a second cruiser which also burst into flames and that in turn cannoned into a third.

The cruisers turned their guns on the Renaissance and in unison they fired. It erupted in flames as thirty to forty Eion Cannons hit it simultaneously. Rennon activated the shielded thrusters and sent the burning ship careering into the enemy fleet. Ships tried to get out of the way but their close proximity meant there was nowhere to go. The burning Renaissance crashed at full thrust into the first ship and the momentum kept it and that ship going until they crashed into the next. Across the panoramic view ships were trying to evade these burning ships and in turn where their inexperienced pilots were unable to control them they ran into other ships. The result was far more successful than Rennon or the Prince could possibly have imagined. Ships began to jump into the corridors and very soon there were very few left in orbit around the planet. Those that were left were either badly damaged or attempting to make a final stand.

The final stand option proved fairly futile as the fleet exited the corridors and the ships were hopelessly outnumbered. As their pilots had had instructions to arrive firing and there was no time to countermand that order they fired on the remaining ships until every one was destroyed.

Rennon just stared open mouthed at the scene in front of him. He scanned and scanned again. According to his scanners what he was seeing was what was there. His eyes and the screens were not deceiving him but he still tried alternative forms of scanning, checked and double checked.

The four stood ready to teleport. Joniel held Kyla's hand and squeezed it tightly. They gave each other a very covert smile when they were sure that Kel wasn't looking and broke hands as soon as he turned around. The Prince was checking his equipment and putting scanners into his boiler suit's pockets.

The Prince stood up straight as they all seemed to be standing still. "Well, if we are ready?"

Everyone nodded.

The Prince took a deep breath and held it. Let it out slowly. "Let's go then." He pressed the teleport and they disappeared from the Argo and appeared on the planet.

The planet was tropical, the sun was warmly beating down and they were on the other side of the planet from where the fire fight had been going on. There were bright sparkles of light in the sky but these were mostly invisible due to the sunlight. None of them looked up, they focused on the area around them.

They had arrived in a clearing in the undergrowth outside the entrance to a cave. The ground was bare, old shells and stones littering the golden sand. The cave was cut from sandstone and matched the golden yellow. Weapons at the ready they formed up. Joniel put his hand on Kel's arm and slipped into the darkness of the cave. Kel looked around at the Prince, his expression questioning. The Prince smiled. "It's how he works best. We'll leave him to it."

Joniel stepped into the pitch dark of the cave and moved around the walls. Once out of the glare of the sun and the entrance to the tunnel system he was able to stand for a moment, his back pressed against the wall. He let his vision get used to the darkness and to adapt so that it allowed him to see the temperature of the rock around him. He couldn't see any detail but he could at least see where he was and where the side passageways were and anything warm and living in the cavern system. When he was satisfied that there were no changes in heat and no obvious traps either electronic or manual he moved on. He had a device in his hand which would have alerted him if it had detected anything, it was set to silent running. He grasped it carefully sensitive to its gentle warning vibration if it sensed anything.

He moved forwards, blaster in hand, silently. He activated his personal shield and his feet raised up so he no longer left footprints and he could move forwards without fearing falling over any stone that remained unseen. He walked swiftly, moving from left to right along the tunnel and smelling the air as it became stale. He turned back and tried another side passageway until that became stale then he tried a third. This took him to a small cave. He could see there were things on the floor but as they were neither a threat nor living he continued on. To the right there was another tunnel and he could see a vague glow at the end of it.

He turned the corner and slipped down the shadowy side of the corridor and came up to the cave entrance. He stopped and watched.

Inside the cave an old man was sitting on a log. He was whittling a boat out of a piece of wood. Around him there were many other wooden sculptures of plants, animals and boats. He smiled to himself. "You think I can't see you? Just because I'm old doesn't mean that my eyesight is going. Come out into the light so that I may see you. I'm no threat to you."

Joneil stepped out into the light, turning off his shield. "I do not wish to harm you."

The old man looked into his radiant blue eyes. The old man's eyes were watery and the lids were red. He had distinct bags under them and he looked tired. "I know you don't. I'm no threat to you either, I'm no threat to anyone."

Joniel smiled but he looked stunned as he took in the old man's age. "How long have you been here? By the way are you Erasimus Deck?"

The old man looked at him and thought for a while. "I am, I haven't heard that name spoken in such a long time. I have been a prisoner here for just over fifty years. You know who I am, who are you?"

Joniel smiled as kindly as he knew how. "I am Joniel D'Aliachi which will mean nothing to you no doubt."

Erasimus shook his head. "You are right. You can't leave you know. Nobody can. If you have come with others you are just as trapped now as I am."

Joniel smiled. "You don't need to worry, I have devices that can get us out of here. May I bring my friends in to speak with you?"

Erasimus smiled. "You can bring them all in, it won't change anything and we might as well start getting to know each other."

The Prince, Kel and Kyla entered the cavern. Erasimus stood up when he saw Kyla. "Well this is an unexpected treat. I haven't seen anyone in years and then I get all of you in a day. I'll say the same again though, you can't leave here."

Joniel smiled. "I don't think that is correct."

Erasimus smiled kindly. "Try it. If you believe you can leave then I'd love to be proven wrong."

Joniel pressed his wrist pad but nothing happened. He tried again and looked in horror at the others. "Its not working."

Erasimus smiled. "Oh its working alright, but you are caught between the dimensions here so it can neither get a lock on you or where you are going to. You, like me are now trapped. I should know, I created the device that trapped me here in the first place."

Joniel looked at him. "Was it a device?"

Erasimus smiled. "It was. It was intended to provide me with my island paradise where I could start a community who lived with the earth in a way that was sustainable and self sufficient. I came here to try out the device and I thought something had gone wrong. Then I realised that there had been nothing wrong with it that hadn't been set up by my assistant. He had long been my right hand man and I had trusted him completely. He came here with me and I found something in his bag when it fell off of the table."

The Prince looked at the old man kindly. "What was in the bag?"

Erasimus got up. "I'll show you but you must promise not to touch. It would be devastating for us here if you do not keep well away from what I am going to show you. Come with me."

He picked up a brand from the fire and took them down a small narrow corridor. At the end of the corridor there was a small cave with a makeshift table in it. On the table there was a bag which was laying on its side. Laying around it and in it were spherical pods. They seemed to be purple balls with holes in them. Through the holes they could see a gelatinous ball with worms swimming around in the liquid. Erasimus pointed to them. "They will not hatch until they make contact with a living being. Then they will hatch and take over that being. This was where the accident happened. My assistant found them on a visit to a planet looking for botanical samples. He had brought them with him here to study them. When the bag fell over one of them touched him. He was sick for days but as I watched he began to change. The gentle and loving boy I'd known became a selfish tyrannical monster. Then I realised that the ball that had touched him was now empty, the worms had sought him out and had somehow got into him. He began to physically change as well. He began to grow a bony like structure over his whole body.

We weren't trapped then. I saw what he was becoming and I knew he would be a threat to anyone he came into contact with so I sabotaged the equipment hoping to trap him or us here. Well I succeeded but I had no idea he had a teleport device so he teleported out when he realised what I was doing, leaving me here. He took my work, my writings about Utopia and my notebook. He got out but I couldn't, he activated the device simultaneously with teleporting out and left me. He left me with nothing, not even paper and a pen to write with." The old man slumped down onto a chair then got up quickly. "We must not stay in this cavern. There may be another accident. Come on lets go back to my cave. We can talk about what we are going to do next."

The Prince sat down on a log by the fire. "I've really screwed up this time haven't I?" His head was in his hands and Kyla sat down beside him and put her arm around his shoulders.

Joniel stepped over and put his hand on the Prince's shoulder. "Not yet. We have the answer, now all we have to do is get home."

Kel grunted. "I wish Rennon was here."

The Prince looked up and a flash of a smile shot across his face. "I'm glad he isn't. He may be our only hope to get out of here. How does your device work?"

Erasimus thought for a while. "It originally worked to shift this whole planet out of phase. When I broke it, it shifted it out of dimension as well and its flashing between the dimensions so it is never in one dimension long enough to get a lock with my equipment. You don't think in all these years I haven't tried to escape?"

Kyla looked down at her hand. The silver ring with the leaves around it was still on her finger. "My Prince, you weren't with us when we first met with Nai though I know he has had a meeting with you since then. Do you trust him?"

The Prince looked quizzically at her. "What do you mean? He has been one of our greatest allies. I would almost hazard to say that I trust him with my life."

Kyla smiled. "Good as you may have to. When we were on Lundy and met with him he gave me this. Is there any chance that it is more than just a ring?"

Kel grunted. "You know when we came back from Lundy I totally forgot about that."

Kyla smiled. "I forgot to log it in when we got back and I forgot to put it in my mission briefing. It is as if I'm only remembering it now."

Joniel picked up her hand and looked at it. "Kyla, you weren't wearing that ring before."

Kyla looked up at him. "What do you mean? I've had this ring since Lundy."

He looked down at her, his eyes fierce. "A faerie gives you a ring, you don't remember it, none of you remember it, I haven't seen it before and I'm pretty good at noticing things."

The Prince ran his scanner over it. "It has a signature, there is definitely power there. I'm amazed that it hasn't shown up on any of the scans on the base."

Kyla looked at him sideways. "I'm amazed none of us remembered it. That is unless it only exists out of dimension."

The Prince hit his forehead with the palm of his hand. "That is how they move things in and out of phase. They are there, but not there. If its here then that means we're on a similar plane or planes as Nai."

Kel grunted to get their attention. "I suppose that was why they were keen to get us here, it was a trap, just not the sort of trap we expected."

The Prince got up. "I don't know how it will help us but it is possible that Nai may be able to pick up that we are here. We could try activating the ring."

Joniel grabbed Kyla's hand as she went to touch it. "Be very careful, it's a faerie thing and they are notoriously dangerous."

Kyla touched the ring and felt around the leaves. Nothing happened. Kyla looked up at Joniel. "I want you to cut my hand."

The Prince jumped over to her and glared down at her. "What? Are you mad? The last thing you need close to those pods is an open wound."

Kyla smiled. "That is why I want Joniel to do it, with a bite. He can seal the wound as soon as he makes it. Why would Nai give me a ring other than for it to be for when I'm in danger?"

The Prince smiled. "I like your logic. If its not an inappropriate thing to say, Joniel, bite her."

Joniel glared at the Prince. He took Kyla's hand gently in his, looked at her lovingly.

The Prince caught his other hand. "No, I want you to terrify her and then bite her."

Joniel looked furious. He glared at Kyla and pushed her back against the wall. Immediately his eyes turned a blood red and his pupils dilated to cat slits. He opened his mouth, his fangs distended, their points razor sharp and ferociously white in contrast with the blood red of the rest of his mouth. His eyes were wild and he hissed at her. She backed against the wall, the breath knocked out of her. He bore down on her hand, biting hard. The pain coursed through her body and she screamed. He had not injected the venom first. The pain was almost unbearable as he tore into her hand. He let go of her hand and held her against the wall, his face close to hers. His fangs touching her neck.

There was a flash in the cavern and Joniel flew across the cave and hit the back wall. The Prince acted like lightning. He leapt in front of Joniel and between him and Nai who stood in front of him with a flaming sword in his hand. The Prince took a deep breath, his face illuminated by the flames from the sword. "Nai, its me, Prince Anathorn. Kyla is not in danger. Joniel is her lover. We needed to get you here as we are trapped out of phase."

Nai stared in disbelief. He turned to face Kyla who was leaning against the wall holding her hand. "Is this true?"

Kyla nodded. "We were lured here and trapped as is Erasimus there. It was all we could think of doing to bring you to help us. We couldn't work out how to activate the ring."

Nai looked at her questioningly. "The ring? What ring? Oh that ring, its pretty and used to be a communication device. I gave it to you because it was pretty. I had been watching the mission and I was on my way here to get you out but I was giving you time to talk to your father."

There was a stunned silence. Anathorn looked at Erasimus who looked totally stunned.

Nai looked slightly uncomfortable. "I guess you haven't talked. Well you can, later. I had better get you out of here."

Anathorn realised he was holding Joniel against the wall. He stepped forwards and Joniel slid down the wall. "That hurts". He was trying to get his hand to his back where he had hit a protruding rock.

Kyla ran over to him and crouched beside him. He smiled at her. "Ok my love, can you fix this one?" She lowered him to the ground and laid him on his front. She took a scanner from her bag and ran it over him. "Do not move." Her voice reflected her panic. "His back is broken. I'm going to immobilise him and hopefully we can do something when we get him back to the ship."

Anathorn turned to her. "When we get him back to our ship, I will get the finest surgeons. We will do what we can."

Kyla had pulled out a rubber blanket which she laid over him and pressed the activation switch. It moulded around his body, tendrils clasping around his front and then went rigid making it impossible for him to move even a muscle.

Anathorn turned to Nai. "There's more. This is Erasimus Deck as you know. He was trapped but it was his assistant who I would assume became the first Follower. He was infected by a pod."

Nai looked concerned. "Show me."

Anathron took him to the cavern.

Nai looked at the pods on the table. "I haven't seen anything like these. They are not of any dimension I have ever encountered but I haven't seen all the creatures and plants of this or any other world. You are now going to want to analyse them and that is going to give us all a dilemma. How do we transport something so obviously dangerous?"

Prince Anathorn thought for a moment. "Can you take them out of phase so we can get a containment unit over them before we bring them back in phase? That would seal them completely with no danger of contaminating anything."

Nai smiled. "I suppose you also want me to contain them and bring them to your laboratory?"

Prince Anathorn smiled. "Yes, I would. After all you are immune to the Follower drug and I would assume that is the source of that drug?"

Nai looked about the cavern. "I'll take you all back now. I'm going to take Joniel to my kingdom. Time passes differently there and it will give your surgeons longer to prepare themselves. With his injury time is of the essence. I will give you as much time as you need."

Prince Anathorn looked concerned. "Thank you for that. He is a loyal friend."

Nai smiled. "That is a high compliment for a Prince to pay to one of his kind."

Prince Anathorn's communicator went off. Both Anathorn and Nai jumped. The Prince looked at Nai. "How can that go off?"

Nai looked terrified. "You had better answer it."

The Prince hit the comms button and the hologram keypad appeared above the device. "Prince Anathorn. RC456934 Queen Isis".

Prince Anathorn nearly dropped the communicator.

Nai's eyes were wide. "Now there's a lady I haven't heard from in generations. Answer her immediately."

Anathorn's fingers were already flying over the keys and he hit send. The hologram crackled. "Prince Anathorn, I send you greetings and I must congratulate you on your great success. It comes at great cost. I am contacting you to make sure that you do not lose a valuable warrior for our cause. That is not something that we can allow to happen. A Daughter of the White Light is with you, she knows me as the White Lady. I will give her the power to help him and I bless their union. The Dark Lord will now speak." Prince Anathorn, Queen Isis KO046893 King Osiris. The voice clearly changed to a deep male voice. "I also send you our congratulations on your success. Our vessels are far from here and we are unable to assist you in your fight as we are bound by ancient agreements. I would see my most loyal subject safely restored to health. I also bless their union." King Osiris KO46893 Prince Anathorn. Queen Isis RC456934Prince Anathorn. Transmission ended.

Kyla knelt over Joniel who was screaming in agony. She stopped administering the drugs and blood. She placed her hands over him and as she concentrated a white beam of light passed through the roof of the cavern, through her body and came out through her hands into Joniel. His screaming stopped and he moaned slightly. The light stopped flowing through her and Joniel relaxed.

Joniel opened his eyes. Kyla ran a scanner over him. "You are healing fast but it will still take time. The healing accelerates your normal healing capability but it is not a miracle cure. But it will heal the damage before there is any chance of it becoming more serious or permanent. The bones will knit, the cartilage will re-grow. Blood will help you but it is going to take time."

Joniel's voice was shaky. He looked up at her. "Don't let anyone who doesn't need to see me like this."

Erasimus crouched down beside them. "Time moves differently here. Stay here. Someone has to tend to the animals and the forest. Keep him here little one, let him heal."

Anathorn turned to Nai. "Is that true?"

Nai smiled. "It is and they are immortal, time will mean nothing and the years they can spend while Joniel heals will be but moments to you in your realm." He looked strangely wistful. "Give them back the time that they lost. Let them have time together here, you will not miss them. You have your replica Joniel and he will be back soon enough. Erasimus, what do you wish to do?"

Erasimus smiled. "It seems my fate is still written in stone and I am a prisoner of it. I must return to the past with the fortune and the knowledge that I have. So that I do not upset the time continuum I must not interfere with the creation of the Followers but I can set up a force to fight them now."

Prince Anathorn smiled. "You did, I mean you will do. You are the founder of Mission Command then, the only reason we are still able to make a stand in the galaxies."

Erasimus winked at him. "Time is a strange thing. So, you are my son are you? You're a handsome chap, just like I was. Perhaps we'll take a little time to get to know each other while we try to sort out our enemies. I would certainly like to see my assistant again. I have a few words I would like to share with him."

In the dark recesses of space many galaxies away two space crafts hovered like giant birds and blanked out the stars behind them. On screens on both ships there was the scene of a man and a woman and their friends in a cave in a tropical forest, all around them was green. The sea lapped at the timeless shores and fish swam in its depths. A stream flowed down from the mountain bringing fresh water and behind the cave a vegetable patch and animals would provide for their food.

A communication channel was opened up and a male voice spoke. "My queen, my sister, my love would you cease your constant travelling and leave these people to their fate?"

The hail was accepted. "My king, my brother, my love would you return to your kingdom and help protect these people?"

The male voice answered. "Then after all these millennia we can still find no solution. Will you stop your earth bound body from wandering? Will you let that part of your consciousness return home?"

The female voice responded. "Not until I know the earth is safe. We should have helped them more. Could you again be the one who defends the earth?"

The male voice sounded sad. "No, I cannot go back. We have made our agreements, we have made our covenant."

A third ship flashed into the area. It was identical to the other two. A communication channel was opened up. "Well my brother, my sister, do you still whine on about the ills that befell you?"

The female voice responded. "My brother Set, will you ever let the Earth live in peace?"

The third voice answered. "I have more than the Earth to amuse me now, I have my Followers." The communication was cut and the ship disappeared.

The male voice cried out. "We gave them our children, was that not enough?"

The female voice answered him. Her voice was serene. "We are bound by our covenant. We must not intervene in the war."

The male voice stated slowly and coldly. "We are bound my queen but not one from the other. We are trapped by our own anger and our own words. I cannot break my bond any more than you can."

In the dark infinity of space two space craft docked. Ships that had not touched in millennia came together united once more by a common enemy.

Printed in Great Britain
by Amazon

79737568R00169